BAD COMPANY

He was short. He was ugly. Troops of nonhuman adventurers had enjoyed themselves swinging through his family tree. Most must have been ... . ous because their desce.... ... ous all the time.

I was face-to-face with Director Relway of the Unpublished Committee for Royal Security. Most people would not recognize the runt if he was snapping around their ankles, but I had butted heads with him several times. He was smiling. That was so unusual that I made sure my pockets hadn't been picked already.

It was too late to make sure that I had an escape route plotted.

The ugly little man commanded more genuine hurt-you power than almost anybody but the queen of the underworld. He could intimidate the King himself, and all the sane people on the Hill. Irk Deal Relway and you could fall off the stage of the world forever.

Irk him badly enough and he might arrange for you never to have existed at all.

PRAISE FOR THE GARRETT, P.I., NOVELS

"A wild science fiction mystery that never slows down for a moment." — *Midwest Book Review*

"Garrett, private detective, returns after too long an absence. . . . Cook makes this blending of fantasy with hard-boiled detective story seem easy, which it isn't, and manages to balance the requirements of both genres superbly." — *Chronicle*

"Cook brings a dose of gritty realism to fantasy." — *Library Journal*

Titles in the Garrett, P.I., Series

WICKED BRONZE AMBITION

AMBITION

A GARRETT, P.I., NOVEL

GLEN COOK

A ROC BOOK

ROC
Published by the Penguin Group
Penguin Group (USA) Inc., 375 Hudson Street,
New York, New York 10014, USA

USA | Canada | UK | Ireland | Australia | New Zealand | India | South Africa | China

Penguin Books Ltd., Registered Offices: 80 Strand, London WC2R 0RL, England
For more information about the Penguin Group visit penguin.com.

First published by Roc, an imprint of New American Library,
a division of Penguin Group (USA) Inc.

First Printing, July 2013

Copyright © Glen Cook, 2013
All rights reserved. No part of this book may be reproduced, scanned, or
distributed in any printed or electronic form without permission. Please do not
participate in or encourage piracy of copyrighted materials in violation of the
author's rights. Purchase only authorized editions.

RoC REGISTERED TRADEMARK — MARCA REGISTRADA

ISBN 978-0-451-46523-8

Printed in the United States of America
10 9 8 7 6 5 4 3 2 1

PUBLISHER'S NOTE
This is a work of fiction. Names, characters, places, and incidents either are the
product of the author's imagination or are used fictitiously, and any resemblance
to actual persons, living or dead, business establishments, events, or locales is
entirely coincidental.
    The publisher does not have any control over and does not assume any
responsibility for author or third-party Web sites or their content.

If you purchased this book without a cover you should be aware that this book
is stolen property. It was reported as "unsold and destroyed" to the publisher
and neither the author nor the publisher has received any payment for this
"stripped book."

ALWAYS LEARNING   PEARSON

1

"Love sucks."

"If you're a vampire." Strafa scattered covers as she struck, diving at the spot on the side of my neck that triggers the reflex. Just the threat of the tickle kicks me into a psycho self-defense mode.

She bounced away laughing, sat up, her eyes the color of stout flecked with gold. Fair warning! Flee, Garrett, flee! Run for your sanity!

Being a skilled observer, I observed, "You're not wearing anything."

"I never wear anything to bed."

"I know. But now I'm officially taking notice."

"Ooh! You wicked man! I see how much you've noticed. Is that all on my account?"

I grunted and tried pulling a sheet over me.

She laughed. "That's why I do it."

Yeah. So I'll notice. So things will happen. The real devil wears nothing, extremely well.

Strafa is as close to the perfect woman as this brokedown onetime Marine can imagine. She's beautiful. She's always cheerful. She's always ready, for anything. She is fun to be with. She is fun to be around. She's even rich. What more could a man ask?

Well, a nicer band of in-laws would help.

The rich is because Strafa Algarda is the Windwalker, Furious Tide of Light, one of TunFaire's premier sorceresses. She has these immense, terrible powers but very little interest in using them. The rest of her family, though . . . Another matter. Definitely another matter. They are weird and scary people, all. And I was on the brink of being pulled in forever.

I dove, tackling her. She laughed. "Distract me all you want, but we still have to go see Grandmother."

"I'll keep you here all day long."

"Braggart. I'll let you try tomorrow. But right now . . ."

Right now time was running out. And even Furious Tide of Light dared not make Shadowslinger wait, so it wasn't long before we started the endless, too brief two-block up-hill trudge to Grandma's house.

2

Strafa's daughter, Kevans, let us in. Kevans has a lot of her father in her. She isn't as slim or beautiful as Strafa. And she insists on being sixteen going on fifty around her mother. "Mom! You two are worse than a cage full of ferrets. You're *old*! Can't you at least pretend to act your age?"

Old is a matter of viewpoint. Strafa was thirty-one, which made for interesting generational math. I ignored it. I ignore the weird Algarda dynamic as much as they let me.

I kept my mouth shut. If I stuck even one finger into the daughter-mother competition, I'd get my arm ripped off and fed to me after one or the other beat me with it.

Yes. The family was the downside to being engaged to the most wonderful, perfect, ridiculously beautiful, loving woman in the world. There was no getting out of having the in-laws included in the package.

Kevans and I get along fine when her mother isn't around. I get along with their father when Kevans and Strafa aren't around. Barate is a smart guy. He really thinks that I'm the best thing ever to happen to Strafa—though it didn't always used to be that way.

Nobody gets along with Grandmother Shadowslinger.

She works hard to make it that way. I am assured, however, that she thinks well of me. As well as is possible, she being Shadowslinger. My most endearing trait was that I was willing to make an honest woman of her spinster granddaughter.

Strafa asked Kevans, "What kind of mood is she . . . ? Right. Stipulated. Stupid question."

"Foul. But not because of anything any of us did, for once."

Like most of the more ferocious magic-users who dwell on the Hill, Constance Algarda, commonly called Shadow-slinger, occupied a vast, gloomy, dark edifice that looked like ghouls and graveyard fetches had thrown it up more than two hundred years ago. A parade of grim residents had installed countless bad smells, dire dust, spiders with webbed accessories, and lots of random clutter. Shadow-slinger was not famous for her housekeeping. She was not your cliché tubby little rosy-cheeked homemaker kind of grandmother.

Most of the smells actually existed only inside my imagination, but Shadowslinger had fixed them there—while wearing a big, greasy, evil grin. A reminder, she said, never making it clear of what. One odor I never failed to catch was that of rotting flesh. It seeped out of the very walls.

Nobody else ever smelled it.

"She does it because she cares," Strafa said. "What do you want to bet she makes it go away after the wedding?" Her eyes were big and blue and filled with self-deluding optimism.

I hunch my shoulders and take what I have to take. It's the price of admission to paradise.

Kevans told us we should follow her, then complained every step of the way till we reached the room where Shadowslinger waited. Then the girl actually smiled for a moment.

Kevans likes her grandmother, though I've never heard her say a good word about the hag.

3

I was startled. Strafa squeaked. She was surprised, too.

Shadowslinger was not alone.

I'd never visited this room. It was big and comfortable and more civilized than any I'd yet seen inside Shadowslinger's suburb of Hell. There wasn't a single torture device, nor even one torturee, in sight. There were rich carpets, richer tapestries, big, ridiculously comfortable chairs, and massive furniture. A fire roared enthusiastically in a fireplace behind Grandmother, who was old enough to be convinced that she was cold all the time. A brace of servants in livery tended to the needs of her guests. I knew Barate, my father-in-law-to-be. He had been half devoured by a monster chair. He had a bone china teacup to his lips when we entered.

He had a relationship with his mother that was as difficult as Kevans's was with her mother. Every little motion he made mocked her unusual efforts toward propriety.

There were another three people present. They were all older than me. Two were older than Barate and might be as old as Shadowslinger herself. I didn't know them. Strafa did. She loosed a little gasp of surprise. I whispered, "Is this good or bad?"

Her right hand slipped into my left, trembling. "All of the above."

A lean man, balding, six feet tall, stood about that far to the left of Shadowslinger. He was armed with another bone china cup. He had an upper-crust attitude on, but his clothing was workaday. He would attract no attention on the street.

Nearby, as though trying to take reassurance from that man's presence without becoming personally involved, was a woman of an age well beyond the thirty-something she artfully strove to project. She was tall, thin to the verge of emaciation, equally plainly dressed but from a high-end source. My first thought was that her hair should be short and silver-gray instead of a grand profusion of chestnut curls.

The final guest occupied a chair like Barate's, a few feet from Algarda. Unlike the others, he seemed comfortable.

A friend of the family.

I looked no closer because Shadowslinger had begun to respond to our arrival.

The ugly old tub of goo was scary just sitting there, behind a massive oak table a good four feet by eight. She would weigh in at three hundred pounds but was only five feet three inches tall on those occasions when she actually stood. She got around aboard a fleet of customized wheelchairs. Strafa said she hadn't been able to stand and support her own weight for more than minutes for as long as she could remember. But Constance Algarda did not need to be a ballet diva. She was Shadowslinger, one of the darkest and most powerful Karentine sorcerers alive.

Rumor suggested that she never ate where she could be seen. I'd never seen her touch a bite, yet she kept on getting bigger.

Shadowslinger's vast, wide mouth expanded into what she meant as a smile. She eyed me in a manner intended to be coquettish. My gorge rose. Gorge. Neat word. You don't get to deploy it very often.

My dearly beloved growled, "Grandmother, behave. Father, be merciful. Tell us what's going on. You've gotten poor Garrett out of bed six months before the crack of noon. You know how hard that is on him."

Barate would do the talking. His mother liked it that way. That made everything creepier.

He sat up straight and slid to the edge of his chair. He extended his right hand, palm upward, toward the lean, bald man. "Richt Hauser."

"Rich?" I said. He looked more like a Ned or a Newt.

"Richt." Hardening on the end consonant. "Hauser." With an "s" as in house, not as in hawser.

Strafa held my left arm with both hands. I was supposed to be impressed and maybe intimidated.

Richt Hauser did not so much as nod. That told me a lot about who he thought he was, which would be the most important man in the room.

Barate then indicated the woman. "Lady Tara Chayne Machtkess."

Seemed I ought to know that name, at least the Machtkess part. She inclined her head in response to my bow, smiling thinly beneath narrowed, calculating eyes. I caught a whiff of something predatory. And, behind that, of something that might be a frightened little girl.

Barate shifted hands. He indicated the man in the other easy chair. "Kyoga Stornes. Often underfoot around here because he's been my best friend since we were kids. But this time he's here because he has some skin in the game."

I knew the name. There were family legends about the adolescent adventures of Barate and Kyoga. At the moment Kyoga looked more like a victim than the perpetrator of malicious mischief.

Karma being a bitch?

Shadowslinger stirred impatiently. "Yes, Mother. Garrett, we need your expertise and resources."

Remarkably polite. But these weren't people I could tell to go away because I didn't feel like working. Which I would never have to do as long as I remained hooked up with my wonder woman, Strafa.

"How so? In what way?"

Shadowslinger got some exercise by pointing at Hauser. Unhappily, Hauser reported, "Signs of preliminaries for a Tournament of Swords have begun to appear. We all have someone likely to be conscripted into the game."

I had no idea what he was talking about. Neither did Strafa. She asked, "What is a Tournament of Swords?"

Hauser's instant response was irritation at being forced to explain. That morphed into an appreciation of the fact that this tournament business was not common knowledge even inside the highest levels of the sorcerer class. "Each few generations an uncertain supernatural process or power arises and compels a contest . . ."

He stopped. Emotion had cracked his cool. He struggled to regain his composure.

Barate took over. "What happens is, a bunch of talented people, usually kids, get chosen to participate. Most come from families in the sorcery business. They aren't asked if they want in. They're conscripted. They're supposed to fight until only one is left. That one wins the prize, which is a device containing all of the power of the defeated contestants combined. Back when the tournament was devised, the families wanted that so badly they all signed on. The final prize, power, would make the winner a minor god."

4

I glanced from face to face. Nobody looked like they thought Algarda was pulling my leg. Kevans made a noise that sounded like a bleat of fear, which might be justified if this was on the up-and-up.

"No bullshit, Garrett. Those two have grandkids that could get pulled in. Kyoga's son, Feder, seems to have gotten the news yesterday. Mother and I, naturally, are concerned for Kevans."

"You've lost me and confused me. Somebody or something picks out kids . . . always Hill kids? And they have no choice?"

"Almost always members of the founding families. But some of those don't exist anymore, as much because of the tournaments as anything, so brilliant outsiders get dragged in to make up the numbers. Or, even uglier, the summons can go out to more than one member of the same family."

That would be cruel. "All right. Cream-of-the-crop kids. And they're expected to murder one another until only one is left standing."

"Yes."

"Crap. How? Why? And how come the whole damned world doesn't know about it if it happens all the time?"

Strafa asked, "How can they make them fight? If they don't want to?"

I said, "That would be a good place to start. Yes."

"You have no choice. Say you're a pacifist and you refuse to participate. Someone will cut your throat just because you make it easy."

"In other words, what it is is an exaggerated and formalized, gamed-up version of what goes on among the ruling class every day, anyway."

That got me unpleasant looks from members of the ruling class.

Barate said, "Some will fight, always, for the prize or just to survive. Some will try to win so they can get strong enough to end the tournaments forever. Whatever, young people will die, some of them horribly. Not all of the victims will be people directly involved in the game. There's usually a lot of collateral damage."

"But the public doesn't notice."

"Mostly it doesn't happen in public. It's no gladiatorial contest, like a bare-knuckles boxing tournament. It's a secret war that, by its nature, can't help having public effects. It leaves corpses and localized disasters. Unexplained magical encounters in the night are common and often lethal."

Not unusual for TunFaire, really, until recently. Lately the city has suffered gut-wrenching spasms of early-stage law and order.

Barate said, "There is evidence in the historical record if you look. You won't need to dig for it. We'll give you a big head start by letting you interview several participants from the last tournament." He extended his hand to indicate Hauser, the Machtkess woman, and his mother.

Kyoga reported, "My father kept a journal detailing his efforts and that of his two Companions."

"But . . ."

Hauser said, "Families were involved. Families hand down oral histories. We refused to play by the old rules. We sabotaged and aborted the tournament. We attacked the devil in charge instead of our friends. And we thought we had ended the tournaments forever."

Lady Tara Chayne said, "We were wrong."

I asked, "All of you?" Kyoga was Barate's age.

Hauser said, "No. Meyness B. Stornes."

Kyoga said, "I said my father. I was still in diapers."

Hauser added, "Five of us rebelled. Meyness disappeared in the Cantard ten years later."

All right. I looked from face to face. Sooner or later they would get around to explaining how they thought I fit. Sooner, I hoped. I was getting hungry. Strafa's eyes had gone yellow with impatience. And Kevans was getting restless.

Hauser said, "We wrecked the last game because our grandparents got cut up bad in the round before that. That one didn't work out according to plan, either, though we never found out why. Everyone involved died before they could explain. Some of us, though, were old enough to understand and friends enough not to want to kill each other over something that we didn't believe was actually real."

Lady Tara Chayne said, "There have been six tournaments, none of which went according to design. Something always went wrong, but a lot of people died anyway. When we were young we thought the whole thing might just be an entertainment for devils. I'm no longer as sure as Richt is that there'd never be an actual payoff, but I'm still set on ending the insanity."

Hauser won no points by adding, "We're all too old to benefit, anyway."

Lady Machtkess said, "It's easier to get in a killer mood when it's your children at risk. When it's you yourself, you don't worry so much because when you're a kid you know you're invincible."

Barate stepped in. "This time we want to abort the thing before it starts and keep on till we end it forever."

I admitted, "I have to confess to being confused. I still don't have any idea of who, what, or why."

Lady Tara Chayne asked, "Isn't that what you do, though, Mr. Garrett? Find answers? I'm told that you're the best." She looked over at Shadowslinger, one eyebrow raised. "Constance would have us believe that you're a genius with a matchless network of shady connections. And that you're more discreet than the Civil Guard."

A rabid mammoth would be more discreet than those guys.

Somebody had been telling tall tales. That it might be Shadowslinger astonished me. She seldom showed anything but contempt. "True." Barely.

A double-hand squeeze on my left arm hinted that it might be in my interest to talk less and listen more, a skill I have honed for decades with slight success.

Barate said, "Mother believes that the tournament will play out differently this time because it will be heavily influenced by survivors from before."

"Um?"

"This round may begin with an effort by the Operators to remove those who helped scuttle it last time."

I pointed a finger at Lady Tara Chayne, Hauser, and Shadowslinger, swinging left to right.

"Us. Yes. Exactly," Hauser said. "We have been remiss, letting the matter slide for so long. We thought it was over forever. Or at least we hoped next time would hold off till after we were gone. But, honestly, some of us might admit fearing that it would come back to bite us someday."

Madam Machtkess said, "Someday has come."

I saw no arrogance here, only confidence and irritation at an outside force that dared try to use them. A common Hill attitude, actually. These were people grown old in treacherous environments.

"So, what shall I do with my special talents and outstandingly shady connections?" Carefully keeping my tone neutral. Strafa had hold of my arm, sending messages by squeezing brutally. In a way, she was thrilled that the man she had chosen, without consulting her elders, was now being welcomed to the family's conspiratorial heartland.

Shadowslinger watched me as if she were cataloging recipes she wanted to try.

Barate said, "First, we should identify the contestants. If we round them up before the killing starts, the whole stupid competition will fall apart. Nobody will have to die."

Hauser agreed. "We could save them all. And if we could identify the Operators . . ."

Shadowslinger summoned Barate close. She murmured into his ear. He then announced, "Mother has to leave us. She suggests that we all give Mr. Garrett whatever information we have so he can get started, especially with identifying the contestants."

Right.

Cynical me, I wondered how much actual identifying and rounding up they really intended.

5

It was dark and hungry out when Strafa and I left Shadowslinger's place, me brooding on the implausibility of a to-the-death elimination tournament involving mostly brilliant teenagers.

Twelve was the magical number of participants. Each would have a sidekick called a Mortal Companion, normally a close friend but sometimes a hired fighter. At some point, somewhere from the shadows, each contestant would attract a supernatural ally as well, called a Dread Companion. Too, there would be entities who chose participants, managed everything, refereed, and delivered coups de grâce if necessary. These were the Operators. They were a mystery. Nobody knew how they got recruited or what skin they had in the game. Evidently death was mandatory for the scheme to work fully. Losers couldn't just admit defeat, they had to die so their power could be folded into the final prize.

Identifying the Operators could give us a means to abort the whole absurd tournament.

My cynical, suspicious side already definitely wondered how the Operators would profit. My villainous side figured eliminating that crew would go a long way toward ending the game permanently, since there would be no one left to recruit a new team.

Though I had been immersed in it all day I remained

both skeptical and deeply confused. It was such a ridiculous way of doing business.

I asked Strafa, "Did you understand all of that?"

"Not so much."

"They talked a ton, and I think they were trying, but when something sounds that absurd you can't help thinking that they're either pulling your leg or not telling the whole story."

"You're right. But I don't think they were holding back. Bonegrinder did more talking than I've ever seen before."

"Bonegrinder?"

"Richt Hauser. His working name is Bonegrinder. He brought it back from his first trip to the war zone."

"And that creepy Machtkess woman?"

"She favors Moonblight. Unless she's feeling randy. I hear she becomes Mistress of Chains then. A play on her name."

"I'll skip finding out why. All righty, then. And they're really your grandmother's friends?"

"As much as can be with their kind. More so, probably, when they were young. Coconspirators is probably closer to the truth now. Where are we going?"

"To my house to check in with some of my matchless resources."

"We're going to go that far, why don't we fly? It's about to rain. We'll get soaked if we take time to walk."

"All right." Reluctantly. "But you don't have your broom." I like having something a bit more solid than air beneath my feet.

"You know I don't need a broom. You're just chicken."

She was right. "You got me. But hold up for a minute. I see civilians." A girl was headed our way, nine or ten, blond, well dressed, very pretty. A living doll. She held the hand of a groll, part giant, part troll, all strength and ugliness, impervious to most weapons but, blessed be, seldom aggressive. Full-grown grolls are big. This one was bigger than most, a good fourteen feet tall. He seemed to be walking in

his sleep, oblivious of his surroundings. The little girl, however, was alert and totally intense.

Strafa backed into me. "Grab on." She was anxious suddenly.

"Always up for that."

"You have a one-track mind, sir. But quit fooling around.
We need to get out of here. Now."

"Whose fault is that? You being you." I paid no attention to the kid, other than to note that she was rich enough
to rate a magnificent bodyguard.

My toes had just left the cobblestones. Strafa turned her
head. I tried to kiss her, for the moment forgetting what we
were up to. She lost her foothold on the sky. We collapsed
into a wriggling pile. The little girl stopped to scowl at us,
then told me, "If you aren't more careful you will be the
first to die."

Strafa ignored her. She sat up. "Gods, I wish we'd met when
I was Kevans's age. We would've had so much more time."

No. I thought not. When Strafa was Kevans's age she
already had a toddler underfoot and I was still shallow
enough for that to make a difference. Too, I was about to
head out for my five years in the war zone.

Chances are, I would have gone off, leaving her with another responsibility about to arrive, which I might have
been low enough not to have acknowledged. I wasn't nearly
as nice when I was younger.

But I'll never tell her we're both better off for life's having kept us apart as long as it did.

The little girl and her monster moved on hurriedly. I
asked, "What was that? Did you get that?"

"Let's just go. It turned out all right." Clearly shaken,
puzzled, and maybe a little frightened, like she had only
just survived a brush with a very dangerous unknown.

I got up, helped her get up, got around behind, and this
time behaved myself while she did what Windwalkers do.

We settled to the cobblestones outside the house where I'd
lived till Strafa carried me off to her mansion on the Hill. It

was dark red, brick, two-story, in perfect repair because my assistant Pular Singe is a freak about detail stuff. My bedroom lay athwart the front of the place, upstairs. Strafa's old habit had been to sneak in the window on the left, above the roof of the stoop.

This time we would go in through the front door, like normal visitors.

I observed, "Old Bones is definitely awake."

I knew because Singe opened the door while we were still getting untangled.

6

Pular Singe is a rat woman, descended from mutants created by sorcerers several centuries back. She stands about five feet tall when she forces herself into her most upright stance. I sort of adopted her when she was an adolescent. She has become the heart and soul of my investigative business. I go out and have fun digging while she stays home managing records, finances, the house, and all the other stuff I let slide because it's boring. She has a genius for it. She keeps everything abovewater.

Singe is also the best scent tracker in TunFaire and, maybe, the best in the Karentine Kingdom. She makes a little cash on her own, on the side, doing contract tracking, usually for the Civil Guard when they're willing to pay up front.

None of those guys work for pride alone, but they seem convinced that the rest of us should donate our time and take physical risks entirely out of a sense of civic duty.

Singe didn't say a word as she let us inside.

My housekeeper and cook, Dean, came out of the kitchen drying his hands. He was ancient. He had begun to develop a stoop and was moving more gingerly than he had just weeks ago. His voice was strong when he greeted us, though.

Dean was a huge fan of Strafa Algarda.

A rattle and thump thundered down the stair from the second floor. The racket ceased a moment before an utterly cool, studiedly indifferent, totally cute little brunette of fourteen stepped into view. "Oh. It's only you. Well, hello." She headed into the kitchen as though that had been her plan all along.

Penny Dreadful is not a huge fan of Strafa Algarda.

She is my partner's pet. Another adoptee of the house.

We're all strays. Even Strafa made some bones that way.

"We came to see Himself," I told Singe.

"There is a surprise."

Dean turned to follow Penny. There would be tea and cakes soon enough. There might be some real food later.

Shadowslinger was too frugal to waste food on visitors.

7

My business partner is a nonhuman beast known as a Loghyr. Weighing in at nearly a quarter ton, he makes Shadowslinger look svelte. His species may be related to mammoths or mastodons. He looks something like a hairless baby mammoth that decided to strut around on its hind legs. He has a miniature version of the snoot.

I'm not sure about the strut. I've never seen a Loghyr on the hoof, and only mine and one other one dead. They are an uncommon breed.

The species has several interesting characteristics. Foremost is a huge reluctance to leave their flesh after they die. My Loghyr, affectionately known as the Dead Man, was murdered centuries ago. With mobility and breath denied him, he developed other skills.

Interesting. A Tournament of Swords. I thought the Hill got over that insanity generations back.

He reads minds. People who know are terrified and tend to stay away. They refuse to believe that he doesn't spy when he isn't invited because they know how they would behave if they had the identical ability.

"You've heard about this tournament stuff before, then?"

Indeed. Marginally. It is the sort of insanity only those afflicted with an insatiable hunger for power would pursue. It is a process whereby power can be concentrated and given

*over to a single wielder. Properly executed, the tournament
would leave its winner strong enough to challenge the gods.*

That, itself, may be why no tournament has yet gone according to design.

Clever Garrett got it in one. "In order for there to be
one big winner, there have to be a lot of losers."

*Exactly. Where losing will hurt a lot more than it would in
the daily lottery. And Hill folk are never the sort to scruple
about doing whatever is necessary to avoid losing. And the
gods themselves might have an interest.*

"The players would all have a good idea of one another's strengths and weaknesses, too, since they all know each
other."

*More importantly, they would know those things about
themselves.*

"It's a wonder TunFaire wasn't destroyed in one of those
matches."

This city has its own protective magic. After a fashion.

I misunderstood. I fantasized some vast oversoul for the
entirety of the polity.

*I meant stupidity! And the fact that though the tourna-
ments are organized, the fighting is not. Its effects are localized. The worst of the clashes always take place on the Hill.*

"Which wouldn't much amaze anyone anywhere else."

Or cause noteworthy despair.

"So. We have a tournament fixing to get ready to commence to begin. Survivors and scuttlers from the last tournament want me to wreck this one before it can come
together."

He wasted no time suggesting that refusing the commission was an option. Not if I meant to forge ahead with
Strafa.

And, perhaps, he had motives of his own.

*The first step may be both easier and more difficult than
you imagine.*

Cryptics. He loves them. In a past life he interned as an
oracle in a cave filled with weed smoke.

"Meaning?"

The roster of potential participants has been narrowed already. Most of the draftees should be identifiable by reasoned elimination. Who from each family is the most likely to be chosen?

Of course. No need to work on that, really. Shadowslinger could tell me most everything I'd need to know.

In fact, she has done that already. You were not paying adequate attention.

She did? She had! My problem was, Strafa had been doing something more interesting close by. Something like breathing fetchingly. Why do I always get distracted? "So what I really need to do is find the Operators and any outsiders who might take places belonging to families that no longer exist."

Exactly.

"Crap. So where do I start?"

I suspect that all you have to do is leave the house to find that out.

He put pictures into my head. Things I had seen without paying much heed. A pretty little blond girl saying something obscure, then an odd smell as Strafa and I lifted off to fly to Macunado Street. And the people in that room at Grandma's house.

They almost certainly involved you with the intention of letting you draw the lightning.

Meaning they might actually put the word out so that unknown baddies would become concerned that Garrett might pose a threat.

"I'm about to marry into a lovely crowd, aren't I?"

It occurred to me that they must suspect the identity of at least one Operator if they were sure they could point out the goat tied to the stake in the clearing and reasonably expect results. Or maybe a lack of results would be equally informative, in its own way.

Please ask Miss Algarda to cease charming Dean and join us. And, while I made the long trek to the kitchen, he sent, *We have a resource today that was unavailable to any previous generation. We will take full advantage of that.*

I got the distinct impression that the Tournament of Swords thoroughly offended his sometimes curious sensibilities.

8

I could not get over the deference Old Bones showed Strafa. He could have touched her mind at will, but, instead, he had me carry a verbal invitation.

I will not give this one any excuse to run away.

I found her not only charming Dean but also eroding Penny's adamant heart. Singe was hunkered down in her office, doing something productive. That girl never took time off to loaf.

Back to the Dead Man's room. *Ask Miss Algarda.*

Miss Algarda demanded, "Why won't he deal with me directly?"

"He might be afraid of you."

Not true. But the suggestion ought to trigger . . .

Very well. Inasmuch as neither of you cares much about courtesy.

He left me out of their exchange. And she did not bother speaking her half of the conversation aloud.

Later, Singe would tell me, "He is smitten with Strafa, you know. He does not want to do anything that will stress your relationship."

Amazing. With the rest of us he shows all the thoughtfulness and sensitivity of a barbarian horde. Which he would deny, of course.

Very well. Dean has a meal ready. Go enjoy that while I digest this information.

I could smell the food. My gut was clamoring already. He didn't have to sweet-talk me.

Dean served up steaming bowls of chicken and dumplings. I wondered how he had managed so fast, but not much. I was used to his kitchen magic.

Once I began to slack off, I asked Strafa, "What did he want?"

"Whatever he couldn't get from you."

"Like?"

"Like what Grandmother told me when we were out of the meeting room at the same time."

"Secret from me?"

"No. But we'll talk business later."

Penny was there with us. So was Dean with his big, hairy ears. What they did not overhear they could not repeat if someone caught them on the street and squeezed. Kind of harsh, militaristic thinking for inside the family, but still realistic.

Strafa was taking this business more grimly than was I. That was scary in itself. Normally, she avoided taking the mystical, magical side of life anywhere as seriously as most Hill people.

She did not want to turn into her grandmother.

Penny understood. She harrumphed, left the table, then left the room. She stomped along the hall, presumably to go cry on Singe's shoulder, or maybe the Dead Man's.

She wouldn't get much sympathy from either.

Strafa observed, "She sure is developing a cute butt, isn't she?"

"Honestly. A guy can't help noticing those things." Especially a guy who is a trained observer.

This guy was on his way to becoming a trained companion, too. He made no effort to defend himself any further.

The hole only ever gets deeper.

"You can notice. I don't mind." With a whole lot of subtext. "She is growing up fast. And she's going to be a heart-breaker."

Strafa is less unreasonable than most members of her species, but fully open-minded she is not. None of them really is. Those who make the claim can be the most dangerous.

9

The Dead Man has multiple minds. He can work on several problems at once and reach some astounding conclusions fast. That's why he makes such a good partner. His athletic skills are limited, though.

I would like to interview everyone who was in that room this morning. I am sure the request has been anticipated. I am equally certain that it will be refused by most. It may be instructive to see who refuses and their choices of excuses for doing so.

I glanced at Strafa. She shrugged. So beautifully.

You are allowing yourself to become distracted again.

I was. "I can't help it. Make her stop."

"Make me stop what?"

"Being you."

Focus, children.

"Yes, sir."

To this point this business has been an exercise in intellect. But a Tournament of Swords does become, by design, intensely physical and violent. The mystery is not mysterious, for the most part. The way to abort the Tournament is self-evident. Shadowslinger has begun the process. The question I would pose, then, is, have the Operators anticipated her effort?

I had one of those moments that are all too rare. "They might be looking for us to collect the contenders in one place."

Probably not the Operators themselves. There was a musing note to his communication, as though he'd just had a new and more disturbing thought. *Yes. We must not put our eggs into one basket. Miss Algarda. Strafa, if I may. Please bring your daughter here. Garrett, I want you to round up any members of the Faction that you can find. Ask them to report here, too.*

"The Faction? Why?"

The Faction is a kid gang of a remarkable sort. Instead of dimwit thugs, the members are all scary smart and not very physical. Kevans is a key member. Her best friend and my sort of surrogate son, another of my strays, Cypres Prose, was their leader. The Faction are as much misfits as any gangster kids but, again, scary smart. And many come from the Hill.

The Faction would be an ideal talent pool for substitute tournament contestants.

"You sure? None of those kids suffers from ambition. All they want is for grown-ups to leave them alone so they can mess around with strange hobbies and weird research."

True. To a point. But we have seen bad apples among them before. The prospect of vast power might lure a few to get some exercise. Power hunger belongs to the culture where they were raised.

Was he poking fun my way? That sounded like something I would say. More, it sounded like a subtle commentary on my tendency to remain an object not in motion.

Still . . . "Any suggestion on how I get them to come here?"

Lie.

I started to say something about how lying adults were half the reason those kids were strange.

You know them. Tailor something to each ego. Once they have come into range, none of that will matter.

I glanced at Strafa. She had been included. She nodded. She agreed with Himself. "It's for their own safety, Garrett. I'll make Kevans come. She'll bring Kip." And Kip's influence would pull in most of the rest.

I might not have to become a major bad guy after all.

Again, and always, we shall have to honor the possibility that our efforts have been anticipated. May, in fact, have been factored into the master plan. Miss Algarda . . . Strafa. Are your grandmother and her associates committed to the extent that they might willingly hire bodyguards?

Predictably, the financial conscience of the household chose that moment to appear. Old Bones had been keeping Singe up to date. She said, "We do not have the money to offer protective services at our expense, nor on spec. And those people often fail to honor their financial obligations."

Strafa said, "I can afford to look out for my daughter. And Kip as well." And the rest of the Faction, too, honestly. I had not been prepared for just how rich the Algardas actually were, and most of that wealth had somehow settled onto Strafa, maybe because the family had made her life so ugly in other ways.

I had not known about the wealth when I took up with Strafa. She had not mentioned it. In fact, I knew about it now only because Old Bones had seen it inside Strafa's head and thought that I should know the full truth about my future wife.

I said, "Kip can afford to look out for himself. He's richer than most gods. The challenge will be to convince him that the danger is real."

Singe bowed her head slightly. "He will be a hard sell."

I foresee possible complications in regard to lifeguarding.

"Well, of course it can't be simple, like we just hire Saucerhead Tharpe and a few thugs and the baddies will leave us be. How will it get complicated?" Both of us denying Singe time to slap on another coat of fiscal doom.

Strafa. Did your grandmother explain about the Dread Companions?

My eyebrows leapt up. Singe's would have done the same if she'd had eyebrows to set a-leaping. Old Bones hadn't winkled out every foul little whiff that Strafa had gotten from Shadowslinger already? His levels of consideration and courtesy were unprecedented.

"She mentioned them without giving a clear explanation. I know they're supernatural allies but not much more."

How could he not have churned up the mental mud by trampling through the gardens of Strafa's mind? What was going on with the old psychic hooligan?

"She went on a lot more about plain old Companions. It's apparently critical to pick someone who can stand up against any pressure. Wouldn't a Dread Companion sort of be the same thing, only supernatural?"

Not quite. Mortal Companions are chosen by Family Champions. Friends, as you say. And it would be useful if they were trustworthy. However, they are not that critical, overall. Dread Companions are, usually, what the tournaments come to be about.

"Wow," I said, applying my best verbal, sarcastic sneer. "Them old-timers went to a lot of trouble to make semiorganized mayhem sound all important."

They did indeed. That would have to do with legitimization and easing of associated guilt.

I am not clear on the complete mechanism. Perhaps no one is. In the earlier tournaments some truly baleful entities, demons, if you prefer, became involved, one Dread Companion for each Mortal Champion. They protected the Champions and did most of the murder. They carried their Champions' powers and, most times, their lives. A few Champions did not perish when they were defeated, but what was left was never worth keeping alive. The results were always final for the Dread Companions. Their powers were collected, too. I never heard of a definitive reason for their having gotten drawn in. Compulsion must have been central, but the how and why remain mysterious, as does the potential payoff for the demonic victor.

I grumbled, "Come on. This is too freaky."

"Grandmother did warn me to watch for demons around Kevans. She didn't think they would be a major threat, though. She says the demon realm is fed up with human incompetence and that any demons who do turn up are likely to be petty gold diggers. Demonic equivalents of purse snatchers, as stupid as your average street thug."

I asked, "Did I just hear some good news?"

Very much to be hoped. It could be true. The tournament that included Shadowslinger, Bonegrinder, and Moonblight was sufficiently low-key that I was unaware of it until now. Demonic manifestations and supernatural combats, by their nature, tend to be flashy.

"The way I see it, we have tons of information that probably isn't the right information. We need to figure out what to expect today."

We could infer that quickly had I access to your grandmother's mind, Strafa.

"I can ask her. You can guess how likely she is to volunteer to come here."

Old Bones has tasted and smelled plenty of wickedness in his time, but I wasn't sure he was ready for Shadowslinger.

Fear not, Garrett. Shadowslinger is more bark and urban legend than she is bite and ugly history. She worked hard to create her legend.

Experience suggested that I trust his judgment. But wow! Grandma was so creepy.

"What do you think, Chuckles? Is it even appropriate for us to get involved? It's sorted itself out without us every time before."

He inserted visions of faces into my consciousness, starting with Kip Prose and Kevans Algarda. He followed up with a real-time look at Strafa glaring at me in disbelief.

"Are you deaf as well as dim, love? There isn't any free will involved. We're in whether we like it or not. We were in before Grandmother asked you to poke around. Please think."

Wow.

You see?

"I see. So, what do you think our course should be?"

Not entirely what your future family seems to be hoping.

*This would be my personal suggestion, given four centuries
of experience.*

He did not include Strafa in what followed.

Old Bones thought I ought to take it outside the family.

He went back to a point he had made earlier, now in
more detail.

*I told you we have resources unique to the modern age. I
posit that, as such, they have not been taken into account by
the Operators.*

"Huh?" Whatever he was on about, it hadn't come clear
to me, either.

*The Unpublished Committee. This is the sort of thing that
it was created to handle.*

"Yes! Ha!" I laughed out loud. He was absolutely correct. I might be able to abort the entire tournament horror
show with one office visit, if I could be convincing. "Deal
Relway will jump all over this!"

10

The evening started out rainy, not in any driving, windy form. Then it became a drizzle of the sort that is more depressing than soaking, a halfhearted weather episode that leaves the world feeling colder than it is and you wanting nothing more than to get inside, close to a fire. It got better later on.

After a nice evening at the Macunado place, Strafa and I split up. She wanted to go flying, then to drop by her grandmother's house to try to arrange for the folks we had met there to visit the Dead Man. She promised to see me back at her house in the afternoon.

After a massive breakfast devoured at a ridiculously early hour, I headed for the Al-Khar. It was raining again. I hunched down deep inside my canvas coat. What breeze there was came from behind. I dedicated my attention to wishing that I had a hat with a more generous brim, especially in back. The beast riding my scalp just then did not keep the rain from running down the back of my neck.

People were out doing make-a-living stuff despite the hour and weather. I spent some pity on them for having to work, then some more on me for getting rained on when I ought not to have to lift a pinkie again.

The great dirty yellow ugliness of the Al-Khar, Tun-Faire's Civil Guard headquarters, hove up out of the mist. They should paint it, or something. Anything to make it less of an eyesore.

I lumbered past a rank of transplanted poplars that would, once they grew and leafed out, slap a layer of pancake over the ugly, then hove to just in out of the rain, in a tunnel-like ancillary entrance. I considered those trees. They said a lot about the Civil Guard. They declared the age of law and order solidly begun. They dared anyone to be bold enough to try converting Guard property into firewood.

The city had been stripped of almost every stick outside the Royal Arboretum, for conversion to warmth, by the impoverished and refugees, before the law and order affliction commenced with a vengeance and became a full-fledged, citywide pandemic.

"May I help you, sir?"

The voice came from behind a small barred window on the left side of the tunnel, just before it was blocked by massive, antique wooden doors. An attractive brunette looked out from behind the bars. Not so long ago I would have been enthusiastic about letting her know that, indeedy-do, she certainly could, in several interesting ways. Instead, I deployed some of the gentlemanly skills I have been polishing since Strafa staked a claim backed by the full faith and terror of the Algarda clan.

"Yes, ma'am. My name is Garrett. I have private intelligence I need to pass on to the General personally."

Silence stretched for several heartbeats. She pushed her face right up against the bars. Damn, she had beautiful eyes. "Garrett, you say?"

"Garrett. Yes, ma'am. That Garrett."

"Well, you're big enough. And you look like you might have been a Marine. A long time ago."

She had to know who I was. Everybody at the Al-Khar knows Garrett. Garrett is a one-of-a-kind . . .

"Haven't kept in shape, have you?"

"Excuse me?"

"I'm sorry. You don't measure up to the hype."

"What?"

"I thought you'd be better-looking, too. And less dinged-up."

"That's just character!" What the hell was this? "I'm sorry I couldn't be what you wanted me to be. Look, I'm not really pressed for time, but I'm not into verbal abuse, either. Or standing around in the rain. And I do think I might have somebody following me. It's possible they could take a wild hair and try to stop me once they realize that this is where I've been headed."

I made the follower part up. It might get her moving.

"I'm sorry. I'm just surprised to see that you aren't a giant. You'll be safe there as long as you stay behind the murder holes. I'll be right back."

An iron plate chunked down in front of the iron bars. I barked a protest but stopped when I heard a crossbow creak as someone spanned it behind one of the murder holes.

Nobody would listen to me and an even smaller population was likely to care what I had to say.

A pair of massive, iron-strapped wooden doors filled the passage a dozen feet back. The walls were not really that thick, though. The Al-Khar only pretends to be a fortress. The exterior walls were the back sides of inward-facing cells and offices, though the stonework at street level could withstand considerable abuse. The passage through was eight feet wide. There was a slim sally port in the left-hand door, so skinny that I would have to turn sideways to get through.

That skinny door opened and invited me in.

I have visited the Al-Khar often, usually on business, occasionally as an involuntary guest. I hadn't used this entrance since they installed the welcoming window and skinny door. The murder holes were always there with guys inside who hoped that this would finally be the day when they got to use their crossbows. I eased through the skinny door thinking I would find a couple of red tops on the other side, waiting to pat me down before they took me to the General.

I slid into an upright coffin instead. The door clunked shut before I could change my mind.

I don't like tight places. Not even a little. I really don't like tight places. It was a miracle that I kept my composure. I treated myself to one lone girlish shriek, then focused on finding creative descriptions of the dams of the motherless dogs who had . . .

Click! Ker-chunk! Screech!

The back side of the coffin swung away.

I backed off on the rhetoric. Some red tops are overly sensitive.

I keep getting smarter as I age. Or it could be that I have developed an allergy to nightsticks.

Four tin whistles occupied the space behind the door. Three were my size, a little over six feet, a little over two hundred pounds of rippling . . . muscle, all equally scarred up. The other one was a big guy who probably ate bricks drenched in acid for breakfast. They carried chains and clubs, pole arms with hooks and thief-takers on the business end, and at least one weighted throwing net.

"Sorry, guys! I maybe got overexcited. I just came to report . . ."

They showed no interest at all.

The big door without a coffin attachment creaked open. Uh-oh. I noted that the tin whistles were dressed for the weather. They were going after my imaginary pursuers.

I clenched my jaw, recalling all those times when my mother reminded me that one tends to learn a lot more a lot faster when one does not have one's piehole open, trying to scam somebody holding a hammer.

Mom was a saint and a sage. And some other things I still get upset about whenever she gets into my head.

The woman from behind the window bars reappeared. She proved to be more interesting in portrait than when seen from head to toe. Everything from just above where the cleavage ought to start, downward, was too wide, too ample, inadequate, or just plain weirdly put together.

She was a personality kind of girl.

I got no opportunity for a more exhaustive inventory. She had not brought me Westman Block.

This fellow was short. He was ugly. Troops of nonhuman adventurers had enjoyed themselves swinging through his family tree. Most must have been ill-tempered and eternally suspicious because their descendant was in a bad mood and suspicious all the time.

But less so than usual right now.

Which did nothing to improve my temper or soften my inclination to be suspicious.

11

I was face-to-face with Director Relway of the Unpublished Committee for Royal Security. Most people would not recognize the runt if he was snapping around their ankles, but I had butted heads with him several times. He was smiling. That was so unusual that I made sure my pockets hadn't been picked already.

It was too late to make sure that I had an escape route plotted.

The ugly little man commanded more genuine hurt-you power than almost anybody but the queen of the underworld. He could intimidate the King himself, and all the sane people on the Hill. Irk Deal Relway and you could fall off the stage of the world forever. Irk him badly enough and he might arrange for you never to have existed at all.

Only some crazy Hill folk and lunatic criminal bosses, like the Contague family, were not afraid of Deal Relway.

Belinda Contague, who headed the main Outfit, had all the power Relway had, and more people she could set to doing dirty deeds.

In his heart of hearts, Director Relway would like to rename his Royal outfit the Unpublished Committee for State Security. But by whatever name his people are the secret police.

He recognizes neither constraints nor limits where law enforcement is concerned. I've never seen him abuse his power for his own benefit, but you surely don't want to be a crook and catch his eye. More so, you don't want to get caught up in any corruption. Relway has a true problem grasping the finer points of baksheesh. He seems sure that a request for a bribe is actually an appeal for a set of broken fingers.

"Why are you nervous, Garrett?"

"I'm usually nervous when people step out of character."

He understood. His grin broadened. His companion was just as nervous as I was. She edged toward her post, hoping to be out of sight and mind before the real Deal came stomping back.

He told me, "I'm just in a good mood, Garrett. Feeling fulfilled. Unless you're on some preemptive mission to deceive us, of course."

Ah. The real Deal was on his way. Only . . .

Only not so much. He twisted the knife by slapping on another happy grin. "Helenia tells me you want to report illegal activity. That's marvelous. It gives me hope that we've actually begun getting through to you." Pause a couple of heartbeats for dramatic effect, not so I could wedge in a response. Then, "But what makes me happiest of all is that you brought me Preston Womble." He extended his right hand to indicate the men who had gone out into the rain, now returning, bringing with them a goofy-looking little bald guy who was ready to break out in tears.

I observed, "Huh?"

"He was the one following you."

The huge man, who had a hold on Womble that engulfed Preston's upper right arm, reported, "He says he's been on the job since yesterday, boss. Picked Garrett up on the Hill last night."

Seemed like Preston Womble, whom I had made up so I could get some attention, was not inclined to keep his mouth shut. Relway would appreciate that.

The Director grunted, told me, "You brought him to us so we could sweep him up. You get points for that. I've wanted to chat with Preston for a long time, but his girlfriend always smells us coming before we can close the trap."

I restated my thesis. "Huh?" How come I never spotted Womble? Was I so distracted these days that I couldn't tell when I was being tailed?

Apparently so.

That wasn't good. It wasn't promising in my line of work.

One of the smaller red tops announced, "He wasn't alone, Chief. Elona Muriat was with him."

"Of course she was. But she got away," Relway said. "Naturally, she got away. She always does. We'll just make do with Preston." He glowered at the little bald man, who tried to melt like a slug dancing on salt. Relway told me, "Muriat is so slick she'll slide out of her own skin one of these days."

I found myself at a loss for meaningful words, but nevertheless managed to croak, "Who are these people? I never heard of them."

"They belong to a new crop of lowlifes that ripened while you were on hiatus."

For one reason or another, mostly the woman who preceded Strafa, I had left the adventurous life till I fell into the mess where Strafa hijacked my future. We had been acquainted before, but neither of us had been in emotional circumstances where we could acknowledge our mutual interest.

"Um."

"Garrett. I like a man who knows when to keep his mouth shut. All right. Details. Preston and Elona are freelancers. Not exactly a couple. Friends with benefits, possibly. They don't always work together. They aren't heavy work types. They're more like you. Nosies. Preston has guts in action but not much courage in static sets like interrogations. He'll tell us why he was watching you if he knows. Or, at least, he'll tell us who paid him to do it."

Interesting that he called them lowlifes, then told me they were in the same racket as me. I would file that as something worth remembering.

One of Relway's beefy boys hustled up. "Preston is babbling already, Chief. Him and Muriat was hired to follow this guy, just to see where he went and who he talked to."

"He name any names?"

"Vicious Min."

Relway did a silent "Huh?" response. "Who?"

I said, "And there is another name that I don't know."

"Marty?" Relway made a two-handed, come-on gesture.

"Preston says female, middle age, very large, giants in the family a ways back, teeth like a piranha that never learned to brush, breath to match, and a real badass attitude. Plus a lousy sense of style. Says he's sorry, but he was so intimidated he didn't take a closer look. Says Muriat can give us more when we catch her."

Relway sneered. "Like that's going to happen. All right. Sweat his ass. We can't charge him for anything because stupid isn't a crime yet, but we can hold him on suspicion, or in protective custody, or some damned thing."

The ugly little man eyed me then, like he thought I belonged in the cell next to Womble. And might have entertained the notion, if for no better reason than that freelancers aren't under adequate state control.

Relway said, "So, Garrett, you think there's a connection between what you want to tell me and the fact that you have some intellectual cousins riding in your hip pocket?"

"Probably. But I couldn't guess why."

Hell I couldn't, considering that I was connected to the Algardas now. I wasn't just going to get the Strafa loving. Everything else that came with a Hill family was coming to me now, too, at least out there at the edge of their dust cloud.

12

The catch crew took Preston to his guest suite. More hospitably, Director Relway took me to his personal quarters, which doubled as his working space. Before he acquired his current status, that space had been two jail cells. Relway had removed some intervening bars and permanently locked the door of one cell. He had no privacy, although no one else occupied space in the area.

I could not be comfortable there, despite having visited before. Relway understood and savored my discomfort. He did resist the temptation to suggest that I reflect on what it would be like to become a permanent resident.

Deal Relway knows that no one else in the world is honest enough and trustworthy enough not to deserve being caged. Deal Relway is the world's lone perfect pillar of righteousness.

I exaggerate, but not much.

His patience, tolerance, and self-control suggested that he had something on his mind. He thought I could help, somehow. He did not explain right away, though. He deferred.

He did say, "General Block isn't in today, which is why Helenia came to me about you." He paused. I didn't shove anything into the silence. "She says you've stumbled across a new criminal enterprise."

Had I said anything to give the woman that idea? Well, maybe she heard that, or at least said so after what I told her fermented inside her head before it came back out in a report to Relway. And the thesis was sound. That was why I had come to the Al-Khar.

"Let me try to tell it in one go and you ask questions after."

"I'm listening." He settled into a chair with very little padding, steepled his hands under his chin, and waited.

Like I said, Relway makes me uncomfortable. Crazy people always do. Though Relway is supposedly one of the good guys, he is also completely loony. Deadly loony.

The twitch in the right corner of his mouth said he was aware of the effect his behavior was having. He was enjoying my discomfort.

I told my story. I left out nothing. He wasn't crazy enough to hassle Shadowslinger's friends. He let me ramble, showing an impressive range of expressions as I proceeded; then he did homage to his normal disbelief by asking, "What did you leave out?"

"Nothing." I have sometimes withheld something. We both knew that. He always ripped me about it and I always lied, claiming that I was doing no such thing. "Really, truly, swear on your favorite religious tract. This is a whole new kind of weird for me. Wait. Maybe I did . . . Yeah. You could say I left out the fact that Shadowslinger, Bonegrinder, and all them probably wouldn't want me talking to the law."

"I took that into account."

I offered a raised eyebrow by way of response.

"Hill folks think they're above the law. I can't reason out why they would set Preston and Elona on your trail, though."

"Me, either."

"Are you into anything else?"

"No. Just Strafa, these days."

"The Windwalker. I envy you, Garrett. I truly envy you, being on a personal name basis with . . . Never mind. Are you sure there's nothing else?" Then he stopped, thinking.

I filled this silence. "Preston Womble. Elona Muriat. And Vicious Min. I really, honestly, never heard of any of them. But heading down to Macunado Street last night, with Strafa, I caught a whiff of Lurking Fehlske."

Fehlske is in the surveillance racket, too. He is a genius at remaining invisible. He is like a ghost. Unfortunately, he is also allergic to bathwater.

Relway waved a hand dismissively. "His sort are in endless supply." Putting me down without addressing me directly. "You still work for the brewery, right? Any possible connection there?"

"Who would mess with Max Weider?"

The brewing king is as powerful as the boss of the Outfit and Director Relway combined when it comes to having the financial wherewithal to impose his will. But Max isn't that kind of guy so long as the world leaves him alone. However, there is no shortage of too stupid to survive.

"Still only the usual minor pilfering, then."

"That never goes away completely, though there's not much of that anymore. I'm good at what I do, Max is a good boss, and jobs are scarce. You don't risk yours over pocket change."

"What I figured. How about Amalgamated and the Tates? That situation has got to be touchy."

That was something I would rather not discuss. But, "Yes, that has gotten complicated."

The Amalgamated Manufacturing Combine produces a range of devices invented by Cypres Prose. Kip. I have a small share in AMC and have been its head security guy since the Combine was formed. Max Weider and Kip are serious stakeholders, too, but the Tates are the folks who run the business. I was involved with one of the Tate women for a long time. The involvement was why Kip partnered up with the family for financial and production backing. There was a lot of drama, high-level maintenance, and plenty of disdain from the other Tates. Then Strafa came along.

Relway said, "I would imagine. How bad do they want you to go away?"

"Me going wouldn't break many hearts."

He nodded, steepled his fingers again. "But they can't

push you out, can they? That would aggravate Max Weider. And Cypres Prose might walk with you."

"I don't know about that. Kip is really serious about Kyra Tate."

"Who is also your pal, if I recall."

"One light in the wilderness." I had the angle of his thinking now. It was plausible, too. He could be right. Preston and his girlfriend, and the Min woman, might have to do with the past instead of the present or future.

"The old boys, the uncles, those guys worship bottom lines. They would suck it up and keep you around because you're good at what you do."

"Why, thank you, sir."

"And one of the things you do best is irritate the shit out of everyone around you. How about the younger Tates? The ones with the bruised feelings? Are they capable of putting a tag on you?"

"Capable? Sure. Likely to do it? No. Tinnie wouldn't turn stalker. She has quirks and hang-ups and twists of mind but only at neurotic levels. Kyra? Not at all. She doesn't care about anything but Kip. And the boys are just glad that I'm gone. They don't have to explain me anymore."

Relway rubbed his fingertips together, wondering.

"I think even considering the Tates takes away from what's really happening. Womble, Muriat, and Min have to have something to do with this Tournament of Swords stuff."

Relway looked out to the hallway, frowning. There was a ruckus out there somewhere. "On balance, I'm inclined to agree. But there is the cousin, Rose Tate, a bad seed with lots of screws loose. Could she be trying to get leverage on the chief of security now that he isn't protected by the rest of the family? Would she try to end your ankle-biting if she thought she could manage it without making Cypres Prose walk away?"

He showed that twitch in the corner of his mouth. In his special way he had just told me that he had a clear understanding of the dynamics inside Amalgamated and the Tate family. He knew that black sheep Rose had been up to wickedness the family wanted kept from the other shareholders.

Cautiously, I admitted, "Rose would be a possibility. Remote, but a possibility."

"The most plausible possibility that I see."

"Unless it has to do with the tournament nonsense."

"Unless. Which, I suspect, we'll hear more about momentarily. I imagine that racket has to do with Womble having given up everything else he knows."

People argued heatedly in muted voices, moving slowly closer. One insisted that the Director had left instructions not to be disturbed. Another argued that it was imperative that he should be. The latter sounded like oddly shaped Helenia.

Relway composed himself, resigned to the interruption. "Did your Hill friends know you were coming here? How important is that?"

13

Everything was about to change. Everything was about to head off at ninety degrees from everything that had gone before.

I had just stopped shaking my head when Helenia appeared outside Relway's den. The Director called his failed gatekeeper off, beckoned Helenia into his presence. Helenia gave me a scared, sad sort of look as she scuttled to her boss, bent, put a hand to his ear, whispered busily.

Them being near each other made me wonder if her unusual assembly specs might not be a result of the same rowdy raids on the family tree that had produced Deal Relway himself.

Toneless, he said, "Shit," language so uncharacteristic that it was as startling as a scream. He tried to appear blank when he faced me, but I could tell that something was wrong. Something was most definitely wrong.

"What?" I demanded.

Relway sucked in several gallons of air. "No beating around it. Never actually softens it. Furious Tide of Light has been killed."

Huh?

It was like . . . Like nothing. No. That couldn't be true. That couldn't happen. Why was he messing with me?

"What?" Like I might have heard him wrong? Like I had heard him from way off in another universe? Or something. He was saying something improbable, so something impossible had to be happening. "I don't get . . . I didn't get . . . That can't be." Head on down to the bottom line of what everybody knows. People can't get close enough to a sorceress like Strafa to actually hurt her. "Killed?"

"Attacked and killed. On the street in front of her house."

Ambush? I knew the perfect place and time. Right when you were fiddling with the pedestrian gate, going into the property. Only . . . What would Strafa be doing going through the gate? She would have been airborne when she arrived home.

"There isn't anything more yet. But she wasn't alone. The woman she was with was injured badly but survived."

"But she may not last," Helenia added, staring hard at the dirty stone floor, probably distracting herself from the intensity of the moment by making cleaning plans. "We will have more information soon."

Of course. An attack on someone from the Hill, especially of Strafa's stature, would make the Guard drop most everything.

I had gone numb emotionally. I didn't know what to think. I didn't know what to do. This was a twist beyond imagination. I had seen some harsh times, especially during the war, but I'd never been smacked between the eyes by something as sudden and evil and unexpected as this. Even when Mom left us, the process had taken a while. There had been time to hone my emotional defenses.

For no special reason I recalled civilians sitting among the ruins of their homes and lives, surrounded by the desolation the people and stuff of those lives had become once the fighting swept through their part the world. Lost souls, every one, every time.

I tried to remember that we humans are resilient. Most of those people came back, eventually.

I tried, but at the moment had little inclination to believe.

"Garrett."

"Uh. Unh?"

"You should go out there, find out what really happened. The reports might be mistaken."

Early reports often are. Usually are. Yes! That might be . . .

There had been no mistake. I knew that right down to the core of my soul. "Yeah. I guess." But I did not get up. I put on my best thousand-yard stare and just sat there, mind empty.

"There might be something you can do. Familywise," he amended, since it was too late to help Strafa.

My response must have seemed too-long delayed. "Yeah. Maybe." I did get up then, still focused only on what was happening on the far side of the horizon.

Relway said, "Helenia, find Target. Tell him to bring Womble. Wait up, Garrett. I'll send some people with you. This may turn out to be a job for my section."

I held up. Even rattled and numb I realized that he wanted to look out for me. But in that state I would just do what I was told, slowly, or I would do nothing at all. I had learned that about me during the war.

In seconds Helenia was at it again with the man who had tried to keep her away from the Director. It sounded like there was a relationship there. Concern underlay everything else.

"Shouldn't take but a few minutes," Relway said. "I know you've seen all this before, even if you haven't lived it. The numb will start to wear off soon. You'll be mad as hell. That's when you really need to watch it so you don't do something stupid. You have to control yourself. If what happened is connected to your blood tournament, the Civil Guard will handle it."

I looked straight into his eyes. And didn't see their color, though I knew they must be . . . brown? I was still empty, but he saw something behind the emptiness. Something that left him exceptionally uncomfortable.

He knew that Garrett isn't somebody you get in front of when he gets hot. It takes him a while to get there, then . . .

"Don't do anything to put yourself on the wrong side of the law, Garrett."

I grew up in TunFaire. Till the last few years, justice was a craft industry. You made it yourself. A lifetime of that wasn't going away because some dreamer wanted me to live up to his ideals.

I said nothing to contradict him, though.

The crew member of unusual size from the gang that snagged Preston Womble turned up quickly. He had Preston with him, Womble scampering to avoid being dragged. The big guy stopped outside Relway's cage. "Set to go, boss," he said. "What do you got?"

Womble lost some color after he looked at me.

I didn't feel it consciously, but the next stage was getting some traction.

Relway said, "Take Mr. Garrett home. I want you both to stick with him. You understand me, Womble?"

"Yes, sir. I do, Director. Yes indeed. How long shall I pursue those instructions, sir? What is my function to be?"

Womble belonged to that class of people who go a long way in very small doses, obviously.

"We'll tell you when you're done. Your job is to look out for Garrett. You will do whatever it takes to keep him healthy and happy. You'll also do whatever Target tells you to do."

"Yes, sir, Director. I understand you perfectly, sir."

"Get moving, then. Garrett, I expect you to control yourself. I'll see you again soon, hopefully with something to report. I must get matters rolling here."

And that was that, a little confusing in the state I was in.

14

I didn't get to ask Target how he got his name. Having been to the war zone, I expect that it had to do with his size and capacity for attracting enemy fire. He clearly did not like being called Target, but he wasn't going to argue with his boss about it.

He led us back to the entrance I had used getting into the Al-Khar, muttering about the damned woman being so damned slow, she should quit playing her damned games with that damned dick Merryman . . .

I caught the stench of horse before I heard or saw the monsters coming, with fiery evil eyes and fangs like the mother of all saber-tithed toogers . . . I have a problem with horses. No, actually, horses have a problem with me. I'm willing to live and let live, but they are equally willing to do what it takes to wrap my story up early. Then they could let bygones be bygones and get on with live and let lie down dead.

These nags were not the worst. No smoke rolled out of their nostrils. After a single flash of contempt, they chose to ignore me.

My companions paid the monsters no heed. Target just stayed near Womble in case Preston got struck stupider and tried to make a break. Helenia and an old red top who would drive the coach hung on behind the pair of scruffy devils. Each led one animal by the harness. I looked for their muzzles and failed to spot any. The coach was not a big one. It was marked but not with any official insignia.

Helenia noted my interest. "We confiscated it under the racketeering statutes."

Um. Yeah. There was a good idea. Give the tin whistles the power to take anything they want from anybody they cared to take it from just by accusing them of being criminals. That had to be too much temptation even for a straight arrow like Deal Relway.

Target told me, "We didn't figure you were up for walking."

He had a good point there.

So. He or Helenia, or both, were the thoughtful sort, belying their looks.

I hoped the coach belied its looks.

It felt like maybe it used to belong to Shadowslinger's evil older sister. It was all black, decorated with carvings of critters who would give voodoo priests the heebie-jeebies, and it had no springs. Walking might be less painful if we hit some really bad streets.

"Let's get rolling," Target said. "You get in first, Womble."

Helenia opened the door on the left side of the vehicle. There was a crest carved there, but the lighting wasn't good enough to show it clearly. No doubt I didn't really want to see it, anyway. It might redouble the kind of nightmares I had already from being around my future in-laws.

Helenia urged me in behind Preston, then came aboard herself. The interior was nicely appointed in silks and leathers. I hoped the latter was sheepskin, not peopleskin.

There was room for four people if three were half my size. Womble did not take up much space, but Helenia was wide at the base and came armed with a big leather case. She said, "I'll be trying to take witness statements."

I figured, good luck with that, even if you can write fast enough.

No two witnesses ever see the same thing.

I heard some creaking as Target opened the gate.

The old man said something in Horse, probably offering to feed me to the beasts if they did what he asked. The coach lurched. Preston and I had our backs to the direction of travel. I almost fell into Helenia's lap.

The coach stopped after thirty feet. The gates creaked again. The old man clambered up to the driver's seat, making the vehicle rock and squeak. Meanwhile, moisture began to sneak in through the side windows even though those were supposedly shut against the weather. I peeked. The rain had grown a little more vigorous, though it was still only slightly more enthusiastic than a desultory drizzle. It was very, very cold, however.

Helenia was chatty. "This coach belonged to somebody off the Hill. One of the necromancer types. His own people turned him in because he was so rotten."

"Sounds like my grandmother-in-law."

Cynical me, I suspected that there must have been legacies and estates involved that someone had wanted resolved in a manner other than the one outlined in the relevant documents. The Unpublished Committee would not back that kind of play, but Relway's crew was still only a small faction at the heart of the new law enforcement.

Helenia continued. "The Director uses it when he wants to keep a low profile."

Yes. Of course. Send out the ugly. Nobody would notice that.

Target cracked the door, poked his mug in. "All set?"

Nobody declared any serious lack of readiness. How do you answer that kind of dumb question?

He pushed on the door. A catch clicked. The coach sagged and rocked despite its lack of springs as Target mounted the footman's backboard.

The coach lurched ahead.

I had recovered enough emotionally to realize that I ought to be glad that Target was not allergic to the damp. It would have gotten tight with him inside, too.

15

There was no immediately obvious sign, in Strafa's neighborhood, that anything huge had happened. There were people around, naturally, but the rain kept the Lookie Lous away and Barate had gotten the key people moved inside. A brace of forensics sorcerers roamed the street out front, pretending to be something else but not convincingly because they wore their red Guard berets.

Our driver took us in under the porte cochere. Target manned the door, helped Helenia dismount. Barate came out to greet me with an uncharacteristic hug.

Algarda said, "Mother is on her way. She's been delayed because there were steps she wanted to take first."

Did I even want to know? He made "steps" sound nastily portentous.

He eyed Target, Womble, and Helenia but kept his expression neutral and did not comment. They had red berets on now, too. Other tin whistles were all over. A squad had a couple of the Hill's private patrolmen cornered and were asking embarrassing questions.

I showed Barate a raised eyebrow.

He said, "There was an explosion on the other side of the Hill. They all headed over there. Those two were dumb enough to come back. The rest have vanished off the face of the earth."

They would be found. They would explain why they had not done the job for which they got paid more than your average tin whistle did. The Civil Guard were hard on the private side lately. Too often the private guys didn't do their jobs or got caught taking tips to look the other way right before bad stuff happened.

Times were changing, though.

The weather was not. It seemed determined to get colder, wetter, and windier. I beckoned Target, Womble, and Helenia. "Let's get inside." I told Barate, "They're with me."

He went right ahead on having no comment.

I failed to notice that Helenia left her case in the coach, meaning it was just a prop.

We were still shaking the moisture off in the ballroom-size foyer when a bug-eyed Preston pointed and declared, "That's Vicious Min!" like he could not believe his eyes.

"The woman who hired him to tail you," Target reminded me.

A very large woman in a very sad state of repair sprawled on a big table brought in for the purpose. It was eight feet long and four feet wide. Parts of Vicious Min hung over all the ends and sides. She was a big girl.

Strafa was on another table, close by. She didn't look all the worse for wear. I probed the sore tooth socket of emotion. I was in battlefield mode, numb and rigidly controlled, saving the hysteria for later.

Min had lost gallons of blood. It was all over her, all over the table, and had pooled on the floor. The leakage had stopped. She was still breathing, raggedly, but her color was awful. I said, "Shouldn't somebody be working on her?"

"I am," said a guy who had, apparently, had to step away momentarily. He looked like he knew what he was doing. I didn't recognize him.

Barate proved he was agile for his age. He kept himself between me and anybody he decided I was bullying unreasonably. He kept reminding me, "Our innings will come after the nosies go. We'll handle our family responsibilities."

I wasn't sure what that meant but did understand that he was well disposed toward me and definitely not so much so toward whoever had hurt his little girl. "Of course," I said. "You're completely right." I noted that Target was sticking close to me. No doubt he had instructions to monitor my every breath.

Preston Womble had no attention to spare for anything but the big woman. He did stay out of the doctor's way.

I could not see what Helenia was up to.

The doctor beckoned Barate, asked, "You know anything about this woman?"

"No. She's a stranger. Ted, this is Garrett. Strafa's husband." He left off the to-be part.

"Nice to meet you." I pointed. "Preston knows her."

Ted deployed that most unhelpful of formulas, "I'm sorry for your loss, Mr. Garrett. I didn't know Strafa as well as I would've liked, but she was a fine woman. A fine woman. What happened here was a crime."

Yeah, well. People can't always get the words out right.

Ted gave Barate a look I took to mean that his admiration for Strafa did not extend to other members of the Algarda tribe. Barate didn't surprise me much later when he told me that Dr. Ted had once had a serious crush on Strafa.

Ted wasn't over that. He was quite intense when he grilled Preston. He got mad when Preston couldn't tell him anything about Vicious Min but her name, that her money was good, and that she was generous with it. I chirped in to ask if he thought Elona Muriat could tell us more if we caught up with her.

Preston didn't think so. Preston was very smug about our chances of finding his girlfriend.

Pular Singe lurked in the back of my mind. Singe was the cure for the elusive.

16

I stared down at the woman I would bury just days before we were to have celebrated our wedding. Anger simmered inside me without controlling me. I had avoided unreasoning rage, so far. I was more drained by my loss and was now approaching the gates of desolation.

Barate had traveled further along the sad road. He had started plucking halfheartedly at future plans.

He eased me farther back into the house, away from other ears. "This had to do with what we were talking about at Mother's house yesterday."

"Did it happen because I went to the Al-Khar?"

He considered before answering, "That doesn't seem likely. That creature, Min, evidently caught Strafa coming home. I think she was here to tell Strafa that she'd been designated the Algarda Champion. Instead of Kevans."

I had myself under control. My mind was working, some. I wanted to bark, "What?" and maybe something about why the hell Strafa when the whole tournament absurdity was always about kids busting each other up . . . ? Except I had enough rationality in stock to realize that I knew no such thing, I had just inferred it from what had been said at Shadowslinger's place. Too, I wondered, "How come you know all that?"

Barate said, "I was on my way here to see Strafa about Kevans . . . I came around the corner while it was happening. If I hadn't shown up when I did, the big woman would have died, too."

"You saw who did it?"

"No. Strafa was airborne but falling. The big woman was on her knees, cursing, holding her chest and bleeding. We'll get into all that once Mother gets here. Strafa was still alive then. She begged me to tell you how much she loved you. She tried to guess who did it. Then she stopped breathing and her heart stopped. I couldn't get anything started again. I don't have the power . . ." He stopped talking, took deep breaths, forced himself to become calm.

He did have that Algarda talent, an ability to manage emotion. To go cold as death when calm and calculation were needed.

He exhaled. "That one was still conscious. She tried to talk. She called herself Vicious Min. She looks mixed-breed, maybe groll, but I don't think she's from this world."

"So that ridiculous tournament thing hasn't even started and somebody jumped somebody else."

Barate nodded. "Yes. I don't think that breaks the rules. I don't think you can cheat, the way Mother explains it. But this would come close. The selection of participants has only just begun and the contest is down a probable Champion, maybe has a Dread Companion dying, and has you, if you're the Mortal Companion, potentially crippled by grief. That has to be an encouraging start for somebody."

I tried channeling the young Garrett who crept through snake-filled, croc-infested swamps to find strangers to murder in nightmares gone by. That Garrett was always scared but never out of control. He got on with getting on.

Once a Marine . . .

17

Shadowslinger showed up while I was dealing with the notion that I had been tagged to be Strafa's sidekick by the Operators. Her Mortal Companion, formally.

There was a lot of formality in this murder game.

The old sorceress arrived in such a dark mood that those who were not part of the family began clearing off as they found plausible excuses. Her reputation was kingdomwide.

The red tops faded fastest, including Target, who seemed content to hand me over despite the charge the Director had laid on him. Preston Womble disappeared even earlier, never being missed till I realized that I hadn't seen him since I'd spotted him leaning over Vicious Min like he meant to kiss her good-bye.

Dr. Ted was among the last to go. He told Barate, "I did what I could, which wasn't much. That woman may be something supernatural. You'll likely have better luck having your own people work on her."

His meaning got through. He meant people like Shadowslinger, who went into seclusion as soon as she arrived. Or Bonegrinder, who had come with her. Or Tara Chayne Machtkess. I had no idea where she fit or what dark skills she mastered. Strafa hadn't explained and it hadn't occurred to me to ask.

Dr. Ted's parting words let me know that, though he lived on the Hill, he wasn't part of what made the Hill what it was. He was just a physician. Probably one of the best since he served such a select clientele, but not a man tapped into the darkness himself.

Nor was Barate. He had been skipped by the family knack. I don't know why. Maybe he had picked the wrong father. Maybe the knack skipped every other generation. Kevans was short on mystical skills, too.

Once the outsiders thinned out, Shadowslinger reappeared long enough to summon the rest of us into the room Strafa called a library. There weren't many books there, actually, though they seemed plentiful to me. Singe would go gaga over the ones dealing with economics.

I have to admit, Strafa's future husband found books mildly threatening, though he would read one occasionally.

The dread sorceress was no longer content to sit, bask in fireplace warmth, and let her son do the talking. "I have made the funeral arrangements," she announced, making it clear why she preferred not to speak for herself. She had a pipey little-girl voice that was completely unintimidating. Put her behind a screen, you'd think a cute eight-year-old was back there chirping. "You will be there. You." She thrust a long, fat, wrinkled, dark, dry, and crooked finger at me.

"Ma'am? Yes, ma'am."

My response amused Tara Chayne and Richt Hauser. They figured I'd gone chicken because I didn't have Strafa to run interference.

There was some truth to that, though less than they thought.

"Your vows were not legally finalized. However, this family will proceed on the basis that they were in place in practice. Arrangements are being made to complete the legal formalities. You are the husband of Furious Tide of Light now, in fact as well as prospect." Her ritualistic tone balanced the baby voice. In fact, it felt like she was casting a spell.

She took time to look for someone who wanted to argue. Kevans looked sour but disinclined to object in words.

Bonegrinder and the Machtkess woman looked puzzled.

Barate's pal Kyoga, silent and nearly invisible today, didn't understand at all.

Shadowslinger said, "This could have significant legal implications someday." She looked me in the eye. "You and I will discuss that later, after the funeral and our war with the people who made this happen."

Little-girl voice or no, anyone anywhere with guilty knowledge had to feel Death's cool breath on the backs of their necks.

Shadowslinger had one of the darkest reputations on the Hill. Today she made it sound like that reputation was understated and was now headed toward a darkness deeper than any visited before.

She kept talking to me. "We aren't going to do anything obvious. You will begin the hunt after the funeral. You will not be subtle, as we discussed yesterday."

We did? When? I didn't remember that. Maybe my knack for getting distracted was betraying me. Or maybe Strafa was supposed to clue me in and never got around to it.

I needed to find out what Shadowslinger really expected.

She told me, "You will find out who murdered your wife."

All right. "Yes. No doubt about that. I'll spend the rest of my life on that if that's what it takes."

"Good. But don't act on it before we have a chance to talk it over. Once you do find out who is responsible, that is. Nothing. Understand?"

"Ma'am?"

"You're a good man. Much too good to have what will happen weighing on your conscience afterward."

I opened my mouth to protest. I couldn't imagine anything that awful. Not at that moment, in the emotional state that I occupied.

She gave me no chance to butt in. She never would. She was that kind of matriarch. In her own mind she was the soul and will of Family Algarda. The rest of us were the feet and fingers that executed the Will.

"You're all too good. I'm not." She closed her eyes and smacked her lips.

Street legend accused her of having eaten some of her enemies. She'd never denied it, but I'd always considered it psychological warfare. Seeing her there dreaming of fava beans and . . . something, though, I was less inclined to be skeptical.

A muted *chunk!* sounded elsewhere in the house, probably not far away. Never opening her eyes, the old horror said, "There is an eavesdropper in your house, Garrett. Deal with her."

18

The eavesdropper led me on a very short chase. She was close enough to hear Shadowslinger tell me to get her. Fear rattled her. I caught her heading for the front door, in the open, apparently wading through invisible mud up to her hocks.

"Helenia? You need to catch up with Preston and Target."

I had forgotten her completely. Preston and Target had stayed underfoot, but she had faded away, out of sight and out of mind. Which might be her special value to the Director. She might be one of those people with a knack for being overlooked, which can be frustrating when you're young, but becomes a priceless skill in the spying and law enforcement games.

I owed Helenia some so didn't feel right doing anything beyond telling her to make herself scarce. "Before those less pleasant people back there take notice." I thought that the most unpleasant of them all probably wanted Helenia to carry tales to her boss. It would be like her to use the Guard and Unpublished Committee to work her mischief.

Pallid, Helenia bobbed her head and backed away, headed for the street. I followed her out, sort of herding her at first, then just accompanying her once we hit the flagstone drive. I stopped outside the gate. She headed west. I noted that the ugly black coach, surrounded by red tops but lacking Target, waited two blocks downhill. So. There had been a plan.

I should have seen it coming.

I was distracted by emotion, of course.

Helenia walked faster as she moved farther away and the mud got shallower. She brushed past people who came out of the lane running alongside the property, flinching away from them.

I forgot Helenia.

Headed my way were the doll girl and groll that Strafa and I had seen near Shadowslinger's place last night. The girl had said something. I hadn't been interested at the time. I had forgotten the incident.

They came up even with me, strolling, neither making eye contact. The little girl held the groll's hand as though they were about to step out in a pavane. One step past me she said, "I warned you."

"What?"

The odd pair moved on while I gulped air and tried to get the watermills of my mind to turn over. I opted for a strategy that had worked in the past. The hell with thought or planning. Charge! Get stuff happening, then sort through the wreckage.

When I moved the groll shed his trance and looked back. Suddenly, Vicious Min looked like a runt. The groll eye nearest me glowed red. A trick of the light, surely, but it was sobering. He was not in a friendly mood.

The watermills *kerchunked*. I did recall that Strafa, far better equipped to deal with the strange and supernatural than was I, had died right here, on this street, twenty feet from where I was about to make a huge, potentially lethal mistake of my own.

I stopped. I watched for a moment. Then I turned, wound up my lazy old legs, and hustled after Helenia.

My new family was pleased to explain, minutes later, that my mind was not yet working right. I should have summoned them immediately. One of them might actually have been able to do something. Shadowslinger seemed particularly interested, especially once I revealed that Strafa and I had had an earlier encounter with the same pair. In fact, she seemed quite disturbed but then closed down on her thoughts except to suggest that those two must be connected to the tournament, maybe as a Champion and Mortal Companion or Dread Companion, working some tactical angle.

When Shadowslinger rolled out, with Barate behind her chair, with Bonegrinder foaming at the mouth and Tara Chayne Machtkess sniffing delicately, there was no pretty doll or ugly chaperone to be seen. Machtkess told us, "Their scent has dispersed." She eyed me like she had begun to question my intelligence.

Bonegrinder felt the surface of the street, shook his head. "No warmth left behind, either."

Shadowslinger said, "He didn't make it up. He saw what he saw." Her head turned slowly. She looked up at me from slitted eyes. "His word is gold." As we headed back up the drive, she told me, "You have been given a thread to pull. Find out who she is, then yank it."

My word needed not stand alone. Helenia and the red tops had seen the strange pair. But there was no need to offer witnesses. I was Strafa's husband. I belonged. Now, with me welcomed by Shadowslinger, there could be no doubts about my report.

Right.

It was a unique feeling, though. Kind of warming. I seldom got as much support or trust even from Dean, Singe, or Penny.

They, though, had been schooled by me and Old Bones alike to question everything and those relationships had grown organically rather than dramatically.

New council of war, family-style, briefly. Shadowslinger chaired and did the talking. She reiterated her strategy. "We will take it easy till after the funeral. We will use that time to tame our emotions and consider our resources. After the interment we will gird our souls for war and rectify the imbalance."

I got a definite sense of understatement there. I pictured an apocalypse developing within her mind.

"We will devour the Operators bite by slow, bloody bite, raw. Do you all understand?"

She was playing off her evil reputation now, maybe hoping Strafa's servants, in attendance as always, would mention her mood while gossiping with servants from other households.

I hoped she wasn't feeling literal. I hoped her reputation was exaggerated.

After speechifying scary the horrid woman handed out assignments, a few of which did make it sound like she meant to eat somebody. The jobs were odds and ends we could pick up, snip off, wrap or unwrap, while we tamed our shock, pain, and crushing hatred, awaiting Strafa's funeral. I got one of the heavier loads.

She thought I ought to keep my mind occupied.

I do have a tendency to brood when things aren't going well.

19

I was not in a good mood. It was the bleakest day of my life.

I stared at the glass-faced coffin and felt sorry for myself. Strafa looked like an angel sleeping, a precious child grown big without having lost her innocence.

It felt like a huge, bad practical joke. She had to be pretending. This was a game in bad taste. She couldn't be dead. Not really. That wasn't possible. She would open her eyes any minute now. They would be a scintillating, teasing violet. Her face would shine in delight at having gotten us with her latest mischief and she would burst out laughing so sweetly that nobody would be able to hold it against her.

The first raindrops plunked against the face of the coffin. It seemed to be the season for rain. Onlookers stirred. Women opened umbrellas. The Orthodox priest started to hurry. Horrid old Shadowslinger shifted her immense bulk a single step his way. If she could stand up in this, he could do his share with proper decorum and pacing.

Father Amerigo forgot the cold, the wet, and his miserable feet. He became determined to make this the finest farewell ceremony ever celebrated in this cemetery.

Strafa's father, Kyoga, me, and my friend Morley Dotes would convey the casket into the Algarda mausoleum. The entrance was fifteen feet away. I had been inside earlier, during rehearsal. I hated the idea of going back. That would declare the whole thing final.

A manicured slope rose behind the gray stone structure

where Strafa would await her reward if she really accepted the Orthodox faith the Algardas professed officially. Which I doubted because the creed tells us we shouldn't suffer the existence of witches, warlocks, or sorcery.

These days most folks cremate, especially the rich and most especially those who dwell on the Hill. They don't want their departed having any chance of making a comeback. My wife's family, though, insisted on old-fashioned interment, unanimously, because Shadowslinger told them that was what they wanted.

I sympathize with those who burn their blessed dead. Unlikely as it may sound, down the road somebody might try to bring them back. Not palatable to me even missing Strafa as much as I did. I have survived collisions with the risen dead. You never get back what was lost, and no revenant ever comes back good.

Ghosts, on the other hand . . . I have had positive experiences with ghosts.

Feral dogs observed the proceedings from the skyline.

Shadowslinger gave them a glance, decided that they were what they appeared to be and, therefore, were of no real interest.

I wondered why they were there. Maybe it was a territorial thing. I was preoccupied with Strafa but I did notice. So beautiful, she, perfect in life and near perfect now. I hadn't prayed since I came home from the war, but I mumbled something, to any god inclined to listen. I would be half a man for a while with her gone.

Our sudden separation was the ultimate cruelty. Each day, each hour that Strafa lay in darkness waiting, she would become more of a stranger.

We grow older and change, no matter how hard we fight it.

Father Amerigo droned on. I cataloged those who had come to offer their respects and support. Strafa, though the most wonderful woman I ever knew, had not had even one friend who had not been one of my friends first. And the only family I had anymore was the one that I acquired by coming together with her: Shadowslinger, blood-hungry; Barate, who had his big-boy fangs out now; and Kevans, who clung to Barate's arm ferociously and would not stop crying.

Her best friend, Kip, Cypres Prose, stood to her left, lightly touching her. He was crowded by his fiancée, Kyra Tate, who, in turn, stood in the shadow of her overprotective cousin Artifice. There were times when Kip and Kevans seemed like fraternal twins with different mothers.

Most of my friends were on hand. Pular Singe and her brother, Pound Humility, known on the street as John Stretch. Playwright Jon Salvation with a three-woman personal entourage: Crush, DeeDee, and Mike, all gorgeous but looking exceedingly depressed. They had been fans of Strafa. Max Weider and Manvil Gilbey, with his wife, Heather, had come over from the brewery. Belinda Contague, girl psycho gangster, remained a little separate and appeared to have come alone, but there would be bodyguards somewhere. General Westman Block wore his dress uniform and headed a delegation of Guardsmen, probably hoping the killer could not resist an opportunity to bask in all our misery. Also there but standing back a little, watching, were my old friends Saucerhead Tharpe, Playmate, and Winger. Dean had wanted to come, but his old flesh had proven too fragile.

Penny was closer to me than anyone, ready to grab hold if I broke down, but she lost it first. She buried her face in my left sleeve when the flood broke. She offered up endless apologies for being unable to stop and for having been so mean.

Penny had worked hard at not liking Strafa so now felt guilty about having seen a secret wish come true.

Singe eased over to take charge of Penny. I wouldn't be able to help with Strafa's coffin if I had a blubbering teenager hanging on.

Hagekagome entered my life.

20

Singe yelled, "Look out!" I looked up, found a pretty, dark-haired girl hurtling toward me, growling.

Penny squealed. The flying girl smashed into me. She hammered my chest with her fists. "Hate you! Hate you!"

Father Amerigo stopped talking. Everyone else gawked, including people you would expect to respond quickly and harshly, considering the event that had us gathered in a cemetery. Morley, Singe, and General Block were the exceptions. Block pulled Penny to her feet. She had done an inelegant sprawl on the wet grass. She was fortunate. She had chosen to wear underwear on her dress-up day.

Still, her dignity had been abused. She would be sullen for a long time.

Morley and Singe peeled the girl off me. She looked maybe fourteen, fifteen, but only eleven or twelve tall. She eyed me like she wasn't sure what she'd just done, or why she had done it.

Her face was one of the most beautiful I'd ever seen, though she was more pale than ever-pallid Strafa even in death. Her hair was fine, black, and hung in an odd, floppy cut on the sides. Her head, even discounting her unusual hairdo, seemed too big for her shoulders.

Maybe her shoulders were too narrow for her head.

Her clothing allowed no real estimate of the balance of her. It was black and white and there was a lot of it.

She shook off Morley and Singe, glared at me from eyes

filled with tears. "Hate you!" Then she ran back uphill, to the dogs. Those followed her once she dashed past.

General Block passed Penny to me. He had, somehow, managed to winkle a nonsullen smile out of the girl.

Somebody asked the question. "What the hell was that, Garrett?"

Singe said, "She looked like a little milk cow." She eyed Penny. "Someone you know?"

Head shake.

Everyone eyeballed me. I insisted, "I don't know. I never saw her before."

They gave me the benefit of the doubt. Family. Especially after some wit tapped the truth to mention that I had been much too tied up with my wife to make any outside friends and, anyway, Little Moo was a good month or two younger than my usual pickup.

He got a few feeble smiles, but, overall, it was not a day for any humor but the foul.

Shadowslinger, I noted, kept staring uphill for some time after the girl disappeared. I wanted to drift over and ask about that, but there was no time. The rain kept falling. The cold kept on trying to gnaw the marrow out of our bones. I would have to ask her later. I would not be getting far away from her for a while now.

Folks wanted to get back to the matter at hand. They wanted to get in out of the misery.

Implausible interruption concluded, the effort to exorcise the pain of the survivors resumed. Father droned his litany of reasons why we all found Strafa so remarkable. Those were plentiful and heartfelt. I shed tears because my friends had found her as amazing as I had.

Father Amerigo finished up. Time for us pallbearers to convey Strafa into the crypt. There were only four of us, but Strafa had been a wisp and her casket was lightweight. We moved it, placed it. I stared down at her, willing time to have a stop, till Barate took me away, back into the rain, so half-drowned, impatient old men could seal the tomb.

I cried some more. So did everyone else who could.

Only Penny had failed to love Strafa unreservedly, but even she had been coming around and now was determined to show the rest of us how thoroughly she had changed her heart.

Strafa Algarda was the love of my life. My heart and soul. She could not have been more perfect had I designed her. Now those of us still in the mortal realm would find out why someone had thought that it would be better for the world if she left it.

I was not fully prepared to buy into the Tournament of Swords idea. It was ridiculous. The Algardas, though, had no trouble believing. But the notion of a last man standing takes all was just too stupid . . . How would you come up with that many players all convinced that there was no way they could lose?

All mysteries would be unraveled. This gathering in the rain consisted of people who loved Strafa and, universally, were convinced that the truth would be found. They were determined to make that happen.

21

Though we were doing things the Orthodox way, at least by pretense, we had not held a wake for Strafa. Shadowslinger wanted to wait till after the funeral. I announced it there, before I broke down, as cemetery employees sealed the tomb. I wanted everyone to come to Strafa's place. We would enjoy a banquet in her honor and share some memories.

It wasn't something I expected to be a draw. My expectations were in error, maybe because Barate circulated vigorously, issuing personal invitations.

He spoke directly to such luminaries as Belinda Contague and General Block, people I expect Constance Algarda might consider potentially useful in the war she was about to launch.

I've never quite been a lone wolf—being the face and fist and punch absorber of the Garrett investigative empire—but I've seldom gone after anything as part of a mass movement, either. I like being my own boss. However, Shadowslinger was doing the shot-calling today. She meant to get every swinging blade she could hacking at the air.

The house seemed a great cold hollow shell without Strafa there. Her two regular servants, assisted by her grandmother's pair and several borrowed from Morley Dotes's restaurants—whence had come the food as well—created a reception that was surprisingly upbeat.

I stayed busy greeting commiserating mourners, me, Ba-

rate, and Kevans gripping hands gently and accepting con-
dolences spoken softly, with Shadowslinger nowhere to be
seen. She saw selected mourners in the library, individually,
as Bonegrinder or Moonblight delivered them.

The old horror could be doing that for show. Kyoga
Stornes hovered near the library door. He picked at a plate
of canapés while he kept watch. He was not good at disguising what he was doing.

Shadowslinger was fishing while trying to forge deadly
alliances.

During a quiet moment Barate told me, "I think she's
about to quit coasting on her reputation."

"Scary thought."

"You can't imagine. Hello, thank you for coming. Garrett, this is Moonslight, Tara Chayne's sister, Mariska.
Mariska, this is Strafa's husband. And you know Kevans, of
course."

"Of course." The woman offered me a hand while sizing
me up more blatantly than her sister had. She did not need
to explain that "Tara Chayne and I are twins." I wasn't so
sure about "But I'm the hot one. Got to go."

Moonblight was headed our way like a tornado-spawning
thunderstorm.

Kevans told me, "They don't get along."

"I picked up on that, kiddo. Not completely senile yet.
Looks like Kip is about to head out. You maybe ought to
say good-bye."

"Yeah. I should."

She made it sound like forever lurked in the back of her
mind.

We had no customers. Barate and I could talk. He said,
"That boy is thicker than a paving brick." Meaning Kip
Prose had no clue that his longtime best friend, who was a
girl, was just as much taken by him as was his girlfriend,
Kyra, a fact that even Kyra suspected.

"He doesn't think of Kevans as a girl." I sneaked a sideways glance, thinking he might have some feelings about his
daughter's infatuation. I saw nothing but parental concern.

"I won't touch it, Garrett. It'll be one of those Daddy-don't-see things."

Kip had a mother out there somewhere. She did not participate in his life except to enjoy the allowances he provided. I was more of a parent, which was scary. Mostly that meant he was raising himself. "That sounds like the best plan. He wants us to think he's a grown-ass man. Let's treat him like one till he asks for help."

Barate grunted. "Not exactly what I was thinking." Since his stake in the matter was his daughter, not Kip. He was about to tell me something when Tara Chayne beckoned.

Time for him to go be Constance's boy instead of Kevans's dad.

I stood around looking dull and feeling like a dim candle, watching my friends stuff their faces and fill their pockets. Staffers and servers pretended not to notice.

They would stock up on leftovers themselves, later, if there were any.

All afternoon, despite all else, either Morley Dotes, Penny, or Pular Singe was somewhere close by, in case I began to demonstrate erratic behavior. Singe and Penny were fiercely uncomfortable in this venue.

I felt plenty of out-of-place myself.

Pockets full, my friends began to move on once the rain slackened.

I considered heading for Macunado Street myself, come the end of the day. I could just run back to my old life. There would be less pain in my old familiar places. Barate could go back to the mansion he'd had to leave a year ago. Plus, at the old place I could have my business partner manage, re-shape, or even suppress the emotions threatening to desta-bilize me now.

I shunned considering the broader situation, instead investing my time in feeling sorry for myself.

Barate returned. "Time to talk to the dragon."

"Huh?"

"She wants to see you."

I pulled a face.

"It's probably not what you think. She probably wants to ask you not to sell this place because of the family history here. Strafa was born here. So was Kevans."

"Sell it? How could I do that?"

"We made it over to you and Strafa after you announced the engagement."

I gulped some raw air and chewed. For somebody in my racket that flashed a big ugly red flag. Motive. A mansion high on the Hill, where the heavyweights live, is worth more than I can imagine. And my imagination has fiddled some seriously big numbers.

"But . . ." I might have heard someone tell me the place was mine without having listened. I was not attentive to the exterior world lately.

"Strafa didn't tell you?"

"She did not."

"That's my little girl. Probably didn't consider it worth mentioning."

Probably. Strafa never had much interest in wealth. Her wants were never large. She never encountered a situation where she couldn't just buy whatever she wanted.

I oozed into the library. Shadowslinger shifted her bulk, turned her massive face my way, smiled hungrily.

Barate said, "Mother feels that it is time to get to work. As soon as your guests leave." Hint, hint.

"I'll deal with that."

22

The overworked staff, while polite, did nothing to encourage anyone to linger. Only Winger and Saucerhead Tharpe were still underfoot and still eating. Neither Penny, Singe, nor Morley quite counted as guests.

I told Singe, "Go if you want. It's going to get boring now." Her brother had left long ago, unable to stand the company of so many humans.

"I do not want. This is family. I will be here for the planning and there for the kill."

I glanced at Penny. As the priestess of a cult now numbering just one, she was tough and fierce. As a girly girl she was timid. She had her angry fangs out right now. "I'm not going home by myself."

No need to look at Morley. He would become my shadow.

Winger and Saucerhead, stomachs and pockets bulging, finally took the hint. Strafa's kitchen and household staff, Race and Dex, saw them off. Those old boys were a couple. I found them creepy but not because of their orientation. They made me think of zombies.

"You'll find those two quite frugal," Barate told me as I returned to the library, indirectly suggesting that they be kept on the payroll. They might be third cousins, or something.

"You want this all back? I'll do a quit claim."

"This is you and Strafa now."

The fat lady nodded.

The Algardas were the weirdest family I'd ever encountered, the full details not germane. And I was a made member of the tribe.

Shadowslinger offered no objection when Morley, Penny, and Singe entered the room behind me. They were family hangers-on now, because they came with me.

While I was out, Kyoga, Bonegrinder, and the Machtkess sisters had moved in, as had Kevans. The room was tight and getting hot. Shadowslinger grew more pungent as the temperature rose. The smell made my eyes water.

Barate said, "Huddle up. Move your chairs into a circle. We'll brainstorm." He gestured impatiently at Kevans and Penny to join the grown-ups.

The family talent for sorcery had skipped Barate, but he had other skills. He shared the olive coloring of his mother. Like her, he was built wide, but his wide hadn't gone to fat. He could pass as a thug, and had done thug work for the family. He had scars as souvenirs of the Cantard War, where he had done two tours.

He had done no muscle work lately. Strafa hadn't been that kind of girl, and Grandma was retired. But he was set for a vengeance run now.

Shadowslinger's beefy lips spread in a sneer when I settled into the chair she had saved for me, next to her. She had fun creeping me out.

Strafa had been convinced that the old witch loved me and was thrilled to have me join the tribe. Maybe. I hadn't been hung from a meat hook yet.

Barate said, "We've had time to vent our emotions. Now let's get rational and start the hunt. All yours, Garrett."

"Huh?"

I do have the occasional profound intellectual moment.

"You're the professional. This is what you do. Tell us what our parts will be."

"Oh." Numb pause. Was he making fun? Shadowslinger

had given assignments the other day. "Let's hear what you all did the last two days."

That turned out to have been a big lot of nothing, which was the case with me, too. I hadn't found the ambition to start. But they supposedly had resources I couldn't even imagine, emotional and otherwise. I grumbled, "I've never had me for a client before."

"Worst client ever," Morley predicted, his pointy elf teeth all a-glitter.

"Probably true. When you're self-employed your boss is almost always a slave-driving dick."

Singe snorted. My custom, historically, was to quiver a finger only when starvation threatened. Her genius kept the Macunado house afloat.

"All right," I said. "I talked tournament with my partner the other night, before what happened happened. He told me to take it to the Guard. They have the manpower resources. Plus, just word getting out that the Guard is interested could put the quietus on the whole damned project."

"An incorrect estimate, apparently," Richt Hauser observed.

"He's only right most of the time. But . . . How would the tournament have gone in your day if there'd been police like we have now?"

Silence till Moonblight opined, "It would have happened anyway, but the game would have been harder to play."

"And deadlier," her sister said. "Some Champions wouldn't have scrupled about killing tin whistles who got in the way."

True then, maybe. Not many villains today were likely to see red tops as disposable annoyances, though. Deal Relway had earned his reputation.

Shadowslinger grunted, stabbed an ugly finger at Barate. He said, "The Guard does enjoy a numerical advantage. They may be able to root out the Operators in no time.

And the men in charge aren't devoted to formalities or individual rights for actual bad guys."

I chirped, "They now have on staff people able to cope with the likes of Dread Companions. Assuming I understand what those actually are."

I wasn't the most popular guy for having brought that up. It suggested that there might come a day when the Guard's wizard teams, working like an orchestra, could handle the mega monsters of the Hill. Hill folks already had their knickers in a twist because the Crown and Guard insisted that they meet behavioral standards expected of ordinary folks.

Barate said, "Mother and I agree that alerting the Guard was sound strategy. The Operators will have to work slower and more carefully. That should give us more time. But did the Guard believe you, Garrett?"

Relway had been intrigued before Strafa was attacked. "Yes. They haven't found anything useful yet, though, according to General Block. What happened couldn't be personal. Strafa got along with everybody and she had no secrets." She had been too open, I thought, glancing from Barate to Kevans.

Singe got up. She couldn't stand a human chair for long. She was bold enough to speak in front of those people, most of whom probably considered her clever vermin. "In the interest of narrowing possibilities, would anyone profit from Strafa's death?"

"It is the tournament," Bonegrinder said. "The tournament and only the tournament. No one bore that child any ill will."

"That is not what I asked. We have established that Strafa was an idol."

Shadowslinger stirred beside me. "No. That is not it." Something had been going on with her, quietly, the past few minutes. Her outer apparel had grown darker. It moved in breezes that touched nothing else. Foul smells leaked out. A massive hand encrusted in ugly jewelry reached toward me. "You aren't looking at this the way you should."

For one mad instant it felt like she was channeling the Dead Man. "How is that?"

"You're ignoring what happened before whatever happened out front." She had the devoted attention of everyone shoehorned into the room.

She opened her hand.

23

A piece of iron dropped into my extended palm. "What is this?"

"Could it be a pork chop?"

Stupid answer to a stupid question.

It was an iron crossbow bolt. The fletched end was missing. It had been designed to rip through plate armor. "This must have weighed three pounds, whole." How do you break a chunk of iron like that? "This wouldn't fit any man-portable weapon."

It was a light artillery bolt made for a small siege piece or an infantry support weapon. It had a hardened-steel penetrator tip.

I wondered, "Any chance it was a stray?"

"Seriously?"

I tried again. "What is this?"

"Tell us what happened at your other house that night."

Penny squeaked. I blushed. Really. I may be grown up, sort of, but I couldn't discuss that stuff with a woman's family.

"Oh, come on!" Kevans said. "It isn't about that. Everybody knows you and Mom were like weasels. You couldn't keep your hands off each other even in front of people. What were you going to be like when nobody was watching?"

"Uh. Yeah. Well. She kind of snuck out, after. There was a break in the weather. She wanted to go flying while it lasted."

She was a Windwalker. Her greatest skills at sorcery centered on flying. There was nothing she would rather do than grab a broom and go walking on the sky. And that was what she had done that night.

"She was restless. She was all keyed up about the wedding. She was sure something would go wrong." And hadn't it just? "And she was even more worried about the reception." That was supposed to have happened in the Royal Botanical Gardens, made available because people she knew in the Royal Family owed her.

She was scared my lowlife friends would get drunk and rip the place apart.

I said, "She grabbed a broom and went out the window. She asked if I wanted to go but didn't hang around after I said no." I'm not fond of going strolling in places where there is a hundred feet of nothing underneath my feet. "She wasn't back yet when I got up. She still wasn't back when I left for the Al-Khar. My partner wasn't worried. It never occurred to me to be."

Plus, I was all distracted by the onrushing tsunami of matrimonial doom.

I admit, I'd found no more perfect candidate for Garrett's wife than Strafa Algarda, forgetting the family weirdness that came attached. Stipulated, the world was replete with better husband material.

Morley finally had something to say, tentatively, being unsure of his right to participate. "Was anything going on that night? Something she might have wanted to see?"

That was some good thinking. Strafa had become a rabid hometown tourist once she roped me in and had someone to drag along. I should've thought of that myself, but my thinker was all clogged up with dark emotions. Never a paragon, it was less sharp than usual lately.

Penny said, "There was an autumn solstice festival in the Dream Quarter. It started at midnight."

The Dream Quarter is TunFaire's religious center.

I asked, "You went?" I hadn't seen her before leaving that morning but hadn't thought anything of it. Penny was often invisible when I was there. Singe said that was because she had a crush on me, which was silly. Penny had made her feelings about me quite clear.

"I had to." She still took her priestess role seriously, never mind that she was the whole cult now. "Mr. Playmate went with me." Stated before I could go all parental and start barking about young girls being on the mean streets after midnight.

If you were a girl and had to be out there, Playmate was the man you wanted to be with. He was big, he was fierce, and he was one of the good guys. And he was a wannabe reverend who never quite got around to making the final leap of faith.

Penny volunteered, "We didn't see Strafa."

Kevans said, "Mom wasn't the sort."

True. She had been less religious than me. Hardly surprising, considering her trade and background.

Penny said, "There was a bad turnout because of the weather. We would've seen her if she was there."

Shadowslinger closed my hand around the bolt. "Relax. Take the advice you give your clients. Stay calm. Use your head till you find a target." She squeezed, grinned a horrible grin. "And then I will take over."

She was right. I was at a stage where I was likely to waste time, energy, and emotion running in circles and whining.

I said, "My partner would like to interview each of you."

That took the warmth out of the room.

After long silence, Shadowslinger said, "Very well. I will set the example. Barate, make sure my carriage is capable of making the journey."

"Yes, Mother. Right away?"

She turned to me. "Right away?"

"Sooner would be better than later. He was fond of Strafa. He will find connections that none of us are likely to see."

"I'm sure that you are correct. Do you all understand? Good. Perhaps you can work it out with Miss Pular today."

Singe said, "He is awake all the time these days, but the

rest of us have to sleep and do chores. It would be best if you visited in the afternoon or evening."

Shadowslinger then told me, "Tell us about the child who attacked you in the cemetery."

"There isn't anything to tell. You saw it all. I don't know who she was and I have no idea what she was up to. Maybe she had me confused with somebody else."

"Possibly. You'll see her again. Treat her kindly and gently."

"Mother?" Barate was startled by the sentiment. The others also stared.

"The child isn't one of our problems. Only Garrett needs be concerned."

Which left everyone curious about an incident that had come close to being forgotten, with me not least among the forgetters. But Shadowslinger had said her piece. She would only reiterate her injunction that I be kind.

After that stuff about me being the man because I was the pro, she had Barate tell them all how they would contribute to my efforts to find my wife's killer. She told the expert how to do his job, in detail.

I nodded a lot. I would do things my own way when she wasn't watching. But I was open to original ideas.

It was the methodology I'd developed in dealing with my mother.

24

The crowd had broken up. They were all gone but me, Dex, Race, and Morley. Penny and Singe had gone sullenly, under orders to report to the Dead Man and to make sure Dean was still breathing. Though his managers kept sending whining messages, Morley was determined to stick like he was my Mortal Companion, while he could. And I felt more comfortable having him close by.

Barate would be back once he had taken his mother home.

Oh, and Vicious Min was still around, stashed in a room big enough to fit, in medically induced unconsciousness. Dr. Ted said he'd check on her regularly. He expected her to recover, but if she did, she was likely the sort who got up and going before she was really ready.

I knew all about that. I'd been known to charge back into the fray before I was physically ready.

I burned some energy helping Dex and Race deal with the wreckage. It is amazing how much damage a few guests can do. We didn't talk much. Those two were more uncomfortable with me than I was with them. They were worried about their jobs. The employment climate in TunFaire had not yet recovered from the outbreak of peace.

They did talk about Strafa. They told me she had come home around sunrise. She ate a light breakfast, then napped for an hour. Then she left again. She said she had to go see a priest. She expected to be back around noon, hopefully before I came home, meaning she had expected me to head here once I was done at the Al-Khar.

Not much to hang my investigator's hat on there. The priest would be the guy she wanted to do our wedding. He had some remote tie to the Algardas through Strafa's mother. He was reluctant. He didn't think either of us showed enough respect for our purported faith.

Barate returned. We settled in the kitchen, where we could kibbitz while Dex and Race did dishes. We drank tea and nibbled leftovers. Finally, Algarda asked, "Have you studied that bolt?"

"I looked it over. It didn't tell me anything. The only unusual thing is that it broke."

"It's more unusual than that. It's what killed Strafa."

"Dr. Ted didn't find any wounds."

"He didn't. The bolt carried a spell. It broke when Strafa deflected it. She kept it from hitting her, but it still got close enough to deliver the spell. That piece ended up tangled in her skirt."

"Oh."

I set the broken bolt on the table. "Barate, this is iron with a steel penetrator tip. Iron, silver, and sorcery don't mix. I've had painful personal experience of that."

Laconically, Morley observed, "I was there to see it."

"They'll mix if a ferromage is involved."

I said nothing. Ferromages are rare, like frog fur coats. I doubted that there were many of either in TunFaire today.

"That was the point Mother wanted you to get. The spell—or spells—would have been laid into the grooves filed lengthwise along the shaft."

There was a trace of powdery stuff lodged there. "A ferromage? That would narrow the search considerably, wouldn't it?"

"Definitely. It would narrow it so fine, and so fast, that no genuine ferromage would involve himself in anything so certainly damning. This iron had a ceramic coat baked on, to separate the magic from the iron."

I confessed, "I'm lost, then."

Dex stepped over, invited himself into the conversation. He picked up the bolt without asking, said, "This is an old piece. More than thirty years old."

"You can tell that because?"

"I was artillery. Date of manufacture, lot number, contract number, all get stamped on the shaft. This one is broken. Only two numbers, a letter character, and the hallmark are missing, though. We don't need them. Only one outfit manufactured these. Smitt, Judical, Sons and Sons. Not the best but they met their deadlines and brought their contracts in without overruns."

I said, "I remember them going out of business when I was little. There was a kickback scandal, or something."

"You're right," Barate said. "Twyla was in on the investigation."

Twyla would be his wife, Strafa's mother, whose ghost I saw the same day I first saw Strafa. She died a long time ago.

"That must have been ages ago."

"Oddly enough, just a little more than thirty years. I remember being worried sick because Twyla was carrying Strafa."

Could a case that cold be germane?

Barate told Dex, "Somebody must have found some of the missing bolts."

"Certainly, sir. Or they may have had them lying around since then."

That seemed unlikely. But. "This mess gets stranger by the minute."

Morley suggested, "Somebody in a hurry grabbed the nearest handy tool. They didn't know the bolts had identifying marks."

Barate said, "They might not have known about the markings, but they spent a lot of time preparing the bolt."

Had somebody been planning to take Strafa down for some time? "Dex, you say you don't need the markings to tell where the bolt came from?"

"Correct, sir. Smitt bolts were cast, dipped, and baked.

The foundry did almost no machine work. Quantity was the goal. Smitt developed a mass production method. You still need the marks to tell when a bolt was made, though. Nowadays, with the war over and the supply scandals forgotten manufacturing dates shouldn't be relevant. Nor even the manufacturer, really. In fact, you'd almost expect newly surfacing bolts to come from a lot that went missing years ago."

"You're probably right."

Dex went on. "If it was me, I'd look for the weapon used to shoot the bolt. There can't be a lot of those around."

A good point. Who had a siege weapon sitting around in the back garden? "Nobody has home access to artillery, right?"

Dex agreed. "Though there are some in private hands, in museums or owned by collectors. Those that are legal have the sear catch in the trigger housing assembly taken out so the string can't be locked back."

"So a legally owned piece won't work."

"Theoretically. It wouldn't be hard to make one functional. I could do it if I had access to a smithy and a machine shop. Any good mechanic could fix one by studying the trigger mechanism. Hell, if you only wanted to shoot once or twice, you could hand carve a wooden sear. We did that all the time in the field. You can't always take a weapon off the line long enough for the armorers to make repairs."

Barate said, "It's another thread to pull. What kind of range are we looking at, Dex? Six hundred yards' flight, four hundred with momentum enough to kill? If we draw a circle with Strafa at the center . . ."

"A surplus antique—which is what this piece has to be—not manned by a trained crew, you're unlikely to see a lethal range over three hundred yards. This engine was probably less than two hundred yards off to get this accuracy."

I said, "Let's get a map, draw different circles, see whose properties show up inside, then winnow the possibilities."

Barete said, "Use a topographical map. One of those

survey maps with all the ground features and structures on it."

Dex said, "Ordnance survey charts are what you're talking about. You can even identify blind spots and impossible lines of fire."

I looked straight at Dex. "You know how to use an ordnance survey map?" Those were for army use originally. They required basic literacy, a lot of training, and on-the-job experience at the point of the spear.

Dex said, "I can use a rural map. I don't know about one for a neighborhood like this. Wasn't a lot of urban fighting in the Cantard."

"I'll get a set for the Hill," Barate said. "What now, Garrett?"

"I go home and talk to my partner. He's sure to have some interesting suggestions."

Barate's expression went blank but cold. Clever me, I figured him out. "This is where I live now, but there's no way I can not think of my house on Macunado as home. That's where I built my life."

Barate said, "Intellectually persuasive but not emotionally satisfying."

I let that slide. "Once I see him I'll hit the Al-Khar again."

"Why?"

Algarda had a full Hill ration of distrust of the Guard, and an abiding disdain for systematized, publicly funded law and order.

"Because if I keep them interested, they can do stuff like find the rest of that broken bolt. They can knock on more doors in a day than I can in a month and be more intimidating asking the questions we want answered. You know somebody saw something. It happened in broad daylight."

"You're underselling yourself. You have more chance of getting good info than any Guardsman."

"You think? Why?"

"You're Strafa Algarda's husband. You're the man chosen to share the life of the only Algarda who shined. The only one that everybody loved. Now you have all the other Algardas, who scare everybody, lurking behind you. Love and fear. Excellent motivators."

Yeah. Only not for whoever attacked Strafa.

He continued. "If you do the asking you'll have your neighbors more willing to help than you might actually want."

From the sink Race said, "That is true, you know."

Dex, erstwhile artillerist, nodded agreement.

25

The light was fading, though it would be a while till sunset. The clouds had thickened. A misty drizzle was back. I hunched some but didn't hurry. I was working my thinking muscles too hard.

Morley had spread out a couple of steps more than usual for friends walking together. "Pay attention! People are killing people. Brood when you have four brick walls around you."

He was right. I had learned during the war. Men who stroll their interior landscapes while the enemy is afoot are begging for an early separation from service. "I've gotten out of the habit."

"I've gotten a little weak myself," he admitted. "Happens when you move up the food chain. But you've been warned. You smelled what I smelled when we left Strafa's place."

"Lurking Fehlske doesn't do hits. He watches and reports."

"Maybe to somebody who does do hits. You have to remember who other people think you are, not what you think you are."

I didn't quite get that. "What?"

"You have a reputation. You're connected to people with darker reputations. It's a sure thing, you aren't happy about Strafa. People who don't know you will make decisions based on what they've heard about you, not on hard facts."

"All right. I get that."

"You're a threat because you're you. You could become the cutout between them and everybody who might help get them."

"Meaning that if they eliminate me, my friends might lose interest."

Killing Strafa might have taken the Algardas out of the tournament, but that now made them a potential source of backflash. Eliminating me should soften the dangers.

So in the moment when I came fully alert, I glanced into the shadows between two brick buildings on my left and saw a pretty little blonde somberly watching. She seemed sad. She held the right hand of the big ugly I'd seen her with before.

I stopped to gawk.

Morley barked, "Get down!"

My instincts had not eroded entirely. I slammed down against the cold, wet cobblestones. Something buzzed and crackled and hummed through the space I'd occupied a moment before. More nastiness ripped through the space I would've occupied if I hadn't stopped walking.

I was focused now, oh yes, I was! I crawled and rolled and slithered toward shadows and shelter with great vigor. A third bolt of crispy whatever singed my waggling heinie and went on to hit a granite watering trough. The water therein turned to steam. A hustling hunk of granite ricocheted off the funny bone on my left elbow. I squealed like that proverbial stuck pig. And I crawled!

The steam became fog that filled the street. Cover! I got some feet under me and sprinted into the alley where the little girl lurked.

The attackers couldn't see me, but I couldn't see much, either. Feet pounded behind me, headed several directions. I heard shouts. I heard cussing. I heard Morley yell something. I heard somebody's startled, sharp cry cut off on a sudden high note as . . . something unpleasant happened to somebody who hadn't expected serious difficulties.

Then I had a feeling, supported by no physical evidence, that some huge and terrible bane was headed my way.

My navigation was less than perfect. I tripped over something, plunged through the fog, scraped my face against the side of a building, fetched up with my nose between an expensive pair of small brown shoes capping the bottom ends of little girl legs in white stockings.

A little girl voice announced, "And here we have proof that being lucky sometimes trumps being smart."

A meat hook bigger than my head caught me by the scruff, set me on my feet.

The girl said, "You have to start taking this seriously. Otherwise you are going to die."

Then her mouth opened into a large O of surprise. I looked behind me.

Tin whistles filled the entrance to the alleyway. There was a fight going on somewhere else. It made a lot of noise. These red tops, perhaps envious, appeared to be looking for a fight of their own.

Two came forward.

A volcanic rumble came out of Mr. Big Thing. The girl said, "Yes. We should."

Then I was looking up as that thing towed the girl up the side of a building using one hand and his feet, which were bare and apelike. They vanished in an instant.

"What the hell?" I said. "What in the hell?"

The red tops backed me in chorus. We were the Alley Cats doo-wop crew for several seconds.

A rebel soul broke off to ask, "Are you all right, sir? I'm sorry we were so slow getting here."

"Huh? I got some abrasions. Hands. Right knee. Right cheek. Got my funny bone rung. Otherwise I'm hunky-dory. You were slow, how?"

"We had to hang back so we weren't noticed by the bad guys, sir. So we could strike unexpectedly, like. The trade-off was, they got a little time to work some mischief before we could begin the roundup."

I wished the light was better. I couldn't tell if the guy was having fun or was just one of those people raised with a stick up his butt.

One fact that I did get quick was that the Guard had used me for bait. They wanted Garrett stomping around knocking things over and ambling into traps, whereupon they could drop from the sky and sweep up the trash.

A studly move fully worthy of the secret police. Or of the commander of the Guard.

I took a last glance skyward and was startled. Little blond doll was silhouetted against the overcast, by herself. The light wasn't good. I could not make out her expression. She was holding a stuffed bear.

The tin whistles prowled the alley in search of something useful. One runty type wore a forensics wizard badge on the side of his beret.

Relway had believed me. The Guard were rolling it all out. No doubt Relway smelled a chance to gain some leverage on the Hill crowd.

The talking red top asked, "Do you know the child or her companion, sir?"

"I do not. I have seen them before, the night before my wife was killed."

How was that for a new Garrett strategy? Utter, complete, total, devoted cooperation, with nearly full disclosure.

The tin whistle shrugged. "We'll find them. People with their skills can't help leaving traces just by being themselves. Let's go see what Karbo caught."

Karbo proved to be the leader of the squad involved in the other ruckus, which hadn't gone well for the ambushers. Three men in cuffs sat on the cobblestones looking thoroughly miserable. Morley was doing the same a few yards away, without cuffs. A medic type attended him. He had some scrapes, nothing serious. He hadn't opened any old wounds. My team leader, Stickman, told the medic to do me next, then went to consult a guy who looked like somebody named Karbo. He was thick, wide, and ugly.

Two men lay stretched out by the three in cuffs. They had the deflated look of the newly dead.

Morley said, "They got downwind of the Specials." Specials being the shock troops of the secret police. "And didn't get their hands up fast enough."

One of the two had been a killer wizard and doubtless the first to die.

I let the medic check me out and salve my scrapes. He gave me rote advice about treatment and how I could expect to have bruises in the morning. He mistook me for a special client but didn't let himself get carried away with the VIP treatment.

I asked Morley, "We know who they are yet?"

"People who don't like you."

"Amazingly enough, there are some of those out there. Don't seem right, a big old harmless, lovable fuzz ball like me. I usually recognize them, though. Dead or alive, these guys are strangers." I nodded then, upwind, to let him know I had gotten his hint about being downwind. These people were out of business, but Lurking Fehlske was still out there.

Just for grins, I asked, "You wouldn't have a jealous husband or disgruntled girlfriend out to get you and I'm collateral damage?"

"I have become seriously monogamous." He had powerful health reasons for doing so, since his main lady these days was Belinda Contague. He had made the grand blunder of breaking his own first law of relationships by getting involved with a woman crazier than him. That beautiful psychopath didn't have much forgive and forget built in.

Better him than me. And it had been me in the once-upon-a-time.

Stickman came back. "We haven't learned much yet, sir. The survivors will be questioned, but the way things work, the ones who give up easiest are the ones who know the least."

"The hired hands."

"Exactly, sir. I do know that the Director has a strong interest, so I'm sure he'll keep you posted as information develops."

"I appreciate that." Look at me, playing the politeness game.

"This incident appears to be closed, sir. There seems to have been no connection between these people and those in the alley. I would urge you, sir, to be more aware of your surroundings. You should get off the street, into a safe place, as soon as possible. You should stay there till the Guard unravels this antisocial behavior."

Morley must have done some growing up himself. He kept a straight face, too.

I said, "Thank you," again, and, "I do appreciate your help. I'll do my best to follow your advice."

Good old Morley kept right on with the blank face. He has skills. But he did look at me like he was wondering who the hell was wearing the Garrett suit.

We made it to Macunado Street without further misadventure.

26

Dean served supper in Singe's office. She and Old Bones had guests: John Stretch and Belinda Contague. They were in related businesses, so some of that might have gotten done during the socializing. Belinda fussed over Morley like he was a toddler with a serious ouchie. The display was revoltingly mushy.

I downed some shepherd's pie and a pint of beer before I told Belinda, "You might not want to roam around on your lonesome, the way things are going around me lately."

She asked, "Why should I worry? You're the target."

John Stretch agreed. "I put the word out to my people when I heard about Strafa." He was yet another soul that my sweetie had conquered.

John Stretch is handy to know. His people go everywhere, doing the dirtiest work, and people pay no attention. They should worry about protecting their secrets.

"Nothing?"

"Not yet. There is a hole in the tapestry. Many on the Hill would like to know who attacked her. None of them do know, or even have strong suspicions."

"That's odd."

Singe added, "I get the feeling that they are not planning anything, they just want to know if there is a danger to them."

That made sense. There have been doctrine-driven insurrections directed at sorcerers before.

Soon I was feeling full enough, mellow enough, and safe enough to collect myself and go to the Dead Man's room—after a side trip to my old office, the broom closet next to the space Singe used, where I put on one of my ratty old sweaters. It can get cold in there with His Nibs.

"Any thoughts?" I asked as I adjusted a chair so I could settle comfortably with my pint. "I see Penny is still learning her oils." The girl is a talented artist. Old Bones does what he can to help her develop her skills.

His pet stray is one of few females, of any species, that he not only tolerates but actively likes.

You have someone worried. More likely, several some-ones, probably all determined to win the Tournament of Swords.

"I have the magical skills of a large boulder. As long as all I have to do is sit there, I'm golden. I'm a powerhouse."

It occurs to me that Strafa may not have been attacked for the reasons that we have assumed.

"Huh?"

She was indeed, Furious Tide of Light and the likely Algarda Champion, but suppose she was eliminated instead in a fool's effort to make sure that you do not enter the game. An ill-reasoned effort that has fired a raging blowback already.

"My head is running slow tonight. Elucidate your reasoning. Pretend I'm a dim five."

Damn! I whipped a flashy word on him and it went completely to waste. Of course, his being able to tramp around inside my head whenever he feels like, he always sees my best stuff coming.

Consider the response to events. Since Strafa's demise the Civil Guard, the Syndicate, the rat people nation, the Algarda family and its allies have all mobilized to hunt the assassins. I submit that it may have been such actions that the assassination was intended to forestall.

"Oh." I got it. Sort of.

Somebody might think the Tournament of Swords game would be rigged against them if I was Strafa's Mortal Companion. My connections could give her an intelligence edge. Take her out and those resources no longer mattered.

"I can see somebody with an upper-class attitude thinking that way. Somebody committed to the premise of the tournament and expecting a win. But it wouldn't be somebody who knows me because I wouldn't buy into the tournament in the first place."

Indeed. At the moment it appears unlikely that the tournament will occur. After the embarrassment those men suffered . . .

"Yes?" There had been more than one embarrassment, I thought. That doll-child had toyed with me, then had gone her way with ease.

Of course, however clever she was, she couldn't remain unseen by all the eyes that would be watching for her now. She would be identified. She would be taken out of the game. Gently, of course. I wouldn't put up with anybody attacking children in my name.

We shall have to come back to this later. We are about to have company.

Damn. I had been hoping to explore his thinking about the girl who had attacked me in the cemetery.

27

Company proved to be Barate Algarda, Kevans, Kyoga Stornes, and one of the Machtkess girls, all of whom arrived in Shadowslinger's coach. The wicked old witch did not come with them.

She had an excuse. Barate explained, "She had an apoplectic breakdown."

It sounds like it may have been a stroke.

We settled in Singe's office. Dean served tea. Lady Tara Chayne and Kyoga were pale and severely stressed by the company, though they didn't know Belinda or John Stretch. They just couldn't be comfortable in a situation where rat people were not only present but were equals—and maybe even the smartest people in the room.

Why hadn't Barate warned them?

He did.

"Got it." Naturally, several people wondered why I would chat with the air.

Mr. Algarda did not know that Pound Humility would be here. He did tell them about Singe. They did not believe him.

I sensed some serious disgruntlement on his side of the hallway. Something was not what he wanted it to be, either.

They are all wearing those silver hair nets.

So what? People have worn those to the house, trying to keep him out of their heads, since Kevans and Kip Prose thought them up. They don't work. Not for long, anyway. Old Bones always finds a way around them.

These are working quite well, below the surface. If they conduct their business quickly, they will be gone before I find a workaround.

Interesting.

They would argue that they did not want the Dead Man to have unrestricted access to the insides of their heads, which wasn't unreasonable. The problem is, no one believes he will stick to peeking only where he is invited, an attitude not based on real-world evidence.

My racket has taught me that most people judge others by the way they think themselves. Claims otherwise are tactics and deception. Villains know we're all exactly as black hearted as them. Naive pacifist vegetarians are sure that everyone else really would rather sit down and talk it out.

There is a bell curve of character from irredeemably vile to blind romantic idealism. The predators on the dark side feed on folks from the other, confident that they deserve it for their idiot outlook.

Which would seem to be inconsistent with the conviction that everyone thinks exactly the way they do. But if you brought that up, the villains would give you a blank stare and fail to grasp your point.

This explains why the world needs us smug-ass sheepdog types from a shade to the bleak side of the median point on the curve.

Thank Singe for that poindexter imagery.

"Why would she have a breakdown?" I asked.

"Anger. Word came, I don't know how, that the Algardas are in the tournament, like it or not, and Kevans is now your Mortal Companion."

The girl had been a zombie since she arrived. Now I knew why.

"What?" Why hadn't Old Bones warned me? "Screw that. But how can that be?"

"Simple. The Operators decided that since Strafa was attacked prematurely, they were free to change up on us. We're still in. You see why Mother was upset."

"And then some. I might do some changing up myself, by means of cranial redesign, once I find these Operators."

Remain calm. Do not say anything more. I believe this is extremely important.

He has me trained. Despite my inclination to rage, I put it away.

The others may have received similar suggestions. Neither John Stretch, Belinda, Morley, nor Singe said a word, though questions could have fallen like heavy snow.

There was some Dead Man gamesmanship afoot. He was hoping to maneuver someone into doing something they did not want to do.

Exactly.

Not particularly comforting. Most times, someone turns out to be me.

Curiously, Kevans has the most accessible mind. Ironic, inasmuch as she designed and keeps upgrading the hair nets. Her father is almost as accessible. He is sure that Shadowslinger's episode was not calculated to avoid this visit. He is close to being paralyzed by dread that it may be worse than the physician reported.

That wouldn't be good. We couldn't have that darkness, as a looming threat, missing from our quiver.

Barate said, "You did ask us to come see your partner, Garrett."

"I did, hoping he would have access to your minds. It's finding things that you don't know you know, and the connections between them, that makes him so valuable. Closed up the way you are with those nets, you may as well not have come."

Kevans was startled. Frightened even.

Had she really thought that we didn't know?

Yes. Really. I did my best to keep it from being obvious.

My bad, giving things away, here.

Me at my age still having trouble thinking things through beforehand.

I didn't expect anybody to shed their protection. I

wanted them thinking about whatever it was that they really wanted to hide. Old Bones could skim those thoughts off the surfaces of their minds. But Barate began untangling the net that had been so artfully installed in his hair.

Old Bones touched me lightly, approving my tactics, offering suggestions, then noting, *This one is deadly serious about this.*

You don't get a lot of tonal information from the Dead Man's communications. There was plenty in that, though.

I asked Barate, "Did Constance have any thoughts about who the Operators might be?"

Algarda was startled. The same question must have occurred to him.

I needed not pursue that now that the mesh was off.

Kevans began removing her net.

Garrett, you smooth talker, you. Look at this. All these people who swim in seas of secrets taking a leap of faith because of the murder of a woman they all loved.

I will not betray the trust they have offered me, even to you. Nor to you, Singe. Gossip and speculate as you will. I shall neither confirm nor deny.

That made his position clear to them, too.

I told my father-in-law, "I got the impression that she had someone in mind but wanted to test her suspicions before she said anything."

Tara Chayne started trying to remove her hair net. That got ugly fast. She was wearing a partial wig with hair extensions. The mesh was integrated into those, which she did not want to do without.

There was some serious vanity there. Or maybe more than vanity. She was partly bald beneath the appliances.

Barate relaxed slightly. "She didn't say anything to me, but I think you're right."

He has mild suspicions of his own regarding his friend Kyoga and someone called Bonegrinder.

The Kyoga suspicion was off to the boneyard already. Stornes had his mesh halfway off. Old Bones assured me, *This one is an empty vessel. Almost literally. The only thing*

*going on inside his head is obsessive concern about the
safety of his children.*

"Plural?" I had heard only one mentioned before.

*There are several. You have encountered two of them be-
fore, as members of the Faction.*

"Egad. Life. Everything ties back into everything else."

I got looks. People aren't comfortable when Old Bones
and I have private sidebars.

*Which point please keep in mind. Mr. Algarda has given
us the complete and literal truth, as he knows it, regarding his
mother's thinking.*

Interesting way of putting that. It might mean that Old
Bones had stumbled over a low-grade suspicion that he did
not yet want to share.

True.

Grumble, grumble. Why do these things have to be so
complicated?

Just once why can't it be easy?

Because the stupid people get rounded up and sent to
the labor camps before their careers begin? Before they get
far enough in life to cause me grief?

An intriguingly solipsist hypothesis.

I stumble over stupid villains like I dodge road apples in
the street. Stupid is the fifth element of creation and, probably, the most common, or else some magnetic power at-
tracts it all to TunFaire.

Penny showed up with fresh tea. She was surprised to
see the size of the crowd. Dean had not warned her. I expected her to flee to the Dead Man's room, her own, or to
the kitchen, but she just backed off to the doorway and
asked, "What's going on?"

Old Bones handled the updates. His responsibility, after
all. She was his pet.

28

I shut the door behind Tara Chayne. That bastion of insensitivity was last to leave, hinting that she needed me to see her safely home.

His Nibs assured me that what she wanted was exactly what I suspected.

He observed, *None of those people knew anything about Strafa's killer and not much of value about the Tournament of Swords. Only Lady Tara Chayne is completely convinced that a new tournament is in the works. The others are taking it seriously only because Strafa is dead.*

Well, hell. Did they think somebody was working a scam?

That could be, though I had some doubts after my encounters.

The scam thesis remains on the table.

He, too, had trouble accepting that anyone would really believe that a Tournament of Swords could be managed under contemporary conditions. "There are people with the talent to run a game on the Hill crowd, but do any of them have the guts?" The consequences could be grim. Might as well mess with Deal Relway or Belinda Contague. Your death would be easier.

It is deserving of reflection. Though not rational, initiation of a tournament is not rational, either.

He shuffled the clutter inside my head. He did the same

with Penny and Singe, Belinda and John Stretch, then proclaimed the obvious.

There is something missing.

"There is a lot that's missing. Like any sense. We've established that already."

He began to muse, allowing the rest of us the rare treat of witnessing the process. It is intriguing to see how his minds work. He sorted through speculations that were entirely ridiculous, like Strafa and Vicious Min having been struck by accidental discharges or having been attacked because of a case of mistaken identity.

He knew the ideas were absurd but wanted to test every conceivable notion. The truth might appear just as absurd at first blush.

The others drank beer and didn't say much. I went to the Dead Man's room and did the same. Penny came in to work on one of her paintings.

I tried picking at the edges of the mistaken identity notion, couldn't make it hold water. Strafa had been attacked deliberately, no doubt about it. Vicious Min had been injured at the same time.

I must see this woman. Race and Dex, as well, but Min most of all, as soon as it can be arranged.

"You've found a thread?"

Perhaps. It has occurred to me to wonder why a Dread Companion, supposedly conjured from a supernatural realm and the only such creature so far actually noted, would arrive before the tournament began. And would then hire persons in your own trade to follow your movements. There is something odd about that.

"Race and Dex? Are you sure? I don't see how they could give us anything. I grilled them good today."

You did indeed. And they may be empty vessels. But it is equally possible that they know something unrelated to what you asked that they did not report, either, and that might reflect obliquely on the situation.

I was skeptical. Those two were neither heart nor soul of the Algarda family operation. They cooked and cleaned.

For example, we assumed that Strafa was coming home when she was attacked. But was she, in fact? Could she have been at home already and was called out? Might she have just gone to see why Vicious Min was loitering out front? Do we know anything about that woman that she did not tell other witnesses herself?

"You could be right. Min told Barate . . ."

Yes. But.

We had only Min's word for anything involving Vicious Min.

The more I think about this demon woman, the more I want to make her acquaintance. She may have had a hand in the assassination. Perhaps she had some bad luck, got hurt, got caught, but because there were no contradicting witnesses, she recouped her fortunes with a tall tale delivered before she passed out from loss of blood.

That is what he does. He sees things from an unlikely angle. That scenario fit the facts. I stipulated as much. "But why would she have me watched?" Preston Womble had known no whys. He had known only that a man needed money to buy food and pay the rent and someone had given him cash to do what he knew how to do best. Elona Muriat would have known nothing more than he did.

I recalled hungry times when I worked under the same blind circumstances. Every client lied about why the job needed doing.

The deception came with the life. You got used to it.

Womble and Muriat are unemployed now. We might lure them here with a job offer.

"Won't work. They won't have anything to do with me."

We will not send you. Have Miss Winger collect the woman. Have Mr. Tharpe . . . No. He is well known as an associate of yours. Mr. Playmate would be better, if his health is up to the legwork. Failing him, try Jon Salvation or Mr. Kolda. They might find the prospect exciting. Mr. Womble or Miss Muriat should not connect this neigh-

borhood with you till they are too close to make their escape.

Only if they hadn't done their homework. I'd been living with Strafa when Vicious Min sicced them on me. Damn! Those two could turn out to be gold mines in the land of things we didn't know we knew.

29

Saucerhead and Winger were onto the payroll, Tharpe definitely doing nothing connected with Womble or Muriat. The Dead Man had him doing courier duty. His first job was to inform Race and Dex that their presence was required here. Mr. Tharpe would show them the way.

I was off to see Playmate, to see if he would lead Preston Womble to the Dead Man. If his health was too fragile, I'd move on to Kolda, whose apothecary shop was just blocks from Playmate's stable. I wanted to see Play even if he couldn't help. I wanted to know what he had seen that night in the Dream Quarter.

Maybe he had noticed something that Penny hadn't.

Plus, I wanted to see how he was feeling. I hadn't had a chance at the funeral or wake.

He had been on the road to a hard death from an aggressive cancer. The combined efforts of Kolda, the Dead Man, and a healing priest named Hoto Pepper had licked that evil, barely. I hoped Play was still out in front of it. He was one of my better friends. And I liked him, which isn't always the case with some of the people we've known for donkey's years. He was one of the good guys, righteous in the sense that the word was designed.

I seemed to have the streets to myself, all by my lonesome. I started out as alert as on a patrol into Venageta's slice of the island swamps. No one showed any interest in me, nor did I smell one. Neither friend, foe, nor Guardsman gave himself away.

I liked that but found it curious.

I followed Macunado east for a while, walked four blocks sideways to Magnolia, took that east to Prince Guelfo Square. That isn't much bigger than a hankie. I stopped to visit Frenkeljean the sausage vendor and had a juicy hot sausage on a bun with masses of raw onion, checking my surroundings while dripping grease everywhere. Frenkeljean sees stuff. He functions more like furniture than people. Folks pay no attention. He has the added camouflage of being only part human.

He is a stringer for Deal Relway, too. I saw him inside the Al-Khar once, reporting. He didn't see me.

I asked a few soft questions, mostly out of curiosity. I really was there mainly for the sausage.

If Strafa had a downside, it was her passion for healthy food. I could never convince her that big fat bratwursts in quantity were real good eating.

Seizing the day, I treated myself to another. Stomach bulging and happy, I resumed my approach to Playmate's stable, now confident that I was not the drum major for another parade. I paid no attention to the dogs that were out. The city has its strays, always there, like rat people, seldom noticed.

Could the lack of interest in me be because somebody really clever had tagged me with a sorcery-based tagalong tracer? Or was it just what it seemed? Nobody cared anymore.

No boost for the ego, that. It meant that everyone, friend and foe, had found something better to do. I was old news.

Even my own life can't be all about me.

I was in the last stretch, headed up a slight hill, puffing and telling myself that I really had to do something to get in shape.

My best exercise happens mostly inside the gymnasium of my mind.

Despite my determination to maintain a level-one alert, I did not, for some time, realize that I was no longer operating alone.

30

I had acquired a shaggy brown twenty-pound mongrel sidekick who had taken station at my right ankle like he had been there forever and that was the meaning of life.

"Head on out, dog. You're too old to hook me with cute."

He awarded me the doggy equivalent of an adoring smile. I noted that he was actually a she. So what? A mutt is a mutt. I don't have much use for any of them.

My brother Mikey brought strays home all the time. Mom put up with it, too, though they usually "ran away" within a few days. Mikey never could do any wrong.

She would have fits if I brought a critter home. Of course, mine were way cooler. A baby mastodon, maybe. Or a raptor thunder lizard. One of the little ones that only come up to your hip and mostly eat rats and cats.

Another sign of the times. We hardly ever see those anymore.

That dog was definitely female. She did not hear a thing she didn't want to hear. She just got on with escorting me to whatever destination pleased me.

I growled under my breath. Brownie growled right back, making good-natured conversation. "Brownie" because I'm so clever, though Spots would have done the job, too. She had a white patch on her throat and another on her left hind leg. Her tail had been broken.

While I was cataloging her charms, another four-legged

lady usurped the place of honor on my left. She was the same size but had a ration of bulldog in her background. She was charming in a maximum ugly kind of way. She did not appear to have a pleasant personality like Brownie.

She suffered from the same hearing disorder.

I was a hundred yards from Playmate's stable. I would hunker down there, see if somebody had slipped a steak into my pocket. I saw Play his own self chatting up a customer looking to board a horse. The nag glanced my way. She made an unhappy noise.

Here we go. They're all out to get me. Nobody believes me, but I never find any proof to the contrary. This mare wasn't issuing a challenge, though. She was just unhappy because she had to be in the same street as that horrid Garrett creature.

Yeah. She knew who I was. She recognized me. Those monsters are connected telepathically.

Little Moo charged out of a dark breezeway. She hit me full speed. She had on the outfit she'd worn in the cemetery. She had nothing new to say. "Hate you! Hate you!" She pounded my chest with her fists.

The dogs danced around us, excited but not really taking sides.

Playmate came running.

I got hold of the girl, tossed her over my shoulder, went to meet him, whereupon he proved that he wasn't going to be any help at all. "Put her down and turn her loose, Garrett. People are watching."

He had a point. Folks aren't always sympathetic to a guy in his thirties lugging a young girl who is kicking and screaming, even when her racket makes it sound like a domestic dispute. The mob might sort me out and consult the facts later, which would give the girl a great head start.

Folks there were slow, though, maybe on account of the dogs. There were four of those now, and they were turning the excitement into a great doggie celebration. They yapped. They yipped. They bounced up and down happily. How could any of that be part of an abduction?

I blathered loud nonsense about how Mom was going to blow her top this time. I put the girl down but hung on to her right hand, which was small, pudgy, and hot. We ducked into Playmate's place.

Play brought his customer and the man's steed inside while muttering, "Kids these days." Then, "Dogs in the office, Gee, not around with the horses."

Gee?

I herded hounds, never turning loose of my new young friend. The mutts were cooperative, the girl just passive. She seemed ashamed now. She kept her eyes downcast and moved sleepily.

She was set to bolt the instant she saw an opening.

I shut the door to the street.

The dogs all sat or lay down. Brownie settled on her belly in front of the street exit, chin on paws, looking worshipful. The others were not so friendly.

Brownie seemed to be the boss female.

I asked the girl, "What's your name?" Still hanging on to her hand.

She looked at me like the question confused her, then down at the floor. "Hate you," she said with little force.

"Not much of a vocabulary, sweetie." I planted her in a chair, stepped away. She wiggled around before she decided she was comfortable.

"No name, eh? Where do you live, then?"

That one appeared to be as tough as the one about her name.

"All right, then. Who are your mom and dad?"

Zip. Nothing. I asked a few more, none of which produced any information other than a sense that she didn't understand what she was being asked. She did, sadly, softly, once remind me that she hated me, but then each question made her shrink in on herself a little more, leaving her a touch more embarrassed.

Playmate joined us. He was not in the most cheerful mood. "I had to lie about you to close that deal, Garrett. So what the dickens do we have here? What's going on?"

"I'd cheerfully tell all if I had a clue."

He settled behind an actual desk that took up about a fifth of the room, faced the girl across its wooden plain. That desk had come to him from his brother-in-law in a debt settlement. The brother-in-law had a history of failures achieved after showing amazing promise, energy, and enthusiasm in the organization and financing of bold new ventures.

Play's expression was skeptical. He gave me the fish-eye, then the girl in the cow costume, and the same to all four dogs, every one absurdly quiet and well behaved. Brownie hid her eyes behind a paw.

I said, "I came over to ask about your trip to the Dream Quarter with Penny. And to see how you're doing. And to offer you a small job helping find the people who attacked Strafa. You know what happened with Little Moo. You watched it happen."

He could not deny that. But he wasn't quite ready to take that at face value. He grunted and waited for me to talk myself into or out of something.

"Things happen around me. Weird things." Things that sometimes sweep up my friends with the dust and clutter.

"Play, I don't know this girl. I'll happily leave her for the Reverend Playmate to sort out. I just want to know if you saw something that Penny missed because she was busy being a priestess."

"Strafa wasn't down there, Garrett. We would have noticed. The turnout was the worst I've ever seen. Religion is dying."

"In TunFaire? This is the most god-ridden city there ever was."

"In TunFaire. There are empty temples on the low end of the Street of the Gods today. The little cults can't make the rent."

Brownie lifted her chin half an inch and cracked an eye like she wondered if one of the two-leggers might do something interesting. Maybe food would be involved.

In a whisper, bashfully, Little Moo reminded me, "Hate you."

"That's all she'll say, Play. Not why. Not her name. Nothing about her family. I don't know if she even understands the questions."

Playmate stood and leaned forward, over the desk. He had his gentlest look on, but even after the cancer had depleted him so badly, he was huge and intimidating.

Brownie opened her other eye and made a sound meant to communicate something somehow, but I did not get it.

Playmate suggested, "Maybe she's slow?"

"It don't seem like she's been abused."

Slow girls on their own don't last long. Maybe this one was doing all right because she lived in the new, law-hagridden TunFaire sprung from the nightmares behind Deal Relway's forehead.

Playmate settled back. "Is there someone else who could help if I turn you down?"

"I was thinking Kolda since he's close by."

"Anyone else? His old lady keeps him on a short leash since the mix-up with the zombie makers."

They hadn't been zombie makers, but I knew what he meant so I didn't correct him. "You see him much these days?"

"He keeps me in the stuff I need to fight the cancer. I buy him dinner at the Grapevine when Trudi lets him out. Who else do you have?"

"Jon Salvation?"

"Probably not your best choice."

"Oh?"

"He'd do it. He'd jump at a chance to be part of another adventure."

I scowled. Did he know something about Salvation that I didn't?

"Really, Garrett. Whatever it is to you, it would be an adventure to him."

"You could be right." It would all be part of a story to Jon Salvation. It would turn up in some future play. And while he was involved in real events, he would be trying to do revisions and rewrites, heading west.

Play announced, "I have animals that need me. And now I have this," meaning Little Moo. "If you can't get Kolda, or anybody else, then come back. We'll find a workaround."

Beer crossed my mind. I hadn't had any yet today. Why think about it now? Playmate was no drinker. He might not have any on the premises. Then I got what my subconscious was trying to tell me. "I could try Max Weider or Manvil Gilbey. Preston would get all excited if he thought he had a shot at working for the brewery."

"And there you go. So take on off. I'll try to get something out of her." Then, before I actually got rolling, he told me, "I don't know what to say, Garrett. I hurt for you so bad. What happened has tested my faith. That girl was the best thing that ever happened to you. I guess I should thank God that you had her in your life for as long as you did."

"I do," I said. "Thank you, Play. That means a lot." It really did, because it is so hard for Playmate to express his emotions. In this case it was especially hard because he had been a huge fan of the woman Strafa had replaced so suddenly.

I still had trouble fully believing that myself.

31

The brewery visit went the way it usually did. Everyone but top management acted like I was a typhoid carrier, though everyone did sympathize with my loss. The disease they really dreaded was a mild cousin of the one Deal Relway and General Block were splashing wildly across the canvas of the city. My own artwork was limited to the brewery floor and storage caverns.

There wasn't much pilferage anymore. Max Weider paid his people well and didn't mind a little personal consumption, so it wasn't often that his security team—me—had much to do. So little, in fact, that I hardly ever showed up, so people worry that there might be a stink in the wind when I do come out of the woodwork. I might get my nose into somebody's business. I made folks uncomfortable.

That was my principal function.

I did drop by Kolda's shop before moving on to the brewery. I never got to the subject of him lending me a hand. His wife scared me off.

She really did want us to stay away from each other. She considered me trouble on the hoof.

Max and Manvil Gilbey were at the brew house together. I made my case. They asked a few questions. Manvil suggested, "We can write the lost time off against your retainer."

Which Max followed by remarking, "Which compensation package we may have to renegotiate. This is the first time you've been here this month, and that's only because you want a favor."

He was correct. I had slacked off shamefully lately, at Amalgamated Manufacturing and at the brewery.

I got all apologetic.

Max told me, "Remain calm. I understand your situation. It wasn't that long ago that I was there myself." Most of his family had been murdered. That was back when I met Singe. "You helped me get through that."

Gilbey said, "Whatever we think of your feeble work ethic and ambition deficit, Garrett, we do owe you. You have been a true friend, to your own cost. We can't be anything less ourselves."

I knew that intellectually. I really did. But I didn't want to weaken myself further by depending on others even more.

I have seen too many people turn passive under stress, then never, ever get up and rely on themselves again.

"So, what do you want done?" Max asked

I explained that I needed Preston Womble lured into the Dead Man's clutches.

"Easy-peasy," Gilbey declared. "I'll handle it. How urgent is it?"

It struck me that if we took the Tournament of Swords seriously—and what could bring the seriousness home more forcefully than the murder of your wife—then I had to take a more holistic approach. I had to view the contest as a societal affliction, not just a familial imposition.

The genesis for the notion was my recollection that Max Weider had a surviving daughter. Alyx was a walking compendium of character flaws common to rich kids. She was also bright and energetic and a good person when the inclination took her. And her daddy was richer than God. She might be the kind of outsider the Operators would conscript into an open Champion slot. She could be an attractive choice if they were feeling vindictive toward me.

I took the attack on Strafa as a personal assault, mostly because it made more sense that way.

Alyx's best friend was the woman who had been my squeeze before Strafa entered my life. Wouldn't Tinnie make an amusing Mortal Companion? Though she was no fighter and couldn't last in a lethal environment.

Nor could Alyx.

"Garrett!"

Both of my companions repeated my name. Gilbey finally got my attention by pinching my right arm just above the elbow.

Max said, "You went all gray. I was afraid you'd need a doctor."

"I'm all right. But I did have a sort of mental heart attack. Hear me out. This is unbelievable. If Strafa hadn't been murdered, I'd have trouble buying it myself. But it's all true and I want you to hear it for Alyx's sake." Then I told them the whole thing, with every detail that I had collected.

Once I started, it seemed entirely rational to pull another of TunFaire's modern power loci in to keep the tournament from happening.

They listened skeptically, as you might expect. They asked questions, as you might expect. They did not refuse to believe.

Strafa Algarda was dead. The Tournament of Swords was why, real or fantastic.

Manvil said, "You should have told us this before."

Max agreed, but admitted, "I don't know if I would have listened, though, before you realized that Alyx could get dragged in."

Gilbey said, "I don't see that happening."

I said, "It doesn't sound to me like the Operators quite have their heads in the present century."

Max said, "Consider us part of the cure, Garrett. Manvil. Let's convene emergency sessions of our boards of directors."

"Because?"

"Because, between us, the Tates, and Garrett's various friends, we can conjure up ten thousand sets of eyes. Nobody can stay hidden with that many people watching."

Not strictly true, but you couldn't stay hidden if you wanted to do something like interact with people. And you really couldn't stay invisible if you wanted to kick off some big, flashy, loud, and bloody elimination game.

Somebody would see you slipping around.

Time was on the side of the good guys. Somebody would spot somebody doing tournament work. I just hoped a finder like Morley, Belinda, or Relway would send for me before they got all ferocious.

Manvil Gilbey can be frustratingly practical sometimes. Like Singe, he asks difficult, emotionally unsatisfying questions. "We appreciate the heads-up, Garrett. This is really disturbing stuff. We'll protect Alyx however much she howls. But a question has occurred to me."

"Yes?" His tone said he was going to ask something that would make me very uncomfortable.

"Your wife was murdered. People have followed you around. They were able to find you when you were on the move, or were able to anticipate your movements. You have been attacked unsuccessfully. So far. Do you have some reason to think that last night's failure was the end of any interest in doing you harm?"

Not quite what I'd been girding my loins to handle. "Not really. Why?"

"Why? Why the hell are you roaming around by yourself, then? Are you deliberately trying to get yourself killed?"

Max's contemplative expression made it plain that he was wondering, too.

"Morley couldn't come with me. He had stuff at work that he couldn't let slide."

Feeble, I know. Even I saw that once I thought about it.

The truth is, there was enough teen left in me that I could still hit the mean streets without thinking ahead.

Practical Manvil said, "Either stay here till we round up a few men willing to walk you home, or sprint from here straight to the Grapevine." That being Morley's hot new restaurant across from the World Theater. "Then plant yourself till he can take you home. Either home. You'll have potent cover at either place."

My brain churned up ego-driven arguments for refusing his invitation to be coddled. But as I sorted through, trying to find one that, at least superficially, sounded plausible, it occurred to me that the Operators, while no geniuses, could be possessed of enough low cunning to see the dragon's teeth leaping up all round and realize that I was the guy doing the sowing. The longer they waited to take me out, the more teeth would hatch.

Max said, "I think he gets it, Manvil."

"Excellent. Thinking outside the moment. It's an art, Garrett. And you've made a start. So. What will it be now? Shall I send for a pitcher of dark for while you wait?"

"Thanks. But no, thanks. I'll take my chances getting to Morley's place. It isn't that far."

"As you wish." Clearly disapproving.

32

I looked around carefully before I reentered the cold and damp. There was no traffic. It was not a day to encourage industry.

I paused again partway down to the street. I could see a couple of pedestrians, but both had their heads down and their shoulders hunched. They were hurrying to get to wherever they were going, which would be inside, out of the drizzle, and probably warm.

I didn't blame them. I thought about going back to take Gilbey up on that pitcher.

One thing about a brewery. Whatever the rest of the world may be suffering, it is warm inside the brew house. Unfortunately, the pungent atmosphere takes some getting used to, like developing an appreciation for stout. It's all good once your senses of smell and taste have died.

Morley's kitchen would be warm, too, and redolent of garlic.

Then I saw Brownie and her crew, waiting. She could barely restrain herself, she was so happy to see me again. I said something grumpy by way of greeting, then something disparaging about Playmate's pooch-wrangling skills, then headed north after a failed look round for Little Moo. She, evidently, had not gotten away.

Brownie took the station that she had made her own. The same surly lady moved into position on my left. The other two ranged ahead, noses to the damp cobblestones. It all seemed militarily precise. And confusing.

I did not obsess, though. Manvil Gilbey's concern had gotten through. I was alert. I was going to get surprised only if it dropped straight down out of the misery overhead.

Even so, my four-legged associates discovered trouble before I had a hint, thanks to their wonderful doggie noses.

They might not be quite as good at tracking as Pular Singe, but they were good at reading the olfactory environment. They snuffled and grumbled. Brownie growled in response. The dog to my left loped forward. Good shepherd Brownie nudged me into a space that looked like it would be easy to defend—and impossible to escape if trouble had the superior numbers.

Some barking and growling ensued, answered by human cursing. Brownie made loud noises that must have been a call to action. Half a dozen strays turned up over the next few minutes, all speaking angry dog and closing on the spot where a surprise had awaited me.

The cursing waxed loud. The growling followed suit, with the growlers outlasting the cursers. Brownie herded me back to the center of the street, took her position of honor. Her crew resumed their former stations. The strays fell in behind. "This is going to cost me, isn't it?" I asked Brownie.

She responded with a snuffling grunt.

"All right. I owe them." But I had to wonder if I'd been scammed. Not once had I actually seen the guys who had been laying for me. They had heeled and toed it out of there first.

Morley's man Puddle answered the back door. I had gone there to avoid disturbing the afternoon trade up front. Puddle gawked. "What the hell?" He couldn't find an appropriate crack.

"Anything you've got, scraps and leftovers, give them to these guys. They just saved my ass from the baddies."

"I give dem anything, dey'll never go away."

And, I didn't doubt, the boys in the back of the shop had their regular customers, bums who maybe made useful spies.

"I did tell Brownie it's only for once. You can put a charge on my tab." Strafa and I had eaten at the Grapevine occasionally. She could afford it.

"Hey! I don' know what ta say, Garrett. 'Bout what happened. Everyt'ing soun's so dumb. She was good people."

"She was. Thank you, Puddle."

"Hey. I could help you do some stuff, you catch da creep what done it."

"I'll keep that in mind. Where's Morley?"

"He's right here," my friend said. He had been summoned by one of the kitchen crew. "And wondering if he didn't raise a slow child. Why are you roaming the streets alone after what's been happening?"

Puddle corrected him. "He ain't not alone, boss. He's got him a whole crew a' sidekicks." Which was a Puddle-style snap joke. He opened the door to the alley to toss scraps and stuff scraped off plates.

Morley looked. "They had better not set up housekeeping out there, Garrett." Then, frowning, he noted, "Some of those mutts were with the girl at the cemetery."

"They were. She turned up again. Ambushed me when I was on my way to see Playmate."

Morley heard my tale. "She won't talk?"

"It's like she isn't sure how, not that she's trying to hide something. I don't think she's very bright."

"That's not good if you're a girl, young, and halfway attractive."

"Playmate has her now. She'll be all right with him. He'll get her to talk, then find her people."

Morley nodded. He didn't say so, but he thought that I was whistling in the dark. The girl lived in a cemetery with feral dogs. She wouldn't be doing that if she had people. "Bell is at her table. Have lunch with her. She might have something for you that she wouldn't share with me."

"Trouble in paradise?"

"No. Just two strong-willed, stubborn people used to having their own ways trying to figure out the couples game. I'm grumpy because I didn't get my way."

Bell was his pet name for Belinda Contague, his current flame and likely his last unless he outlives her. Which isn't implausible, considering her career.

33

Belinda beckoned me right away, already aware that I was in the house. She indicated a seat opposite her at a table she had to herself. "You look a little ragged."

I gave her my morning's sad tale of woe, studying her as I jabbered. Time was not being kind.

She was a beautiful woman, but, then, her father had collected those when he was younger. Belinda's mother had been one of the great beauties of her time. Belinda herself had extremely pale skin and dark hair technically augmented to be even darker and glossier. Her eyes were a stunning blue. As always, she wore intense scarlet lip coloring. Today she was dressed as though she was as rich as she was, instead of the usual down.

She seemed tired.

We're friends because I saved her soul back in a day when she was determined to avenge her mother by indulging in self-destructive behavior. She meant everything to her father, Chodo. Bad behavior was a way to make the old man hurt. We had been more than friends for a while, then friends with occasional benefits till we settled into our present people-we-can-always-count-on friendship. There were times when she could creep me out as thoroughly as Shadowslinger did.

She wasn't really sane. Like the worst sociopaths, she could fake sanity almost perfectly.

"So how are you doing otherwise?" she asked. "Handling it?"

"Doing all right, I think. Better than I expected at first. I guess experience helps even when it comes to grief."

"Most people get on better than they expect. I think it's built in. Once the crunch does come, we soldier on for the sake of the other survivors."

Interesting that she could see the social interconnectedness of our species even though she was incapable of participating genuinely herself.

Morley brought a freshwater prawn, clam, and mussel platter that I loved but could not afford. He placed it in front of me. I could not lie. "God, that smells good." They hadn't been miserly with the garlic.

Morley settled into the chair nearest Belinda.

The lunch crowd, mainly from the theater across the street, envied me this sign of favor. Morley Dotes was a celebrity as a restaurateur.

He told me, "I sent a couple men to backtrack your route. I doubt they'll find anything, but they could get lucky." He was more than the restaurateur he pretended. I had stopped looking at the horse's teeth years ago. And he was a lot more laid-back about his shadow behavior these days. Putting years and ounces on, in a business environment suffering from an ever more intense case of law and order fever, might be why.

"Thanks. You didn't need to do that. I can get Singe to . . ."

"Yes. I did need to. I owe you for the zombie thing."

I tried to wave him off. That was no big deal. We were the next thing to brothers. Better than brothers. I never got along with Mikey as well when we were kids.

And Belinda wanted to talk.

She had a hard time starting, but she is nothing if not willful and determined. "How is my sister doing, Garrett? Really?"

Well. That was a stunner. I exchanged glances with Mor-

ley. She had not been inclined to address this ever before.
She was becoming more human. Morley's influence?

Penny Dreadful is also Chodo's daughter. She shares
nothing else with Belinda. The father hunt had drawn Penny
to TunFaire originally, but that had ceased to matter much
once she figured it all out. It hadn't meant much to Belinda,
either, from the indifference she had shown till now.

Her showing any interest was a surprise.

I didn't editorialize. "She's doing good. You saw her at
the funeral and the wake. She's pulled herself together.
Dean, Singe, and the Dead Man all helped. She'll be a fine
woman someday." I was prepared to leave it at that.

So was she, probably thinking that she had shown
enough weakness for one day.

Morley did feel compelled to add, "She's an excellent
artist, too."

I stabbed a clam with my fork. "This is really good, Morley. You changed the recipe."

He understood. It was a new subject time. "I had them
add more crushed garlic and replaced cow's milk with
goat's milk in the sauce."

Belinda added, "They started putting in some kind of
grub you get out of rotten logs, too." She used her own butter
knife to indicate a clam strip that did look a little like a grub.

I made a face. "I'm out of practice on the jungle gourmet . . . Damn!" I realized that she was messing with me.

The woman could keep a straight face.

Morley's jaw tightened, though not because his kitchen
was being disparaged and he had no sense of humor about
that. He was looking toward the front door. A rowdy crowd
had begun to roll in. They came from across the street, from
the World. They were in a good mood, collectively. A dress
rehearsal had gone well.

One was a skinny little guy in doublet and hose. He
wore his hair long under a goofy floppy hat with a peacock
feather sticking out in back. The costume was not suited to
the play or the street. He spotted me, abandoned his crew,
headed my way.

Jon Salvation, playwright. I had to thank him for making time for the funeral. . . .

My throat filled with a sudden lump. If this was the crew from his new play, *The Faerie Queene*, then . . .

That explained why Morley had gone green around the gills.

He moved so Salvation could sit. Belinda did not object. I finally grasped the fact that Salvation was not in costume. He was outfitted weirdly on purpose, making some kind of statement.

He had been weird from the beginning. Weird before he found out that he could slap his tall tales down on paper as cracking-good stories for the stage.

Morley told him, "It's good to see you back, Jon. I'll go see if the boys need help handling your mob."

What he did was place himself between us and that crowd in case my ex did not have her hatches battened, her ducks lined up, and her screws sufficiently tightened.

Tinnie had the lead role in *The Faerie Queene*. Jon Salvation had created the part for her unpredictable self. *The Faerie Queene* was Tinnie Tate as Jon Salvation thought he knew her from an extended acquaintance.

Tinnie Tate is a high-maintenance redhead with a quiver full of quirks, but she is good people. She would be in pain, still, because of Strafa, and, no doubt, she was confident that I had abandoned her simply because Strafa was more pliable.

And there she was, looking good for a heartbroke woman.

Our gazes met. Her laughter died, but what replaced it wasn't hatred or anger, it was sorrow. She knew what had happened. Her niece Kyra had come to the funeral.

She inclined her head slightly, then moved on with her crowd, one of whom was Max Weider's daughter, Alyx. Alyx did not have a sympathetic look for me. She and Tinnie were longtime friends. She was Tinnie's understudy for the Faerie Queene.

Jon Salvation observed, "I guess that went well."

"You disappointed?" Belinda asked.

"Oh. No. Not me."

I asked, "How has she been doing?"

"She's doing all right, Garrett. Staying wrapped up in her work. She'll manage."

"Good. That's good. I never meant to hurt her."

Belinda gave me a profoundly curious look, like she couldn't believe I could say that and believe it.

But Salvation chirped, "She gets that. Part of the time. She's her own worst critic. Speaking of former girlfriends . . . How is mine?"

"Winger? She's Winger. She's sharing a place with Saucerhead, just to save on rent. There's nothing else there. The Dead Man has her running errands. Singe hires her when she has something that isn't time-sensitive."

Friend Winger gets distracted easily.

34

Satisfied that there would be no drama, Morley returned. Jon Salvation eased his chair back, said something to Belinda about saving her a premier seat for the opening of *The Faerie Queene*. He started to rise, had a thought, sank back. "I ran into something weird this morning. I was at that thief Pindelfix's shop, Flubber Ducky. I was scrapping with the tailoring crew about the fairy costumes . . . Never mind. Those she-men are just going have to learn that I use real girlie girls to play my female roles and real girls have got bazooms. Anyway, I overheard a discussion that happened on the props' side of the shop. Two old men were looking to get some ceremonial outfits made. They insisted that they had to have some bronze swords to go with them."

"Bronze swords?" I asked. That was strange. Bronze weapons had been state-of-the-art in the once-upon-a-time, long ago, but not so much since somebody clever came up with iron, then figured out how to make steel. Bronze works better than wood or stone, but it doesn't hold an edge very well and even "soft," freshly smelted iron, can damage bronze weapons easily.

Interesting factoid: That sort of antique cutlery fascinates the black magic crowd. A bronze blade is ever the choice of the shady character who goes in for stinky black candles, songs in dead languages, and human sacrifices.

Salvation said, "That was what the clerk at the shop said, I think mostly because he couldn't imagine what kind of play would call for actual bronze swords instead of painted wood. He goes, 'You really gonna use them for props in a play?'

" 'Something like that,' one old guy says. 'But we do need a dozen functional swords, made of bronze. Well, no, actually, we need five. We have seven. But those will need reworking by the same smith who makes us the new pieces.' Then the other old guy goes, 'Maybe we should go ahead and replace those with new.' "

"Interesting," Morley said, musingly. "The number twelve comes up."

My first thought was of how much trouble the prop shop guy must have had keeping cool. Selling all those swords, custom-made, might guarantee a profit for the month, and why should he care how they got used, anyway?

Then I got what Morley meant. "Twelve, eh? Interesting."

The laws about edged weapons don't include religious relics, antiquities, or reproductions of antiquities. A fine point, of course. You go to the magistrates because the red tops took your antique reproduction blade, you'll win your case and get it back—in about two years. And you'll spend the rest of your life on the Guard's list of people who get special treatment.

"Interesting indeed," I said. "Did this old man mention any reason for wanting bronze swords?" Had to be something ugly. And we were hunting ugly.

Jon Salvation was getting exasperated. He had given me what he had and was in no mood to play interrogation games. "I thought they might be doing a revival right then."

I pressed him whether he liked it or not. "Did you get a look at anybody?"

"Only a glimpse. I wouldn't be able to pick anybody out of a group."

"Well, hell. It's something. Thanks. Tell you what, you find yourself with time on your hands, you could take that to the Dead Man. He'll mine out the clues you caught but didn't notice consciously."

I didn't have to explain. He was a veteran of the Dead Man's operations.

"I'll work that in later. After the show." Besides the play in rehearsal, Salvation had two more running, one of those also at the World. The World was unique in that it could put on four plays at once, often a nightmare for everybody but the audiences.

I started to ask if he could have Alyx Weider come to the table for a minute, but then there was no need. Her father came in from the street with Heather Gilbey. Manvil's wife managed the World, which was owned by the brewery. Morley's people found them a table instantly, to the disgruntlement of a couple who had been waiting. Heather braved the theater crowd to ask Alyx to join her and her father.

There would be no need for me to brave the furious solidarity of all those womenfolk yonder.

Resolute, I turned my back.

Belinda snickered. "That Alyx is a piece of work."

I raised an eyebrow inquiringly.

"She's down on you for hurting her friend when she tried to get you to wrestle, what, maybe fifty times?"

"As I'm sure she'd tell you, that was a whole different bucket of monkey guts. Have you learned anything I might find useful?"

She didn't challenge my presumption. We both knew she'd help with the hunt. I'd do the same for her in personal circumstances, and had. I wouldn't help her with the kinds of problems that resulted from her business, nor would she ask.

"Nothing yet. It's early. Anything as big as this is will cause ripples of some kind, though."

No doubt. Before long we should be hearing lots of little things like the request for bronze swords. Most would have nothing to do with Strafa or the Tournament of Swords, but they would have to be noted, investigated, and studied by the Dead Man.

"Patience is the name of the game now, Garrett. Impatience will get you laid down beside your wife."

Even Belinda had become a Strafa fan.

"I know that with my head. It's my heart that's giving me trouble."

Morley said, "I'll go visit that shop Jon Salvation told us about."

Belinda shook her head. "You stay here and wrangle your eggplants, lover. Keep faking good citizenship. Let the real bad guys break the rules."

Morley's lips went tight and white till he grasped the fact that Belinda wanted to protect him, not to rob him of his manhood by henpecking his social routine. He relaxed, nodded, said, "Somebody has to make sure the leader of the pack here gets home with a minimal number of bits missing."

"Which thinking I do appreciate, Morley," I said. "But . . . Bell, when are you thinking about visiting that shop?"

She raised her eyebrows. She did not have the skill set needed to do just one by itself.

"If it was soon I'd tag along. I need to work on getting my edge back."

Belinda glanced at Morley. Something passed between them. Belinda said, "How about after you finish your lunch?"

"I've got nowhere else to go but home."

35

The shop was one of those places with airs and a clever name, Flubber Ducky. Which I didn't get. Maybe no one else did, either, because I didn't get an answer when I asked around. I never got to ask anyone inside. I came close to getting no chance to open my yap at all. Belinda wanted me to stay in the background and keep quiet. She didn't want me asking questions that could be interpreted only as part of a quest to unearth the Operators.

There was more to her thinking, but she wasn't inclined to share it.

With little more than an eyeblink and a wave of her fingers, she conjured the Contague family coach and half a dozen very large, hard men who would drive, ride the footmen's running boards, or trot along ahead or behind on horseback. That she had only six escorts today told me that peace reigned in the underworld—for the moment.

Belinda faced more challenges than her father ever had simply because she was a woman. So many ambitious villains just could not believe that she was as ferocious and crazy as she really was.

We reached the shop Jon Salvation had mentioned. It really was called Flubber Ducky. It had a sign outside saying so. Amazing. Belinda's thugs isolated it without being given specific instructions, establishing a unidirectional customer flow. There were no complaints. These were the kinds of guys who got their way just by standing around looking grim.

There were only a few customers inside, all on the costumers' side. Belinda isolated the elder of two men working props. He fit Jon Salvation's description of the clerk who had dealt with the men who had wanted bronze swords. She moved in close enough for her hot breath and buxom proximity to be intimidating. "Two men came here looking for bronze swords. Who were they?"

The clerk did that dumb-goldfish-tasting-the-water thing while seeing nothing but Belinda's fierce red lips and strange blue eyes, all within licking distance. Could dread hetero possibly be catching?

Belinda used a soft, gentle, terrifying voice to suggest, "Talk to me while you still can."

The clerk chewed on the air. A breeder storm had fallen on him out of a cloudless sky. He didn't understand, except that this might be the start of something bad.

"Talk to me," Belinda urged in her deadly mommy voice. "Who were they?"

"I don't know, ma'am. They never said."

I winced. Belinda's ego was not yet ready for "ma'am." Like Lady Tara Chayne Machtkess, she might never be ready.

She said, "They bought stuff."

"Yes, ma'am. Robes. Other ceremonial-style stuff. Best quality."

"Which will have to be delivered somewhere."

"No, ma'am." He gulped some more air. "They said they would pick everything up."

"When?"

"A week from yesterday. They paid for priority service."

"Did they say who would do the picking?"

"They said they would come themselves."

That didn't sound smart.

Maybe they weren't villains. Or maybe they were sure that nobody would be looking for them.

The tournament thing was so completely anachronistic, why not?

Belinda kept pressing but didn't get much more, other

than to extract a copy of the order that the old men had placed, after which she wheedled the old clerk into telling her where the old men went to get their bronze weapons made.

"Normally we would commission the blades ourselves, passing them on at a big markup. Those men didn't seem concerned about costs, but they were creepy. Scary creepy. I wanted them out of the shop. So I sent them to the smithy we use for specialty stuff. I sent a runner to tell Trivias to set the price high and kick back a sucker's fee to Flubber Ducky."

Belinda gave me a warning look. I was getting restless and was making inarticulate noises indicating that I had something to say. When she could take it no more, she snapped, "What?"

"We need to find a way to have this fellow visit my house."

Belinda's frustration faded. "Of course. That makes perfect sense. I should've thought of that. Elwood." She turned to the largest of her large men. "Load our witness in the coach and take him to Mr. Garrett's home in Macunado Street. Wait for him, then bring him back when he's done visiting."

"No, you don't! Oh no, you don't!" A skinny little guy, barely five feet tall, mostly bald but with hair six inches long where he had any hair at all, bustled in from the other side of the shop. He carried what looked like a naval belaying pin in a left hand that lacked its two outermost fingers. His eyes were a washed-out, watery blue, but they were fierce and fearless.

His sojourn in the Cantard was a long time gone. He was out of practice at the killer's trade. He had lived in the tailor's world since coming home. But he had not lost his courage, nor had he gained a grip on reality.

Nobody who had that grip would tie into Belinda's crew the way he tried.

He did have the advantage of surprise. Briefly.

Belinda's heavyweights broke some stuff, not including

the tailor but that only because their boss insisted that she just get his attention. She examined price tags attached to the damaged goods. "Those were just display pieces, right?" She slipped a gold angel into the left-side pocket of Mr. Feisty's blouse. "Take this one, too, Elwood. Leon, help wrangle. The rest of us will visit the man who is going to make those swords."

Elwood and Leon, gently for thugs, showed the craftsmen to their transport. The rest of us gathered on the street, to debate the best way to get where we wanted to go—except for one normal-size but scarred and remarkably ugly character called Bones who stayed to explain to the staff that the damage they were about to put right could as easily happen to people who could not overcome a compulsion to whine to the tin whistles.

It had been said that Bones had gone for a run through the Forest of Ugly blindfolded on a moonless night and had banged into every tree before he got to the other side. With the scars added he was one intimidating character. It was not often that he was forced to act.

There was a tin whistle in the street, half a block west of Flubber Ducky, deftly ignorant of any miscreantcy that might be happening within rock-throwing distance of the Chodo family coach.

36

Closer to hand and ecstatic about seeing me again was my pal Brownie. Her number two, which I had decided would be called Number Two henceforth because of her number-two attitude, wasn't nearly so pleased. The other two ladies didn't care, one way or another, but they were happy that Brownie was happy.

The strays from earlier hadn't stuck with the crew.

Belinda asked, "These your friends from in back of the Grapevine?"

"Yeah."

"They were at the cemetery."

"Yeah. That odd girl was with them, too, when they caught up with me near Playmate's place. Her attitude was still the same. Playmate has her now. He's gonna try to find out who she is and what we ought to do with her."

"She was pretty." She checked for the mouse in my pocket.

"She was." In fact, on reflection, I thought she had looked a lot like Belinda might have when she was still a fresh fourteen.

Elwood, Leon, their guests, and the sullen driver of a coach drawn by four Garrett-contemptuous drays headed westward toward my Macunado estate.

Belinda said, "That's enough of that. Let's walk."

I glanced at her, thought about Little Moo, wished I had known Belinda when she was that age. But I would have been that age, too, then, which meant my head would have been on sideways.

Belinda's remaining troops spread out. Brownie took her usual place, forcing Belinda around to my left. That did not sit well there, but Number Two kept her displeasure contained. She sensed that Belinda's level of tolerance for uppity canines was quite low.

We hardly got our bad selves sorted into a traveling formation, reminiscent of the squad diamond of my defense days, when we got to the shop where most of the theater industry's custom metalwork got done. Belinda invited us all inside despite the protests of some apprentices who, after considering the odds, put their hands in their pockets and stuck to muttering.

Belinda told them, "I want your master out here. Now."

So I was expecting a master smith on Playmate's scale, high and wide and muscle-bound. Instead, we got a guy who had some elf and a bit of dwarf in him, about five feet tall, who ambled out of the forge shed cleaning his hands on a rag. I was looking past him for the burly guy when he asked, "You wanted to see me?"

Me, Belinda, her crew, and the dogs all snapped to a higher level of readiness. He sounded like a martial arts master, confident, at peace, absent any concern. This was somebody who could be dangerous if he wanted.

Belinda said, "You were asked to make replicas of antique swords. The men who commissioned them were involved in the murder of this man's wife." She indicated me, gaping at the mad queen of crime being polite and reasonable. "We want to find them so we can ask them a few questions."

The smith eyed me, considered Belinda, cataloged her thugs, even checked Brownie and her crew. I got the impression that he saw more than what was immediately obvious— in keeping with the martial arts master image. With those guys it's always all about perception. He said, "I see." Slightest of frowns as he took another look at Brownie. Puzzled, "The dogs have nothing to do with that, right?"

He was mumbling to himself, so nobody responded.

He took a single step toward me. "Please tell me your story. It would be best if you don't edit."

I grinned, slipped into the mode I use while reporting to the Dead Man, confident that this man deserved complete honesty and respect. I gave him exactly what I had given Deal Relway. Belinda's troops grew restless before I finished.

The smith said, "You cleave to the truth as you know it. I did get a negative feel while those two were here. Also, I will stipulate that I know Tournaments of Swords used to take place, but I thought the last one happened about eighty years ago."

"There have been others more recently. Tries, anyway. My wife's grandmother helped mess up the last one."

"As would appear to be the case again. One wonders why the Operators would go ahead in the face of such poor odds."

"One does wonder."

The smith considered the dogs again, obviously intrigued. I wondered why. The mutts clearly were not pets.

He was even more intrigued by Belinda. She had not identified herself, but it was plain what she and her men must be, if not who.

The smith said, "I hold no brief for the tournament concept, especially in a form where the contestants are expected to die."

Belinda made a tiny gesture meant to caution me. Impulse control was no problem, though. I could see that the smith needed space to lead himself on.

I had witnesses. We could declare a day of celebration later: Garrett kept his big damned mouth shut for a whole damned minute . . . How long the miracle might persist remained to be seen.

"My problem would be diminished if the participants entered the game of their own free will. But even then there is the ugly prospect of so much power ending up condensed into one person smart enough and ruthless enough to slaughter all the others, some of whom would have been friends or, at least, lifelong acquaintances."

I had to break my silence. "Wow!" The fighting and killing longtime friends might be a key reason why Shadowslinger and her friends were determined to sabotage the process. That last man standing would be a very dark personality indeed.

And maybe I was last to really get that. Belinda had seen it right away. Enlightened self-interest might be moving her more than friendship was. That kind of villain, running loose, would not benefit her shadowed interests.

It occurred to me suddenly that Strafa could have been murdered by someone she thought was a friend. That would explain how the killer got close enough to hit her with a big-ass crossbow.

The wee smith told me, "I can't control my curiosity. Tell me about the dogs."

37

Something about Trivias encouraged me to talk. Plus, I saw that Brownie and friends were interested in him, too, once he focused on them.

Belinda and crew weren't as inclined toward patience with the pups. They kept their attitudes restrained, however, she because she'd known me long enough to understand that most anything could turn out to be relevant in anything connected to me, even what just looked like "stuff happening."

In life, though, stuff usually happens without being a cog in a carefully constructed plot.

So I was forthcoming with Trivias despite knowing nothing about him other than that he felt comfortable. Belinda's crowd closed in to listen while Brownie's bunch decided to become fans of the smith. He gave all their ears a scratching and demonstrated killer skills as a flea catcher. He asked, "You did some thinking about the girl?"

"Definitely. But I still don't know who she is or why she hates me."

He considered the dogs. They considered him back, body language apologetic because they were with me and therefore not free to commit themselves to him.

I asked, "Do you have any idea what's going on?"

"In a folklore sense, perhaps, but not in a quotidian world sense."

Oh my. Only the Dead Man ever uses words like that. I

wasn't sure what "quotidian" meant. I grunted, mostly to prove that I was listening.

"I'll think about it. The tournament is something of a folklore artifact, too, but I doubt there's a connection. Your grandmother was right about the girl, though. Whatever the strain, whatever she does, be kind. That's the only way to win through." Having thus spoken with sybilline clarity, or the precise exactitude of a wizard, he patted Brownie and Number Two, and added, "I do wish I could be more help."

Belinda said, "You still could be. The bronze swords. How about I leave someone to greet their buyers when they pick them up?"

"Oh. Yes." The smith mimed thought, nodded, said, "And now for a better idea. You." He jabbed a finger at me. "Exploit your family connections. Have your grandmother produce tracer charms I can put into the hilts of the swords."

"That's a damned fine idea!" Shadowslinger could then follow the weapons around. We could identify anyone who carried one.

Belinda, being Belinda, wasn't happy with being out-thought but was never so long on pride that she would burn a good idea because somebody else came up with it. She stipulated, "Good thinking." She did give the smith a suspicious look. Craftsmen are supposed to be clever with their hands, not their heads.

Trivias obviously was more than a hammer-and-tongs kind of guy.

I said, "I'd better get on that part fast." I had a feeling that there was little time to waste even though preparing the grips of swords would be among the last steps of the manufacturing process.

"Where you going?" Belinda snapped, the way you might interrogate a three-year-old demonstrating an inclination to wander off.

"I need to see Shadowslinger."

"And you're going to head on up there by yourself?"

That was the plan, yes. If plan there was. I would have Brownie and the girls for company.

"How many times has somebody tried to kill you in the last few days?"

Again? People have been trying to break me or end me for years. I'm still upright. But I have been lucky and I have had the backing of good friends. Skills and quick thinking help occasionally, too, but only some.

"Honestly, Garrett. The dogs have a better grasp on life outside the moment."

She wasn't far off the mark. I just didn't have that war-zone edge.

I said, "I'm starting to wonder if I shouldn't find a new line."

"If you make it a hobby you'll only get killed quicker."

Too many women have said the same thing the last couple of years.

"You can't do deadly stuff part-time, Garrett."

Yeah, yeah. I knew it in my head.

The smith said, "I'll start binding the grip of the first sword sometime late tomorrow."

Little hint, there. I grunted. All right. Time to move on. Time to stop acting like a hobbyist.

Actually, time to start thinking like a professional.

Smith said, "I wouldn't need every tracer right away. Spread them out over three or four days if you have to. But . . ."

"Sure. Don't waste time. Look. It probably won't be me bringing the tracers." I offered descriptions of Winger and Saucerhead Tharpe.

"Very big people, sure." In his world most people would qualify.

"Let's move, Garrett," Belinda said. "I hope Elwood doesn't waste time. These aren't the best shoes for walking."

Trivias the smith performed a ritual of parting with the mutts.

Belinda would be better served hoping Old Bones didn't waste time exploring the boys from Flubber Ducky. Their heads might contain a lot of stuff he would find interesting.

Boys and girls and puppies, away we hiked.

One of Belinda's goons spotted a red top working ever so hard to look like the last thing that might ever interest him was a mob of thugs and mutts. Then Belinda, I, and the crew all caught a whiff that said a man of unusual talent was in the neighborhood.

Belinda and I exchanged looks. No words needed saying, but she observed anyway, "I'll have someone look out for the smith."

Trivias would be at risk if Lurking Fehlske was reporting to the Operators.

38

Elwood and Leon didn't get the borrowed tailors back to Flubber Ducky before we returned there ourselves. That business was plugging along without them or us.

"Guess that makes sense. They had farther to go than we did."

On the other hand, though, the Dead Man could manage his interviews faster. He didn't have to work out who was lying and why.

Trivias had put on a great show of cooperation, but I was not convinced of its sincerity. I should get Trivias together with the Dead Man.

"You're thinking again!" Belinda snapped. She had begun to limp. We were headed toward Macunado Street, to meet her coach in transit. Her footwear remained inappropriate for hiking. "Why is it so hard to pay attention?"

A damned good question. "A damned good question. I don't know. I just wonder about something and suddenly everything else goes out of my head."

"It worries me. It can't be healthy."

No kidding. Intellectually, I knew with absolute conviction that distraction could get me killed. A lot of things could, at the best of times, but most lethal stuff can be ducked if you pay attention.

I confessed, "It scares hell out of me sometimes, getting lost inside my head trying to figure out why I keep getting lost inside my head."

Belinda cursed her shoes, then said, "I'd rather not lose you, Garrett. You're precious." Which earned her an odd look from the nearest bodyguard.

She didn't mean that the way it sounded. That was all a long time ago. But she did count on me as an emotional and moral resource.

"I know. I'm precious to me, too."

"Can it be because you can't get your head out of the hole left when Strafa went down?"

"Probably, but that can't be the whole story. It was a problem before."

"But not so big till the last few days."

"Yeah." And I went away—till she hammered me on the right biceps. "Damn! You got a vicious punch, girl."

She scowled.

"You're right. It's worse lately. Maybe the Dead Man can straighten me out."

"Maybe he can fix you so you'll help yourself stay alive."

"Maybe." That was worth consideration. . . . "Ow!"

She hammered me again. "I just had an idea." She looked downright evil.

"That sounds dangerous."

"Oh, it is. Especially for wiseasses. But you'll thank me later. Assuming you live. Assuming I don't kill you myself."

Some people don't get my sense of humor.

This Belinda reminded me of Mom and a covey of aunts, mostly related by friendship instead of blood, who had rejoiced in doing stuff for my own good when I was a kid.

I couldn't resent Mikey in that area. He'd gotten it worse than I did.

Punch!

"That's going to leave a bruise!" She had hit me in the same spot.

"Good. It'll be a reminder. Meanwhile, nap time is over. Here come Elwood and Leon."

The Contague coach rolled up. Belinda yakked it up with her brunos. Me and Brownie and the girls roamed the immediate neighborhood, staying inside rock-chucking distance. Good on me, I was alert the whole time.

A whiff of Lurking Fehlske helped my concentration.

Brownie pawed at her sensitive nose, trying to make it stop.

Belinda finished. Her coach rolled on. It had to make a delivery to Flubber Ducky. I rejoined her, suggested that Tribune Fehlske might not be the only watcher. A couple of clever loiterers, dressed too well to be homeless, felt like Civil Guard Specials. Then there was a woman, I think in brown, only glimpsed in the corner of my eye, come and gone so suddenly I couldn't tell anything. Old Bones could work on that. Even her sex was just an assumption. She'd been done up in old-woman dress.

I'd never done a job as a girl, snarky accusations on the part of the jealous aside, but it was a traditional, respected false-flag ploy.

"Do I have to slug you again?"

"I'm awake, Mom. I'm on the job. We're being watched. Tracked."

"I'm not surprised. Let's hope they don't work for your Operators."

"Crap! That wouldn't be good."

"It wouldn't. I'll make adjustments once Elwood gets back from dumping those poofs."

I grunted, checked Brownie, wasted a second on wishing that she and hers were pliable dire wolves. I could have them go round up . . . Right. How would I deliver my instructions? I don't speak fluent dog even after several quarts of beer.

Punch!

That arm was going to be useless if I had to defend myself.

39

I eased into the Dead Man's room. "So, did you get anything out of those guys I sent you?"

Belinda yowled loudly enough to be heard from across the hallway. Dean had her planted with her feet up and was working on her blisters. She had raised a fine crop. The man was a saint, working that harvest.

They knew nothing useful immediately. However, they had picked up several small clues that will help pick those old men out of a crowd. Faces appeared in my mind. One was a generic old man, but the other had wild white hair almost a foot long, plus a nasty wen inside his hairline, above his left eye.

"They might be brothers."

One of the visitors had the same thought.

I started to ask if he thought it would be useful to interview Trivias. . . .

Of course. Arrange it. Relax for a moment. I need all my attention elsewhere.

I chewed some air.

Well. These people are quite careful about not coming too close. But there is too far to be caught or read and there is too far to be detected. They have failed to stay back that far.

Well, duh! He wouldn't know about the ones who were smart enough to stay far enough away, would he?

You are correct, sir. And you can forget those ambitions immediately. I will have Singe do whatever tracking needs to be done. Your task will be to return to the Hill, both for your

*own safety and because that is where the crime took place.
You have reports to make and tracers to be created for the
smith's employ.*

He was scheming something. I wasn't sure what. He was
too preoccupied to break it down. But he did get back to
me eventually.

*Our heart-line task must be to unravel and requite what
was done to Strafa. The Tournament of Swords is an interesting abomination, of course. It must be stopped. But it is of
secondary import to us right now. Do you understand?*

"In a personal, emotional sense, of course I do. But I
don't see how we can separate the one from the other."

That argument does have some odor.

Huh? "It will have a big, fat stinky-cheese smell to any
Operators or players who get into the game seriously."

*Even so, we should try to separate, or at least distinguish,
the two, till we are given no other choice.*

Odd. He made it sound like he'd had a hunch and
wanted to chase it without sharing it or even admitting its
existence. He didn't like having to confess when he guessed
wrong.

I was vaguely aware of the front door closing. "Where is
Singe headed?" She, I assumed, because I hadn't heard
Penny blundering around like a mastodon on crutches.

The girl has trouble being quiet.

*In fact, that was Miss Contague departing. However,
Singe did leave the house earlier.* He did not elaborate.

I didn't think about that much. Singe did the shopping
because Dean no longer had the stamina.

"Have we gained any ground other than where I stuck
my nose in? Did you see Race and Dex?"

*I did. They were of less value than I had hoped. They
merely confirmed my speculation about Strafa having gone
out of the house to deal with Min. Ah yes. The point whence
the killing bolt was launched has been determined, adding
nothing to our knowledge.*

Information washed into my head, in no good order. He
seemed distracted. I glimpsed the city through Singe's eyes

and nostrils. She was involved in an exchange with one of the Specials outside. The vision slipped away. Old Bones got me involved in a hypothetical reconstruction of what had happened with Strafa.

His scenario hinged on the known facts. Two women had been injured, one severely, the other fatally. One broken bolt had been discovered. The engine necessary to cast that bolt would take a minute to crank to full draw.

Both women must have been injured by the same bolt.

Footnote question: Could there have been a second engine?

"I call 'miracle shenanigans' because somebody moved one engine without being seen." "One bolt takes everybody" is one of those implausible things that seldom happen anywhere but in a war zone.

Old Bones had decided that a bolt meant for Min had ricocheted off bone, breaking as it did, the tip half then going on to bring Strafa down.

The plausibility factor was weak, but he could not come up with a hypothesis that fit the facts better. And, as noted, more absurd stuff had happened in the Cantard every day.

I made sure. "Vicious Min was the target?" No way Strafa could have been that at fifteen feet up in a one-missile theory. "I'm confused."

Nor are you alone. Your problem, however, is that you are determined to force a pattern onto an inadequate information array.

"I know. Do the outside pieces first. Did somebody say that the red tops found the other half of the bolt?"

I do not recall that. If so I have not been so informed.

I mused, "I need to take a closer look at Vicious Min." Again we faced the fact that our only witness to murder was someone who might be vested in avoiding the truth.

The Dead Man put nothing in concrete form, but he was thinking the moral equivalent of "Don't teach Grandma to suck eggs."

He offered a scenario in which Vicious Min was the assassin and the sniper was there to protect Strafa.

"Logically absurd," I said. "Anyone trying to cover Strafa would have started making excuses before she hit the ground. Speaking of grandmothers . . ."

As he sent, *Speaking of Vicious Min . . . Be careful out there!*

I needed a moment to get that he meant that for Penny.

"You sure you want to let her go out?"

She will be at less risk than you would be. She will pay attention to her surroundings.

I stomped my pride down. "Yeah. About that . . ."

40

I wasn't listening well. I missed Penny's return till she came into the Dead Man's room to say, "I could only find Dollar Dan."

"I have an ever higher regard for you, too, girl-child." Dollar Dan Justice oozed past her. He is a rat man. At five feet six he is a hulking brute of his kind, but, like Singe's brother, whose second in command he is, he is more than a thug. He is a thinker and definitely a would-be lover.

Dan said, "John Stretch is away on business. He left instructions to help you any way we can."

Dollar Dan was eager to be my pal, more so than Singe's brother was.

He had an ulterior motive.

He announced, "I have a detail waiting outside."

It had been a while since I had seen Dan. He had begun trying to upgrade himself. His apparel was finer, more stylish, better kempt, and less garish than usual for rat men. I saw no yellow, orange, or electric green whatsoever.

Singe was why.

Poor guy. He was spitting into the wind with those hopes.

He knew it, too. But where there is life there is hope, as some word slinger once claimed.

I asked, "A detail?"

"Six good rats and true."

To accompany you on your progress to the Hill, where

you will take up that more valuable part of the investigation. There being no one else available to guard your back.

"My progress to the Hill, eh?"

Miss Contague and her friends have departed. As with Mr. Dotes, she has other demands on her time. Those occasionally trump her devotion to you.

He was being critical in some shadowy, oblique way. Didn't she owe me? Didn't I just save her sweetie from the zombie masters?

"Aren't I old enough to take care of myself?"

He sent me a one-second vision of a ridiculously powerful sorceress lying in a glass-face coffin. *If you insist on suicidal actions because of an inability to control massively misplaced adolescent pride . . .*

Before Strafa's death I might have pitched a snit. Before Strafa I could've altogether thrown a heavy-caliber tantrum out of dimwit pride, yes. The woman had taught me to get past my worst knee-jerk responses.

And I had a mission. I had to stay above the grass in order to put some Operators under it.

"I've got hold of the reins. I'll be a responsible adult, cautious and rational at all times. I will consider consequences before I speak or break anything."

Rat men can't grin. Dollar Dan would have been ear to ear if they could. Penny did so, with some skepticism. Himself was amused. And all full up on "I'll buy that when I step in it."

Excellent. So. Here are some angles you might pursue.

What he wanted to see get poked was obvious, mostly. See if Shadowslinger was avoiding him. Likewise, Vicious Min. He wanted to get together with Min as soon as she could survive the haul to Macunado Street. I should consult Dr. Ted in both cases, get a read on him, and get him to come with one of the women.

Ah, Dr. Ted. I'd been considering having a chat with him, even if I had to hunt him down.

41

Brownie and crew were not fond of rat people. Dollar Dan and his pals felt the same about dogs. Good thing those mutts weren't rat terriers.

The tribes came to a silent accommodation. Brownie and Number Two got to stick to me, at their usual posts. The other two ranged ahead, in nervous pairings with a brace of young bucks far too proud of their gang connections. They put on way too much swagger.

I cautioned Dollar Dan.

"They have to learn the hard way."

John Stretch was a power only inside his own community. Plenty of beetle-brow humans would not be intimidated, regardless. The possibility that they should be would be beyond their ability to grasp.

The boys didn't learn their lesson while I watched. We ran into no one inclined to teach them.

We did collide with some attitude, though.

A fat man about forty, wearing the cap of the disbanded City Watch, intercepted us soon after we passed the bounds of the Hill, a private security type. He was shorter than me, sloppy because a master tailor would not be able to make clothing flatter his shape, and maybe a little dangerous in the way that Saucerhead Tharpe is dangerous.

He looked like a guy you could hammer on all you wanted and he would keep on keeping on, with no skill but definitely with a long supply of stubborn. He did not favor the presence of known felons within the bounds he was pledged to defend, his root assumption being that all rat people are criminals.

That stereotype isn't far off the mark, actually. That's how rat people have survived since their forbears escaped the laboratories where they were created.

I glanced past the man, who didn't seem to understand that he was outnumbered, and, bam! There was the pretty blonde and her humongous friend, half a block ahead. She glanced our way, maybe startled. She said something to her companion. He scooped her up and headed out at a pace no horse could match.

"Who was that?" I asked the guard.

He scratched his head. "Who was who?"

Dollar Dan, his crew, and the girls had not missed the kid. Dan spoke softly. Two of his guys and Number Two scooted around the patrolman and sniffed for a trail.

I said, "This is good. This will get us somewhere." Whistling in the dark in broad daylight.

Meanwhile, flustered, the patrol guy fussed and blustered. He left me no choice. "You got a problem with me, take it to my grandmother. Shadowslinger. She'll satisfy your needs. She's been thinking a lot about you people lately."

Hardly fair of me, really.

He blanched.

The guards would know that the Algardas were looking for goats to roast because of Furious Tide of Light. More than one jaundiced, angry eye was focused on the overpaid muscle that had failed to protect her.

Shadowslinger had been sharpening her teeth in public.

The man in the retro hat stepped aside. "You shoulda said who you was, sir." Feebly trying to salvage some face while sweating grease.

Yes. My Algarda connection was a tool I should remember to use.

Half a block later Dollar Dan said, "That fool made a good point. You should not hesitate to use the old witch's name."

"Old habits are tough to break."

"Oh, do I not know the truth of that!"

42

I took Dollar Dan into the kitchen of my place on the Hill. *My* place. That was a tough one. Race and Dex were enjoying an afternoon snack consisting of a gallon of fortified wine. Me and my troop of rat man gangsters didn't rattle them. They had heard all about me. Plus, they had been nibbling that lunch for a while.

Dex sealed the bottle and put it on a shelf too high for Dollar Dan to reach. Race gathered knives and silverware and everything else small enough to fall into a pocket. Neither showed an inclination to be apologetic.

I considered a crack indicting them, of all people, for prejudice but chose to save my breath. They wouldn't get it. "You two the only ones here?"

Some folks just can't answer a question directly. They're made so they have to go somewhere else to get the job done.

Race said, "Barate was here but he left. He went up the Hill to visit."

"I see. One of you go fetch Dr. Ted."

Dex had had lunch enough to fuel a spark of attitude. He considered arguing. Race took him by the right elbow, burying a thumb in the joint, got his attention.

I said, "Dex, there are some dogs in the garden. They're with me. Give them something to eat. Race, get the doctor." I deployed my sergeant voice, the voice of the god that admits no possibility of debate.

The arrogance of my assumption that Dr. Ted would drop everything never tickled my consciousness.

In the nethermost background of my directions, unstated, was the fact that Race and Dex were facing the arbiter of their continued employment. Dr. Ted was, too, some, because of my Shadowslinger connection.

Dex said, "He's probably at the old witch's house with Barate." For Race's benefit, not mine, as he gathered scraps suitable for doggie dining.

Despite a major onset of the surlies, both men got busy.

Rat men tagging along, I went to have a gander at Vicious Min.

There was no Vicious Min.

There was an empty bed where a demon woman was supposed to be laid up. "Dan, get that clown I told to feed the dogs."

Dex turned up fast, eyes bugging. "What the hell? Where did she go?" He began to shake.

"I was hoping you could explain, Dex."

He swallowed some air. "I don't know. She was in that fracking sack twenty minutes ago, when we was trying to get some soup inside her. She looked the same old, same old, in a coma. Worse than before, even. We figured she'd be gone in a day or two. You could smell the pus."

"And then there was a miracle," I grumbled.

"I guess." Dex stirred the bedding like he might find that big beast hidden in the fold of a blanket. "This is still warm."

He was right. Min had cut out moments before I walked in.

Dex said, "She must have been faking. But that would be tough to do, man."

I agreed. I was suspicious. But in my racket you're always suspicious. If you're smart you keep a jaundiced eye on yourself. "Dan, there any chance your guys can follow her?"

"Garrett, take a whiff. You could follow this one."

The bedding certainly reeked. "You give me too much credit. I just smell sickness and infection. Dex. When was the last time the doctor was here?"

"The day she went down. You was here."

"Not since then? Why not?"

"Shadowslinger said."

I didn't get it. "She say why?"

"She didn't want that thing having no outside contact with nobody."

There might be some logic behind that, but I missed it. "I'll ask why when I see her."

Dex chose to reserve his thoughts about that. His employment was at risk already. "I hope she's in good enough shape to talk. She looked awful when I saw her."

There was a ruckus elsewhere in the house, which turned out to be Dollar Dan running into Race and Dr. Ted.

"Damn, Race, that was fast."

"We said he was just up at Madame Algarda's."

"I thought it would take longer. Thanks for coming, Doctor, but things have turned sour. The patient has absconded."

Dr. Ted sighed, shook his head. "She must be tougher than I guessed. I expected her to die."

"I wouldn't want you wasting your time, especially if you were working on Shadow . . . On Constance. Who is doing how well, anyway?"

"She's making progress. I'm cautiously optimistic, though I can't quite say why. She's in a vegetative state right now. With a will as massive as hers, she'll probably bull her way through."

"That's good news." The expected response, but I wondered if some folks might not consider it discouraging. "Can I visit her?"

Ted eyed me as though consulting a checklist of possible motives. "A visit should be all right. Don't expect a response. Remember that even fierce people with hard hearts deserve consideration once they've been struck down. She might be aware of you. That could stiffen her resolve. But no business. No pressing. No bullying. I'll throw you out if you try."

I couldn't stifle a grin at him doing his damnedest to be fierce. I could get to like the guy. "Where did you do your five, Ted?"

Nobody over twenty-two would misunderstand. When we were young anyone who turned eighteen still equipped with an approximately appropriate number of limbs and digits and a working eye could expect to spend his next five years trying to enforce the Karentine crown's will on Venageta. For more than a century, that war was as much part of life as weather and the seasons. When I was a boy, even the concept of dissent had no life anywhere. Evaders were rarities held in contempt by all.

The state and polity still struggle with the consequences of victory. The end of the long war caused huge dislocations.

Ted reddened, did one of those indirect answer things. "I volunteered for a maneuver unit. Twice. Both times they told me I was too valuable to risk in a combat zone."

Translation: His skills were such that they wouldn't be wasted on less than the most exalted among us. Those days would have been when he made his connections on the Hill.

"Thank your patron god." Guys like Ted, never stewed in the cauldron of blood, would be best suited to pilot Karenta into the postwar age. We who had seen the elephant knew only one way to cope.

Our Shadowslingers, who had been to war many times over, had to be heralded for their courage, but that sustained exposure seriously distorted their thinking.

Ted said something that I missed. I had wandered into the wilderness of my mind again. That was getting irksome. "Excuse me. I zoned."

"Understood. I have flashbacks and never got closer to the fighting than Full Harbor with Prince Rupert the first time he went. I was a medical orderly then, officially."

Naturally. He would have been taken into service before he finished hopping through all the hoops. "Your father was a physician, too?"

"Both parents. My mother was a medical genius. She never became a doctor officially. They didn't accredit women back then. But she was a pet of the Royals. She saw to it that women can get accredited now."

He probably started learning his stuff while he was learning to walk.

He observed, "There is no reason for me to stay here, the patient having chosen to desert."

"Right. I'm sorry. I'm rattled. Dex, should any rat men turn up here, tell them I've gone on to the old woman's place. And ease up on the wine." I've never understood why some people prefer rotted grape juice. I can't quite trust their sort.

Dex restrained himself. "Yes, sir. As you wish, sir."

"Good. I'm sure we'll be glad we decided to keep you, Dex."

43

Ted flirted with the dogs all during the short journey to Shadowslinger's place. He found a friendly side to Number Two that she had hidden from me. "Are you sure that these are feral dogs?"

"They were till they adopted me. They live in the Orthodox cemetery." I gave him a rundown on them and Little Moo.

"Really? That's strange. And there was no connection with Strafa?"

"Not according to Constance. And she could tell if anyone could."

"No doubt. No doubt. I was never that close to her."

I liked Ted better and better, for no definable reason. He was just a nice, comfortable guy, rather like Strafa had been.

"You were interested in Strafa, weren't you?"

"I was." Confessing made him uneasy. "Once upon a time. Barate didn't approve. She could never defy him."

"I see." Best to drop it. Aspects of that were too creepy to discuss.

Ted was ready to let it go, too. He had smelled the same shadows.

Shadowslinger's place seemed deserted. Ted and I headed upstairs, to the witch's hide. The dogs and Dollar Dan stayed down, on guard.

I'd never left the ground floor before, but encountered no

surprises. Upstairs was as grim as down till we entered Constance's own bedroom. And that was only slightly better.

Barate Algarda was asleep in a fat chair beside his mother's bed, troubled even while out. He started awake.

"Garrett. Hi." Sleepily. "Ted. Excuse me. This is kind of rough."

"I understand. No problem."

"Hey! Ted says he thinks she'll come back." The ugly old tub of goo lay on her back, upper half slightly elevated, arms and hands lifeless beside her, atop a quilt probably sewn for a pittance by some refugee even older than Shadowslinger herself.

I studied her hands. They were slightly deformed, the way arthritis does. Chronic pain might explain why she was always cranky. Ted and his kind, and magical healers of the quality accessible to someone of Constance's status, might not be enough to beat that bitch. It was one of those things that could be immune to sorcery.

Some things just naturally are resistant, and some people, too. Penny has the knack, a little. A few metals and minerals disdain or even negate witchery. Iron and silver are the best known.

Still muzzy, Barate asked, "Where is Kevans?"

I shrugged. "I haven't seen her."

Ted said, "We didn't see anyone. No one answered the door. Is she supposed to be here?"

Worried, Barate said, "Kyoga should. And Mash and Bash."

"They the staff?"

"Mashego and Bashir. Yeah. They live here. They never go out."

They had gone to Strafa's to help with the wake, but I got it. Their odd, cadaverous builds, bountiful ritual scars, and religious tattoos would be social liabilities—unless they put on some serious disguises.

They weren't Karentine. Shadowslinger had brought them home from the war zone. They were male and female, husband and wife, but I wasn't sure which was which.

Barate jumped up too fast. "We've got to . . . Crap!" He wobbled, trailed off.

"What?"

"My little girl is a genius, Garrett. But you know she doesn't have a lick of sense."

"I can't argue with that. I've got the scars to prove it. But she's a good kid. She just . . ."

"She was whining about having to stay cooped up. She just can't make the connection between what happened to her mother and something that could happen to her. This stuff isn't real to her. It can't happen here."

At which point his mother's left forefinger twitched. A quarter of an inch, last joint in the digit. I started to tell Ted, but he was staring at it already, smiling big.

Barate didn't miss it, either.

Ted peeled back an eyelid. We all watched her pupil respond to the light. Ted muttered, "Most thoroughly excellent."

I told Barate, "If Kevans is gone she probably went looking for Kip."

"I hate repeating myself," Algarda said. "But she has got to realize that she's never going to beat out the red-haired girl."

There was nothing encouraging I could say. Kip was as dense as granite when it came to realizing that Kevans wasn't only his best buddy but also a living, breathing, feeling, female-type girl.

"Are you really worried? I have some rat men with me. They could track her."

I expected him to wave me off. He was a proud man, stubborn when it wasn't Constance pushing, likely to think he ought to handle all his problems himself. He surprised me. "You could arrange that? Would it cost much? Maybe I could have them hang around her all the time."

"Cost? I don't know. I'd need to ask. You're sure?"

"We lost Strafa. Mother . . . Maybe. I couldn't take it if Kevans . . . Of course I'm sure. I want a flight of guardian angels. What do you call a gang of crows? A murder? That's what I want. A murder of black-hearted guardian angels, hungry for human flesh."

"I'm not sure that rat men can meet that level of expectation."

He grinned. "Then they can just hang around wherever she goes. She won't notice if they don't wave and shout."

"I'll talk to Dollar Dan." Dan would milk it, certainly, but he wouldn't be unreasonable. He would see a chance to make a valuable connection.

Never hurts to have a Shadowslinger in your debt.

"Doctor, I was meaning to ask and got distracted. Could the missing half of that broken quarrel be inside Vicious Min?"

"What?"

The nasty old sorceress twitched again.

Ted grinned again.

"Here's my thinking." But before I leapt I asked Barate, "Am I right about you using survey maps to work out where the ballista had to be to make that shot? There couldn't have been more than one, right?"

"Yes and yes. There had to have been a misdirection spell hiding the ballista, too. You don't cut somebody down with a monster engine and nobody sees you unless you're working some heavy concealment sorcery."

"My thinking exactly. So. Ted. I'm guessing the forensics sorcerers never found that bolt because it's inside Min. And that's because Min was the real target, with Strafa as collateral damage."

"What?" Ted and Barate said that in perfect a cappella harmony.

"Look. Somebody shoots Min. The bolt maybe hits a collarbone, breaks, and the tip half ricochets up to get Strafa."

Shadowslinger twitched again, now with the fun finger of her left hand. Barate said, "That may fit the facts, but it doesn't feel right."

I didn't think so myself, but only because I wanted Strafa's death to mean something more than just "shit happens."

Ted said, "You find the demon, I'll take a closer look. I thought the wound was through and through, but that was what I expected to see."

"We'll find her," I promised.

Barate settled back into the fat chair. "Go see about covering Kevans."

"Consider it done. You think Mashego and Bashir could visit the Dead Man?"

"No. Not because he's what he is. I wouldn't warn them. But they won't go out while Mother is laid up. . . ." It occurred to him that they were out right now. "They won't. I'm sure."

"I understand."

44

All the rat men but Dollar Dan were on assignment. Well, Dan was, too, but I was his task. Dr. Ted and I were sitting on the steps to Shadowslinger's front porch. There had been a flirtation with sunshine earlier, but the overcast was now back and I expected rain. TunFaire had become locked into that cycle.

Ted and I played with the dogs. Dan stood around looking left out. The mutts had not yet warmed to him, which was no surprise. And he didn't exactly hunger for canine affection. Ted and I didn't talk much, but we were trying to like each other because of, or in spite of, our having had Strafa Algarda in our lives. We talked around most everything of consequence while hiding our true selves, each trying to learn something interesting about the other.

Dollar Dan suddenly stood taller, slamming into a better mood suddenly, like everything he valued had just begun to shine.

"Oh. Ah," I observed, in the secret cant of the polished modern philosopher.

Singe had eased through the pedestrian gate into Shadowslinger's gaudy front garden. Penny tagged along behind, nervous, gawking, surprisingly well dressed. Her style set off the fiscal alarms. I wondered when she and Singe had gotten together.

Penny got distracted by the flower beds, which I had paid no heed before. That sort of thing isn't usually germane. I asked, "Ted, does Constance have a gardener? Maybe I should talk to him."

Ted considered the flowers. His gaze lingered uncomfortably on Penny. "I've never seen one. But I don't spend that much time here. I suppose she would have to have one, wouldn't she?"

An accented voice said, "She does the gardening herself, with help from Bashir and me."

Mashego was home. Silent as midnight death, she had moved in behind us. She—I was by then confident that Mashego was the she—went on. "We are trying to keep up, but as you can see, absent her direction we are losing ground."

I couldn't see that at all. But all I know about plants, farming, gardening, whatnot, is that I have a championship black thumb. Crabgrass and kudzu die when I want them to grow.

Mashego asked, "Who is that girl? She is quite pretty. A few strategic tattoos would turn her into a total heartbreaker."

I sincerely hoped that tattoos never became fashionable. One look at Constance Algarda was warning enough that an appalling future awaited anyone who acquired body art.

Singe kindly gave Dollar Dan a moment while waiting as I explained about Penny. Done with that, I told Mashego, "If you like, I can find somebody reliable to help with the garden." I was thinking Saucerhead Tharpe. The man has some surprising skills.

Once I paid attention the garden began to grow on me. It wasn't just pretty and perfectly kempt; the plants and plantings had been laid out artistically. That was what had caught Penny's eye.

So for the dozenth time since I became involved with Strafa, I had to recalibrate my estimate of a member of her family.

Mashego told me, "No need for that, sir. Master Barate has made arrangements for part-time help."

"Of course." People who would inspire his confidence.

"Good enough. So, Singe, true heart. You tracked me down. Is it critical?"

"Critical? I doubt it. Simply a report of general success. Lurking Fehlske has been taken into custody. Deployment of enough red tops can negate any individual advantage."

I showed her my raised eyebrow, in interrogative mode.

"In such wise, Elona Muriat has been located and surrounded, too. She should be on her way to the Al-Khar by now as well."

The underlying smugness said that she considered herself responsible. Equally, something in Dollar Dan's stance said that he wasn't so sure all that was something of which a rat person ought to be proud. Rat people and the law were natural enemies.

Singe winked at him, then dropped down and started scratching around Brownie's big old floppy ears. Brownie not only tolerated it; she leaned into it. If she'd been a cat she would have purred.

Five seconds later every mutt but Dr. Ted's favorite was in the love scrum.

Brownie backed out and came to sit watch beside me, abandoning her troops to their pleasures.

Dr. Ted observed, "Dogs are one of the good things the gods have given us. We're always more relaxed and content when they're around."

"I'm not a dog person by nature. Never had one myself. But I do get what you mean."

My remarks seemed to surprise Ted and Brownie both. Ted's expression was one almost of pity. Brownie's, adjusted for doggie nature, looked like serious confusion.

I told Singe, "Dan has some people out tracking. We're basically loafing till we hear something." I told the story.

"Vicious Min just got up and ran for it?"

"She was faking good enough to fool him." I indicated Ted. "But I'm pretty sure she couldn't do much real running."

Ted agreed. "She lost a lot of blood. She couldn't get far."

He was distracted.

Penny began to play with the dogs, too. They really went for her. She won Number Two's heart completely while gushing about the magnificence of Shadowslinger's garden. She was inspired to try gardening in our tiny backyard at home. I thought, good luck with that. Those few square yards were a desert where weeds went to die.

Dr. Ted and Mashego both eyed Penny with an appreciation equaling what the girl showed for the flowers.

Singe winked at me, amused by the daddy stuff she knew must be going on inside my head. She was, probably, building haikus about karma.

While I had them there and thought about it, I asked Dr. Ted and Mashego to go see my partner.

Neither begged off, though Mashego probably understood the risk. I sensed strong reluctance. Dr. Ted, though, just wondered, "Should I stay away from Constance for that long?"

"The time will be in the journey. Old Bones is a clever interviewer. He gets right to the heart of the matter. And he's a master at discovering clues and connections that you don't realize you've made."

Ted asked for directions. I provided them, considering Mashego as I did so. She didn't want to get involved but was afraid that refusal would make her look guilty. Of something.

45

Kyoga Stornes trotted through the pedestrian gate, halted a dozen feet away, surprised by the crowd. He looked unhappy with a misery that had come with him, not because he had plunged into a mob.

"Is Barate here?"

"He's up with his mother," I said. "What's up?"

"Moonslight. She's been kidnapped. Maybe killed. But maybe they wanted Moonblight and got the wrong sister."

"Eh?" I noted then that he was wet in spots, dirty in spots, and his clothing had come the worse for wear. "They go after you, too?"

"Uh . . . Hell. Maybe so. I never considered that. If they'd hit us ten minutes earlier, they could've gotten Bone-grinder, too. He took off because one of his grandkids came after him. Family emergency."

Singe gave me a look. So did Penny. They waited to see what I would do, for different reasons. I asked Singe, "You want to get started?"

"I'm on my way." She started moving.

Kyoga blurted, "Hey! What's that about?"

"She'll backtrack you to where this happened. Then she'll follow Moonslight, whose odor she remembers from Strafa's wake. And she will be very careful not to attract attention." That I said loud. I didn't want her to miss it. She waved a hand in a "yeah, yeah" gesture.

Penny and Dollar Dan decided they wanted to tag along.

I yelled. Penny held up, scowled back at the interfering fuddy-duddy. Dollar Dan ignored me and Singe did not tell him to go the hell away.

"Well," Kyoga observed. "Well. That was intriguing."

Dr. Ted began checking him over and cleaning his abrasions — while giving Penny a more appreciative exam.

I ground my teeth.

The girl was not hideous, but . . . Mostly, I was just used to having her underfoot, considering her the Dead Man's pet kid.

Kyoga grumbled, "I'm gonna live, Ted! Let me go see Barate."

"Barate has come to see you."

Indeed he had arrived, alerted by Mashego. Kyoga told his story in detail. We listened attentively. Barate asked the question that had occurred to me right away. "Why was Mariska there instead of Tara Chayne?"

"Not sure. Something to do with Tara Chayne needing to be somewhere else. Her youngest daughter was having her first baby."

Wow. Hill folk could get excited about the same stuff as real people.

Kyoga said, "You know those two. They figure they're interchangeable to the rest of us. Even if they feud all the time."

Suddenly, I realized that Strafa and I would never see grandkids of our own . . . I shook it off. It could consume me. "Barate, one reason I'm here . . . I almost forgot . . . I was hoping Constance would be getting it back together, some, because . . ." I explained what we'd learned at Flubber Ducky and from Trivias Smith. "It's a solid, genuine lead."

Kyoga was disappointed because my belated news topped his. Still, he was encouraged. "Bonegrinder or Moonblight — either one can make a tracer you could hide inside a sword's hilt."

"And Mother won't be making anything but poop for a while," Barate said. "You trust this smith, Garrett?"

"Not really. No reason to." But I wasn't always sure about me. You get cynical in a racket where everybody lies to you, the majority are psychotic, and you run into them during the worst days of their lives. "But I got as good a feeling as I have from anybody lately. Belinda will check his background." I doubted that she would find anything bleak.

I should get Trivias together with the Dead Man.

Singe came shambling back, mumbling to herself. "I need something to track that woman after all. I can't separate her scent from her twin's." Of course. Maybe. Or maybe she just wanted to stall to keep an eye on Penny.

Dollar Dan looked miserable. It took only moments to figure out that Singe had changed her mind about letting him tag along.

Kyoga looked confused.

I promised him, "She really is the best. But even she has limits. If we get her started before the rain comes back, she'll find Moonslight." That should hold off till evening, though.

"Oh. All right." Kyoga let Singe take him aside. He kept one distracted eye on Penny. Penny's body language suggested that she was aware but not particularly conscious of his scrutiny.

Barate called Dollar Dan over to ask what it would take to surround Kevans with a cloud of ferocious rat men.

Mashego bent down to whisper, "Not to worry on Master Kyoga's account, sir. He would never attempt anything of that sort."

Barate overheard. "That's right, Garrett. It's not what you think, anyway. What's got him going is, she's a dead ringer for Scatura at the same age, wearing that outfit."

"Who is Scatura?"

"His wife. She died a long time ago. I find the resemblance uncanny myself." He considered Penny so intently that I got uncomfortable all over again. Barate Algarda did have flaws where relationships with females were concerned. "Any chance there could be some connection?"

I couldn't see how. "I doubt it. We have stuff to do."

"Yes. We do. Ted. Take another look at Mother before we go. Update Mashego and Bashir about anything special they need to be doing. What about you, Garrett? Want to check on her one more time?"

We? "Well . . ."

Dollar Dan announced, "Here comes Firé Esté, meaning we are about to hear something concerning Vicious Min."

A rat man hovered in the pedestrian gateway, unsure if he ought to come ahead without a specific invitation. Dollar Dan beckoned impatiently. I backed him up.

This Esté was new to me. He turned out to be a stutterer. It worsened around people he didn't know. He needed several minutes to tell us what Dollar Dan had predicted.

"What do you think?" Barate asked, since the plan had been to go see Moonblight about her sister and the tracker inserts for the swords. I preferred her to Bonegrinder for those.

"The man is creepy," Barate admitted. "It's his special charm. Don't take it personal."

"If you think he'll do better, I'll defer to your wisdom."

"No. Moonblight it is. For professional acumen, not personality."

Acumen? That was one from the Dead Man's lexicon.

Algarda awaited further remarks. I had none. Nor did anyone else. He added, "She can be quirky, too."

"Really? Well . . . She should act her age . . . What? What did I say?"

Penny snickered behind her left hand. She pointed an indicting finger, also left-handed.

Yeah. She was a southpaw. So many artists are.

"Girl, I liked you better when you were scared of me."

She still was, enough not to banter.

She had a point, though. I wasn't being gritted teeth and steely eye enough. We had twenty things in the air and I had no control. I was letting stuff happen when I should be out kicking down doors.

If I just had some idea where to start kicking . . .

Nobody could do better than me right now. Shadow-slinger was in a coma. The Dead Man was still dead—though he did have people out looking for likely doors. Likewise, Belinda, Morley, and Director Relway.

I felt useless, even so.

Barate tapped me on the spot that Belinda had pounded into bruise pudding. "What's on your mind?" I kept my scream to a girlish bark.

"I'm trying to throw a saddle on all this chaos."

How clever was that, bundling horses and bedlam?

It went right on by him. "You should plant yourself in a safe place and mastermind things from there."

Probably the sensible course, but I found it emotionally barren. "I don't know how to sit. I have to do stuff."

"Running in circles, flapping your arms and shouting. Then getting killed. That's sure to help."

I could argue honestly, "It's pretty much always worked. Except for the getting killed part. You bang on things long enough and loud enough, the bad guys will try to do something about you. Then you nail them."

"Unless they're smart enough to nail you before you know they're there. How long do you suppose that'll take this time?"

"Huh?" I puffed up like a big old toady frog, ready to argue: Look at me, still standing after all these years! But I had had tons of unreasonably good luck, as recently as this morning.

Even Brownie had a comment, a small doggie whimper. She leaned against the outside of my right thigh. Yeah. I started scratching ears.

Those beasts have selectively bred us for thousands of years.

Realization: I almost totally depend on friends to manage parts of my life. I cannot make it on my lonesome.

Old Bones might claim that, while not hive insects, humans are social animals who have to belong in order to function properly.

"He was kind of a loner."

"Nobody knew him very well. He stayed pretty much to himself."

"He always seemed like a nice guy, quiet, but he never had no friends that I ever seen."

The neighbors, as the red tops start dragging the bodies out.

Crueler, though, is when they're winkling the tortured girls out of their shallow graves and the guy showing them where his playthings are stashed is a good family man, five kids, a deacon in the church.

Pain exploded down my right arm. For half a second I thought it was the Big One, swooping in a couple of decades early, out to reunite me with my beloved. Then I realized, wrong arm, and noticed Penny Dreadful backing off, anxious and smug at the same time.

She had delivered the strike with military precision.

"What the hell? Why did you do that?"

"You were spacing out again. Singe says we don't want to lose you. She told me not to let you go drifty. Do whatever it takes, she said."

Everybody had a fierce grin on, including Mashego but excepting the rat men, who lacked grins only because they weren't made for grinning. They expressed their grand amusement by wiggling their whiskers, the sort of laughter that, in a human, would have looked like somebody choking on a chicken bone.

Part of me wanted to drag the kid across my lap and get to paddling, but I'm supposed to be too mature to yield to impulse. Besides which, that was sure to be misinterpreted, and beyond which, I wouldn't have gotten anywhere. Penny had won a lot of hearts with one slick move.

She's also a nasty infighter.

The hidden story of my life. Always a plaything of women.

Even Brownie's sympathy was entirely pro forma.

46

So there we were, outside the place where Vicious Min had gone to ground. Supposedly.

"What a dump." Dr. Ted had invited himself along after a final check on Shadowslinger. And a dump it was. And I was wondering if I shouldn't have visited Moonblight first.

I joined Penny, Barate, Mashego, Dollar Dan, and his troops in agreeing with Ted. Only henchrat Firé wasn't there to opine. He had gone back to John Stretch headquarters to gather the murder of rat men that would lifeguard Kevans once her whereabouts was determined.

I grumbled, "Yeah. I've never seen worse."

It was a brickwork shell with half a roof, most of the wood stripped out to burn and the metal stolen to sell for scrap. I was surprised the bricks themselves hadn't been carted off.

Barate suggested, "Something must have been done to keep looters away."

I saw no bleached bones scattered around. The protection must be moderately subtle. "If Min actually lives here, that might be enough. I wouldn't mess with her if I didn't have to."

"Perhaps," Barate conceded. But that meant Min would have been there awhile, in turn meaning that she could not be a recent immigrant from a demon realm.

The dogs did not want to get any closer.

I said, "We've seen a place like this before."

Barate nodded. "Where the kids did their bug experiments."

That had happened in a bespelled ruin with secret cellars underneath. Kip, Kevans, and gang had indulged in such socially useful tasks as the creation of giant bugs. As if the roaches we have already, big enough to toss small children across their backs and abscond, aren't magnificent enough.

I explained for the others. Dan suggested, "I smell exaggeration."

"Maybe some. But ask somebody who was there. Those bugs were bigger than these mutts."

"Nor will I argue with you, Garrett. I have heard such claims from others. Sadly, I missed out." He eyed Penny.

She nodded. "They were big. It was scary. I'm so glad those kids didn't make any giant spiders."

Barate chuckled. "A sentiment often heard. Can you imagine a camel spider or banana spider jumped up as much as those other bugs were?"

We all took a moment to be grateful.

Giant spiders have to be some kind of universal human nightmare.

Dan said, "I hear there was some good eating on some of those bugs."

Half the people in the world, even when they aren't really people, are the glass-half-full kind.

Mashego asked, "Is it your intent to stall and reminisce indefinitely, or will we actually do something?" Her accent had thickened. "I do have work waiting at home."

I did not remind her that she was with me at her own insistence.

"Same goes for me," Penny said.

I restrained a petty remark about never having seen her do much. I really had no idea what she contributed. On reflection, though, I doubted that Singe or Dean would let her freeload.

I asked, "Barate? Thoughts?"

"We're here. And she can only get healthier."

"Um." On the other hand, I could just relay news of her whereabouts to the Civil Guard.

I had questions I wanted to ask myself, though.

Dollar Dan suggested, "We should probably do it while we still have some light and the rain hasn't started."

An excellent point. The gloom kept getting thicker though the rain continued to hold off.

Penny stated my feelings for both of us. "It's been a long, long day."

It was unlikely to be over soon, either.

47

The anxiety all proved needless. Vicious Min was in there, yes. But she was unconscious, exhausted. Ted couldn't get a flinch out of her.

Penny hit me with the obvious. "We should ship her over to Himself while we can manage her."

And while she was still available. I feared that she might have stressed herself to a point where she could die on us.

"Oh. Oh! Yes! We'll need to transport her somehow."

"Big as she is, we'll need a wagon," Barate said.

Ted added, "Preferably with springs."

"So. People. Spread out. See what you can find." This was not a neighborhood I knew. "Ted, stay with Min. Keep her breathing. Keep her asleep. Damn, she's ugly. Penny, you stay, too."

Naturally, she argued.

"Dig through her stuff. You're the only one who knows how to investigate. You'll know good stuff if you see it. I'll help find a wagon."

She accepted my contention but didn't believe me. What I said was true, but I really just wanted to keep her out of harm's way.

Then I began to wonder if I should leave her at Ted's mercy.

Hell. I had to trust her. She was a big girl. She could make choices. And other whistling-past-the-graveyard thoughts.

I had to get out there. How likely were Dollar Dan or Mashego to come up with a wagon? They lacked a trustworthy look. And Barate was from too far up the Hill to have a clue how to connect with real people.

Only . . . How likely indeed?

Both Dan and Mashego scored before I got my first lead—which led me straight to the wagon Dan already had on offer from a rat person with soft connections to John Stretch.

Mashego found a carter from the old country who was willing to do night work.

It is truly all about who you know. I knew no one around there, in the shadow of the Bustee slum.

We chose the rat man's wagon because it had the longer bed. Only a yard of Min would hang out the back.

The dogs were anxious to go. They could not stop prowling nervously and eyeing me like they wondered why I insisted on wasting time hanging out where members of the tribe might get eaten.

Once we had Min in the wagon—an all-hands adventure shifting her, it was—I asked Ted, "Is she likely to wake up during the ride?" It was two miles to Macunado Street. Farther if we stuck to smooth pavement.

Ted was helping Penny load stuff to be looked at later. Min had a lot, mostly junk, some of which suggested that she liked to play at being a girly girl when nobody was looking.

"Couldn't say for sure. Why?"

"I was hoping I could get you to stick with me and Barate for our visit to Moonblight while Penny and Dan take Min where she needs to go."

Dollar Dan announced, "Dollar Dan will not go anywhere that Garrett does not go. Dollar Dan Justice's task is to keep stubborn, uncooperative, and ungrateful Garrett alive, not to transport prisoners."

Ouch.

Penny snickered. "You notice he didn't mention anything about making sure that you stay healthy?"

Ted hadn't brought a full doctor's rig, but he did have a small emergency kit. He tried to tell Penny how to use some chemicals and a wad of wool to put Min to sleep if she started to come around. She suddenly got dumb as a stump. He finally decided to go with her instead of me. "I'll head for Shadowslinger's place once I'm done with this."

Grumble, grumble. "You do that."

Meanwhile, Dollar Dan had a heart-to-heart with the wagon's owner, who did not trust rat men enough to let his only means of making a living out of his sight, despite his own connection to John Stretch's organization.

"All set here," Dan announced.

I sighed, wondering why everything always has to get complicated.

I know why some guys become loners. It simplifies things.

48

It would be full dark soon. The dogs were nervous and hung closer than during brighter times. They were far from familiar ground when the time of greatest danger was approaching.

As a stray you had only what protection you could invent for yourself. Darkness could harbor dangers day walkers never noticed.

Undead mutts? Vampire pups? Doubtful, that. But maybe nocturnal predatory thunder lizards. Thunder lizards have become uncommon in the city, but we still sometimes hear of incidents outside the busier districts, especially at night. Mutilated carcasses turn up, savaged by something bigger than rats.

Singe intercepted us as we neared the Hill, in company with the balance of Dollar Dan's crew. She was worn out but not yet complaining. She fell in beside me, brought me up to date on all the successful arrests. Elona Muriat alone remained sullenly unimpressed by Deal Relway and refused all cooperation. Preston Womble, on the other hand, could not shut up despite having almost nothing to say. He had had an epiphany. He had become born again. He was trying to bring his partner into alignment with the new law-and-order facts of life.

Singe asked, "You do realize that you are being watched, tracked, and studied by the Specials, don't you?"

"I haven't paid much attention, but I don't expect to operate in a full vacuum. Do we know who hired brother Tribune?"

A drop of moisture hit my cheek. The rain would not hold off much longer.

"No. But they have not yet threatened him with soap and water." She made a rude noise after stumbling over a nervous dog who wanted to stay really close. "The Director means to let you work while counting every breath."

"Doing his job for him."

"More like he wants to see what you will stir off the bottom of the cesspool."

"And Kevans? Any word on her?"

That was exactly what Barate and I had thought it would be. Kevans had gone looking for Kip Prose. She had hung around with him till Kyra's scowls and boredom reminded her that she had an obligation at Grandma's house. She remained unconcerned about her own safety.

The rat men now watching over her had not attracted any attention.

They also reported that she had had other watchers already, now chased away.

Their description was vague, because it came from rat men, but it was intriguing. An attractive pair of youngsters, the girl a young man's fancy while the boy was a father's nightmare.

I exchanged looks with Barate. He said what I was thinking. "A Champion and Mortal Companion."

"Know anyone who fits the description?"

The rat men did smells better than visuals. Smells . . . We would have to have those two sniffed out.

How might I leverage those two into the Director's embrace?

Other trackers had determined that the little blonde and her sidekick moved between several hiding places on scattered rooftops. They had a knack for disappearing not only visually but nasally, but not indefinitely. They could not long elude a determined team of rat men.

We also got a fix on Moonslight, though the severity of her durance seemed questionable. The rat men thought she was more a reluctant guest than a prisoner, and might not have been confused with her sister at all.

Singe opined, "They will exercise deference whichever sister they have. Any wickedness could come back a thousandfold should their employer lose courage or have a change of heart."

That side of our system irks me. It might never even occur to a victim to savage the man who gave the orders, if he was of noble standing, but woe be unto his hirelings, who were only in it to make a living.

"Garrett?"

"Huh?" So. There I was, gone again, this time yearning toward Relway's ideology.

Singe suggested, "There is another possibility."

"Which is?"

"That they only want to keep her from interfering if they do think that they have Moonblight."

"That would mean that somebody knows Moonblight wants to sabotage the tournament." It occurred to me then that it didn't matter which Machtkess the villains had, that being the case. Either would provide leverage and leave Richt Hauser as the last high-power enemy of the Operators.

Was Shadowslinger's condition the result of hostile action?

I broached the possibility to Mashego, who seemed to grow slighter and less obtrusive as the day faded. "I will think about that," she promised.

As would I. And I would try profiling the minds behind the tournament. I had a hope that I did not consider even slightly forlorn: The Operators, by nature, must be discounting, even disdaining, Mr. Furious Tide of Light.

The Garrett beast was, after all, a no-account, bottom-feeding, common-as-it-gets, blood-sucking nothing. A flea.

God, or Gods, Above and Below, let their minds be locked into that way of thinking.

It wouldn't take long to gobble that kind down.

I tripped over Brownie. "Damn it, girls! Spread out!"

The dogs did so, with no enthusiasm, and only for a few minutes.

49

Moonblight's place was surprisingly unremarkable considering her standing and public persona. It was a small two-story on a modest plot, square, white-painted stucco with green trim, green shutters upstairs, and a green tile roof. Like Tara Chayne herself, the place seemed past its prime, about to go to seed. I told Barate, "I expected something more flamboyant."

"Tara Chayne Machtkess the person is actually a little timid and lacking in confidence."

The big green front door swung inward.

I asked, "And her sister lives here, too?"

"Mariska, yes. There are some younger sisters without much talent elsewhere. Mariska and Tara Chayne split the upper floor. They stay out of each other's way. They don't get along. It goes back to when they were girls, to a squabble over a man. I don't know for sure, but that was either my father or Kyoga. Or maybe both. They were supposedly pretty loose."

I said nothing but noted that here was another scandalous disclosure involving an Algarda. Any old affair had to have taken place after Barate's dad married Constance. "There was mention of a grandchild's birth."

Dan and crew were doing a quick sniff round and posting sentries. The dogs crowded toward the light. Singe was indifferent to anything but her own exhaustion. I hoped I didn't end up carrying her home. Mashego was no longer with us, having headed home to Shadowslinger's place.

"The twins both married. Tara Chayne had a son, Harou, right away. Harou didn't come back from the war. He wasn't smart and he wasn't talented. He let himself be talked into trying something beyond his skill level. There were two daughters, Haroei and Haroa, the younger. Haroa had the baby. She came along after Harou died. Tara Chayne likes to think that Harou's soul lives on in Haroa."

I grunted, impressed only by the fact that Moonblight had named all her kids with variants on a root meaning precious. Similar tragic histories you can collect by the score if you search.

"Mariska had no children, by choice, after seeing what Tara Chayne went through giving birth to Harou. Mariska is not known for being unselfish or for willingly suffering inconvenience or discomfort."

"What happened to the husbands?"

"They're around as career remittance men. The girls have nothing to do with them anymore except to pay them to stay out of the way."

Dollar Dan let me know that he and his guys were set. We could go on. Nobody had smelled any disturbing odors from the house. "Shall I keep an eye on Singe?" Asked in wan hope.

Singe managed a head shake. "I am good. For now." To me, she added, "You may end up carrying me home, though."

"If I have to. If I can't find somebody to buy you. But who is going to carry me?"

Barate informed me, "Denvers is getting impatient."

"Denvers?"

"Tara Chayne's man. There in the doorway letting in moths and mosquitoes while we stand around jawing."

"Oh. That guy."

We started moving.

Barate went back to "The younger Machtkess girls have no talent. . . ."

Light flared on the far side of the Hill, setting the belly of the overcast on fire. It faded, was followed by the grumble of baby thunder. A few raindrops hit me, but there was no connection. The grumble faded. Then flashes backlighted the skyline, accompanied by a racket like divine swords clashing.

It took no genius for Dan to declare, "That's sorcerers fighting!"

Sparks flew in showers, as though from holiday fireworks.

Barate mumbled, "Damn!" The rest of us just gawked.

It lasted several minutes. The whistles of Civil Guards and private watchmen sawed shrilly at the night.

"Oh my! I guess it's started." Moonblight had joined her man in the doorway, face pallid, eyes wide. She was not happy.

The dogs crowded as close as Denvers would let them. They might be feral, but they carried millennia of racial memories of shared safety with two-leggers in huts and caves.

"What is this?" Moonblight demanded.

"They're scared of the dark."

She considered the excitement yonder. "That might be smart tonight. Let them into the foyer, Denvers. Find them something to eat." After brief consideration, she added, "The escort as well."

Dollar Dan moved his guys inside reluctantly, yet with relief. Being invited into a sorceress's house was scary, but staying outside could turn out much worse.

Moonblight cut me and Barate out of the crowd. "Come with me."

I gave a sad shrug to Singe, whose offended look turned into mute appeal. Tara Chayne had exceeded herself already to accommodate my nonhuman companions.

It would do Singe good to spend time learning to deal with Dollar Dan. She would face that problem for a long time, and other rat men would want to stake claims of their own. She was a huge prize.

50

Moonblight led us to a sitting room where a female servant was setting a table for three. It featured glasses, carafes of wine, and a platter of cheese bits and sausage chunks. I drooled. I was ferociously hungry. And tense. And sore.

I had roamed more than usual in a normal month. And the day was not over yet.

"So, why are you here with a mob instead of . . ." She glanced at Barate, chose to turn it off in front of my father-in-law. Barate Algarda might become unpleasant if he was offended.

"The mob's job is to keep me alive. People have tried to do ugly stuff to me. I came to ask some questions, to see if you'll help with a couple of things, and to let you know that your sister has been kidnapped. But I imagine you've heard about that."

"I have. An unpleasant visitor brought the news this afternoon. He said that Mariska will be hurt if I keep trying to sabotage the tournament."

She seemed content with that. I prodded, "And? What else?" There had to be more. I should drag her off to see the Dead Man again.

"I wished him luck. I told him I hoped they had fun. I suggested a few things he could do, mostly on the lines of don't throw Mariska in the briar patch. He didn't like my attitude. He got belligerent, so I had Denvers thump him and stuff him in the dustbin out back."

Was she that sure the villains wouldn't hurt Mariska? Or did she really not care? "Did you see anything that might help us identify him?"

"I know who he is already. No. Wait. I know what he is. A priest. Orthodox. From the cathedral in the Dream Quarter. I've only seen him from a distance there. He never noticed me. This was the first time I ever actually talked to him. He had no idea that I'd seen him before."

"And you, being a clever girl, didn't clue him."

"Yes. Me being a clever woman."

I must have started to glow. Was there a connection? A priest. Strafa had visited a priest the morning she died. We all assumed that was about the wedding. She and Father Amerigo had issues. But maybe she had gone to see a priest causing difficulties of another kind.

I should put Father Amerigo on my interview list. Or the Dead Man's, even better.

I needed to remember that Playmate and Penny hadn't seen Strafa in the Dream Quarter, which proved only that they hadn't seen her, but it was suggestive.

"Any chance you'd know this priest's name?"

"None. But a visit to Chattaree Cathedral ought to turn him up. He's easy to spot. Or describe. He has a huge wen." She tapped her head.

I wanted to exchange "Aha!" looks with somebody but had to do without. Barate hadn't been there when the wen got mentioned before. I treated myself to an evil laugh. "I do believe we've got one!"

Barate asked, "Got one what?"

"Operator. A guy with a big-ass wen was one of the gobs who commissioned those costumes and the swords we're going to booby-trap."

Tara Chayne eyed me like I had just begun to shine with a howling madness.

"Sorry. Listen. That's the other reason that I came to see

you." She looked hopeful, but only for an instant. "By the way, what do you want to do about your sister?"

Moonblight burned through Tara Chayne Machtkess. "We know where she's being kept? Good. Let her marinate."

"Say what?"

"All right. Have somebody keep watch. Rat men would be appropriate. I'll pay for their time. But let her sit, otherwise. We'll do something if things start to fall apart for her."

"That's really what you want?"

"I'm fine with letting the dumb bitch stew."

Hardly charitable toward your sister. Not my place to judge, though.

I got busy telling about Flubber Ducky and Trivias Smith, ceremonial costumes and imitation antique swords.

"And you want to sabotage those weapons."

"Yes. No. Not exactly. Hell . . . That's a good idea. If you could fix it so they'd just bend if you tried to stick somebody . . . Ugh."

I thought I had galloped blind into verbal quicksand. The woman was in no mood to play with it, though. Or she didn't have a mind as skewed as mine. She said, "Creating a hilt insert to make them traceable can be done. Anything more would be a huge challenge. Barate, how is your mother doing?"

"I'm more optimistic. Her fingers have begun twitching. Ted says that she may be aware."

"If she's even halfway conscious, she'll be back. She's too strong and too bullheaded for anything less."

Barate nodded. "She won't go before she gets even for Strafa, that's for sure."

I decided we should get back to the man who had tried to strong-arm Moonblight. Pretty daring, that, going at somebody from high on the Hill. "Lady Machtkess . . ."

"Tara Chayne." She did not simper.

Barate nodded minutely, eyebrows up. He was surprised. Moonblight had accepted me into her in-crowd.

"Tara Chayne, then. Once I'm done here I'm heading

home. I'm exhausted. I'll report to my partner, then collapse. But . . . if there is some way you can make yourself do it, could you come with me? He could mine a fortune in information from your encounter with that man . . ." I stopped, certain I was wasting my breath. She had let herself be violated once, and that was once too often.

She stood up. "You two get busy on that platter. You must be starving. I'll be right back."

She went into the foyer, talked to somebody, I thought Singe. Maybe Dollar Dan, too, then silence, soon followed by whispering.

I asked Barate, "What do you think?"

"About what?"

"About everything in general and her in particular."

"Tara Chayne. She's letting friendship and a conscience usually in hibernation influence the image she shows the world." When I didn't respond, he added, "Most Hill folk are better people than you expect, once you know us."

I stayed shut up. He might smack me if I didn't agree. And that is a problem with villains. The better you know them, the more you get why they are the way they are. You may actually suffer a sympathetic reaction.

Which doesn't mean you shouldn't crack skulls and cut throats anyway. You have to deal with the monster that is, not the victim that was.

Tara Chayne came back. She announced, "I have everything I need to make the tracers. I do wonder, though, who you meant to do the following. You don't have the talent. Neither does he."

I hadn't considered that. I glanced at Barate. He shrugged. "I didn't think that far ahead. You and Richt Hauser are all we have left."

"Then I suppose it will have to be me."

I wondered if I shouldn't ought to be suspicious. She was awfully cooperative.

People who cooperate enthusiastically usually turn out to be up to no good. They're trying to con you. But, on the

other hand, Moonblight had been into the conspiracy
against the tournament before Strafa and I got recruited.
And the days since then had delivered us all plenty of motive to get some licks in before the Operators got their production rolling.

51

The rain arrived as drizzle, better than the soaker I'd expected but still enough to leave the cobblestones dangerously slick.

Barate headed for his mother's house from Moonblight's place. He had business with her and Kevans both. The rest of us headed for Macunado Street. The dogs were not thrilled with the weather. They would have been happy to grace Moonblight's house permanently. There was some good eating there.

Tara Chayne wasn't ready to adopt.

On the upside, Singe was getting along under her own power.

Dollar Dan was disappointed.

"What is that odor?" I asked. Something lurked behind all the ripe aromas stirred up when it rains.

There was a pale fog with something like thin smoke mixed in. I caught notes of sulfur and something metallic. The keen noses around me might be able to explain.

A rat man said, "Something to do with that sorcery from before." The air wasn't moving much, but it was drifting from that direction.

Dan and Singe agreed but had nothing to add.

The hired wagon stood in front of the house. Min was not aboard. The owner had to be inside. Likewise, Penny and Ted. The team seemed to have been struck stupider than is usual in the dim and bloody-minded horse tribe.

They looked like anybody who wanted could just lead them away.

Only, their barrels-of-rocks dumb and lazy show was happening in front of the house where the Dead Man denned up.

I wondered if Himself wasn't using them as bait.

I grumbled, "Stinks like wet horse around here." I followed Singe up to the stoop, she peeking back in case Dollar Dan suddenly could no longer restrain his passion. A questionable concern considering the proximity of the Dead Man.

Old Bones didn't touch us, but he was awake and aware. Penny knew exactly when to open the door. She had exchanged the stylish outfit for her usual raggedy tomboy look. I heard voices from Singe's office, as did Singe, who registered alarm. That was her turf. No trespassers allowed when she was out.

Penny told us, "Dean has some potato sausages warming." Which, tell it true, was what I most wanted to hear right then.

"Those and some beer and I'm down and gone to heaven."

Singe kicked up a cloud of dust in her haste to go defend her patch. I got there three steps behind.

Her office contained John Stretch, Saucerhead Tharpe, his totally nonromantic roommate Winger, Helenia from the Al-Khar, and a man I didn't recognize. But no Dr. Ted. And where the hell was the rat man who owned the wagon?

Vicious Min, I assumed, would be in the room next door, which had been my office before I grew up and left home.

Winger, heavier now, more worn, and seedier than ever, fed my ego by reporting, "You look like shit on a stick, Garrett."

"I feel worse than I look. I haven't done that much walking since boot camp."

I stayed in the doorway, watching Penny politely thank Dollar Dan while hinting broadly that he ought to go so the folks who lived here could crash. I checked John Stretch.

His ears were good enough to follow the exchange. Dan wasn't getting the message. But then he loosed a weird squeaking noise caused by the Dead Man's direct touch. He wasted no time getting gone after that.

I felt Old Bones paging through my memories, suggesting that it would be a good idea to hit the sheets. Tomorrow would be another long day.

Even so, I started to get on Saucerhead and Winger about not having done the work we had given them.

His Nibs showed me a condensed version of their adventures.

They owed their lives to the fact that Deal Relway was a sneaky psychopath driven by an abiding need to know and a further compulsion to meddle.

Specials had been watching most of my closest associates—a matter of public policy nowadays if Old Bones could be believed.

Anyway, both had gotten into tight spots. Both had been rescued by swift Guard responses, leaving them tormented by mixed feelings about the law-and-order outbreak.

Both had been celebrating, using their newly won time to indulge in an effort to empty my beer kegs before somebody named Garrett cut them off.

"Thought you were going on the wagon," I said to Winger. She had embarrassed herself with her drinking after she and Jon Salvation parted ways.

"Shit, Garrett! Today I foun' out that life is too goddamn short to waste it trying to be somebody you ain't. 'Specially, if it's somebody somebody else wants you to be."

A sentiment with which I did not disagree—though I had begun to realize that doing only what you feel like will make life unpleasant in the long run. You'll make a lot of people unhappy.

I asked John Stretch, "Did you find out anything useful?"

"Almost nothing."

Penny and Dean brought food. Singe chivvied her brother out from behind her desk, cleared clutter enough to make space for her tray. I settled onto a hard wooden chair with mine aboard my lap. "Nothing? That's amazing."

"It is. But there are no rumors, even . . . Let me start over. Other than the excitement in the families being pulled in—and we identified only two of those—there is an information vacuum. There is no discussion outside the families involved, which they don't want to be but are afraid that trying to ignore the mess could just make their Champion easier to kill."

I turned to Helenia, already wilting under Singe's regard. "Why are you here?"

"The Director sent me." She sipped from a mug that had the look of one she'd been nursing all night.

You can't trust sippers. They always have a hidden agenda.

"Why?" After she failed to say anything else.

"To be liaison."

I pulled in a deep breath, then decided to save the air. I turned to the stranger. "Who are you?"

"I'm with her."

"That's an unusual name."

"Merryman. Clute Merryman. Corporal of the Station for Criminal Statistics. Day watch. I tagged along to look out for Helenia."

Penny brought in a folding chair. I glowered. She told me, "They were here when I got home. Yell at Dean." She nodded toward the Dead Man's room. "Or him." Letting me know the visitors were here on Himself's instructions. "They helped with Vicious Min." Now she nodded toward the small room next door.

"Ah. And what happened to the wagon guy? And the doc?"

"Visiting across the way."

John Stretch stirred uncomfortably.

There was nothing for me here right now. The Dead Man would get anything worth knowing faster than I could. And I needed sleep.

"I might as well hit the hay, people. Soon as I finish these wonderful sausages. Good stuff, Dean." I used my fork on the last little chunk, waved it as the old man rolled a cart into the doorway. The cart carried beer pitchers and fresh tea. I wondered when we had acquired the cart.

Dean passed me my favorite mug, so ranked because of its capacity. "Oh my! Select Dark. I'll hold off wasting time on sleep for now."

The Weider Select Dark is good stuff. Really good stuff.

Business talk resumed. Other than to wonder what Old Bones might have gotten from Vicious Min, I didn't concern myself much. It took only one capacious mug to free up thoughts of Strafa that I had been keeping suppressed for several days.

52

Singe was there beside my bed, armed with my favorite mug. It was filled with medicated black tea. Something had reached inside my still throbbing coconut to waken me. It withdrew after easing the pain a little.

"Did I make a total fool of myself?"

She raised a hand, thumb and forefinger narrowly separated. "Close. But not quite. Drink this. It's from Kolda. You have work to do."

She'd been up long enough to go see Kolda? I seemed to recall her gobbling the dark with enthusiasm herself.

Must be something she'd kept around, just in case.

She said, "You left the dogs out without food or water." Apparently a crime, though I didn't get it. Dogs are dogs. They belong outside.

I swallowed some tea. The medicine hit fast. Kolda knows his stuff. But it didn't change my attitude toward the mutts.

"You just cannot do that sort of thing, Garrett. You have accepted responsibilities."

I wound up to protest and argue.

She stepped all over me. "Go downstairs. Things need doing."

Old Bones brushed me, mildly impatient.

"Huh?"

"That sorceress is here with the tracers for the sword-smith."

"Huh?" Again, now with startled oomph! behind it.

"Moonblight? I didn't think she'd come within a mile of here ever again."

"Himself says she is all business this time. Something happened on the Hill last night . . . Oh! You were there, too."

Intuition, maybe subliminally fed by the Dead Man. "All that flash."

"Apparently. He has not filled me in."

Interesting.

Kolda's herbs did what they could, but a low-grade headache persisted. I've had some experience with the hangover phenomenon. This day might not be filled with sunshine and joy. I started it with the traditional vow never to do anything as stupid again until the next time. I was too old for this crap.

And we have heard it all before. Please move along. Wear comfortable shoes.

He was trying to scare me.

There was a grand conspiracy afoot. Penny waited to play her role at the foot of the stair. She herded me toward Singe's office, no stalling or side trips allowed. We met Dean coming the other way. He said he had delivered breakfast for me and a light repast for our guest. I glanced into my old office as I passed. Vicious Min lay splashed across a couple of old mattresses, on her back, totally disheveled, in a coma induced by the Dead Man. My attempt to stop for a look failed. Penny and Singe both pushed me on.

"But what have we learned from her?" I demanded manfully. Though Singe claims I whined.

Very little. Her mind operates differently. She deals with situations by translating from our ways of thinking to hers. Her rest state, or ground state, is wholly alien. I am trying to work my way into her mind by tracing one memory at a time.

"Oh, come on!" My exasperation did not target him so much as the perversity of the universe where I was stranded. If reality was a solipsist bubble, the chief engineer needed his butt kicked till he got his mind right.

She may be a demonic immigrant after all.

An immigrant. Right.

53

Dean had not gone out of his way to provide a gourmet breakfast. He *had* whipped up something good for what ailed me—assuming I was clever enough and man enough to keep all that biscuitry in heavy sausage gravy down.

Moonblight said, "Good morning, Mr. Garrett," far too cheerfully.

Nobody should be bright and cheerful that long before the crack of noon.

I tried to stifle the acid surging in my gut. "Good morning, ma'am."

Which didn't get so much as an eyebrow twitch. She was here on business. She was dressed for business. Sensible shoes and clothing suitable for travel by horseback or hiking in the woods, all top quality, genuinely meant for rough usage.

I tied in to breakfast with more enthusiasm than seemed reasonable considering the state of my hangover, all the while wondering what the old gal had in mind.

She told me what. "I will be joining you today, Mr. Garrett, to make sure nothing happens to you."

Wow. Other than Strafa by circumstance, I never had a heavy-hitter Hill type for a bodyguard. Cool. Sort of. But scary.

Singe poured me more thick black Kolda tea, tapped the rim of my mug to let me know that I had no choice.

Everybody wants to be my mom. Even Dean.

There was extra spice in the sausage gravy. Another Kolda contribution, no doubt.

Penny brought a beaker of chilled water. Always smart to drink lots of water after a night spent processing proof that the gods do love us.

I grunted a response to Moonblight. If Old Bones hadn't run her off, he must think her company wasn't a bad idea. And my ego's defenses were down enough that I could entertain the notion that it might be useful not to work today's mean streets alone.

I faced Singe. "I take it Morley . . ."

"As occasionally happens with your acquaintances, life got in the way of his babysitting obligation."

Hurtful. "Babysitting" was not her exact phrase. It was what she meant, maybe hinting that my friends could be feeling a little overutilized.

Which could be a problem in need of address. My friends do have lives of their own.

It is possible that the Operators have used hidden influence to generate distractions, too.

"Those nut jobs could be that well informed and organized?"

They could be. Crazy does not mean stupid. It does not imply an absence of genius tactically, strategically, or organizationally. However, it is far from certain that they are manipulating your environment.

"I'm not sure that helps."

We will have a more certain perspective by the end of the day.

Which I took to mean that, yet again, I'd be out drawing fire while folks like Winger and Saucerhead, John Stretch, and others would slide around in the dank and dark looking to sneak up on the truth.

I swilled a final bitter gulp. I understood. There was a plan afoot. A scheme. Childe Garrett would appear to be the main operator. Maybe Old Bones had cooked something up with Tara Chayne so she would go dancing between the raindrops, playing chicken with the lightning, with me.

She observed, "You're moving faster and showing better color. Feeling better, then?"

I was. Some. "I can manage the random linear thought. Smiles are a ways off, though."

"Smiles? We don't need no stinking smiles."

Excellent. Images flooded my noggin, beginning with my itinerary, a jagged line that started at the house and zagged mostly eastward, toward the river, before it plunged down south to the Dream Quarter. _A visit to the Al-Khar is not necessary but could be useful on the off chance someone there has learned something they are willing to share._

Nothing useful had come of Helenia's visit. The presence of the boyfriend had been stifling. Not that she had had anything useful tucked inside her vacuous head. Nothing Old Bones cared to share, anyway. I'm sure he learned something useful about the secret workings of the Guard. Meanwhile, Helenia and the boyfriend abused my hospitality by about two gallons' worth.

His Nibs took a cavalier attitude toward the expense.

First job would be a run to Trivias Smith's place with the tracers—and a Moonblight eager to meet him. Then we would go to the Dream Quarter to find a man with a wen. If we located him, somebody might deliver a robust midnight invitation to a conversation with my partner. Relway would disapprove, being a born-again authoritarian, but he would get over it—fast if there were laurels to be won.

Next stop would be Playmate to see how he was holding up. Too, Old Bones hoped that Playmate had done better wrangling Little Moo than he had Brownie and her crew. He wanted to meet the girl.

He had some ideas that he wasn't ready to share. He doesn't like putting something out there that he might later have to admit was incorrect.

If all goes well, we may have some interesting developments by this evening. He then reminded me that, given the chance, he wanted direct interviews with the people we'd see today.

"Good luck with that," I told me under my breath. I didn't see anybody but Playmate volunteering.

Lady Tara Chayne observed, "You appear to be stalling." When I didn't respond fast enough to suit, she added, "I'm getting no younger. And Shadowslinger is moving toward recovery."

She would come back, wouldn't she?

Moonblight made a statement of objective truth sound totally sinister. Had my partner contributed a touch of emotional harassment?

No.

She had delivered that dose of dread all by her own self.

She did come from way up high on the Hill.

54

Brownie and two of her gal pals gamboled round, yapping joyously. It was the beginning of a great day!

Number Two shared my bleak attitude.

I blurted, "What the hell?" I stared. I shuddered. I started to sweat. I turned back, but the door had shut behind me. My hands trembled. My knees knocked. "What in the hell?"

There were horses tied up at a street-side hitching post just downhill from my steps. Intuition shrieked that they were there because of me. I am cursed with a powerful instinct when it comes to the darker blessings. Just seeing those monsters guaranteed that all things dreadful were about to come down.

My reaction was maybe a wee bit melodramatic. The fact remained: I should have vandalized that post as soon as the neighborhood association put it in. Hitching posts attract horses the way horse apples attract flies. Right now my stretch of Macunado was suffering a surfeit of all three.

Moonblight announced, "We will cover more ground faster if we ride." My vote having no real weight. She strode manfully to the larger beast, a gelding whose ears brushed the bellies of the clouds. She checked its tack, swung aboard with the ease and grace of a feline cavalier.

The lesser beast was a mare, old, saggy, not much bigger than a kiddy-ride pony. She gave me a sideways look three seconds long, all sad and resigned, smoothly masking the evil in her heart. I psyched myself up to commence to fix to begin working my way closer.

"Will you stop dawdling? You could get annoying if you insist on being a drama queen."

Oh boy. Struck to the macho heart.

Tara Chayne's stallion pranced and caracoled impatiently.

All right. Her gelding shuffled sideways a little while my ego shrank till it could slither under the bellies of night crawlers. I stepped in, checked cinches, bridle, and stirrups like I knew what I was doing. The saddle did not fall off while I levered myself aboard and, age of wonders, settled facing the same direction as the nag. My toes did not quite drag the cobblestones.

"That isn't so terrible, is it?"

Curses. She knew that I suffered a slight neurosis concerning horses.

Yes. It was terrible. The view from way up there was . . .

I bit down on that. I needed no aggravation from anyone who suspected my secret foibles.

The mare stepped out, sadly trudging along beside the sorceress and her beast, one step back like a good Venageti wife. Brownie and the gang, no more enthusiastic about horses than I was, moved out with us, in synch with the monsters despite being ill at ease. Number Two and another roamed ahead, scouting. Brownie assumed her standard station a foot outside the range of any surprise kick. The remaining mutt fell back as a one-dog rearguard.

I clutched saddle and reins and awaited the dark moment when my steed commenced her mischief.

It is gospel absolute. Sometimes "they" really are out to get you!

The mare might be working for the people who had been out to get me the past few days.

I worked on my nerves, using relaxation techniques learned back when I was a national hero in training. I reserved a fraction of my attention for taking advantage of my new high vantage point.

TunFaire's streets teem by day when, as this morning, rain is only a threat, though come nighttime, some areas turn into deserts. By day it can be easy to follow someone through all the busy, and more so if they rise above the press on horseback. A professional eye, however, can discover followers. They will be the frequently seen people impatient with folks who impede their parallel progress.

It helps to be operating with clever dogs, too. They notice things when you don't if you're preoccupied with feeling sorry for yourself.

Hangovers and horses. Could it get any worse?

Of course it could.

"Lady Tara Chayne, we're being followed. And not by guardian angels."

"Tara Chayne will do. Titles get cumbersome."

I grunted.

"I'm not surprised. Your partner warned me that we might be stalked. He sensed watchers who weren't close enough to read. Are they friends or enemies? Enemies might be more fun. Guardians? I see a lot of rat people." Her tone suggested that she found being of interest to bad people particularly flattering.

"I don't know. You're right about the rat men. I don't recognize them, though. They're grays. John Stretch would use ones I know. And his own kind." I didn't recognize any of the humans, either.

The followers weren't together and seemed unaware of one another.

Me. Me. I wasn't alone. Moonblight had people interested in what she was doing, too. We might each have our own stalkers.

Hell, for that matter somebody could be watching those weird dogs. Or they might be agents dedicated to exposing equine treason.

I had to admit that equine treason was a stretch, even in an unlimited universe.

Moonblight shifted course next intersection.

She had been hot to get those tracers to Trivias Smith.

But, more than I, she didn't want the transaction witnessed. Why mark the swords if the creeps who took delivery had reason to be suspicious?

My steed stomped on in the lee of the gelding, resolutely indifferent, just getting through another day. I wondered if she wasn't blind and navigating by sound and stench.

Tara Chayne's beast definitely had a horsy pong.

55

Moonblight headed for the Al-Khar, to that same entrance I'd used before. We found the watch post womaned by the usual greeter. Helenia looked "rode hard and put away wet." I couldn't help saying, "I hope you had half as much fun as it looks like."

"I'm hoping with you. But I'm not holding out much. I don't remember much after you turned up. I woke up in my own bed, alone, and don't remember how I got there. I don't know what happened to Merry. He didn't show up for work. Why are you here?"

"Barnacles?"

"Huh?"

Tara Chayne watched and listened and didn't say anything. Odd. Her mouth had run nonstop till now. I told Helenia about the folks slowing us down without mentioning our destination. I said I thought that the Guard might be interested in some of them. I was still explaining when Target and half a dozen heavyweights stopped to gather relevant points before charging out into the weather. How had Helenia summoned them? A capability worth keeping in mind. And why, before she heard my full tale of woe? Because she knew Moonblight was accustomed to premium service?

That I doubted.

This was Relway ground.

The devil himself turned up. I had to go back over the

high points. Meanwhile, Target and his playmates exfiltrated to the street.

I was wrapping my sad tale when the prisoners arrived, three men and a woman. Target announced, "The rat men scattered like rats, boss," ever so proud of his wit. "Just being close to our place had them spooked."

I reminded Relway, "They were grays. Not John Stretch's people."

The little thug's brushy eyebrows leapt up. "Yes?"

He assumed he was about to hear a confession.

"I need somebody to run a message to Pular Singe." That smelled like a way around an admission of trafficking with undesirables.

"Certainly. Target, see to that. Helenia, give Mr. Garrett what he needs to write his note." He struggled with a self-satisfied smirk. "And you two." He wheeled on the captives, isolated a man and the woman. "I thought I made myself clear yesterday."

At which point I penetrated Preston Womble's excellent disguise. The woman, then, must be his habitual associate, Elona Muriat. She was tricked out as a homeless immigrant. I could get no fix on the real her inside the rags. She wouldn't stand out on a busy street.

How come she hadn't lived up to her reputation for being elusive?

Which wakened a curiosity as to how people were tracking me so easily.

So. Pals Womble and Muriat had been tagged, without noticing it, while they were in custody before. I had been tagged, too, somehow, probably more than once, since Strafa and I made our first visit to Shadowslinger's place.

Had that little blonde gotten close enough? No. Little Moo? She'd been all over me twice, but I had Shadowslinger's guarantee that she wasn't part of the tournament mess. I checked the dogs, all staying close and low-key. I wouldn't be able to blame anything on Brownie, either.

When or how didn't matter. Neutralization would be good enough.

Helenia showed me where I could scribble a note to Singe, which I did assuming that Target would sneak a peek. I stated the facts. Unknown rat men were following me. They were grays who did not seem friendly.

John Stretch would be interested. The sneakers weren't his people. That meant that someone out there dared risk his wrath.

John Stretch hadn't been challenged since he became top rat. Rat people liked his ways.

Moonblight went on not saying much but stared hard at Relway. Her self-satisfied smile assured everyone that the Director was an open book. Relway himself showed discomfort, so even he could be intimidated by Hill folk who were there to look him in the eye.

He took it out on Womble and Muriat, who had made bail by agreeing to sneak for the Unpublished Committee.

Tara Chayne smirked at Relway's back.

I folded my message and handed it to Target, no seal. No point making the Guard's specialists bust their butts to make it look like it hadn't been opened. Target understood. So did the Director. There would be no rowdy secrets hidden in there.

Hell, knowing that, there was no point to looking.

But he would, just to make sure that I wasn't counting on him not to because it wasn't worth the trouble.

Thinking so much makes my brain swell up and the backs of my eyes hurt.

Relway asked, "Want a couple of my men along while you wander?" not being the least thoughtful except toward his own people. They wouldn't have to work as hard if they could just tag along.

Preston and Elona hadn't been freelancing. They had made the mistake of letting themselves be noticed.

"Not necessary," Tara Chayne said, lapsing fully into Moonblight mode. "Show us an exit point away from where we entered."

"An excellent strategy, ma'am."

Ma'am? Really? That got my attention, and Tara

Chayne's even more. I was startled and amused. She was . . .
One eyebrow began to twitch. Relway's eyeballs were
about to get boiled in their sockets.

He looked as bland as milk soup.

Tara Chayne had the lastest, biggest, and stinkiest laugh.

Relway told Helenia to take us across the heart of the
Al-Khar to an exit opposite her home post, a level down
because the Al-Khar stood on sloping ground. Our critters
made the journey with us. Both horses insisted on delivering proof of their innate evil by leaving handsome piles in
the busiest work areas.

Tara Chayne, being what she was, dared tell Helenia,
"Be glad the dogs are all bitches." She glared at the oddly
built red top, perhaps suspecting unauthorized thought-
usage of a female descriptive/pejorative in a nearby Civil
Guard mind.

Good boy me, I kept a straight face.

56

We were coming up on Flubber Ducky. I kept fighting the snickers. We had no shadows at the moment. Tara Chayne was not feeling talky. I was positively chatty. For me.

Moonblight pulled up, eyed the costume and props shop, finally spoke. "That was fun, pulling the little man's ears."

"It was," I admitted. "But don't make a habit of it. Deal Relway is the most dangerous man in Karenta because he's one of those guys who knows he's right. The gods themselves are behind him. He is the anointed voice and fist of justice. He has no reservations and doesn't care who gets in his way, except tactically."

"Stipulated. He could be dangerous. But I suspect you exaggerate that danger as much as you do everything else. This is the shop, correct?"

"Yes."

"I'll look inside." She swung her mount in to the horse trough and hitching post. "Did anyone touch you while we were inside the Al-Khar?"

She had been insultingly reluctant to allow anyone near her.

"I don't think so."

"It could be important. You had two tracers on you when we started. You picked up another passing through the Al-Khar. We'll tamper with that one so it looks like it doesn't always work right. That might be handy later."

I chewed some air, surprised. "Helenia touched me a few times. Light brushes. I didn't pay attention."

"Because you're used to women touching you during a conversation."

Well, yes. That happened. Tara Chayne had done it herself sometimes when there wasn't room for me to increase my personal space.

"They have a good book on you at the Al-Khar."

"Oh." I hadn't thought about that before, but it exactly fit Relway's character, tracking the habits and foibles of people of interest.

I dismounted without embarrassing myself, to the amusement of the sorceress. She had a book on me herself, inside her head. "We'll have you cavalry-qualified in no time."

Oh my gods! I suffered a horrified flashback. What if they had put me in the cavalry when they called me up? What a nightmare, that would be rolling along still because I would still be down there slumbering under the cacti right now if I hadn't been lucky enough to have become a Marine.

"Get it together, Garrett. I'm beginning to see why Strafa fell so hard. You're as distracted and flaky as she was. How have you stayed alive so long?"

"You aren't the first to ask. I don't know. I wasn't always this way."

She shrugged, indicated the shop door. We waited as a party of eight came out, stage crew folk from the World led by Heather Soames-Gilbey. Heather eyeballed me, Tara Chayne, the mutts, and the horses. "Garrett." And that was it. She focused on the horses, stifled a grin. She knew about my horse allergy.

The World gang moved along, Heather shaking her head.

Tara Chayne and I seized the opportunity to operate the otherwise unoccupied door.

The first native we encountered was the little baldish

guy I'd nicknamed Feisty, real name Pindlefix, that Belinda
had sent to party with the Dead Man. "Welcome to Flubber
Ducky, sir and madam." He pronounced "madam" old-
fashioned, so it sounded like "my lady," from ages past. Pretense was part of the Flubber Ducky ambience. "How
might we be of service?" He recognized Tara Chayne's status. But then he decided to see what her man-toy looked
like, recognized me, and became all attitude. He sputtered
instructions to me to get my ugly butt out while trying to
summon some security thug to chuck said homely delecta-
tion into the nearest horse apple pile. Somebody hunt one
of those up if none was readily available.

Moonblight extended a delicate, timeworn hand to
Feisty's throat, as though to make sure that nub really was
an Adam's apple. Pindlefix continued his rant in silence.
People gathering for some flash entertainment suddenly
lost interest.

It took Pindlefix a few seconds to realize that his voice
box was hoarse de combat. "Frog in your throat, buddy?"

He was fresh out of interest in me. Life was all about the
dread in front of him: a Hill creature who could silence him
with a touch.

A mercurial sort, Feisty adjusted, becoming deeply ob-
sequious in just a few heartbeats.

Moonblight told him, "Gently, sir. Gently. A good customer service attitude is critical to business success. Don't
you agree?"

Feisty mouthed, "Yes, ma'am!" and bobbed his upper
torso as if she were a foreign dignitary, or he was from one
of those countries where their heads are always wobbling
up and down.

"Much better." She touched his throat again. He regained the power of speech, sagged in relief. "I can make
that permanent."

Feisty stopped trying to suck up by expressing his grati-
tude.

I let him know, "We just want to browse."

"As you will, sir. As you will. Summon me if I can help. I will be close by."

I told Tara Chayne, "I wish I could do that trick." Hoping my envy wasn't totally obvious.

"It takes a special talent. Otherwise every husband would do it." Grinning, she began to wander, pushing her fingers and nose in everywhere. Pindlefix stuck close, usually staying ahead to warn everyone to look out, till someone came in talking a sizable order. With Feisty distracted, Tara Chayne invited us into a back room normally closed to the punters. Teams of seamsters were building costumes. Tara Chayne found one little man stitching a long, heavy, hooded robe, vaguely clerical, in dark umber with planned embroidery rough-sketched in yellow chalk. She asked nothing and touched nothing but made the little man intensely aware of her presence. She got scary close, maybe shedding girl cooties.

He worked slower and slower. She watched for several minutes, then told me, "I've seen enough. Almost time to go. But first." She snagged a seam ripper, pushed me against a wall, and began to pat me down. I remained polite and tolerant on the assumption that she wouldn't make an unwelcome move in public. Though she might not be able to resist the absurdity of trying in the middle of this particular crowd.

"Turn. The other way. Stop." She poked around behind and above my right hipbone, used the seam ripper. The tailors stopped work to watch. She showed me a small canvas patch. "Tracer One, gone."

"I saw that but never thought anything about it. Singe is always fixing stuff without telling me."

"Turn a little more. Did that Helenia creature put her hand in your pants?"

"No."

"The Guard tracer got in there somehow." She tugged at the top of my trousers.

"We were going to keep that one, remember?"

"Spoilsport. I wanted to go fishing. Another quarter turn, please. Perfect." She patted my left calf down, down, and down. "Weird. Where did it get to? Hey. Pull your pants leg up."

I did that. She frowned some, thought some. "Lift your foot but keep your toe on the floor. And here the devil is!" Then, puzzled, "But how did they manage this?" Using fingernails and the seam ripper, she worked on something on the top center back of my shoe, above and behind my ankle. "Did you have some bimbo hanging on your leg while you were fighting the zombies? This one has been there awhile."

I no longer bothered arguing that they hadn't been zombies. "You told me to wear comfortable shoes. But I didn't."

"What?"

"I didn't. I forgot. These are the ones I always wear. That patch is really clever. I don't know when or how the damned thing . . . you wouldn't notice it even if you were looking."

"Not with untrained eyes. Besides tracer elements, there are spells making it hard to see. Which didn't work against me."

"They do say it ain't bragging if you can do it."

She gave me the fish-eye. "I'll let that opportunity slide." She held both tracer patches to the light. It looked like the clouds might be thinning outside. "These are first-rate."

"Same craftsman made both?"

"I think so. Someone compelled to engage in commerce."

Behind that lay prejudices seldom encountered anymore. Times are tough and even the gentry likes to eat.

Moonblight did something quiet and clever that stopped work while the tailoring crew boggled. She summoned a rat, a big bull that didn't want to play. He fought her. He lost. He responded to her will. He came to her.

She had just finished working a tracer into the rat's back fur when Feisty arrived with smoke streaming out his ears. He bellowed, "What the hell do you people think you're doing?" Bellow being relative, considering his limitations. "Enough is enough. . . ."

Moonblight's fingers wove patterns in her lap. Pindlefix approached her showing the same ferocious reluctance that the bull rat had.

Tara Chayne welcomed him with love talk he'd never heard from a girl, so deftly that I failed to mark the transaction when she fixed him up with his own inherited tracer.

Scary, scary, scary once I got to brood on it.

The woman might be able to manipulate anyone that way.

Maybe I should have Kevans Algarda rig me a custom anti-Moonblight hair net.

She told me, "Don't worry your pretty head. You're special to me. Well, look here. It's time to go."

57

Second time running I boarded my horse without error or mishap. Brownie yipped happily, impressed. Admittedly, though, my dressage needed polish.

As did the mare's. She was strictly economy transportation.

Moonblight asked, "Did we learn anything useful there, professional investigator Garrett?"

"Yeah." Like, don't underestimate Tara Chayne Machtkess. She was more than just another dirty old woman.

I said, "It was your idea to go stir them up."

"But isn't that your special technique? Don't you always do that before you show off your formidable skills as a survivor and observer?"

She was playing with me again. "There was nothing to observe. My partner already interviewed the noisy little man and one of his associates. They were exactly what they showed the world. Pretentious, sure, but only peripherally involved in the tournament absurdity and ignorant about what happened to Strafa."

Why couldn't it be simple? Just once. Just march straight to whoever hurt Strafa and hurt them back with usurious interest.

Tara Chayne said, "The red tops have caught up." Proving that she could be attentive when she wanted. I had only just glimpsed a brushy-haired, bearded Preston Womble myself—though why I was sure that was Womble in the underbrush I couldn't explain.

"The Director was blowing smoke when he yelled at Womble and Muriat. He was just irked because they got noticed."

"Oh yes. He is a bad, bad man."

Sarcastically said, still having fun.

We headed for the Trivias smithy. Master Trivias came out personally, maybe sensing that someone of standing had arrived.

Moonblight offered him a cloth-wrapped object the size of the box lunch you can purchase from street vendors. "There are six pieces."

"That should do." Trivias was more deferential than I figured he should be. He placed the box on a massive wooden workbench, untied the cloth, unfolded it, opened an actual used lunch box gently. Inside, on white cloth, lay six teak-colored cylinders three inches long and less than half an inch in diameter, like fat sticks of dark chalk. He was impressed. "Oh! And you created these overnight?"

"I did. It's a knack." She was pleased by his reaction.

They commenced what sounded like people in vaguely related trades talking shop. I took the opportunity to roam the smithy and try picking the brains of the staff. Most were happy to explain their trade to an old guy who wasn't just interested when he wanted to yell at somebody for not having been born perfect. I learned from them and played with the dogs till Moonblight said something about the swords needing to be peace-bonded in their sheaths, which the law demanded, so the tracers would activate when the swords were unsheathed the second time. Trivias ought to discourage experimentation by his clients when they took delivery. If one of those old men was sensitive, he might feel the surge when a tracer went active.

So I volunteered, "Don't deliver the damned things sheathed. Lay them out like you want them checked over. Let them sheathe them, then bond them and bum-rush them out."

They eyed me with that numb look people get when they have missed the snakebite obvious. It was a look I knew well because it turns up on my clock most every damned day.

Tara Chayne snickered. "Now you see why I keep him around."

Trivias nodded. "I had an intimation that it couldn't be for his prowess in the night lists."

Ouch!

Brownie distracted me. She remained a big fan. And she still wanted to play. I followed her out of the shop. We amused ourselves by playing "Where's Womble?"

Tara Chayne joined us. "I'm finished here."

"Were you actually hitting on that little man?"

"I was. I had to give up on you."

I felt my cheeks get warm.

She laughed as she readied her gelding. "Let's go find the priest with the knot on his head."

So. Yes. Off we went, horses, dogs, and people, with spies behind, probably aware that they had been spotted but going through the motions anyway.

58

"I've been thinking," I told Tara Chayne, around a mouthful of a particularly nasty vegetable mix, foully spiced, inside a wrap, the principal ingredient of which seemed to be gritty sand.

"I worry when you do that."

We were having a snack at a place called Sasah. She was known there. She had enthused about the menu till I agreed to stop in. I regretted my weakness. I blurted, "This stuff is awful!"

Probably not the smartest reaction, which I realized a moment too late. So, naturally, I dug the hole deeper. "It has peppers in it. Bell peppers. Everything here has peppers in it. That's sick. When I'm king of the world, as soon as we finish off the lawyers, we're going to torch the pepper fields."

She managed a strained smile. "You'll just add a new angle to the underground economy. Your friends will start planting secret pepper patches, picking and packing by the peck."

I answered with a gagging noise.

The nearest staffers, having overheard, looked baffled. Mental defectives every one, they couldn't imagine anyone thinking that peppers were anything less than a blessing from the gods.

This town is afflicted with way too many freethinkers.

It does take all kinds, granted. But the world could get

along fine without those nasty vegetables and, more so, without people compelled to put them in stuff that actual living, breathing human beings have to eat.

Sasah's was a sidewalk café. It was in a fine part of town, just outside the Dream Quarter, including many big homes owned by top priests suffering through their vows of poverty and service. The mutts were right there with us, drawing scowls from other patrons and passersby. Staff did not have what it took to face us down, though.

Tara Chayne spotted me trying to slip my lunch under the table, where I had no takers. Not even contrary Number Two was hungry enough. "I rest my case. These are stray dogs. They never skip a chance to eat."

"I believe I get it. Bell peppers don't suit your taste."

"Yes, dear. That's true. Anyway, what I was thinking? Should we be making a move on this priest before his crowd collects those swords?"

She chomped down a gob of pepper chum like it was good. I tried to keep my reaction off my mug but couldn't help recalling that she'd wanted me to kiss her.

She gave me a big smile. Her teeth needed work. Surprising, that, what with the options available to people with all the wealth and power she had. Colorful bits of pepper had gotten caught between several teeth.

"What are we going to do about your sister?"

"She's good right where she's at."

"But . . . family . . ."

"Yeah? You try being her kin."

But they lived together.

"Hell, Garrett, she'll be fine as long as they think they can use her. Her personality being what it is, she might gloom them all into committing suicide before they figure out that she's useless."

She slapped some coins down. Too much. Showing off. "Sorry you didn't enjoy it. Next time you pick, your treat. Let's go find our man."

While I was working out which foot went into which stirrup which way, I glimpsed Helenia, in ineffective disguise. Her crew included Womble and Muriat. The Director must be letting Helenia hone her field skills.

Family evidently meant a little something to Deal Relway.

"I have a cunning plan," I announced. "Once we spot our man we turn him in to the Unpublished Committee. The Specials can handle the dirty work. They can make him disappear and then turn up at my place to chat with my partner. The Operators would never know."

If she and I weren't obviously involved, we would retain our freedom of action. Relway sticking an oar in anywhere wouldn't surprise anyone who followed current events. That was what the man did.

Nobody, not even the Palace, could get him to stop.

I added, "The more I think about it, the better I like that."

"There is a problem."

"Yeah. It might look like Relway was being manipulated. He wouldn't want anybody to get that idea."

"You're entirely too cynical. And you ignore the benefits of open communication."

"Huh?"

"Just explain what you'd like done and why. Clearly. In short, declarative sentences. No asides. No parenthetical remarks. No historical justification or moralizing. The way you wish clients would talk to you."

That sounded like . . . Hell, I don't know what. Maybe just something too sensible, simple, mature, and unlikely for human nature, especially if the nether half of the transaction was a nut job like Deal Relway.

"Overwhelming as a concept, isn't it?"

"What is?"

"The idea of just stepping up and saying something."

She was messing with me, ringing the wind chimes of a lesser and tangled intellect. She pranced back to her original point. "There would be a legal problem if our man is a priest. Clerics are supposed to be handled inside their churches even when they commit civil crimes. That goes back centuries."

I understood. There had been a stink about exactly that a few years ago. The Courts of Resolve ruled for a temple where a priest had committed rape, citing past practice, common law, and the fact that the cult was signatory to the Canonical Accord of the Synod of TiKenvile.

Life gets stupid once politics become involved.

"Got you. But what do you want to bet the Unpublished Committee doesn't give a rat's whisker?"

It wouldn't go down in total secrecy, either, if ever it happened. Relway would want the priests to know that they enjoyed no more immunity than any other criminal class.

Yes. His branch of the Guard probably felt strong enough to begin eroding clerical privilege employing a time-honored tool: divide and conquer.

Every cult wanted to cut the rest down. There were hundreds to cut.

Relway might see a chance to establish the primacy of the Unpublished Committee because one of the Operators was a priest in TunFaire's biggest denomination. If we told him.

59

We were clip-clopping along the Street of Dreams now, nearing its head and the great brooding mass of Chattaree, epicenter of the Orthodox rite. "Been a while since I've been here," I said. There had been a case involving a bad magister back before General Block, Deal Relway, the reform of the Watch, and the founding of the Unpublished Committee. Hardly anyone knows about it. The Church handled its own dirty laundry, as ever it had. I told Moonblight the story, without nostalgia. We had by then dismounted and established ourselves on a public bench across from the cathedral.

"I knew a little about it," she said, never asking why we were sitting when we could go inside and do. Chattaree was open to anyone who wanted to wander in. That was part of its function. "Constance had your background examined when it became obvious that Strafa was smitten and determined."

That surprised me but should not have. I said so.

Tara Chayne responded, "Strange as the Algarda family dynamics are, they are a family. Insular in the extreme, yes, but you're right. Constance is thorough. She probably knows more about you than you remember yourself. Her unreserved approval must have surprised a lot of people."

Did that make me uncomfortable? Yes, it did. "It stunned me. I expected to be chopped into dragon chow first time Strafa took me to meet her formally."

"Presumably Constance saw something no one else but Strafa did. Quickly, anyhow. I believe I'm starting to get it." She gestured, including Brownie and the girls, which only made me feel more lost.

She chuckled when I moved a few inches away. "Garrett, sweetheart! You're safe here. I don't do my business in public."

Must be stamped on my forehead in big red letters that don't show up in a mirror: THIS IS GARRETT, BORN TO BE GIVEN A HARD TIME. ENJOY. And, yeah, lately I've been working on clearing enough upper-level forehead to make room for all that.

I concentrated on Chattaree, which was as much ugly citadel as it was cathedral. Never much for ambling through TunFaire's remoter past, I didn't know why the original builders had gone for hideous instead of sublime. And, as I did every time I beheld it, I wondered, "How many millions of old-time marks did they spend to pile all that limestone up that high?"

"Do you really care?"

"Not much. It wasn't my money."

"The elders are still servicing the loans taken to finance the construction."

My opinion of Chattaree was down there with snakes' balls. It was like the architects and artisans had made special efforts to generate the maximum in repulsion, but then had changed their minds partway through the project. They had started with a step pyramid, but once they got thirty feet above ground level, new management decided to plant a cathedral where the rest of the pyramid ought to go. That part was all soaring spires covered with curlicues and gargoyles.

Chattaree dominated the skyline for miles around.

I considered the steps. There were forty, of irregular height and width. Brownie came and rested her chin on top of my right leg, considered me with big brown, soulful eyes. Wishful thinking took me back to the unreasoned devotion Strafa had shown. I missed her bad. "You think Strafa and I would have made it?"

"I don't see why not. She was devoted to you."

"I got that part. But for a total genius she was a little simple. Somebody promised me she would be trouble because of the way she lived before we got together."

"The Algardas put that darkness behind them."

"Not the family complications, just the fact that Barate never let her grow up."

"Because she was spoiled, you mean?"

"Partly that. And she never developed any life skills. Though I'm not quite sure that nails it, either. Kind of, the way she lived before she met me was the only way she ever lived, so that's the way she'd always expect things to go on being."

"I see. You could have seen some of that. But don't forget that when she was much younger and even less worldly, she managed a line tour in the Cantard without anybody to hold her hand. She bore down and dealt when the fire began to burn."

"Oh. Yeah. I didn't think about that. Where was she? Never mind. I don't want to know. I'd hate it if it was somewhere even worse than where I was. She never talked about it. Not even once."

"Do you talk about it?"

"No." Since I never see any of the guys I was down there with anymore.

"Case closed. You worry too much about stuff that doesn't matter."

"You aren't the first to notice."

"I don't think our man is going to come out to us. Let's go find him. We do have other stuff to do."

60

We took the steps in stages. I was uncomfortable leaving our four-legged associates unsupervised. Horses can be counted on to do whatever is evilest, while dogs are easily influenced by those who are dedicated to doing evil—although, honestly, I was more concerned about rustling than I was about critter misbehavior.

I wasn't sure why.

Tara Chayne was probably right when she insisted that our Civil Guard shadows would take care of any problems. They needed us as stalking horses.

They might even defend the dogs against the sort of refugee retards who thought pups belonged in the communal pot.

We ran into an old priest coming out of the cathedral, long, lean, and tired looking. He would have gone to the old priests' home by now if there were any young blood taking the cassock. The lack was surprising considering the state of the economy.

Most of the traffic consisted of religious personnel. It was the middle of a workday in the middle of a week. Honest parishioners ought to be occupied elsewhere—unless somehow involved in preparations for the upcoming holy days, Day of the Dead and All Hallows'.

This old boy had one foot in the next world and was thinking on the wonders ahead. He nearly jumped out of his frock when Tara Chayne asked, "Father, can you help us?"

Rheumy gray eyes focused. His gaze darted, assessing us instantly and possibly too accurately.

He opined, "I suspect that I don't have enough time left. I do have an assignment. But helping is the mission that God has given me, so I must do what I can." Meaning he would go through the motions, though he would be wasting time on spiritual deadbeats.

Old people can be scary the way they read you, and this one was old even to Tara Chayne Machtkess, who said, "We're looking for my father's cousin, Brooklin Urp. Which was his name before he took orders. My father is dying. He had a big fight with his cousin when they were young. I don't know what they fought about. A girl, probably. I just care about getting it all settled so there aren't any problems with the probate."

She lied smoothly, with conviction, sounding like a complete weasel, which I noted and would not forget.

Unskilled liars focus on details and try to put a shine on their own part in whatever they're trying to pull together.

The priest said, "I don't know a Brooklin Urp, madame. I've been at Chattaree forty-nine years." And now began to show more interest in me than her. Frowning. "I've seen you before."

"I'm no regular but I do come to services." The absolute truth. Only God Himself could fault me.

I didn't remember him, but that didn't mean we hadn't collided at some point. My most recent visit to Chattaree had been full of excitement and had taken place under cover of darkness.

Tara Chayne pulled it back to her. "He changed his name after he turned into a priest." Which was not unusual. New priests often want to break with their pasts. "Dad says he should be easy to find because he has this big thing on his head, over his eye." She touched her hairline, indicating the wrong side.

"Bezma? I didn't think . . ." He shut up. His face shut down. "That doesn't sound like anyone here. I'm sorry. Now I do have to get on along to my shut-ins."

We let him go. He had given us something. And I could pick him out of a gaggle of old priests if I had to drag him off for tea with the Dead Man.

Tara Chayne said, "Bezma must be important."

"Maybe scary some, too."

"We maybe ought to look into that. Why scary, I mean. He didn't scare me."

"But you're you."

She agreed. "There is that."

I grunted, said, "I guarantee, some of the people here, back in the shadows, are very scary. Was there a connection between the tournaments and the Church before?"

"Not obviously. But we never got the angle on the Operators. The ones we saw were dead. Those who weren't dead made the bodies disappear before we could use them or identify them."

Shadowslinger, I recalled, had been accused of being a necromancer. Of course, there was little that hadn't been laid on her at some point.

Might the Operators not have a last-man-standing game of their own going?

61

Once inside we approached a lay brother near the confessionals. His task seemed to be to control traffic and to provide information. Cynical me, I suspected that his real function was to separate the faithful from those who came looking for the truth—whatever that might be in any given case. He might be skilled in estimating the depths of pockets, too.

Tara Chayne repeated the truth she had created for the elderly priest out front, so convincingly that I was halfway ready to believe that she had a cousin lurking here.

I don't know what the lay brother thought. He nodded and delivered the occasional friendly smile that did not synch up with anything being said.

"There is no Brooklin Urp here, ma'am. But I am sure that you want to see Leading General Select Secretary for Finance Izi Bezma. I didn't know he had family outside. The consensus here always has been that he must be a virgin conception hatched out of a gargoyle's egg."

There was an inside joke involved, for sure. It seemed some Chattaree people were not enamored of Izi Bezma. "What kind of name is Izi Bezma? Is he some kind of foreigner?"

Moonblight hit me with a ferocious look. The man was supposed to be family!

But he was Brooklin Urp when he was one of us.

"Don't know." He did not miss our exchange of looks. "His ancestors came to TunFaire before the war."

That would've been a ways back. Maybe far enough to coincide with the start of the tournaments.

Maybe we had lucked onto something.

Maybe this mess wouldn't be all that hard to pick apart after all.

"I'll just go see if Magister Bezma is in." He snickered.

Tara Chayne asked, "Is that funny?" with a compelling quality in her voice.

"It is. He's famous for never leaving Chattaree. He hardly ever leaves his office suite. He has his meals brought in. You can expect the Hammer of God to fall if the Leading General Select Secretary for Finance visits you on your patch." Then he explained, for the uninitiated, "The joke is, he's never not in. But that doesn't mean he'll see you. Back in a flash, folks. Anybody wanders in with a question, tell them I'm on my way. They need to confess, the confessionals on the ends are manned and neither priest is busy."

"Got it." I gave him a thumbs-up. He went. I reminded Tara Chayne, "He never leaves the premises."

"As far as our new friend knows. There can't be many hundred-year-old priests with the same disfigurement."

Couldn't be many people at all anymore, outside the blisteringly poor. Cosmetic sorcery has become a competitive field. You can get subcutaneous cysts, small scars, and the like eliminated for the cost of a meal now that there is no demand for sorcery in the Cantard.

I thought back to my Chattaree-related case. The villain then had not tried to disguise what he was, but he had laid on layers of misdirection. Shouldn't I expect the same this time? Or more since the tournament scheme involved legally unsanctioned violent death?

A thought out of nowhere. "Don't know why I haven't asked this before. What was all the excitement on the other side of the Hill last night?"

The humor fled her face. "It was what we guessed. Two young people from the Hedley-Farfoul family—fraternal twins—lost their lives, quite nastily. The little blonde you described, and her companion, were in the neighborhood but not involved—though Chase found one witness who said that they had attacked the attackers, too late to help the Farful kids." Chase would be her man Denvers.

"A thing that might have been a wolf-demon, its ties indeterminate, got torn up as badly as the twins. It escaped lacking an ear, some scalp, its tail, and its right forepaw up to whatever a wolf's fetlock is called. The patrol collected the pieces but had to give them up to the Civil Guard. The corpses, too. The forensics sorcerers are still working the area. They wouldn't cooperate with Chase or Orchidia Hedley-Farful."

"Don't know that name."

"It would be strange if you did. The twins' mother. She keeps a low profile. She was an assassin-mage during the recent unpleasantness. The best there ever was."

"The Black Orchid?"

"Her."

"Bless me." Nothing would express my amazement any better. "I thought the Black Orchid was like an urban legend of the combat zone."

"At least nineteen people on the Venageti side wish she was made up. Not to mention all the unknowns who got between her and her targets."

"So, basically, the Operators didn't think things through and maybe screwed the pooch."

"They did that when they killed Strafa. But yes. Orchidia was never more than a rumor here. No one who hadn't worked with her knew much about her. Once her obligation was fulfilled, she hung up her blades and became a housewife who did consulting work for the Crown. And I don't mean consulting as a euphemism. So. Last night's events will definitely bring the Black Orchid out of retirement. We may be in a race to avenge Strafa before she avenges Dane and Deanne."

I vaguely recalled an odd girl the kids called Deanne Head running with the Faction. She hadn't found what she wanted there and had moved on. "I might've met the girl."

"She and Kevans were acquainted. I don't think they

were friends. Deanne may have had her eye on Kip Prose, too, for a while."

I sighed. "So the stupid tournament really has started."

"It's started. It'll get uglier if we can't abort it. The Guards who cleaned up weren't Specials or Runners. Could that mean anything?"

It meant she had a fine paranoid mind tuned to sniff out wicked possibilities.

Suppose those first red tops weren't the real thing? Suppose they were agents of the Operators cleaning up so no useful evidence would be left for the real tin whistles? That might be why the forensics sorcerers were working the scene now.

Clever, maybe, but foolishly lethal to try—unless you got away with it. But till some mob found themselves drowning in a pond of their own blood, showing the world the full price of stupid, it was sure to happen eventually, probably sooner than later.

I didn't think any professional bad guys would be dim enough to yank the Director's beard that blatantly. They tried to get along. Even Relway knows when to pretend not to see. It would take an amateur convinced of his own brilliance to try, one with a built-in case of supreme upper-class arrogance and disdain. Or maybe someone who had spent his whole life isolated inside a cathedral, never getting any true flavor of the real world.

62

Tara Chayne said, "It occurs to me that it wouldn't be bright of me to challenge anyone as powerful as this one might be, here in the seat of his power."

"And he would recognize you, wouldn't he?"

"He would. And that greeter called him Magister."

"He did, didn't he? That isn't good."

The title indicated that, in addition to the job with the long-winded title, our man had been accredited as a magic user inside a denomination that doesn't like wizards or sorcerers much.

Moonblight said, "I'd better go check on the horses."

"Good idea. Brownie might not be able to hold off a determined band of rustlers. I'll stay here. It's been a while since I've confessed."

The confessionals remained unused. Only the end two showed signs admitting that a priest was available.

"Excellent thinking." She took hold of my right ear, tugged. I tried to yank away, not knowing what game she was playing. She held on. "Hold still. You want to be able to hear." She muttered something harshly melodic, tugged again, then slipped a little finger in. I am nothing if not the consummate professional. I endured.

"This will be good for about a quarter hour."

The hearing in my right ear became ten times as acute, difficult to believe and hardly comfortable since it now seemed I could hear the tiniest scratch or creak within a dozen miles, including Brownie's fleas farting. I'd have to get used to it fast or not be able to take advantage.

I started to ask for advice.

Advice was not available. Tara Chayne was gone.

She'd been on my left. I hadn't heard her go.

Intriguing.

Murmuring voices approached from the direction Greeter Man had gone. Feet scuffed limestone. I wondered why the builders hadn't used a more durable stone where there would be heavy foot traffic. And I got myself into the priestly side of a confessional booth several doors from either one that was supposed to be in use. Seeing in would be tough. Seeing out was almost as feeble. The booth reeked of cheap wine and urine.

Every priest might not be at ease with the filth that he had to hear, so ugly, yet, ultimately, banal.

Few sins are unique.

Not a time to philosophize, Garrett. Time to act. To eavesdrop.

The greeter said, "And they're gone."

"It is quite impossible to deceive your sharp eye, Niea."

"There is no need to mock me, sir."

"No need, but . . . Apologies. You are correct. You were doing your job. It seems that these people offered no cause for more suspicion than is normal with street people. Street people are, after all, why we're here."

I thought it sounded like somebody was being sarcastic.

I found an angle where the seeing out was better. I saw enough of the newcomer to understand that he wasn't the man we'd hoped to find. He was younger, browner, and had no huge blemish growing out of wild, curly black locks just starting to go salt-and-pepper. He turned slowly, all the way round, frowning. His gaze did not linger on the confessionals.

"Curious, Niea. Very curious. I wonder who they were." Not what we might have wanted.

The greeter offered descriptions that Old Bones would have applauded, and a surprising analysis. "The woman was older than she pretended and thought she was important but wanted to hide that."

"Nobility?"

"Not quite that feel, but there was that level of self-assurance."

"The Hill, then?"

"Probably. It wasn't as obvious as usual, though."

"And the man?"

"A cipher. Not what she was. A hard case. Not a bodyguard, though. He dressed badly and was poorly groomed."

"So. That would make him single. Was he her Jodie?"

"No. He was the senior partner despite pretending that he was dim and darkish. He paid closer attention than he let on."

"Civil Guard snoop? A Special, maybe?"

"Maybe. But why would they be interested in Magister Bezma?"

"Why indeed?"

I tried to get a better look. The guy expressed himself by tone quite well. He had made that sound like the query was rhetorical to him but a real question to the gatekeeper.

I tried to recall the description of the man who had traveled with the old boy who owned the wen—Magister Bezma—to Flubber Ducky's and Trivias Smith's. No one had done well delivering one. The wen had been a huge distraction to people not much interested in the first place.

I reached back for images passed on by the Dead Man. Even people not paying attention might have noted something useful.

Yes. They had. But not enough. Just enough to make me suspect that this character hadn't been with Bezma.

He told Niea, "Go out and see if you can't find some trace of them." His tone said he thought there was a good chance we wouldn't be making a run for it. "Wear your cap. I want Almaz able to spot you."

"You think they were spies?"

"We should find out if we can."

"Of course. The more I think about that guy, the creep-

ier he feels. His eyes were like a wolf's. Like back behind
the dull and friendly was somebody really looking forward
to hurting somebody."

"You're known for your discerning eye, Niea. It's why
we have you working here. You're probably right. So I have
to wonder why this man and his beard would be interested
in Magister Bezma."

Niea wanted to speculate. The other guy wasn't interested. "Put your hat on and get out there, Niea."

"Uh, yes, sir. On my way, sir."

He never named a name. I'd been hoping to hear one.

He shuffled to where he greeted visitors, produced a yellow flop hat so bright that it ought to glow in the dark. You
had to admire the genius who came up with the dye. For
several seconds I lost interest in anything but curiosity
about that. Whence had it come? How had it been applied?

Niea left the cathedral.

I didn't doubt that he would spot Tara Chayne quickly.
She had no reason to try for anonymity. She'd probably returned to that bench. There was no good reason not to
have.

Niea's boss paced. He held a brisk conversation with
himself but too softly for me to catch a word in five even
using my enhanced hearing.

He wasn't fussing in vernacular Karentine, anyway. He
was using either the liturgical tongue or something foreign.
Probably the former. It sounded vaguely familiar.

When you're a kid you know damned well you'll never
use any dead languages, or any of that dull religious stuff,
once you're dealing with the real world.

Now I grew impatient. I wanted out. I wanted to make
sure Moonblight didn't get caught in some unexpected
deep doo-doo.

63

I had a serious backup of beer dregs by the time I made my
getaway. My luck was in. Garderobes were available inside
the main entrance. They were a public relations gimmick.
The barons of the Church could point and pat themselves
on the back for that glittering example of the benevolence
of their corporation. Anyone could stroll in and use the pot,
no charge—though there was an alms box handy, painted
scarlet, flanked by saints famous for having distributed
their fortunes to the poor once they got religion.

Nothing said that they had beggared themselves for the
benefit of the impoverished rather than the Church, though.
The professionals are always all about tithing, then giving a
little extra for the building fund, the education fund, the
this fund, the that fund, the other fund, the fund-raising
fund.

How much of the poor box fell into clerical pockets instead of finding its way to the truly needy?

So. I shared space with stench and flies for a bit, then
eased on out of Chattaree, not far behind the man called
Almaz, whom I had heard receiving instructions just before
I was finally to make my toilet run.

Did Niea know what Almaz really was?

He was for sure not your everyday parish priest.

And he was no longer alone, which explained why he
was only now getting around to heading down all those

steps, toward Tara Chayne and that bench, which she shared with a fellow sporting an incredibly bright yellow hat.

Two feet separated Niea and Tara Chayne. Niea had his hands planted on his knees, sitting at attention, staring straight ahead like a nine-year-old in deep trouble. Moonblight was being conversational. He was being all "Yes, ma'am" and "No, ma'am."

It would have been amusing had not Almaz and three unpriestly priests been bearing down.

I hung back, both curious and calculating the value of an unexpected arrival. What would Moonblight do?

She registered the approach of the ill-wishers. She did nothing to tip Almaz and his gang.

Brownie and her pals were invisible. Had they gotten bored and gone home to the graveyard?

I couldn't have that kind of luck.

In fact, it was time for luck of a whole 'nother kind.

Almaz never got a chance to bark because Moonblight waved some fingers and said something my wonder ear heard but my brain couldn't process. All four men hit an unseen wall ten feet from the bench. In plain Karentine Moonblight said, "You can come out now and deal with this."

People sporting red berets spontaneously generated. Those hats all carried the Specials badge. One was Target. Another was Helenia. Preston Womble and Elona Muriat were not among the others.

No one said anything. The Specials just got busy.

If ever I'd doubted that Deal Relway was on a mission from God and knew no fear, the last doubt died. Only insane lawmen would arrest Chattaree priests on their front steps without so much as offering a charge. Almaz and his henchmen were boggled. They surrendered meekly, neither arguing nor resisting, only Almaz asking what was happening but going no further when he got no answer. He did toss a long look back toward the cathedral entrance.

Struggle was pointless. They were sure to be released shortly, probably before these red top idiots drove them all the way to the Al-Khar.

The man who had sent Almaz out watched from above, his anger obvious. Brownie and the girls joined me as I moved to a better vantage, still close enough to jump in if it looked like Moonblight needed help.

A few gawkers clapped when the Specials bound the priests' hands behind them. The clapping spread when the red tops tethered them together in a coffle.

I should roam the Dream Quarter more often. This was something new. Somehow these priests had managed to make themselves detested.

There was some laughter when Target sent the prisoners off herded by one woman not much bigger than a gnat, armed with a knobbly walking stick that she plied with the skill of a sword master. She needed to do so only once.

Target and the Specials removed their caps and vanished.

Was Relway getting crazier?

He had just challenged Chattaree to a pissing contest. Being Deal Relway, though, he wouldn't have pushed that boldly if he wasn't damned sure that the results would be happy.

First criminals, then priests. How long before he went to work on the lawyers?

I told my girls, "Let's go see Tara Chayne."

The red tops hadn't bothered Moonblight or Niea. Niea still couldn't get his mouth all the way shut.

He was staring after his comrades when I arrived. I sat down the other side of him from Tara Chayne, leaned back, spread out. "Be a great time for lunch, we'd thought to bring one."

"What about Sasah's?"

"Wasn't lunch. More like punishment for my sins."

"Plebe."

"Born and raised. Me and Brownie, too."

Big doggie eyes sparkled. I was talking about her.

"While you were hiding your light under a bushel, I introduced myself to Niea Syx here. A cool name. I'm sure he made it up. I presented our case. He doesn't believe me, but he's pretending to see the light."

"Which light? Not the one under the bushel?"

Number Two settled to her haunches in front of our new friend, stared like she was waiting for him to offer her something to eat.

"The light he'll follow will be ours instead of the one belonging to the Civil Guard. Otherwise we hand him over to them."

"We can take him home for dinner."

"Just what I was thinking."

Brownie popped up suddenly, growling.

64

Civil Guard Senior Lieutenant Deiter Scithe, an old acquaintance, appeared as though having stepped out of an alternate dimension. The hedge wizards the Guard used must have been working on stealthy projects. Scithe said, "Make some room, Garrett." Then, eyeing Brownie, "That's one ferocious killer hellhound you've got there."

"Able to bring down a woolly mammoth with one snap of her jaws. Easy, girl. The lieutenant is all right. He's just not smart enough not to name names in front of strangers."

"It's Brevet Captain these days, Mr. Garrett. And since when are you worried about folks knowing who you are? You always have your dukes up telling the world to bring it on."

"You might have heard, life hasn't gone so great lately. Just between us, some bad people have been giving me grief."

"I have heard. They've heard on up the chain, too. The Prince himself is pretending that he cares."

Tara Chayne's ears pricked up.

Mine lay down like those of a nervous mutt. I asked, "How come you're out here? You don't usually hang out with the Runners or Specials."

"Special assignment. Monitoring the Director's favorites." A sweeping gesture included Target and others who could no longer be seen.

I wondered where Helenia had gotten to. She had been the last to disappear.

"Oh, snap! And you with a family to worry about."

"Things aren't like that anywhere but inside your fevered head. I'm not here to critique their behavior. I'm supposed to monitor their judgment. Inquiring minds want to know, are the boys being deceived by the tricksey, dastardly Garrett, or does his tall tale have any real substance?"

"You're kidding me." He had to be. Strafa was dead. Shadowslinger was laid up. Moonslight had been kidnapped. There were sorcerous battles in the night. People kept trying to kill me. They thought I might be working a scam?

Senior Lieutenant—Brevet Captain—Scithe couldn't suppress a grin. "Now you know what it feels like."

"I don't get it." But I did.

He eyed Tara Chayne, Niea, and the dogs again, lazily, but asked no questions. "You need to learn to relax, Garrett. Bad as things get sometimes, they're never as bad as you make them out. The situation in the Guard isn't complicated. The Director stretches the boundaries of the law to make it work more effectively, but he never deliberately violates it."

"That could be a matter of perspective."

"Really? When only the perspective of the Guard actually matters?"

And there it was. The iron truth.

He asked, "How has it been going?"

"You just made it sound like you know that better than I do."

"Yes. We have been watching."

"No! Really?" Sarcastic.

Moonblight reached across behind Niea to pinch me. She asked, "You mind telling us your special reason why?"

Niea was trying to polish his invisibility skills. He wasn't a master, but he was good enough for the brevet captain, who took him for some random civilian who had picked the wrong place to loaf and now wouldn't run because he was afraid that would attract attention.

"Because Garrett is Garrett. Where he goes, weird shit

happens. The hierarchy doesn't like weird shit. And when the current crop of weird shit is considered, it looks like some serious villains might ooze out of the woodwork if we just stay quiet and wait."

"The hierarchy? That would be?"

He eased back, suddenly cautious, probably recollecting having been briefed about me maybe running with some grim enigmas off the Hill. "The Guard leadership. Ah. I see. You're thinking factionalism inside the Guard. I promise you, that's nowhere near as sharp as a professional paranoid like Garrett might think. Our disagreements are familial. We don't quibble about what needs doing, just about how to do it and how soon we should get it done."

Man, that sounded like he was borrowing sentiments retailed to some other pain-in-the-ass outsider recently, by somebody like the boss who had sent him to monitor the behavior of Relway's boyos.

Scithe went on to assure us, "It is a matter of inalterable policy at the Al-Khar, high and low, to see someone swing for what happened to Furious Tide of Light."

"You don't need to waste any public treasure making that happen."

"It's part of a larger picture, my lady."

I made a decision. I told Moonblight, "I'm going to tell him about your sister."

Her response was a knee-jerk natural. She began to puff up to argue, but then she reached a conclusion of her own. "That might be best." She rested a hand on Niea's shoulder, keeping him quiet while the rest of us talked. "Go ahead. I'll fill in if necessary."

So I explained why we had come to Chattaree.

"Interesting," Scithe said. He was a long, lean man now so sprawled and relaxed he was like a scattered pile of sticks at the end of the bench. "You knew this man but he didn't know you, Lady?"

"I knew I'd seen him before here. Because of his deformity. He had no reason to recognize me. He didn't seem like the kind of priest who gets out in front of the punters."

Niea stirred uncomfortably, his eyes grown big. He wanted to say something, but Moonblight's grip reminded him to keep his opinions to himself.

The poor boy was in the grip of professional angst. He had a powerful inclination to defend what, more and more, looked indefensible. And Tara Chayne wasn't going to let him argue his case.

More, he had begun to realize that we couldn't just turn him loose to report that he had heard Magister Bezma ratted out.

Scithe said, "I'll pass this on to the Unpublished Committee."

He didn't explain further.

I kept getting distracted by concerns about the relationship between Relway's crew and the rest of the Guard. Brevet Captain Deiter Scithe was Westman Block's creature. General Block was the voice of moderation and convention. But Scithe wasn't uncomfortable being surrounded by the Director's devoted thugs. Presumably the contest between moderates and extremists did not yet feature animosity.

Human nature being human nature, that would change once the Guard achieved the luxury of not having to stand united against everyone else.

I asked the air, "Isn't there some way we could lure Bezma out?"

"They might have a good reason for him not to," Tara Chayne said. "I didn't know he was a magister till friend Niea let that cat out."

Priestly sorcerers of magister status would find few friends on the Hill. Hill folks who started their own cult would find no sympathizers among the organized defrauders of the Dream Quarter.

Bezma would be safe from outsiders as long as he stayed inside Chattaree. His position there was perfect cover for one of the Operators.

Even Shadowslinger lacked a set big enough to try bringing him out against his will.

I did not miss Deiter Scithe's secretive smile.

Maybe Magister Bezma wasn't so secure after all.

I told Tara Chayne, "We blew a chance here."

"Stuff happens. Think positive. We have a name and location now. A thread to pull. A big-ass mooring cable kind of thread. It's only a matter of time till the tournament scheme collapses. If we can convince the right people to keep their emotions in check."

What did that mean? Was she just whistling past the morgue?

But she had her evil smirk on.

Lots of folks were having thoughts they weren't sharing.

Ha! I had the cure for that!

Niea looked lost.

Brownie and the girls didn't care. They did look hungry again, though.

Tara Chayne suggested, "We ought to take our new friend back to your house. Your partner will be thrilled to meet him."

The thrill would not be mutual.

Niea Syx knew plenty that he wouldn't want to share with outsiders.

65

We headed back north, me now particularly conscious that a cloud of Specials must be swarming around us. The others, excepting Niea, were relaxed. Scithe chattered incessantly, digging into how Strafa's passing might touch my connection, or lack thereof, with my former woman. Despite being married, with children, Brevet Captain Scithe was thoroughly infatuated with Tinnie Tate. Not that he would ever push past flirting—but he would certainly look out for the pretty red-haired lady.

I neither encouraged nor discouraged him. Tinnie was outside my personal orbit but not gone from emotional recollection. I lugged around a satchel full of guilt about the split. I like Tinnie. She is good people. I wish there was a way we could stay friends.

Belinda Contague crossed my thoughts.

We had stayed buds.

Belinda was unique, though. She was crazier than most.

Tara Chayne asked, "Working on your suicide program again?"

"Huh? My what?"

Then I got it. I'd drifted away again, escaping dread reality.

"I'm awake." I checked to see where we were.

We hadn't been wandering. We were only blocks from Playmate's stable. I felt like I'd forgotten something important but hadn't lost track of the fact that I needed to see my friend and to check on Little Moo.

Her I expected to be gone. Playmate was kind, caring, and gentle, but knew less than I did about the nurture of teenage girls. Especially those who were intellectually and emotionally challenged.

Lucky me, I had Dean, Singe, and Old Bones to help chip the edges off a reasonably normal Penny Dreadful.

I suffered a sudden blow to the right biceps. "Ow! That hurt!"

Not nearly as much as it might have had Tara Chayne not been older than stone and punching sideways off the back of another horse. "Stop fantasizing. Death is afoot."

"What?" I didn't see anything unusual. We were a block from Playmate's place in one of the quietest neighborhoods in TunFaire. My encounter with Little Moo could be the biggest excitement there in months. "What do you mean?"

"Just trying to get your attention."

One thing had changed. Helenia had joined us, limping badly. "Blisters," she said when I caught her eye. "I'll need to wear better shoes if Deal keeps sending me off on these fool's errands." She grimaced at each fourth or fifth word.

"Hang in there, eighty yards more. Then when we get rolling again I'll let you ride."

I should have been down off that monster already. We couldn't travel faster than Scithe and Niea could walk.

"Trouble coming," Tara Chayne warned, shifting to Moonblight mode. She hadn't lost her edge since coming back from the Cantard.

I felt the change, too. The air became charged with crackling imminence and a touch of ozone. The dogs, Scithe, even Niea felt it, as did our hitherto invisible escort. Several materialized, drifted in around our party.

The imminence faded. I sensed irritation, frustration, and impatience tempted to take a chance.

More red tops revealed themselves. They had an idea whence those sensations had come. They closed in fast. In moments they were chasing several people.

None of my companions gave in to the impulse to join the chase.

That caused another wave of irritation.

Moonblight ripped off a peal of laughter right before she gave away the fact that she was a heavyweight off the Hill.

She said something in a demonic dialect that consisted mostly of grinds and clicks and consonants. The pure jet ink of a living centipede shadow materialized overhead, legs churning, body undulating like that of a snake in a hurry. A cry of despair rose somewhere between us and Playmate's place. Moonblight spoke again. The centipede scuttled off after whoever or whatever had run away. It walked on air fast!

Moonblight said, "I've been looking to use that ever since they misspulled me in." "Misspulled." I'd swear that's what she said, though she promises that she said, "Since this mess pulled me in."

Some awful noises started up in the direction that the centipede had run. The roar of a panicked crowd followed.

"Caught them!" Moonblight crowed. "We're having fun now, aren't we?"

She didn't mean that quite the way it sounded. In midchatter she had shifted attention from the sounds to some red tops bringing two prisoners our way. They weren't coming to meet us. They passed by on their way to the Al-Khar, which lay back behind us. They nodded courteously to Scithe and winked at Helenia.

The prisoners wore clerical mufti. Collars proclaimed their professions. Civilian clothing declared them off duty. They belonged to the same litter as the prisoners taken in front of Chattaree.

Niea froze. He blanched. He stared at the bowed backs of the captives.

"Friends?" I asked.

Apparently not. "I know what they are. I've heard the rumors."

Smiling enough to reveal her need for dental attention, Moonblight said, "He's marked." Which I understood. She asked him, "Are you carrying some token that your bosses insist you keep with you all the time?"

"I don't understand."

"It could be anything. Jewelry. A badge. A uniform bit of clothing. A handkerchief with a Church monogram. Anything. Just something they gave you and told you to keep on you."

He got it, turned to gape at the departing prisoners. "They were here after me. Maybe they were supposed to kill me!" He fumbled in a shirt pocket, produced a painted wooden plaque bigger than a playing card but smaller than those used to read the tarot. It slipped out of his shaking fingers, clattered on the cobblestones. Brownie gave it a sniff. Her hackles went up. She began to growl.

Number Two and the others hurried up the now empty street, formed a skirmish line. Tin whistles who had been nearer the source of the trouble had all dematerialized again.

Niea took hold of his death card, passed it up to Moonblight. He began shaking so badly he could hardly move. More than to the terror he was reacting to the opening underfoot of a depthless abyss of betrayal.

The thing that was a hundred-legged absence of light returned. It circled above Moonblight, widdershins of course, legs flailing like the oars of a galley where the rowers were totally wasted. It looked fatter than before.

Scithe opined, "I think a new Special just got born."

"Recruit him if you want. My partner gets to see him first, though."

Moonblight studied our surroundings. Some red tops from earlier reappeared buildings up ahead, each of two pairs carrying a corpse slung from a commandeered pole. Tara Chayne muttered, "And I guess that will be that." She swatted her centipede. It shattered into a thousand fragments, each of which faded to amber and evaporated.

I had to admit, "That was impressive."

"Thank you. It was all show. I don't get many chances now that we're not at war anymore."

"Can't say as I feel sorry for you."

"Don't get me wrong. I don't want the excitement back.

I enjoy the quiet life. My sister is the one in mourning because of the peace plague."

"Then she's having a good time today, isn't she?"

"And that's why I want to leave her where she is. Hoping she'll suffer enough to realize that she's too old for this shit. You're all goggle-eyed. What now?"

I pointed.

Little Blonde stood atop the peak of a roof tree up the street, hands tucked into her sleeves in front of her, untroubled by the fact that she was three stories above the cobblestones and the weather was about to get damp again. She wore an aquamarine winter coat with a white lace collar. A little white pillbox of a hat sat cocked atop her head. Her shoes were out of sight, but I didn't doubt for a second that they were shiny black leather over low white socks. Very in for the well-to-do girl-child these days.

She offered me a slight bow and a small smile once she saw that I had spotted her. I didn't see her sidekick but was willing to bet the farm he was within stabbing distance.

Moonblight said, "I know her." Her tone was one of awe.

"Who is she, then?"

"I don't know."

"Uh . . . That don't make much sense."

"Right. All right. I've seen her before. Somewhere. But I can't remember where or when."

That was no help and I said so.

She wasn't going to apologize. "She the one who turned up before?"

"She is."

"She's cheating. She isn't what she seems. She might even be a spirit or demon."

66

We had been oozing toward Playmate's stable since the fallen had gone by, presumably off to spend quality time with the forensics sorcerers at the Al-Khar. I wondered if General Block was bold enough to have a real necromancer on staff.

Target materialized as I was about to quiz Tara Chayne. "You'll be uncovered for a while. Every swinging dick will be busy cleaning up. Be careful. Helenia? You doing all right?"

"I'll make it. They're going to let me ride."

"Keep an eye on our boy. And keep the stupid under control. The boss don't want to lose him yet."

"I'll do my best."

Target trotted after the body haulers. Those guys were drawing local attention.

I was just realizing that Target had disrespected me when I noticed Playmate and Little Moo up ahead, a whole fifteen feet away, waiting outside his office's street door.

Brownie and friends started bouncing around Little Moo. She had acquired a fresh outfit. Not something new, nor stylish, nor even that fit particularly well, but it was clean and didn't draw attention. Her expression was less bewildered. She was happy to see the dogs. If Playmate hadn't said something, she would have gotten down and rolled around with them.

Tara Chayne grunted, startled, then muttered, "Well, that was just a little bit remarkable."

I glanced over. She was looking up rather than at Little Moo. I decided to help her stare back at the sky. "What?"

The baby blonde was gone, a "So what?" to me, being accustomed to not having her in my life anyway. "And?"

"She flew away. Well, floated, if you want to be precise."

"She's a Windwalker?"

Moonblight shrugged. "Not a talent we usually see before puberty."

"Not to mention, it's just damned uncommon. That ought to make her easy to identify."

"You would think so, wouldn't you? Windwalking being so unusual that everyone on the Hill always knows the people who can."

"I have a bad feeling."

"Good guess. Furious Tide of Light was TunFaire's only active Windwalker."

"So there might be another sorcery at work."

"There must be." Her interest waned as she considered Playmate and Little Moo.

Playmate wasn't much to see, just a tall, bony black guy gaping because he saw me on a horse. He was at a loss for words except a mechanical "Bring your mounts inside. They're worn out and hungry."

"I don't have much cash."

"Singe is good for it. And it'll be at cost. I owe you big."

"Speaking of. Himself wanted me to see how you're doing."

"I'm good. Better than anybody had any right to expect." He rested a hand on Little Moo's shoulder, lightly. She stopped doing whatever it was he thought she shouldn't do. I hadn't caught what. "You don't need to keep fussing over me."

"Sure we do. You're important to us. He wants you to come by so he can check on the cancer. He might want to see Kolda, too."

"And he wants to meet the girl."

"Yes. He does."

We managed physical business while we talked, taking

the horses inside, loosening their tack but removing only their bridles. Play brought water and oats. The mare looked at me like she might be having second thoughts about my fitness to be sharing the world of the master race.

Little Moo helped Play. She said a few words, not clearly, not to me. They didn't have "Hate you!" among them.

Playmate crouched, examined my mare's left side. "You're right. You have a good eye, child." He conjured a pail of stinky salve, grabbed a handful, and slathered it onto a raw spot developing where the saddle's left-side fender had rubbed. He wanted to chide me about it but restrained himself. I couldn't know any better. I hadn't spent time in a mounted unit.

And I was known for my bad attitude toward the equine tribes.

Playmate is the goodest guy I know, but he does come afflicted with bizarre prejudices where animals are concerned. They're freaking animals, Play!

We would get into a tiff if we kept on about horses. Time for something else and I was more interested in the girl.

So was Tara Chayne. She seemed captivated and awed, uncertain, determined to be disbelieving, and professionally confused.

I told Playmate, "You've obviously been a good influence. What happened?" And, to Moonblight, "What? You see something interesting or do you just have to pee?"

"I'm not sure. Eight of one and four of the other. I can't believe it's what it looks like."

In TunFaire we see the improbable and implausible every day. The impossible comes up once a week.

Playmate said, "It just takes patience. She's a good kid, eager to please. Truly slow, though." Said softly.

"And?"

"And what?"

"Who is she? Who are her people? What's her story? You got her into less ridiculous clothes. You managed some kind of communication."

Meanwhile, Tara Chayne extended a hand, gently beckoned. Brownie and the girls surrounded Little Moo, looked to her for cues.

Playmate said, "The name she gave, once she understood what I wanted, was Hagekagome." Hah-gay-kah-goh-may.

"Really?" Definitely not TunFairen, and not likely Karentine.

"Really."

"That's a strange one. But . . ."

"You think you've heard it before."

"I do. Oddly enough."

"I do, too, Garrett. A long time ago. Near as I can tell—she is truly confused—she thinks you should know it because you used to live together. And she loved you very much."

I opened my yap to declare that completely impossible. Tara Chayne laid a forefinger across my lips. "No." Then, "As Constance told you, be kind, be gentle, and be patient. It won't cost you a copper."

"Why?"

"You would prefer to bruise feelings?"

"I'd prefer to know why I'm getting special instructions."

"She's a special child. Like none other."

"Special how?"

"Consider her your challenged little sister. That's enough to know."

I flashed Playmate a look of appeal, saw that I would get no help there. He said, "She's coming along but she's still confused. She can form sentences part of the time but doesn't make much sense with them."

I showed him my best baffled frown.

"She'll keep getting better if she's treated well."

Tara Chayne agreed. "She will. For a while."

Plaintive, I demanded, "What does that mean?"

"It means that you will treat her well, treat her right, and be gentle and loving for as long as she's with us. If you don't, I'll hurt you."

Ooh! I felt the steel behind that.

"Damn it, if . . ." No. *Rein it in, Garrett.*

I got skills. I got resources. I got the Dead Man to slash and burn through the smoke and mirrors.

I said, "Play, come by my place as soon as you can. And bring Little . . . Hagekagome?"

The girl stopped playing with the dogs, stared at me with big, sparkling brown eyes, thrilled because I'd used her name. She waited several seconds to see if there would be anything more, then turned back to the dogs.

Number Two gave me a hard doggie glower before jumping back into the fun.

Playmate said, "We'll be there. I'll have my brother-in-law cover. What time is supper?" He had to yank my leash.

Everybody but Hagekagome snickered.

67

We still had places to visit, people to see, things to do, but I declared, "We'll head back to Macunado Street now. Helenia, Captain Scithe, we'll drop you off on the way."

Those two had been keeping quiet, trying to go unnoticed, with ears the size of saucers. Helenia, though, was pleased. She now knew she wasn't a fieldwork kind of girl.

Scithe made himself look as bland as wild yogurt.

I wouldn't be rid of him as easily.

I told Playmate, "I'll let Dean and Singe know you're coming." I might have Dean boil up a kettle of grits if I had to feed a crowd.

Playmate touched Hagekagome lightly. "Would you help me in the stable?"

She bounced up, grinning, eager to help.

I looked to Tara Chayne for a reaction.

"You're trying to be clever. Get your answers from your partner."

Something smelled funny there.

"He'll tell you what he thinks you need to know."

And there it was. She thought Old Bones would keep me in the dark, too.

It made no sense.

But why did it have to now? A dab of patience would bring whatever knowledge I needed. I just hated waiting.

Playmate and the girl readied the horses. I installed

Helenia aboard the mare, who finally betrayed her true self by nipping me.

Playmate, Hagekagome, and Helenia all barked at me when I popped the monster in the snot locker. Brownie put on the same look of disappointment that my mother used to get when she was unhappy about something that I'd done.

I asked her, "You weren't my mom in another life, were you?"

Niea gasped, horrified, reminding us of his presence. Reincarnation theory was anathema to all true-believing Orthodox.

The mare just looked dumbfounded.

We delivered Helenia to the Al-Khar. Scithe did drop out there, too, only asking once if he could take Niea with him. He took "No" for an answer. The Specials faded away, too, probably because their shifts were up. We weren't far along before I spotted Preston Womble again, though.

He didn't care if he was seen, probably because he didn't care what we were doing. He was working because he had been given no choice.

I chose to go past Frenkeljean's roach wagon, where I treated everyone to sausages, including the mutts—though they got surplus that had been around too long for people to eat. Grease running up my arms, I told Tara Chayne, "Now, this is what I call good eating. Yo. Frenkle-man. Give me another one."

Tara Chayne's reaction to her sausage approximated mine to her pepper-based abomination. She took a few bites, made ladylike retching noises, and passed the rest to Number Two, who totally agreed with me. How could anybody not love a big old juice-dripping pork sausage?

Frenkeljean filled me in on local gossip. That didn't take long. My activities hadn't gotten any rumors started. Folks didn't care what happened on the Hill as long as the Hill didn't include outsiders as collateral damage.

It was an attitude I knew well. I'd shared it before Strafa came into my life.

From Prince Guelfo Square it was a short trek to Macunado, where several red tops deliberately showed themselves. I heard grumbling from neighbors who objected to the possibility of excitement.

Tough.

The Dead Man was awake. I began to feel him when we were a block away. He was playing ambush predator, but why wasn't clear. He might not know that himself.

Penny opened the door. She said something nice to Moonblight, looked down to where I was trying to make the horses comfortable. She told Brownie, "I'll get something for you guys in a minute." To me, "Can you put them in back?"

I asked the air, "What happened to the real Penny Dreadful?"

Your Church friend is most intriguing.

"What have you got?"

It is too early to concern yourself. Do as Penny suggested.

"Huh?" Did she suggest something? I must have missed that.

The dogs! With exasperation.

That let me know that I really did have to get it together. A lapse so small shouldn't trigger the impatience of someone normally little pressed for time. There must be a frustrating pattern.

Well, of course. Especially since I'd lost Strafa.

I kept recognizing it, then failing to do anything about it.

"Come on, girls. Follow me." Down a narrow breezeway alongside the house stood gates into my garden and that of my neighbor to the left. I had not, literally, been back there for years. I expected masses of windblown trash and the rotted memory of a gate. I found neither.

The breezeway was clean. The gate was new. "That Singe," I muttered. "She's spooky efficient."

The breezeway had been cleaned after someone had tuck-pointed the mortar on the side of the house. A few missed slate chips told me that some roof repairs had been made, too.

The girls and I found Dean on the back porch, juggling bowls. Penny was there to help, a pot in each hand. She must have opened the back door. Dean couldn't budge it. It seldom gets used and is stubborn about sticking shut, then is tough to close again once you do get it open.

They set out four bowls of mutt grub in ridiculously generous portions. Penny's pots held water. Somebody had gone out of his or her way while I was off earning a living. Sic. Such as that was.

The pay had been lousy lately, and, being self-employed, I had me a really cheap-ass boss.

Penny reddened slightly, patted a couple of canine heads on critters too busy to notice, grumbled, "Got to go answer the door."

There was no point raising my concerns with Dean. That old boy has no shame when it comes to spending my money.

"You girls be sure to thank the nice man." I glanced around, saw essentially a desert the size of a handkerchief. Dean had started an herb garden once upon a time but couldn't keep it up. Singe kept talking about creating a fancy flower garden, but she never got past the talk. She was too busy.

Penny and I were too damned lazy, and I didn't care, anyway.

Gardens are nice when somebody else does the planting, watering, weeding, and grooming. I used to hit the Royal Botanical Gardens about once a year, then more often after I hooked up with Strafa.

I went back around front wondering if we should put the horses back there, too, and arrived just in time to see Penny close the front door behind Dollar Dan Justice, then to spot a slowly moving Playmate, with a patently worried Hagekagome, turning onto Macunado off Wizard's Reach.

With no audience but the girl, Play was revealing how weak he really was.

I should have a man-to-man with his dopey brother-in-law.

Accumulated circumstantial evidence suggested that the jerk just wanted Playmate to hurry up and die so he could get hold of the assets, sell them, and squander the proceeds on fool get rich schemes. He had done that with Play's sister's inheritance.

68

Penny was waiting to let me in. I heard talk from Singe's office. John Stretch was using his deadly calm, lethally reasonable voice. I thought he would use that voice to explain why he was going to kill you. He was the only one doing any talking.

I raised an eyebrow to Penny. She shrugged, raised one hand with all five digits up, said, "The others are over there," indicating the Dead Man's room, then stepped around me to wait for Playmate and Hagekagome.

She knew they were coming, though I hadn't said anything and they were still out of the Dead Man's range.

Old Bones was peeking again.

Dean had not brought out any refreshments. Maybe our guests were less than totally welcome.

Perhaps he was being encouraged to restrain his natural hospitality.

I could endorse that attitude wholeheartedly, and about time, too!

You are dithering.

And not even recognizing it. I checked Penny. She was on tiptoe at the peephole. Satisfied, I advanced boldly on Singe's office.

It was like a rat people clubhouse in there, minus the weed smoke and beer smell. There was plenty of rat smell, though, all with anger and fear behind it.

Singe was at her desk, making notes. Her brother stood

beside her, dressed to the nines for a rat. Dollar Dan Justice and an unfamiliar mutant almost my size stood to either side of the doorway. The rest of the room was filled with four smaller, poorer, rattier rats who were much more gray than my friends. They were a different breed.

There are three kinds of rat people. Most humans don't pay attention, but the two breeds that aren't John Stretch's and Pular Singe's kind are uncommon. The differences hark back to the species of rats the creator sorcerers used in their experiments, and to the methods they used.

There are only two species of ordinary rat, ugly and uglier.

Rat eyes turned my way. I wasn't stricken shy. "Some of these guys were on me and Tara Chayne a while ago."

John Stretch said, "They were. They've never been so bold. I thought this might be a good place to ask them why. And thank you for sending word."

"Best place in town for asking questions." Speaking of Tara Chayne, what had become of her?

She is in the kitchen with Dean.

So at least one of his minds was not fully occupied.

Singe rewarded me with her most penetrating look. "Tara Chayne? Really?"

"Moonblight, if you prefer. Got to call her something."

Her look shifted subtly. The subject would be tabled. It would come up again. I didn't get why. She had to know that the sorceress wouldn't be that kind of problem.

I asked, "What's their story?"

Singe said, "My apologies on behalf of the rude interloper, gentlemen. This is Garrett. He owns the place and on that he tends to presume."

The sleekest gray said something in dialect.

It is impenetrable to me as well, though I will pick it up. It descends from Karentine as spoken by the poorest poor two centuries ago.

John Stretch hunched his shoulders, nodded. He had been included. He was not yet used to hearing voices inside his head.

Singe bobbed her head, too.

Tara Chayne strolled in. She had equipped herself with my own favorite oversize tankard. It was filled with fragrant Select Dark. My mouth watered. She said, "Stinks like the monkey house in here."

The grays cringed.

The other rat people were not much more at ease.

They all knew what she was, and maybe who. Her forbears might have had a paw in the creation of their lines.

She asked, "Have we learned anything yet?" Then slurped.

His mouth watering, too, John Stretch said, "Friend Evil Lin here was just starting to tell us a story."

Singe said, "Perhaps you could translate, Humility."

"But . . ."

"Is anyone better qualified?"

"No." He just did not like to admit that he had contacts as low as these people.

Everybody has somebody to look down on.

"Evil Lin?" I asked.

"They favor names like that. Wicked Pat is his littermate."

Wicked Pat. I knew that name. He was a gray tribal leader.

I'd had nothing to do with grays before today. The opportunity hadn't come up.

69

"This is what we learned," John Stretch said. "They were sent to keep an eye on Garrett, the thinking being that even my people would pay no attention. They have a long history with this employer, whose identity they would not give up, possibly because they don't know it."

"Cheap," Moonblight grumbled, evidently to herself. Her intensity said she thought she might know who. Maybe she knew somebody who had a habit of employing grays. She didn't want to share, though trying to hide anything in my house was futile.

Or maybe she was just feeling the beer.

She should have eaten that sausage.

She thinks her sister was responsible. The timing is intriguing. I cannot determine when contact could have been made. Grays have almost no grasp of time, relative or exact. Past and future become entangled with the present.

But?

Indeed. Oddments in Niea's mind suggest Moonslight made occasional nighttime visits to Chattaree.

So why didn't he react to Moonslight's twin when we showed up?

He never saw her. He is the day man. He heard talk. Nor did Moonblight behave as though she was intimate with someone inside. He has not developed a conscious suspicion, but he has begun to feel an itch.

That's what Old Bones is good for. Making connections,

probably not only with stuff from inside Niea's head but also clutter from the shadows in Tara Chayne's, spiced with whatever he got from the rest of us.

Tara Chayne began to grunt and scowl. She muttered, "The more you get done, the more they want you to do."

Penny stuck her head in. "The dogs are done eating. I'll get them ready to go."

So. Playmate and Hagekagome had arrived. Penny had put them in with the Dead Man.

Exactly. Get a move on.

"A move on? What, where, and why?"

"We are now off to see my sister. To rescue her if we're asked. Actually, maybe, to capture her and drag her bony ass back here."

I was confused.

Not unusual, sadly. Please hurry.

"Just me and Tara Chayne? Against the Operators?"

Indeed. They are old. You are fast on your feet and fierce, and you will be accompanied by four savage hellhounds. And, likely, by half the Specials and Relway Runners infesting TunFaire.

"But . . ."

Quickly. Speed is essential. They may move her when they hear that these four have been captured.

Damn! Oh yeah! More of their kind might be coming around.

Singe said, "Then I have to go, too." She worked herself out from behind her desk, then through the crowd. John Stretch gestured to Dollar Dan. Dan nodded. He stepped into the hallway to await the body he would guard.

Singe snarled in exasperation.

She doesn't want to be treated like a girl.

I said, "Don't waste time arguing. Put on your walking shoes."

Penny announced, "I want to come, too."

I need you here, dear.

"I can take care of myself."

Indeed. I would not question that for a moment. You

*should certainly do better than some members of the party.
You use your head to a purpose higher than damaging fists
and nightsticks. But I do require your assistance. Singe and
Garrett will be out of the house while we have outsiders on
the premises. Dean cannot handle them if they become un-
ruly.*

Meaning Dean was too feeble to chuck the bodies out
by himself if badly behaving guests had to be tossed overboard.

Penny turned surly but acquiesced.

I wondered if Himself did truly need her or just wanted
his pet kept out of harm's way.

He didn't clue me in. He did give me a swift mental kick
to get me moving.

Pouting, Penny headed for the back of the house. Tara
Chayne and I scouted a route to the front door. Dollar Dan
twitched nervously while watching for Singe to catch up.
He lurked in the open doorway while we two stood snarl-
ing on the stoop, watching an unfamiliar teen boy mess
with the horses in full view of a couple of tin whistles who
did nothing about it.

Moonblight spat, muttered angrily, considered doing
something that would have been unpleasant for the boy.
Then she cocked her head, listening.

The Dead Man was on the job. The boy eased past us on
the steps, eyes on Penny, who awaited him with a smile. He
was too scared to appreciate that, but he couldn't make
himself stop.

Old Bones didn't waste mental capacity letting me know
what was going on with the boy. Nor did I much care just
then.

Brownie and crew charged out of the breezeway. Well,
she and the nameless pair charged. Number Two sauntered,
not at all eager to seek further adventure. She wanted to be
napping in the shade while the flies buzzed round.

I told her, "Stay here if you like."

Big, dumb-eyed stare. And maybe a doggy sneer. No. No
way.

I needed to get shot of her. Really. She thought I might do something wicked to her pals if she wasn't there to stop me.

Tara Chayne fished something out from under my saddle blanket. "Oh, lookee." It was leather, sticky on one side, had odd figures inked onto the other, skin side. They might have been tattooed there while the skin's owner was still warm. "You and the bitch certainly are two of a kind, aren't you? My. This is another tracer from that same craftsman."

Number Two and I glared at each other. That snap had been hard on us both.

Tara Chayne cocked her head again. "Ah. He was just paid to install the patch. He doesn't know what it is. He doesn't care. He was hired by some generic 'old guy.'"

Ah, the sharp eyes of youth. "That does reduce the suspect pool."

Tara Chayne tucked the leather tracer into a pocket. "I'll use it to start a false trail later."

"Think it was the Operators?"

"Probably. But you have to wonder how the little girl does it, too."

I should. Now that it had come up. It seemed she only watched, but how did she know where to be?

"Where is that woman of yours?"

Woman? Of mine?

It took a few seconds.

Amazing lack of prejudice in the old gal now, when there were no rat people to witness. She meant Singe.

Dollar Dan missed it. He was still on the stoop, getting restless, too.

Tara Chayne said, "We'll walk the horses. They're worn out." And our rat companions couldn't keep up if we rode.

Singe turned up wearing a complete new outfit. She had gone for an adventuress look, tan and plain, with one of my old hats slit to fit her ears. She carried a staff that I hadn't seen before, made of bamboo strips bound and glued together. It had to be eight feet long. I stared but didn't comment. Maybe she had a blade for its end hidden down her pants leg.

Any red top who got close would wonder, too.

Singe would have been grinning were she made that way. Her body language practically screamed that she was in a great good mood. She went out of her way to be nice to Dollar Dan.

Dan had decided to back off and bank the fire. He would become part of the environment, which was his job assignment anyway.

Singe was amused. She was bright enough to recognize the new strategy.

I think she was secretly flattered.

I began to suspect that there was a marginal chance that Dan could wear her down.

On the other hand, I doubted that he had enough time. He was mortal.

70

Tara Chayne said, "Let's take these beasts back to their stable. It's practically on the way."

"Suppose your sister isn't in good enough shape to walk?"

"We can only hope. We'll drag her. You grab one foot, I'll grab the other, and we'll both hope she's wearing a skirt." She faked a dreamy look. "And no bloomers."

How much of that poison was real?

The Machtkess girls certainly had an eccentric love-hate thing going.

Singe fell in beside me. "I just had to get out of the house."

"Huh?"

"It is getting stressful. I am not equipped to mother a human teenager, nor do I have the force of personality to manage an old man who refuses to act his age."

"Problems with Penny?" I faked an anxious look around. "Actually, she's pretty well grounded. Just don't let her know I think that."

"She is. Near as I can tell, being younger than her in actual years."

There was that. Singe was a full adult rat person, but in universal time she was two years younger than Penny.

Her people grow up faster, living shorter, harder lives. Ninety percent have been dead awhile by the time they reach my age.

"Hey. How has it been with Vicious Min? I never even thought to check on her."

"Dean handles her with help from Humility's women. I have other things to do."

Her distaste was plain.

I shrugged. "Whatever works."

"Penny helps a lot, too."

"Good for her. She's finally making herself useful." I was jabbering on semiautomatic. Something didn't seem right. Brownie and the girls weren't happy anymore, either. "Has His Nibs gotten anything out of her?"

"What he has gotten is frustration. He says something inside her keeps adjusting as he finds ways in, as soon as he begins to probe."

We stopped briefly while an old-style Sisters of the Biting Oracle party, playing brass instruments, crossed an intersection in front of us. That took a while, not that they were deliberately holding up traffic. They were old. The youngest was Tara Chayne's mother's age—and she was strutting out in front of her grandparents.

Sons and grandsons helped carry the instruments.

Tara Chayne said, "I enjoyed their music more when I was Penny's age."

"The nuns probably enjoyed it more when you were Penny's age, too. And that was wicked of you."

She had attached the leather tracer from under my saddle blanket to an instrument case being lugged by the last grandson in line.

She might have been my kind of girl when she was Penny's age, too. Unfortunately, back then I hadn't been old enough to be born yet.

Singe and the dogs were sniffing the air now, and Dollar Dan's head bobbed like a pigeon's as he looked for something. Only Tara Chayne seemed at ease.

Then I spotted the gargoyles.

They were watching from atop a white limestone building up ahead. There were eight of them. Their heads bobbed the way Dollar Dan's head was.

I told Moonblight, "That looks like more your expertise than mine."

"What does?" Then she spotted the critters staring at us in apparent confusion. "I see." She laughed.

"What?"

Neither Singe nor Dollar Dan got the joke, either.

"You thought they were demons, didn't you? Real gargoyles, maybe? But they're regular animals. We just don't see them inside the wall anymore."

Closer and looking from a steeper angle, I could see that she was right. Those were flying thunder lizards and yes, of a sort not seen inside the city lately. Other people were beginning to point and wonder, too.

The gargoyles seemed unhappy about being on the city stage.

We kept moving. They kept fidgeting, watching us in a way that left me sure that we were the reason that they had come to town.

Moonblight told me, "You are one lucky son of a bitch, Garrett."

"It ain't luck, it's mad skills. What did I get right this time?"

"You lucked out. You caught that boy marking your horse. If you hadn't spotted him and I hadn't slapped that tag onto that baboon's bassoon—"

"It was a two-reed flute."

"—those monsters would be all over us now."

I was getting my mojo back. Instead of screeching, tearing my hair, and refusing to believe her, I observed, "That would constitute a whole new angle on the art of murder."

"Well . . . Not really. But this might be the first time in your lifetime that anyone collected flying lizards and imprinted them with a target."

For no rational reason I thought aloud, "The Black Orchid."

"Not hardly." Amused. "Orchidia is a hands-on girl. If she wants you dead you'll be smelling the cognac on her breath when your lights go out. This was set up by somebody who wanted to be far away when the excitement started."

"Me for sure?"

"Yours was the horse that got marked. Though I will stipulate that the kid might not have known it was your horse. And the baddies probably want anybody with you to go down, too. To ease the pressure later."

I grunted. The boy probably figured that the smaller horse had to belong to the woman.

We were just yards from being directly in front of the limestone ugliness. The thunder lizards were three stories up, making noise enough to be heard a block away. Had they had any brains, you might have thought they were arguing about what to do.

A singleton squawked and flapped clumsily off toward the musical nuns.

You could still hear them playing, faintly.

71

Moonblight revealed her talents once more, showing no originality at all. Her best trick seemed to be that giant flying centipede of darkness.

Singe asked, "Is there an alpha with those things?"

I did not understand, nor did Moonblight.

Dollar Dan, that clever fellow, did. "Most flying thunder lizards do not show gang behavior. Flock behavior? Those up there feature a red-and-blue crested helmet growth. I believe that makes them a carrion-eating breed."

I was lost. But he was right about what looked like big tumors on top of their heads. They were buzzards that would kill something when nature's rhythm let them down.

I was big on thunder lizards as a kid. You saw more of them back then. I thought I knew all about them. Now I knew that I didn't.

Singe explained, "I believe they hunt singly but call each other when they find a carcass, cooperating to fend off competitors. My question is, in a group situation does one animal take the lead? If so, we should capture that one and have Dan take it to the Dead Man."

"Good thinking, Singe!" Truly excellent. Scary excellent. Though Dollar Dan wasn't excited about the role she had chosen for him. He didn't argue with the logic, though.

While we convened our committee, the gargoyles got on with business, the main feature of which was a massed plunge straight down.

Moonblight's centipede bought us precious seconds by wrecking the foremost monster and rattling the others.

I produced the lead-weighted oaken head knocker I supposedly always carry, and actually had remembered this time. It was my favorite instrument of applied mayhem. This time it didn't give me the reach I wanted. Those things had wingspans of five to eight feet, the widest I'd ever seen inside the wall. Plus, they had plenty of claws and thickets of teeth that stuck out at seven different angles. I thought Dollar Dan might have been optimistic about them being carrion eaters.

Dan produced a truncheon similar to mine. He would be in serious trouble if the tin whistles caught him carrying that. Not that he was breaking any formal law.

The common law, the unwritten law, the law that says humans get to make it up as they go along where the Other Races are concerned—especially with artificials like rat people—was being badly abused here. Nobody wanted to see a rat man armed with anything resembling an actual weapon.

A rat man with a nightstick might get the idea that he could hit somebody back, or even whack somebody just for being an asshole.

Singe, however, had that staff that would cause less comment, she being a girl, and it had some real reach. Plus, as instantly became obvious, she had snuck in some training in the art of fighting with big-ass sticks. She destroyed three of those ugly turkeys in about that many seconds, stepping, grunting, twisting, thrusting, and thumping like she was working her way through a floor exercise.

The rest of us would have backed off to watch, mouths agape for flies to nest in, if those gargoyles not yet demolished hadn't decided to get the hell gone.

A particularly bold monster, the one who had gone to scout the nuns, stayed to watch from the flock's original perch.

A tin whistle whose uniform had shrunk in the wash arrived. There were no longer any weapons in evidence. Dan and I were cleaning cuts and whining. Singe was leaning on her staff looking dreamy. Moonblight was poking fallen gargoyles and rifling pockets in the weird net vests they wore strung between their long necks and the hips of their stubby legs. The fat red top was too winded and stressed to grab witnesses who might not tell him the same lies we would. He puffed, hands on knees, staring in disbelief at the scattered beasts. A widening circle of emptiness developed as potential witnesses made themselves scarce.

Folks just didn't want to spend their afternoon telling red tops something the tin whistles didn't want to hear.

Moonblight drew the fat man's attention by bringing in her centipede. That made clear what she was. "None of these creatures is dead, Officer, but they're all broken. There's another one up there."

I thought she meant the watcher but then noticed bits of ragged brown felt hanging off the edge of the roof. Her centipede had gotten one more as the gargoyles made their getaway.

She added, "I can have it brought down if you like."

"No, ma'am. That is entirely unnecessary." She being what she was, he was eager to please and to avoid inconvenience. He didn't give a rat's patootie about the rest of us. We must be servants. She was between us and him, anyway. "Other Guards will arrive soon, I'm sure. They will clean up and see what the witnesses say. How may we get in touch if it becomes necessary that my superiors disturb you?"

I had trouble keeping a straight face. I almost lost it when Moonblight gave him her sister's name. I got an ugly look for that.

The moment the fat red top turned to greet the next tin whistle, Dollar Dan asked, "Does this mean that it is too late to take one—"

Moonblight silenced him. "We didn't get the right one."

We looked up.

The remaining gargoyle wilted slightly, then concluded that it might have a brighter future elsewhere. A demonic centipede might be sent to visit if it stayed here. It launched itself in a frenzy of flapping.

"Did you see?" Singe asked. She was staring up at the building beside the limestone ugly, a redbrick pile almost as hideous. It stood some taller with its sloping roof and whatever was above that.

"I did not. What? I was engrossed in the gargoyle's getaway. I was hoping it would smack into that half-timbered place over there. What did you see?" I figured she'd seen some other exotic from outside the wall, meaning maybe we ought to get braced for another adventure.

"There was a little girl up there. Just standing on the slate. Dressed too heavy for the season. A nice blue coat. She went away walking with nothing underneath her feet."

"I see."

Tara Chayne nodded thoughtfully. "Hmm." But she kept looking in the direction the gargoyle had fled. "It might behoove us to fade away before someone with more status, nerve, and initiative, who doesn't care who we are, turns up."

Yes. Some Guards wouldn't be afraid to hold us up all day for having committed the sin of making them work.

Tara Chayne gestured at Singe and Dollar Dan, got them moving, then me and my mare, then moved out herself, walking rearguard.

We hadn't gone fifty feet before I found myself swarmed by dogs.

They had vanished while gargoyle weather loomed. They crowded in close now, not confident of the threat's end.

I suspected that they might have some dark collective memories of deadly hunger from the sky.

We nearly made a clean getaway, but the dreaded somebody with the exaggerated sense of self-importance did turn up and start hollering for us to hold it right there. He had a big, shiny Specials badge on his beret.

"Nonsense," Moonblight said. "Turn into that alley."

Dollar Dan did so. Singe followed. Garrett and pack, with pony, chugged along behind, neither arguing nor questioning. Surprised, Singe asked, "Are you feeling all right?"

"No need to be a wiseass," I snapped, and kept moving, thinking I knew what Moonblight intended. And she did it, putting up a visual barrier that would make it look like we had dashed into that alley and off the face of the earth.

She was in a generous mood. She left no booby traps, humorous, humiliating, or dangerous. She caught up. "A shift in plans. I want to see Barate before we go after my sister."

"That will cost time. They could move her."

"I understand that. I'm trusting your associate to live up to her reputation."

Singe preened.

"We can. Home it is, then."

72

We were near where Strafa died when I realized that I had called her mansion home. Well. Wasn't that interesting?

Barate wasn't there. I hadn't expected him to be, but it made sense to check and not have to backtrack. Now we had to hope that he was at his mother's place. We didn't have time to hunt him down. If he wasn't at Shadowslinger's, I'd agitate for forgetting him.

We found Race and Dex in the kitchen. They lacked sufficient work. They were mildly pickled and had yet to think about starting their suppers. We warned them to look out for unfamiliar visitors. Tara Chayne told them to take our horses back to the stable where she had hired them.

We grabbed some small loaves of hard bread and traveled on.

Singe warned me, "The dogs are getting worn out."

"So are mine."

The joke didn't work. Mine seldom do. My sense of humor doesn't work for anybody but me. "They can drop out whenever they want. They can stay here, go back to the last place, or head for Macunado Street. Or they can even go back to the cemetery. Nobody is making them follow me."

Tara Chayne blew out a couple of gallons of air in otherwise unregistered derision.

I tried to ask why, but she wasn't inclined to be conversational. I had disappointed her. And we had reached Shadowslinger's door.

Singe and Dollar Dan had to stay with the dogs but weren't resentful. They were all allowed inside the entry foyer. Tara Chayne and I went to see the sorceress. I was anxious to move on along. It looked like it could rain later. Singe can have problems tracking in the wet.

Barate and Dr. Ted were in with Shadowslinger, who looked as awful as ever even in a coma. Both men seemed worn down but in good spirits. Barate volunteered, "She's showing progress. She's moving fingers and toes. She even opened her eyes once."

Ted said, "She wasn't seeing anything, though. Her pupils responded to light, but she didn't track."

Tara Chayne said, "You're wasting too much worry on her, Barate. She's indestructible. She'll be back making us all miserable long before we're ready. Probably by the weekend."

"Harsh, but I hope you're right."

"Of course I'm right. I'm always right. The only time I'm not right is when people don't agree that I'm right. I'm still right then. I just lose an argument to a fool who isn't. Garrett wants to tell you about our day."

Not really, but I did so anyway, in detail, same as I would have with the Dead Man.

Barate announced, "I'm getting curious about that little girl. Tell me more about her."

"There isn't anything more to tell. Ted. Can Constance hear us?"

He shrugged. "I can't get a response. But that might only mean that she can't respond. Why?"

"Just curious." Then I did try to tell Barate something else about the little girl, but I didn't really have anything.

He mused, "That all sort of rings a bell somehow. I don't know why. Windwalkers don't go active that young. Strafa was precocious but she showed no promise till she hit menarche." He grinned at Ted.

Ted said, "Look at you, using fancy words like you know what they mean."

"He's always had a knack for faking things."

We all turned, startled.

Richt Hauser stood in the doorway, but he hadn't spoken. Kyoga Stornes had, from behind him. Kyoga looked decidedly grim.

Barate asked, "Did something happen?"

Bonegrinder said, "We've been standing here listening."

Both men came in. The room was getting tight. It threatened to get tighter. Mashego stood in the hallway, ready to do servant stuff if needed.

Then Tara Chayne said, "Those kids last night! Oh! Richt, I'm so sorry!"

So there I was, totally lost. Bonegrinder wasn't married. I hadn't heard about any illegitimate kids.

He was generous enough to explain. "The twins were my sister Margete's grandchildren. We all doted on them."

I hadn't paid close attention but thought I'd heard that an allergy to marriage ran in the family.

Once again it appeared that failure to marry was no guarantee against catching parenthood.

Bonegrinder muttered, "Their mother will lose it. There'll be hell to pay now."

He didn't explain. I didn't understand but didn't get a chance to ask.

Satisfied that I had gotten friends and family updated, Tara Chayne said, "I was hoping you would come with us when we go get Mariska, Barate. Kyoga, Richt, you're welcome to join us. Kyoga? Are you all right?"

Pale, Barate's friend had settled onto a chest. He sat there hunched over like a man suffering grievous stomach pains. He did not respond the first time Tara Chayne spoke to him.

"Kyoga Stornes." She employed a distinct Hill lord's voice, arrogantly certain of its power and rights. "Speak to us."

"Uh . . . Uh . . ." He was struggling with some huge conflict. "I don't get it. It isn't possible. I've got to be wrong. But what if I'm not? I can't let Meyness . . ." The battle was leaking now. It made no sense even with him trying to articulate it. Even Barate couldn't guess what the hell his problem was.

Tara Chayne said, "Barate, I'll defer to you. You're the polished Kyoga-with-the-vapors wrangler. Do something."

He had these fits all the time?

Sighing, Barate stepped over. He clapped a sympathetic hand on my right shoulder as he passed. We were now comrades in tragedy.

Ted eased closer to Shadowslinger. I did so, too, feeling slightly odd. Not that long ago I'd spent days that seemed like months sitting watch over Morley while he was in a coma. Now my grandmother-in-law was roaming the twilight between here and the other side. Another creature, in a similar state, lay in the house on Macunado, in the very room where Morley had begun his recovery.

Too many people I knew were hanging around death's doorstep lately, after too many others had gone on through already.

Barate gripped Kyoga's shoulder the way he had mine. He squeezed hard.

Kyoga barked, "Hey! Barate! What the hell?"

"Come back to the land of the living. Let us in on the secret."

"Secret?"

"What the drama stylings are all about."

Kyoga looked around like he was suspicious about finding himself with all of us.

"What was that all about?"

"You didn't get it? You really didn't feel it? Tara Chayne . . . Didn't you have a thing with my father when you were Feder's age? About the time when you were involved in your own Tournament of Swords?"

This was the first I'd heard about that. She denied it. "That was Mariska. She's had round heels since she was twelve . . . Oh. Oh my God!" Her eyes grew improbably huge, or so it seemed because normally she tended to squint. "No way! That's just plain freaking impossible! Meyness died in the Cantard!"

Dr. Ted looked as lost as I felt. Barate and Bonegrinder looked stricken numb, and, watching from outside the doorway, Mashego definitely looked bewildered.

"You're right." Tara Chayne shuddered dramatically. "It was him! It is him! Why didn't I see that?"

"Maybe because he's forty-some years older and everybody knows he's napping six feet down a thousand miles away from here?"

Tara Chayne went on working it out for herself. "They never sent a body back, but we all knew he was dead! And yeah, he is an old man now. And a priest. But the wen . . . Gross. It should have made me think. But back then it wasn't much more than a birthmark and he kept it covered with his hair or a hat."

All right. I saw the shocker now. We all did. Our pal Magister Bezma could be Kyoga's missing papa, Meyness Bismar Stornes.

Bonegrinder blurted, "The priest who warned you off the tournament because he has Mariska . . . He's Meyness?"

Kyoga launched the perfectly reasonable and critical question, "If that priest really is my dad . . . why the hell hasn't he been in touch?"

Moonblight assured him, "We'll ask him about that, Kyoga." She went silent. We all did. Constance made some kind of weird noise. It might have been her stomach commenting. Moonblight moved to where she could stare down at Shadowslinger, thoughtfully. "I wonder . . . No. Can't worry about that now. Let's go get my sister. That would be the biggest inconvenience we could offer the Operators." She shoved through the crowd. "Garrett. Come on. Who else is with us?"

Everybody, initially. Even Dr. Ted, after tarrying to instruct Mash and Bash, both of whom had collected in the hallway outside Constance's bedroom.

73

When we left Shadowslinger's hovel, we hustled straight to Moonblight's place. She wanted to pick up some tools that might come in handy if we ran into supernatural trouble.

That took only a minute, but during that minute Kyoga and Bonegrinder had a change of heart and deserted us. I'm not sure why. A second minute went to Tara Chayne giving Denvers special instructions. Then it was a quick trek southeast, Dollar Dan leading, essentially reversing the route we would have taken had we come straight from Chattaree to the Machtkess house. The place where Moonslight was supposed to be was barely five blocks from Prince Guelfo Square and the home of Frenklejean's porkly magic. The area featured masonry operations and those who prepared the brick and stone that masons used. Too, there was a place that produced tombstones and one that burned specialty cements for mortars. The neighborhood had a distinctive odor after a productive day. In among the shops and storage buildings and manufactories were the homes of the owners and a few tenements that offered housing for workers. It was a glum and dusty neighborhood on the best of days.

It was late enough that most places had shut down for the day. Dusk threatened. A glance skyward left me suspecting that we would be getting wet again soon.

Dollar Dan's arrival spontaneously generated rat men. He and they chatted. They were nervous because of the human crowd. They were awed, too, because Dan could hang with notable humans and Pular Singe, too. They were afraid to get close to Singe. She was next to royalty among rat-kind. She should not be troubled by peasants.

I had no difficulty considering her royalty. There never was a rat person like her. Only John Stretch came close. She was a celebrity. She was a heroine. She might become a saint.

She was a huge source of pride to all ratkind and better known there than her dim-candle sidekick, me.

She had no brief for what of that attitude she did notice, which she blamed entirely on Dollar Dan.

Dan came over. "They are getting ready to move the woman. They have been doing that, off and on, all afternoon." He raised a paw. Moonblight wanted to launch an immediate sortie. "Patience, please. Hear me out first. Orders for the move came hours ago. Then those orders were countermanded. Then, just a while ago, someone angry rolled in wanting to know why the move had not been made, apparently because Moonslight's keepers are supposed to be able to anticipate their boss's desires."

I have worked for bosses like that.

My jaw hung. It wasn't alone. Singe rasped, "Who are you, Poindexter, and what did you do with my Dollar Dan Justice?"

Dan lapsed into drooling idiocy instantly. Pular Singe had praised him. She had called him "her" Dollar Dan Justice.

He got over it fast. He was back to business in seconds, describing the inside and outside layouts of Mariska's "prison."

Barate whispered, "Did they just roll in there and map it?" The information was detailed.

"Some rat people have some amazing talents." Singe, while unique, was not alone in not being a big lump of dumb with whiskers and ears. Barate had seen it himself, back when, but I chose not to remind him that some rat men can commune with their unmodified cousins and use them as scouts. That shouldn't get spread around, especially on the Hill.

An intelligence resource like that would be massively useful to any villain. And I'd bet that the possibilities hadn't gotten past Singe or John Stretch. They probably had plans for dealing with the evilly ambitious.

I asked Dan, "Have they scoped out the tactical situation?"

Again Dan failed to commit to stereotype. "They have a plan and an alternative plan, in shock-and-awe style."

He produced a map, crudely drawn on ragged-ass scrap paper. The lighting left something to be desired, but the damned map worked.

I said, "One change, I think. Instead of taking the risks that come with a break-in, why not let them come to us? The only way out, if they want to sneak, is through the storage lot to the alley. Which would be perfect for an ambush. Right?"

Dan said, "Let me talk to Mud."

Ted whispered, "Why wait? Why not just blast in from three directions? They couldn't handle that."

"Coordination problems. Somebody would go early. Somebody else would go late because they didn't hear anybody else moving. And the baddies would be ready because somebody would make noise and give the whole thing away. Plus, we could end up fighting each other in the dark."

Dan came back. "Mud Man says you are a genius, Garrett."

Singe said, "Which shows you how well Mud Man knows him."

I said, "Well, of course I am. My mom always told me so."

Actually, she was talking about Mikey when she said that. Me she told, over and over, that I would end up in the gutter unless I made at least a half-ass effort to live up to my potential.

Oh, sigh. The past is never as shining as we like to remember. And it never turns us loose.

Whispers ran among the rat men. There was a stress-out squeak from Tara Chayne as regular rats of unusual size scrambled around among us. So. The little scampers made the dread Moonblight nervous.

Dan said, "They're about to move out, exactly the way you guessed. We need to be ready."

74

Four people accompanied Mariska Machtkess, surrounding her in a loose rectangle. Front left and right rear were gray rat men of the sort we'd seen earlier. Neither Dollar Dan nor Mud Man had mentioned their presence.

Deliberately? Probably. But it didn't matter much.

Moonslight didn't look like she was under duress. She was talking steadily, too softly to hear but obviously deeply unhappy. I wished I had my magic ear back. Be interesting to know why she was feeling blue.

We should know soon enough. I meant to drag her straight to Macunado Street.

I gave the ever-so-clever signal: "Get them!"

Pounce! And multipounce! The bad boys got neutralized before they understood that they were being hit. Likewise, and especially, Moonslight. She, for one breath, looked like she meant to resist, then lapsed into a resigned "this is too good to be true" attitude.

"Tara Chayne. You're getting sly in your old age. I never felt a thing. And you my twin." Dramatic sigh. "I'd given up on you."

Moonblight replied, "You were always covered. My rat man friends were there all the time. You seemed safe enough. But when things started happening elsewhere, I decided to get you back."

Last light was almost gone. It was hard to tell, but I thought Moonslight looked a little gray.

I exchanged glances with Singe. We definitely had to fix her up with the Dead Man.

Singe's eyes widened. I spun to see why.

The light was awful. Flecks of rain had begun to fall. Even so, there was no mistaking the little blonde atop the cement maker's shed.

Singe stepped close, grabbed my left arm with both hands. She had a sudden case of the sniffles. She got up on tiptoe to whisper, "We are no longer alone."

Brevet Captain Deiter Scithe stepped on her line. "So, what is this all about, Garrett?"

He had not turned up alone. Shadows moved all round, closing in.

I had to get rid of that Civil Guard tracer.

"Don't you ever stop working?" No point mentioning that I didn't find it useful to have the Civil Guard in my hip pocket all the time. He would refuse to be convinced.

"They won't let me stop while you keep getting into mischief. Guess who my wife hates more than her mother-in-law?"

"Somebody kidnapped Moonblight's sister. Singe's connections helped us find her. We came to get her back."

"I'm beginning to understand why the Director and General Block get hysterical about you. That feels like it's true but smells like it's only a fraction of the truth. That's work that should be left to the Guard. It should have been reported when it happened."

I shrugged. "You're another one with serious trust issues."

"Well, duh. You have an interesting mix here."

I thought he meant my companions, and maybe he did, some, but he was staring at the baddies when he said it.

"Yeah. You hardly ever see gray rat men working with another race."

"As you say. My bosses will be interested in that."

I concentrated on self-control. This was where being the usual me might earn me a difficult row to hoe later on.

Scithe said, "Here's a thought. The Director won't like it,

but I am the senior on the scene, with full situational discretion. And, honestly, you and your friends did all the work. It would be less than fair to confiscate your whole harvest, however much I have the law and courts behind me."

I put my hands over the seat of my pants. Somebody was about to get bent over.

It took me a moment to realize that Scithe was messing with me. He was wasting time deliberately. He suggested, "Let's split the haul. You take a rat and a thug, I'll take a rat and a thug."

"Works for me."

Brownie took a stance in front of Scithe, bared her teeth, growled a growl that made her sound more exasperated than threatening.

Scithe grinned. "Ferocious sidekick, Garrett. Going to pee my pants leg, girl?"

"You never know," I said. "She has character."

Clever, clever, ever-slick Tara Chayne Machtkess used the distraction to ease Mariska away from the Brevet Captain. Mariska did nothing to make that difficult. She was disinclined to head into durance in a place unlikely to be hospitable. Denizens of the Al-Khar had been born again into the faith of the law. She preferred traditional privilege.

One or both sisters did something intended to make themselves less notable.

Scithe was not fooled. "Miss Machtkess, ma'am, I understand that you want to share an emotional reunion after a successful rescue. But your sister should come see us at the Al-Khar as soon as she can so we can collect information about the scofflaws involved." He winked at me. "That will give you time to get your stories straight."

He didn't quite mean what he said. He was, actually, counting on the Dead Man's superior interrogation techniques.

He winked again as a rogue raindrop the size of a robin's egg smacked him square in the third eye.

He yelped. "Steng, Split, snag that one and that one and let's go. Maybe I can get my supper before midnight."

Brownie growled again. So did her henchmutts. This time, though, she didn't care about Deiter Scithe. The dogs all glared at the cement maker's heating tower, where the little blonde's good buddy stood silhouetted against what little gray light remained. He stepped off the back side and vanished.

Tara Chayne asked, "What was that?"

"I'm really starting to wonder why that girl turns up whenever my life gets interesting."

"Does she? Every time?"

I shrugged. Maybe not. "Well, no. Frequently." There had been times that I hadn't seen her. But that was all that meant. She might have been watching. "I'm just really wondering why."

"Let's take sis to dinner at your place."

"That's a great idea."

75

I wasn't totally gone in the wastelands of my own thoughts—years of being the butt of practical jokers who scheme beneath the seat of the three-holer in the sky guaranteed that we would see an ambush before we got to my house—but I was nibbling round the crust of a slice of curiosity. What should we do with our captives once the Dead Man was done burglarizing their brains?

We must have them stacked in like cordwood by now.

Tara Chayne could do whatever she wanted with her sister once we were done with her. Maybe the Guard could pass the rest along to the labor camps.

Barate smacked us hard with the obvious. "It's dark." He had helped himself to some lumber from the storage lot, a broken piece of form board. He swished it around like a practice sword.

I protested, "I'm alert."

Singe and her big stick were more ready than I was.

The dogs were close in and halfway slinking, expecting trouble.

"There was that ugliness with the Hedley-Farfoul twins last night. That must have been the first official clash of the tournament. Right?"

"So I understand." I looked around nervously. "You're getting at something specific?" We did not have the street to ourselves. There was civilian traffic and plenty of movement rolling with us. Tara Chayne, though, didn't seem particularly uneasy, so I assumed that movement must be friendly. Nominally. Like Specials hoping our honey would draw more flies. Honey, I say! Not horse puckey. Not any kind of puckey, horse, chicken, or bull.

In the outbacks of my mind, a puckish imaginary being ticked the box next to Bull, Commercial Grade.

Barate said, "We should consider the likelihood that there will be more action tonight. Possibly several incidents, all extremely violent."

"Yeah."

Things were moving faster than we or the Operators liked.

"You should, then, be more concerned than you have been showing."

"Eh?"

"As far as we know, you're still Mortal Companion to Kevans's Family Champion. The Mortal Companion should be close enough to support the Family Champion, especially when the Dread Companion isn't around. Do you know where Kevans is?"

Oh. No. I did not, not in the least. I couldn't think of anything to say and Barate was a worried dad snakebitten already by a nasty loss. "We should work on that once we get these villains delivered." I unlaxed even more, and upped the pace.

Moonblight, I noted, was psyching herself up for something, too. Even Dr. Ted appeared to be readying himself.

Moonslight, though, appeared to be relaxed.

That seemed like an evil portent.

I was, by then, comfortably confident that she was connected to the Operators.

Tara Chayne softly whispered, "Mariska and Meyness Stornes were a hot item back in the day."

I missed the hint in the fact of the whisper because I was thinking that nostalgia becomes a potent driver as we age and spend more time snuggled up with our regrets.

The workings of Moonslight's mind were less a mystery than were those of Meyness B. Stornes, whose own grandson could become one of the victims of his cruel scheme.

Maybe the eldest Stornes planned to cheat in favor of his descendant.

"Hey," I said to Tara Chayne, not using my inside voice. "You think anybody besides us has any idea who Magister Bezma might be?"

"And the inimitable Garrett steps into another big, steaming pile," Singe muttered. "Really, Garrett? Don't you ever think before you blurt stuff out?"

No need for her to explain. There was Moonslight, till now brilliantly unaware that we knew, her eyes widening in horror and her head jerking as she looked for some immediate opportunity to escape.

"Not often enough," I confessed. "Not nearly often enough. I'm a Marine. It's hey, diddle, diddle, straight up the middle, smashing things till the job is done."

Some of my companions could think on their feet. Or paws, as the case might be. First the dogs, then Dr. Ted and Barate closed in around Moonslight. Ted helped her up after she tripped over Number Two while making a sudden, brief bid for freedom.

She went from confidently calm to panic in seconds. Was that only because we knew about Meyness B. Stornes? And did we, really? I didn't feel like that had yet fully passed the frontiers of speculation.

Tara Chayne slapped me across the back of the head. "Genius." Then, "Gods, aren't you lucky that you're pretty?"

That stung. That was sarcasm at its pure, crusty finest.

"I do my best," I protested. "You should have suspected the worst when you heard that Strafa picked me."

"That would be on her, not on you."

Dollar Dan said, "Can we keep it down? There may be people interested in your problems, but none of them are here. We want to keep an ear on what is happening out there in the darkness."

Singe's whiskers wiggled. She snuffled up little chunks of air.

Tara Chayne and I exchanged looks. Dan must have taken a fistful of courage pills. He'd never been so forceful, nor as responsible, come to that.

I whispered, "Something is about to happen."

Moonblight nodded. "Dan, whatever happens, don't let anybody get away."

Dollar Dan puffed up. A major Hill player had just spoken to him by name, like he was a real person.

When the something happened it didn't happen to us. A light show, with bangs and roars, broke out over toward the Hill. Whips and staves of light lashed and slashed the darkness, making the scattered raindrops sparkle like descending diamonds. Every glow tossed off a splatter of fading shards when it hit something.

Stunning. Beautiful. A great distraction, suitable for leaving everyone oohing and aahing, but it didn't distract us completely. We were not unready when the flood of gray rats arrived.

There had to be forty in the swarm, maybe the majority of their kind. The attack made no sense. I saw males, females, preadolescents to hobbling elders. None were armed with anything more dangerous than a stick. I might have felt sorry had they been jumping somebody else. The assault seemed that pathetic.

I didn't let my lack of understanding keep me from cracking heads. I didn't let my eye or conscience distinguish the stick-wielding adult male from his stick-wielding mate or granny or pup. Doing that could only lead to pain.

Ted did scruple. That doctor thing about first doing no harm. It cost him blood and bruises and us all the loss of Mariska Machtkess.

Weight of numbers nearly did for us all. Luckily, gray rat people are not big. They do not have much mass going for them.

Swamping was the point, of course.

The rush wasn't about liberating Mariska; that was just its result. The object of the thrust was our gray rat captive. We would learn, later, that he was Wicked Pat, the grays' John Stretch. Wicked Pat had been clever enough to conceal his identity and so avoid having to meet Deal Relway.

Pat would be of definite interest to the Director.

His friends and family weren't clever enough, though. Only Mariska Machtkess benefited.

The rat tide left me wobbly and blessed with a thousand new aches and bruises. I just wanted to lie down and feel sorry for myself. Ted was in worse shape. He didn't have enough oomph left to help himself, let alone the rest of us. He asked, "What should we do about these people?"

Meaning the rat folk who had been left behind. The light was poor. My count only approximated, yet I had eighteen feebleminded fools scattered about the street, conscious and unconscious. I hoped none were dead or badly broken.

"We'll take a couple along so my partner can find out what moved them. The rest are fine right where they're at."

Singe, Dollar Dan, and the rest all panted a lot and said very little. Barate was down on one knee, bent over a puddle of lunch. Some rat had given him a solid whack to his pride and joy. Tara Chayne, between huffs and puffs, battled a case of the giggles.

"What's with you?" I demanded, taking a break from sucking left hand knuckle abrasions. I couldn't remember losing the skin.

"The joke is on Mariska." She fought for breath. "I put a tracer on her a while back. Not the one from your saddle, the old Guard one. If she ran I figured it would be funny if she just got into it deeper with the tin whistles."

Yeah. That's the kind of thing you do to your siblings, just for the hell of it. And it was funny till you considered possible real consequences.

The fugitive was Moonslight, a Hill-topper sorceress. She didn't have many resources, but the red tops weren't Hill-toppers. She had skills, and her lack of an arsenal could be rectified quickly.

A general with troops to burn would rush a battalion to the Machtkess house with orders to sit tight and wait. Mariska would show. She had to show.

Moonblight didn't say so straight up, but she considered my reasoning simplistic and naive.

76

We were on Wizard's Reach, outside the Dead Man's range, approaching the intersection with Macunado from the south. Singe was in a dark mood over the behavior of the gray rat people.

I tried to talk her down. She was determined to be angry. She had influence enough with John Stretch to spark a war. That could not possibly turn out well for the grays.

Her brother's people were everywhere. There were a lot of them. Mostly they went unnoticed by the folks they wouldn't be shy about hurting if the boss rat lapsed into his own dark mood.

If he did, though, he might set off Deal Relway. Director Relway and General Block have a far larger gang.

I was working myself up to whine because John Stretch hadn't contributed more to the current effort when I suffered an epiphany. That complaint would be unreasonable to the point of absurdity. John Stretch didn't work for me, nor did he owe me feudal service. He was a friend taking time out of his own life to help because his sister had tied herself to me. Hell, he had had his number-one guy leave his regular work to hunk around with me and Singe. And, most of all, this was only our second day of vigorous operations.

It seemed like we had been at it a lot longer.

"That does not look like it will resolve itself soon," Dollar Dan said as we reached the intersection. The light show continued sporadically. Glistening diamonds continued to fall. The rain had neither increased nor diminished. The drops remained exceptionally large.

Tara Chayne suggested, "That smells like a forced conflict between matched opponents who didn't want to fight in the first place."

The rest of us hoped she would say more, but she had nothing to add. We weren't the only watchers.

No one should have complained that it was less than a hell of a show, but a certain personality type did feel compelled to belittle the demonstration. Someone who had been to the Cantard and survived had to tell everyone that they had seen bigger, flashier, louder, stinkier, and most certainly deadlier, in take your pick of major battles down there. And, though sprung from a petty mind, the claims were solid. When major sorcerers butted heads in the Cantard, the earth itself boiled and screamed. The sky tore. Shredded flakes of reality fell like crispy black snow.

Moonblight said, "I begin to suspect that we're seeing what they want this to be. A show."

"Um?"

"We did the same in our day. When I went against Constance we favored smoke and noise and temblors, but the strategy was that prolonged drama might bring the Operators out where we could hurt them."

Barate asked, "Did it work?"

"Some. We roasted three like chestnuts. The tournament began to come apart. The other Operators went underground. We only ever found two more."

I said, "We've got good stuff going and we already know who one of them is. If we catch him and get him to the Dead Man, we can break the whole mess up and zero in on the dick behind what happened to Strafa."

Moonblight wasn't listening. "Our problem now is, Meyness was a big player when we pulled our stunts. He won't be sucked in by stuff we did back then. He was never a real team player—I remember thinking that he would've played our cycle out if he'd thought that he could win. He's surely warned the other Operators."

I supposed. With so many survivors of the last tournament still breathing, the Operators would have to account for them in their schemes—especially when those survivors started pushing back even before the tournament began.

I wanted to ask how many survivors were still with us, but we were close enough for the Dead Man to feel us coming.

He let us come a hundred feet farther, then, *Inside quickly. There are enemies about with deadly intentions.*

Enemies, huh? I couldn't pick them out, but I did spot Target and another red top. Whoever took a whack at us would start a battle.

Indeed. And numerous innocents will become collateral damage. I will fog the minds of those nearest the house, but please do not dawdle. I cannot spare the attention for long. Once you are inside . . .

I did not find out what then. His attention did turn elsewhere.

I explained to my mob; then we went, straight on like good Marines hell-bent, everyone holding on to a prisoner. Then I tripped over a dog. I couldn't make out which one. They were all frightened and crowding close. I blamed Number Two because she was my least favorite.

Barate used his free hand to help me up while Singe broke her staff over the head of a weasel-faced, dried-up little guy about fifty who had popped up with one of those needle-bladed daggers meant to slide through links of chain mail. She might have killed him, she hit him so hard. We didn't stop to give first aid. Target and his troops could clean up.

I wasn't sure if I should treasure or be horrified by the look on that man's face when he realized he'd been laid down by a girl rat.

One more villain tried. Target snagged him off a tangential dash, by the collar, and had him in restraints before he knew what was happening.

Inside. Feebly, like he had no more strength to spend. *A battle may break out anyway.*

Penny opened the door. Her eyes bugged at the parade of gray rats, dogs, friends, and allies on the steps.

A crossbow bolt struck sparks off brick beside me, so close it clipped a bit of hair. I ducked, looked back, could not pick out the shooter, who would be in for a truly bad time if Target caught him.

Then came a dull boom, huge, from an uncertain direction and indeterminate distance, then a long, muted grumble. The ground shook. Things rattled and clinked in Singe's office and the Dead Man's room. Something fell in the kitchen. Another crossbow bolt, as close as the first, slashed my right sleeve and thunked into the door, narrowly missing Penny, too. I dove past her. Ahead, between legs, I saw Dean, who had been watching the invasion develop. He hustled off to rescue his pots.

With scant help from the invisible force, we got everyone settled and, more importantly, quiet. Tara Chayne and Barate migrated into Singe's office. Dollar Dan and Dr. Ted loomed over the prisoner collection, Ted failing miserably to look like somebody fierce.

Another distant rumble shook the house. Being about as brilliant as a human being comes, I opened the door and stepped back out to see what I could see. What I saw was a baby riot as red tops chased villains among gawkers watching the show on the Hill. I didn't see anything to explain the rumbling.

I didn't get shot. The sniper had moved on. It would not be in his personal interest to get caught with an illegal weapon.

I congratulated myself on being clever enough to get home just before the rain began to get serious about answering its natural calling.

Can you come assist me, please?

77

The Dead Man's room remained untainted by the chaos burbling in the hallway. He was not alone, though. Penny was there pretending to work on a painting, escaping the confusion herself, and making a statement. If we wouldn't let her play with the big kids, she wouldn't do anything else that she didn't have to.

Penny was the only one conscious there. There were leftovers from other roundups. They weren't stacked in, but they did take up most of the available room.

In fits because he was running near capacity, Old Bones informed me, *I need your . . . assistance clearing . . . out. Too . . . much of my attention . . . is consumed by the . . . need to manage them.*

"So why not have Penny . . . ?"

Penny . . . does not have the strength or . . . physical skills needed to . . . handle one of them . . . if my control slips.

Penny did that girl-kid thing where she sticks her tongue out the side of her mouth while pulling down a lower eyelid with a single finger. I've never figured that out and didn't see how it fit the current situation, either.

I was pleased that she was no longer afraid to act like that.

The gods don't want us to understand kids, nor are kids supposed to understand us—our lack despite us having survived kid-dom ourselves.

I suppose that, like childbirth pain, it just drifts off into the ether.

I noticed some friendlies behind the crowd, Playmate and my friend the poisoner . . . Excuse me. My friend the apothecary, Kolda. He and Playmate must have become inconvenient to have underfoot, though I thought Playmate would have been useful removing no longer wanted houseguests. Maybe Old Bones was so distracted and pressed and frustrated that he had added them to the people freeze because that was easiest.

I glared at Penny. There was no way she couldn't have managed those two just by making puppy eyes.

She asked, "Did you see what they did to the door?"

"What?"

"You're going to need that Mr. Mulclar again."

"Door? Mulclar?" Mulclar has an enduring problem with gas. I could smell him already. Feh! "What did you do?"

"I didn't do anything. Some people tried to break in. Some of them weren't human. Himself had so much going he couldn't totally deal with them. He only had me and Dean to help."

And me standing there looking at Playmate and Kolda. Kolda was no ax-swinging barbarian, but Playmate, even weakened by cancer, could handle his weight in wildcats.

"It got exciting. He had to keep all these idiots controlled while he held off the people outside. They were working on the door with pry bars when some red tops finally stepped up."

"I see. So. Who were they? Do we know that much?"

"No. At least Himself didn't tell me and none of them offered a calling card. Probably had to do with those Operator creeps."

"They didn't know about the Dead Man?"

"Maybe not. Maybe they didn't care. We didn't get to ask."

They would care if they knew.

She added, "Maybe the red tops will tell you what they get from the ones they caught."

Maybe. I didn't think I'd hold my breath.

That should've been the Dead Man's cue for a comment

about my cynicism. He forbore. Or he was too damned busy.

"Penny, how about you give me a hand clearing these deadbeats out?"

Playmate and Kolda looked like their minds were beginning to unfog.

Old Bones managed a feeble *Do not . . . waste time. Big pressure . . . has begun . . . to develop from . . . outside.*

Meaning he would have no attention left for doing anything with or to the new intelligence sources I'd brought in.

Exactly.

And that was his last word.

78

I chose a villain who looked ready to be returned to the wild, suggested, "Pick one, Penny. Then lead him out ahead of me and mine."

Grumbling, she did as I suggested.

"Wait by the office door. I'll get Barate and Ted to help." If nothing else, somebody had to stand by at the front door in case of comebacks while the bad boys were being ejected.

We were at the door. Penny was set to spring it. I got caught up in one of those speculation loops, wondering what had become of Hagekagome. I'd seen no sign of her. Had she run away, been turned loose, or been chased off? Unlikely. Playmate was still here. He'd never let anyone that vulnerable roam around unprotected.

And what about Vicious Min? Was she still in that induced coma?

Penny poked me, hitting a pain point perfectly, no doubt having learned by observation. My once-upon-a-time, Tinnie, had been a master at finger-poke torture. "Wake up, old man! You're the one who says we have to do this."

"All right. Sorry. I took a second to worry. And to let Ted and Barate catch up. Go on, now. Open her up."

She unbuttoned and flung the door wide—then put every ounce of her ninety-some pounds behind the shove she gave her victim.

He flipped over the porch rail.

"Damn, girl, I hope you didn't break him." I moved my

man out more gently, then backed against the wall so Barate and Ted could evict their own.

"Why?" Penny asked. "They work for people who want to kill you. Who already killed Strafa."

Barate shared her level of anger. He got a lot of muscle behind his toss.

Dr. Ted, though, wussed out. He still had trouble getting past that first-do-no-harm twaddle.

Then we were all tumbling over one another as we tried to get the door shut before something bigger than Vicious Min or the little blonde's companion, wearing a head like a squid, got a tentacle in there among us.

Ted had no trouble going to work on that with his knife.

"What the hell was that?" the sweet young thing among us demanded. "That was one ugly fu . . . freak!" She was panting and shaking.

I was panting and shaking. Barate was panting and shaking. Ted was panting and shaking but had not gotten distracted from keeping eighteen inches of writhing severed tentacle pinned to the floor.

I said, "That thing had twenty arrows in it." Though, really, most had been crossbow bolts. Whatever, they should have slowed it down.

The street had been seething with excited red tops, some of them Specials armed for military-style action.

I had some military tools of my own. I was tempted to break them out. If I did, though, Deal Relway would insist on knowing why I had them and where I'd gotten them, after the dust settled

Penny asked, "Would salt do any good?"

We once had an encounter with a tentacle-thing that had responded to salt like a snail or slug.

"I doubt it. That was a whole different kind of beast."

Ted said, "You could experiment on this piece, though."

That hadn't stopped wriggling.

I said, "How about let's get us some fresh victims?" I stepped to the doorway to the Dead Man's room.

Shifting four bodies out hadn't freed him up. He now had nothing with which to offer an explanation.

Penny guessed, "He's busy holding off that thing out there."

Almost certainly. The people still in the room had begun to stir. Then some heavy-duty thumping started up somewhere else in the house, maybe over where Vicious Min was supposed to be sleeping.

"Penny, run across and tell Moonblight . . ."

I didn't have to finish. Mr. Tentacle had put the hoodoo on the kid, big-time. In seconds Moonblight was headed up the hallway looking grimly angry and as scary as Shadowslinger in a sour mood. She told me, "Stay out of the way, candy-ass!" Then, "My gods! I am going to blister that girl's butt when I catch her."

She knew what was out there and who to blame for its having come around. So. Here was more family squabble, of the sort where somebody was supposed to wind up hurt. Moonblight flung the door open and to hell with being fussed about what might be out there.

Tentacle-boy was right where we left him. But he-she-or-it wouldn't be aggravating anyone else any time soon. Something had happened. Something that wasn't all those bolts and arrows totaled up.

Something had carved off big chunks, including tentacles, legs, an arm, and a head. One big eye still had a dagger lodged in it, tip stuck solidly in the creature's weird, cartilaginous skull.

Moonblight opined, "Well, hell, this isn't so good."

"Looks good to me," I had to say. The contest in the street was breaking up. Bad boys had begun showing their heels with verve and enthusiasm. Tin whistles were putting the captured and fallen into restraints, ignoring wounds, taking no chances on dead guys only faking it.

There did seem to be an excessive number of fatalities. Red tops try to take their men alive. Prisoners can be passed along to the labor camps, where they pay their debts to society by contributing to public works. Plus, the camps pay prize money for breathing bodies.

79

Target and three battered friends came to the foot of my steps. Target's eyes were up high enough to see Brother Tentacle's remains. "Damn, that thing was ugly. Tough, too. We barely slowed it down."

"How did this happen, then?"

"Some little old granny lady . . . Never seen nothing like it. Hell, I couldn't see her at all, most of the time. There was just flashing steel and flying blood and screams in the street, like a bow wave headed here. Which ended with this mess. I only saw her clear for a couple seconds. She just stood there staring at your door. Then she sort of shimmered and went away again, leaving a couple more villains shorter by a head as she went. Very selective about who, too."

"Sending a message."

"She is for sure one seriously pissed-off old lady. I hope the Director don't decide he's got to hunt her down."

"He wouldn't be happy if he found her." I looked to Moonblight for confirmation.

"Yes. Officer, do hope. Pray. That was the Black Orchid, come out of retirement."

Target's sudden pallor told us that he had been to that part of the world where the Black Orchid had made her name.

Moonblight continued. "She would be after Mariska. Thinking she might be here, but informed by your thing inside that she isn't."

So maybe Old Bones had gotten a little capacity freed up now. Or maybe he had let go of something else so he could deal with a deeper threat.

I said, "Folks, we need to get some more villains out of the house. Target. Buddy. I've got some more baddies for you. Some Scithe sent over. Some your boss sent. Some we caught on our own. They all have something to do with this creepiness. We don't need them anymore. I'd be generally grateful, for minutes or more, if you could take them away."

He sighed. "They'll end up in the camps. Poor bastards. Most of them wouldn't have gotten into this if they could've found any other work."

A red top capable of sympathy and empathy? The wonders never cease. But, then, I was considering letting Niea skate. That poor bastard hadn't done anything but his job.

Target told me, "Fine. I'll take care of them. The Director will want to know what you got."

"That was the deal."

"In writing if you can. Memories are somewhat fallible."

The Dead Man's memory was perfect and it came with sounds and smells and kinesthetic cues. "I'll ask Singe to create a report. But we've been out all day. It'll take her a while just to catch up on her own stuff."

He gave me a skeptical look. "Do what you have to do. But don't waste time. Things are moving fast."

He had that right. Developments were coming faster than we could make sense of anything.

Target and his boys clambered over the dead thing, which seemed severely deflated now and already smelled like calamari gone bad. The Specials avoided physical contact while easing past Moonblight. I said, "The ones we need to move out are in the room behind the door on the right. The ones cringing at the end of the hall still need to be processed."

The newest arrivals were crowded back close to the kitchen door. Dean blocked that line of retreat. At some point Penny had dashed back to post herself on the first step of the stairs, cutting off any flight upward.

I glanced back outside.

Moonblight was on the porch trying to get the dagger out of the demon's eye, if demon the critter was. Conversationally, she said, "We need to pick up this mess, throw it in a big pot, and cook it down so there's no chance it'll death-spawn."

"Is it female?"

"I don't know. How do you tell? But why take the chance?"

"I got to admit, I'm not sure what you're talking about."

"These things sometimes squirt out all their eggs if they die suddenly. Thousands of eggs that can hatch in hours. The hatchlings look like whiskery little yellow grubs. They feed on the carcass till they can get at something alive. Only a few will manage, but the ones that do will make like botfly maggots."

Botflies I knew. Botflies I remembered. Ugly, ugly stuff. The god who thought those up was one twisted . . .

I didn't get the cooking part. I guess that would kill the larvae.

Some nobility types had gotten that treatment after they died in the field, so that their relics could be sent home for interment with family. Us ordinaries remained where we fell, of course. Unless we had friends who cared enough, and had time enough, to put us down deep enough so the scavengers couldn't get us. Or, where there was wood to waste, they might burn us down to ashes and ghosts.

I wondered what the jackals and buzzards were doing now, in a time of famine. Waiting on each other to starve?

"Garrett? Are you there?" Target asked.

"I'm awake. I promise. What?"

"That's Harmon Kolda in there. The poisoner. How did you catch him? We've been on the lookout for him for months."

But not trying very hard, I didn't say. Kolda ran a shop not far from Playmate's stable. He had an apothecary sign outside with his name on it.

"The Director has always been interested in his client list."

Harmon? Really? I couldn't recall ever having heard Kolda called anything but Kolda, even by his wife.

"Sorry. He isn't a prisoner. He's a consultant. He's helping treat a friend with cancer. Maybe he was in the poison racket one time. I keep hearing that. But he isn't now. He makes good money as an apothecary."

Target radiated a fog of skepticism.

"Anyway, the Guard's writ doesn't run to anything that happened before the Crown issued its charter. Right?"

"I never figured you for a barracks lawyer, Garrett. But I won't argue."

Yeah. If he really wanted Kolda, he could just wait outside. Kolda would head home eventually.

Maybe Target was really testing the Dead Man. He'd done a comedic double take when he got his first glimpse. Maybe he was trying to see if that lump of weird's reputation was solid.

I looked over Target's shoulder. And began to wonder if there was anything to the stories myself, in the sense that I couldn't feel Old Bones at all.

I was concerned.

In modern Karentine that meant I was worried a whole lot.

We had worked through some grim times, off and on, but I couldn't recall a time when there had been such an overwhelming demand, stressing his capacities and talents so severely.

He might be gone.

Gone in the sense that he was deeply asleep, recovering, not in the sense that he was gone gone, like into forever sleep.

I couldn't see that coming up in my lifetime.

Target said, "If you insist I'll just be too busy to notice the poisoner in the back."

"Thank you, sir." And cut it off there, with no sarcastic

color commentary. "Maybe you'd better take the rest of these bums, too. The ones in the hall that I was going to hang on to. My partner is out of it now. We can't do anything with them. He used himself up on that thing on the stoop."

Which was the undecorated truth, as far as I knew, but Target was skeptical. I repeated Moonblight's suggestion about cooking the thing down. He was skeptical some more, but less so. He had seen some stuff in his day, too. "I'll see to it." Still . . .

There seemed to be a fundamental assumption underlying Civil Guard culture: If Garrett is talking, he's telling a tall one.

I know. They feel that way about all civilians. But it's just not fair in my case. They're wrong at least forty percent of the time. They should consider each statement on its own merits and in its own context.

Target eased past Moonblight so he could lean out and yell for more men, which made me real nervous. How did I make a big crowd go away, once it got in, without Old Bones to back me up?

Renewed thumping came from my old office. Something like an elephant gargling gravel bellowed a curse. It shook dust off the ceiling.

Singe leaned through the doorway to her office. "You want to do something about that?"

"I'm open to suggestions."

"Think!"

"Not part of my skill set. Tara Chayne? How about you? Anything you can do?"

"I'll try. Give me a minute. I'm working on calming down. I still can't believe Mariska did that! All our lives I've made allowances and excuses and covered for her. I've even bought people off for her. Then she goes and sends her favorite familiar after me. Her practically godsdamned diabolical supernatural husband thing, K'thool Hoo C'Thug himself! Damn her, I've had it! Sister or not, twin or not, I'm not going to pretend to be blind this time!"

Renewed, ever more vigorous thumping and cursing came from the room where Vicious Min was, apparently, trying to get onto her feet and back into the business of whatever her business was.

Still muttering, Moonblight headed off north to slay that particular giant.

80

So there I was. . . .

A lot of my stories start that way, and then beer or some lesser form of alcohol gets involved. I was hoping some of that might be involved here soon. I waved without enthusiasm as Target and his crew hauled the last bad boys away. The dead and wounded from the street scuffle had ended up aboard a big wagon that was a cell on wheels, where they were piled three deep.

Those healthy enough to shuffle under their own power had left already, tied together in a coffle.

Though the red tops took a few with them, nobody seemed to know what to do about the balance of the gray rats. The half-ass consensus was to turn them loose and let the rat community sort them out. Meaning a blind eye would turn to the moon while John Stretch did what he wanted to restore order, social norms, and tranquillity among the under-people.

As they sometimes do, my thoughts drifted. I was agitated because Old Bones did indeed appear to have gone into hibernation. That could last for weeks or even months.

This was not a good time.

It never is.

This time he had gone without passing along anything learned from Min, Hagekagome, or any of the gang folk we had rolled past him.

There was yet another outbreak of thumping and cursing in my old office, the verbal part more enthusiastic than the physical. I picked out a few words in no language I recognized but, doubtless, not the sort one used while having tea with one's mother. Not my mother, anyway, even where she was likely dwelling now.

Don't get me wrong. I love my mother plenty, I've just never had any illusions about her being a saint.

Well, she might have been to my goody-two-shoes baby brother.

Vicious Min had control of her faculties but not her flesh. The racket slowly declined.

The old homestead would need a thorough cleaning after this. How much could I pass off onto Penny?

She had scooted up front and had the door partway open, checking the street. Singe was helping her rubberneck, likely watching for her brother.

Dollar Dan lurked a few steps behind Singe, clearly nervous. It wasn't clear why. I had no complaints. He had been a good man to have on the voyage.

Tara Chayne stepped out of my office-turned-infirmary. "That's all I can do. It won't last. You want her kept controlled, you need to get your partner back in action. Or convince Ted to do something."

Ted sneered but did not dignify the suggestion with a response.

I said, "Based on experience I can say I don't have a good feeling about that."

"Then hand her over to the Specials, too. You won't be able to manage her yourself."

I started to say something, realized I had nothing to say. I broke precedent by actually not saying it.

Tara Chayne continued. "She's mostly recovered. She has an inhuman vitality. It'll keep getting harder to make her sleep. Ted won't help and I'm not moving in to handle her for you. I have other squid to fry."

She wasted no innuendo on the move-in remark. It was time to go on. She had a sister who needed to be found and spanked. That sister was tagged. How far ahead had Moonblight been thinking? Had she thought that Moonslight might lead us somewhere interesting?

Had Target figured out that the tracer had migrated? Might he and his be launching their own hunt?

Moonblight thought they might be. She was getting antsy.

No way she wanted them getting to her sister first.

"I understand. Anything else you can do before we go?"

One eyebrow rose slightly in response to that "we." She withheld comment otherwise. She did gesture toward the Dead Man's room.

"Like I said, he could be out for months."

"There is another resource in there."

I didn't understand. His Nibs was alone now, except for Playmate, Kolda, and Niea, all caught in the twilight between sleep and consciousness.

"The poisoner can render her pliable. Or, if not pliable, then weak and manageable. Or constantly unconscious."

Maybe he could. I didn't think it was reasonable to ask him to break any more laws on my behalf.

"Singe, are you expecting John Stretch?"

"I am. He will appear once he knows he can get here without being seen by the Guard. He will be interested in hearing what we know about the involvement of the grays."

He would. "Too bad Old Bones is out of it. He probably had all the answers."

Dollar Dan said, "Singe and I can give a few. We learned a lot that would not be obvious to a human observer."

Singe nodded, then eyed Dan like she still wondered who this imposter might be.

I bit down on a grin.

You had to give the guy kudos for studly determination. He was willing to transform himself into a total rat man Poindexter if that was the price of gaining Singe's favor.

His quest was poignantly, sadly foredoomed, but I was willing to pony up a pail of points for perseverance.

I said, "Tara Chayne, Ted, Barate, and I will be heading out shortly. . . ."

Ted said, "I've been away from Constance for too long."

Barate nodded. "I still need to find Kevans and get her locked down where the gods themselves can't get at her."

Tara Chayne wasn't as thrilled with the prospect of my company as once she had been. Luminous intuition suggested that this might be because I tried to do the right thing in the tight places. I was too much into ethical folderol, even after my loss.

I told her, "I'll try to keep my big damned mouth shut."

She would catch Mariska, sure. Things might turn problematic then, though I was sure that Moonblight would prevail. I did hope to ask Moonslight a few questions before big sister took the process too far.

"All right. If you want to tag along. But I'll hold you to your promise." She moved in, looked up at me from as close as she could get with her clothes still on. "I hear any of your usual lip, I'll sew your mouth shut with catfish tripe."

"Gah!"

"You won't have the Algarda angels hovering anymore."

I took that as a reminder rather than intimidation. "Got you."

"That I'll believe when I see it."

I turned away, chastened. Tara Chayne Machtkess had a little Mom in her. I told Singe, "See if you can't get word to the Al-Khar suggesting that we might be willing to turn over Vicious Min. Penny . . ."

The girl was tired. She turned surly. "I don't want to hear about it."

"But—"

"Not about any of it."

"All right! Dean. I need you to come up with a special diet for this one. Something with less sour in it."

Dean grunted. He had nothing else to say. He was pushing his cart. Somehow, while everything else was going on, he had found time to make sandwiches. He offered me a fat one.

Singe turned from the front door. "Humility is coming."

"Means we can go without attracting any attention."

Of a sudden there was a racket on the stair. Four scruffy mutts tumbled into the hallway, ready to join the new enterprise. Number Two did a perfect imitation of a tame hound's sit-up-and-beg maneuver.

Dean said, "Pay no attention. They've been fed."

I wanted to blather at him and my girls about cleaning up dog hair and any gifts the critters had left but then glimpsed Hagekagome peeking round the corner at the bottom of the stair. So. She had been hiding out.

She stared at me like she was determined to commit my face to memory. Very intent and, yet, the slightest bit confused.

She didn't charge, telling me how much she hated me.

I told Penny, "Take good care of her, too."

"I will." No arguments. No attitude. No nothing at all but a straightforward statement of intent.

Did she know something that no one had bothered to share with me?

Probably. A lot.

Everybody knew stuff about stuff that they didn't bother to share with me. That was the nature of my business. That was the story of my life.

81

The street was quiet. The show that had brought the crowds out was long gone. The cobblestones were still messy, though. Brownie and her friends found a hundred places deserving of sniffing and pawing. Some looked like patches where somebody had lost bladder or bowel control. A few stains might have been spilled blood.

Local civilians wanted nothing to do with it. Some wanted to arrange it so nothing like it ever happened again. A fierce committee of two upright subjects and three busy-body goodwives engaged us in the street. They explained in no uncertain terms how insistent they were that I not bring any more such intolerable nonsense into the hood. In fact, it would be best for the hood if I just packed up and . . .

Tara Chayne stepped up to the grim-faced harridan who was the grit round which this pearl of displeasure had formed. "I don't like people like you, you sour old witch." She waved a hand on which fingers danced inside wisps of indigo mist. The unhappy woman's hands leapt to her throat. She made choking noises. Her eyes expanded more than could be accounted for by choking.

Despite everything that had happened tonight and all that she had ever seen, that old woman never really believed that what touched me could also reach out to her.

She went to her knees still fighting for air. Moonblight patted her head as if she were a small child. "Anybody here having trouble understanding? No? Good. I didn't think you would. In a nutshell, it's mind your own business." She dropped her fingers to the choking woman's head, lifted. The woman floated up as if she weighed four ounces.

Her choking never quite became life-threatening.

"There. Have some air. That's better, isn't it? Are you listening now? I'm going to say something important after I remind you that Mr. Garrett is now part of one of the senior houses on the Hill."

The entire committee cringed.

"Are you listening?" Moonblight asked again.

The biddy could only nod.

"That's good. That's what I wanted to hear. You need to listen and remember. What you're experiencing now will stay with you forever. I'll loosen it a little before we go. You should remember that it's there—though I imagine that it will remind you frequently. I know your type. You'll never stop cursing and complaining, so you'll guarantee your doom. Once we go, that spell will tighten a little every time you say Mr. Garrett's name."

Moonblight squeezed the woman's shoulder. "It's up to you. I don't think you can save yourself. You're too rigid, too sour, and too bitter. But I could be wrong. Maybe you can change. My sister did. Let's go, gentlemen."

The only person of the male persuasion handy was me, and I'm no gentleman. Barate and Dr. Ted were long gone. Tara Chayne had been having too much fun to notice.

We left those people flustered, intimidated, outraged, and frightened. Which one in what combination depended on individual characters.

Out of earshot, with Tara Chayne hogging Number Two's place to my left, I observed, "You weren't very nice to my neighbors."

"They were going to be nice to you? I'm constitutionally incapable of being polite to that kind of butthead."

"But . . . Well, I've always tried to get along with them." Sadly, I can't control the bad behavior of people who come around trying to cause me misery. "Making it so she can't even say my name seems a bit harsh."

"Pussy."

"But—"

"That was all bullshit. Nobody can cast a spell that fine."

"But—"

"You sound like you're doing background vocals for one of those street-corner singing clubs."

"But—"

"It's too complicated to craft a spell that specific. But she doesn't know that. We work hard to make people believe that we can wiggle our ears and make any damned thing we want happen. She'll believe it. She'll feel the noose tightening every time she starts bitching about you ruining the neighborhood. And when she does she'll believe in it even more. She could end up strangling herself using her own imagination."

I couldn't help blurting, "You're evil!"

"You ain't seen nothin' yet."

I hoped I never got into a position where that truth might affect my well-being. And then I wondered if she wasn't trying to do to my head what she'd already done to that of my neighbor.

Probably. She was a natural-born voodoo woman. She'd been doing it since she was a toddler. She had started doing it to me the moment we met.

She said, "I wonder what all the excitement was a while ago. Up the Hill, I mean. Remembering what we're involved in."

It felt like she was playing some game with me again.

"Are we going to go find out?"

"Not hardly. We still have Mariska to catch."

We weren't headed toward the Hill. I should have understood that without having to be told.

I was tired.

I was going to get more tired. Or even tireder.

She said, "We're not out here alone again anymore. Again."

"Again?"

"Again."

I sighed. "Any idea who it is?"

"It might be the curly top."

I saw nothing but darkness. "No rats? No red tops?"

"They figured we'd quit for the night."

"Why is this kid so interested in us?"

"A good question. Let's hope we get a chance to ask." Some seconds passed. "I think the big thing is with her. Or someone showing an interest."

I suspected that "the big thing" was always close by, whether or not he was visible.

Was he her Mortal Champion or Dread Companion? Where was the other member of their team?

82

Mariska Machtkess kept moving. We walked and walked without catching up. Each time Moonblight thought we were there, we found that Mariska had gone on.

"She's just being careful," Tara Chayne said. "While she's waiting for something. She'll settle somewhere eventually."

We burglarized a couple of Mariska's stopping places. Neither was occupied. Neither produced anything of interest.

The last place looked like it had been tossed already. Tara Chayne observed, "The Operator organization may have slipped into panic mode. Mariska may not be the only villain on the run."

"We rattled them good, then."

"Maybe. I hope so. But I'm more inclined to think that somebody familiar with the Black Orchid recognized her work. Orchidia Hedley-Farfoul is a lot scarier than either of us. Scarier to some than even Constance."

"Gah!" That was pretty scary.

"Exactly. With Orchidia there is no hype. She is as bad as your imagination can make her, and then some. Unlike Constance, she doesn't look the part. Constance wants you to know, at one glance, that she is terror on the hoof and the only safe place is where she isn't. But if you ran into Orchidia on the street you wouldn't give her a second glance—

though your chances of actually doing that are slim. She's been a recluse since she came home from the Cantard."

Common enough. TunFaire is a vast, bustling, rowdy metropolis, but you really only ever see a fraction of its people. There are day people, night people, morning people, twilight people, all forming their own tribes. There are humans and nonhumans. Each affinity constitutes a city within the city. And then there are those who came home damaged, members of a tribe that is little seen. Their bodies came back absent something left to haunt the mountains and deserts and ten thousand jungle-cursed islands of the south.

It's out there, all round, seen but not seen daily. Any veteran will recognize it at a glance. But I have to confess that I have never completely understood it. Granted, the war wasn't pleasant. We saw ugly things. But I'm back home, it's over, and now I deal with things equally ugly here.

In part, I guess, I haven't vested myself in being a victim. Meaning, I do run into veterans who have made a career of suffering from aftereffects of what they survived. Not saying that isn't real for some. Just thinking that a certain kind of personality feeds on the drama.

A lot seems to have to depend on where you wear your face. You manage all right if you have it on looking forward, but not so fine if all you want to do is look back.

Tara Chayne nailed me with the dreaded finger poke. "Think you can stay out of Fairyland long enough to deal if we get jumped?"

"Uh . . ."

"That's what I thought. I'm wondering if I might not be safer working alone."

Brownie made a snuffling noise. For a moment I thought that was a rude opinion. But up ahead there, whichever mutt was scouting had stopped to stare into a grove of unnaturally dense shadows. Her fur was up and her teeth were showing, but she wasn't growling. Yet.

Tone amused, Tara Chayne punned, "Point taken. You do have your more reliable auxiliaries."

Whatever was out there, it did not terrify my girls. Number Two spread out left, the other unnamed mutt went right, and Brownie made like a good Marine, heading straight up the middle. All three laid on some fierce growling.

Moonblight called forth her spirit centipede. You'd think that thing would be invisible in a moonless dark. It wasn't. It's navy-indigo presence was hard to spot when it didn't move, but when it did it coruscated with dull violet highlights. When it scuttled fast it shed random little purple-lilac sparks. Fairy sparkles trailed toward the shadow orchard, fast. I got the feeling that our potential antagonist had not been aware of what Moonblight had at her beck.

The dogs stopped, settled onto their haunches. They saw no need to get close enough to risk becoming collateral damage.

83

"You know this man?" Moonblight had a globe of glowing air perched on the tips of the upheld fingers of her left hand. It had the slight greenish cast of firefly light and was no more intense. Her right hand held a scented handkerchief pressed to her face. Her eyes were watering.

"His name is Tribune Fehlske, but people call him Lurking Fehlske. He's the top surveillance man in TunFaire. He's been watching me, or us, off and on, since before Strafa died. He's hard to spot and impossible to catch."

"First time for everything, eh?"

"I guess. His odor is his weakness. It's how you know he's around. Or has been around. He doesn't notice it himself. It's like he's had a lifelong allergy to soap. Maybe this will change his mind about hygiene." Unlikely, though. He had had the lesson before and never learned.

"One can pray."

"He isn't dead, is he?" I didn't have issues with Fehlske that went that deep.

"He'll be fine except for a headache."

"He was using some kind of sorcery, wasn't he?"

"He was creating a lurking place but not very well. He let us spot a place where the shadows were too thick."

"A natural talent, then?"

"Low-grade."

"I always wondered how he could be so good at not being noticed."

"He has talent that he doesn't understand consciously. I expect that he just thinks he's really good at what he does."

Lurking Fehlske was good. That was beyond debate. How he managed that didn't much matter to me.

I mused, not for the first time, "Why would he be watching us?"

"An excellent question and one for which I can offer no answer."

"How could he know to be waiting for us here? Even if there was a tracer on one of us, we only just decided to cut through here a few minutes ago. Yet there he was. Waiting."

Tara Chayne raised her glowing hand slightly, extending her forefinger to suggest that she needed a moment.

I backed off a few steps to reduce the chance that the smell would establish itself in my clothing. After the hustle of the day, I had worked up a good enough pong of my own, thank you very much.

The dogs went with me. They had had enough, too. Then Brownie found an excuse to take them off to scout "the perimeter."

Tara Chayne said, "Here is what probably happened. He was cheerfully larking around, keeping track of us, being the other thing I sensed. We caught him completely by surprise when we suddenly came this way. He couldn't get away without being seen, so he hunkered down and hoped we would go on by. It didn't work."

"Fits the known facts. Maybe we should wake him up and ask him questions."

"I don't think so. It's been too long a day already. My feet hurt. I'm happy to leave him napping." Shuddering, she slipped something inside Fehlske's shirt. She needed light to see by so had to use the hand that had been holding the handkerchief. She gagged but did not lose her lunch. Finished, she shook her hand violently to rid herself of any vermin that had climbed aboard.

She regained control. "We can find him if we need to talk to him. Now let's find Mariska and get this day over with."

"I won't last if she keeps moving."

"I think she's worn down herself. We were gaining before this."

Nice to be kept up to date, I didn't say out loud.

I was getting cranky. I was sure she must be, too. "We
should see about finding a snack, too."

"If the opportunity arises."

We covered a block, straight ahead and slightly downhill, and reached an intersection with a street I can't name
because it was dark and I didn't know the neighborhood.
Tara Chayne made a sudden stop.

"What?"

"Quiet."

Then I heard it, too.

Something was going on, quietly, back the way we had
come.

I couldn't see but was sure it was happening where
Lurking Fehlske lay.

Maybe somebody with no sense of smell was rolling him.

Moonblight's centipede scattered purplish sparks as it
scurried across the faces of several buildings, going to see.
When it stopped moving it was invisible.

Tara Chayne touched my arm. "Only a quarter mile to go."

The centipede caught up before we got there. She and it
communed, and then she sent it off to scout ahead.

The dogs weren't willing. They were nervous and staying
close.

"So," she muttered. "That's it."

"That's what?"

"Oh!" Like she was surprised to find me still with her.
"They didn't notice the tracer I put on him."

"They, who?"

She didn't want to discuss it. She pointed to a darkness
looming ahead, where the street we were following ended
as the trunk of a T. As yet there was no other light than that
shed by an immense number of stars, the cloud cover having cleared away. The place she indicated felt big and ugly
and exuded a psychic bad odor. "Mariska is in there. I think

she's asleep. I'll make sure." She gestured and whispered. Her centipede sparked into motion. Betraying sparkles falling off made for an interesting effect.

"Don't let me fall asleep while we're waiting for it to report." I had settled down with my back to the side of somebody's front steps. Brownie halfway climbed into my lap. The rest of the pack snuggled up, ready to sleep in a big, hot pile. Everybody was exhausted.

Very little time passed, but Tara Chayne had to use a magnum finger poke to bring me back. "Mariska is in there, alone." She was uncomfortable for some reason.

"What's wrong?" Groggily.

"The property belongs to the Hausers. It's empty today, but I remember visiting the place when I was a kid."

That left me with a sinking feeling. "Does that mean . . . ?"

"I'm hoping it just means Mariska ran to a place she knew would be empty, though she had to penetrate some ferocious wards to get in."

Obviously. Otherwise the place would have been reduced to a hole in the ground long since.

"I don't want to think that Richt might be one of the Operators."

That didn't seem plausible. Not sure why. My brain was working at ten percent. "Let's just load the wagon and worry about where the mules will come from when we need them."

"What? Oh. I got you. A little borrowed country wisdom."

"Wisdom, anyway."

"About earlier. I didn't mean to shut you out. I was preoccupied. The people messing with your Fehlske creature were Big Thing and Curly Top. Big Thing poked Fehlske a few times. When he didn't respond, it picked him up and took him away."

"Whoa! That thing is a better man than me, then."

"Perhaps it hails from a plane where such odors are perfume."

"Yeah. Sure. I'll buy that." The little blonde had begun to collect people from outside the tournament? Why?

More twists. More nonsense. And me such a simple, straightforward kind of Marine. "Let's do what we need to do." I lived through the struggle to get to my feet. "And here we go, girls."

The centipede hurried ahead. It wasn't worn out. The rest of us limped and dragged.

The first door we tried was protected with physical locks backed by magical wards. Nobody felt like looking for an easier entry. Moonblight used what energy she had left to break the locks and crack wards put in place by somebody as wrung out as we were.

We found Moonslight snoring on a braided rag rug in a huge room otherwise naked of furnishings. The entire house lacked any furnishings.

84

That finger poke, one more time. It was morning. Light didn't improve the ambience of the vacant house, nor did it increase the appeal of the witch with whom we shared it. The floor—my mattress—remained as soft as chert. Tara Chayne showed me that she had the stamina of a sergeant major, last to retire and first to rise.

It was morning. Light was getting inside somehow. I grumbled, "Why the hell do you keep doing that? It hurts!"

"Because it works. Get up. Time to go. We've been in one exposed position for far too long."

That made it feel like a recon mission back in the islands.

Misery, curdled, then double-dipped.

She did have a point. That little nasty was out there with her giant-ass friend, plus who knew what all else with a bad attitude where we were concerned?

Obviously, Tara Chayne Machtkess didn't just sit around Force headquarters when she'd gone down South. She was here for this morning because she'd learned her lessons then.

I sat up. "I feel like death on a stick and we never had anything to drink."

Brownie whimpered, maybe in sympathy but more likely in hunger. We'd been a team for no time and already she and her crew were spoiled.

I observed, "This is the hardest damned floor I ever slept on." The room itself was as big as a barn. A ballroom once, I suppose.

Some thumping then, from beyond Tara Chayne.

"And your little sis agrees." I leaned forward for a better look.

Mariska remained well and truly bound and gagged. She wanted to say something. She seemed desperate to speak. It might not be what I first thought. I could smell well enough to get that what she really wanted to do was complain.

Tara Chayne observed, "If you'd just stuck with us last night, you'd have woken up in a real bed, clean and dry."

Thump-thump. Thump-thump!

I said, "I believe I sense some anger issues."

"She can be that way sometimes."

"Last night we said we were going to take her back to your place today. That made sense at the time. But couldn't it be a little risky?"

"It could be. Yes. But I've already informed Denvers. Things are in motion. We'll stick to the plan."

She sent a message? How?

No sooner wondered than answered. The centipede thing.

It curled around Moonblight's neck, whispered into her ear. Then it unwound and slithered into a corner, where it faded from sight.

Tara Chayne grumbled, "Get your butt up so you can help me get up."

Oh. All right. She was in a foul mood because, despite not being bound, she remained a prisoner of her body. She resented the infirmities of age. More, she hated showing those where others could see.

Aching everywhere, I shifted my bones. I helped the sorceress. Between us, muttering and whining, we got Mariska upright, too.

Tara Chayne grumbled, "At least you didn't sleep on a bare floor." Not that the rag carpet would have given Mariska much comfort.

I growled, "Can't we just shut up and go? We're all hurting. This whining doesn't help. And I'm starving."

Mention of hunger, even if not by name, got the interest

of the dogs, all of whom made noises showing that they agreed with me.

I limped to the door. We had left obvious signs of break-age. We—in the form of Tara Chayne Machtkess—would have to apologize to Richt Hauser and make restitution. I took a cautious look outside, saw nothing suspicious, nor anything likely to attract attention—other than the coach rolling up. The coachman was having trouble staying awake.

"Oh, excellent!" Tara Chayne barked. "Most excellent. Here already, Chase gets a bonus. Let's move out. All aboard!"

She crossed to the coach boldly, indifferent to curious looks from a passerby, leaving me to manage Mariska. I would be the great hairy thing remembered if a kidnapping story began to circulate.

Tara Chayne opened the coach door, chucked dogs in-side. That offended Mariska's dignity. With hands bound behind her and wearing a gag, she still managed to make her displeasure plain. Stray dogs were so far beneath her that they did not belong in the same city, let alone the same vehicle, where they would shed mangy fur and parasites all over her.

Tara Chayne told her, "I could tie a rope around your neck and let you run along behind. You think you can keep up?"

Mariska allowed me to help her board.

Every facial twitch thereafter, as she sat facing us during our ride, betrayed a determination toward paybacks once the tables turned. And she was confident that they would.

These girls had been in this contest for a long time.

Mariska might be with the Operators more because Tara Chayne had chosen to oppose them than for some other irrational reason, including nostalgic romance.

I fought down a grin on imagining Mariska blaring mad laughter and yelling, "Retribution shall be mine!"

Neither woman was pleased when I couldn't keep the grin off my clock. But I would survive. Brownie still loved me.

85

The coachman dropped us in front of the Machtkess place while sunrise remained a looming threat. Denvers was waiting. He had no question or comment. Mariska was in a bleak mood. Her future could be nothing but a plunge over a precipice into the abyss.

Tara Chayne exploited the captive audience situation mercilessly, needling Mariska, trying to winkle out details by taunting her twin with what we knew already.

The technique was new to me. It might be proprietary, working only inside the Machtkess crew. Whatever, it did work in that Mariska became unable to keep her mouth shut. Still, yammer as she might, she didn't give us anything really useful. In the main, she just hemorrhaged emotionally.

Maybe when you're twins who have been at each other for three generations, you develop a shorthand script for cutting each other up.

Denvers was an amazement. He was the miracle man I always wanted Dean to be, with a better attitude. He had a breakfast ready when we got there. He began serving dogs and all as soon as he sent the coach on its way. He freed Mariska without comment, settled her in a chair that snagged her bony butt and held her down. She and Tara Chayne both seemed embarrassed around Denvers, like children who had done something naughty and expected to hear about it. Their manners toward each other were impeccable and ignored everything that had happened before they settled at the table.

The oddest thing was, Chase Denvers was younger than they were by more than a generation.

The dogs were settled and happy. Mariska picked at her food. Tara Chayne wolfed hers. I proceeded at a workmanlike pace. Denvers posted himself behind me. I sat opposite Tara Chayne. Mariska was between us, at the side of the table, to my right. He announced, "Madame Hedley-Farfoul wakened me in the night, having evaded and slipped our best wards."

That pleased neither sister. It bothered me less because I didn't know the woman. Mariska stopped eating altogether. Tara Chayne asked, "What was on Orchidia's mind?"

"She was obscure. Her principal interest seemed to be locating your gentleman friend here, however."

I pointed at my chest. Me? Couldn't be me, surely. But Tara Chayne took a cue from Denvers and nodded.

Not good. Not good at all. "She say why?"

"She did not. As I reported, sir, she was opaque. Nevertheless, it did seem related to the tragedy involving your spouse."

"How so? Wait. Never mind. Question withdrawn. You said she wasn't forthcoming."

He nodded, expression bland. The dummy was catching on. "She most certainly was not, sir."

"Any cues in her attitude?" I was hoping she hadn't gotten any crazy ideas about me or mine being connected to what happened to her twins.

My own twins had distant looks. Mariska cocked her head like she was trying to hear something faint from far away. Tara Chayne whispered to herself. Only her centipede heard her. It came out from under a sideboard, swam away through the air.

I wondered if she would ever put that thing away again.

Why would she in these exciting times?

Or maybe it wouldn't let her.

Too often sorcery works that way. Once out of the bottle, it stays out.

Denvers considered carefully before telling me, "I believe she just wanted to talk, sir, about your mutual losses. But she did seem to feel that patience had become a luxury."

Been there a few times. You just want to hurt things and break people till your own pain and anxiety go away.

"Then we'll hear from her soon," Tara Chayne said. "And she'll make her interest clear. Chase, you've outdone yourself. I'm almost tempted to give you a raise."

"Almost, ma'am?"

"Almost. If I actually did you'd be making too much to be hungry enough to always do your best. You'd start slacking off and then I'd have to fire you."

Denvers said, "Very well, ma'am. Perhaps you are correct."

"Of course I am. Never in the history of opinions have I been wrong, except for that one time when I thought I was wrong."

"Yes indeed, ma'am. It is an amazement, how you can be so perfectly right in every instance, even when you disagree with Madame Mariska, who is also correct on every occasion." Denvers turned to Mariska. Maybe she was supposed to threaten to hire him away, but her head wasn't in the game. She was wandering the wilderness of her thoughts.

Tara Chayne said, "Harumph!" An expression you hardly ever hear these days, unless you're around folks way older than you are. "All right. You're safe for now, Chase. Tell me what you learned about the conflict on the Hill last night." Sounding thoroughly confident that Denvers would have something to report.

Denvers launched a lengthy exposition that made it sound like he had directly witnessed two discrete incidents, one of which had dragged on for an hour, generating substantial collateral damage, then ended in a no-decision when the neighbors turned all buzz-kill on the duelists.

I observed, "Once again youthful high spirits are stifled by old sticks in the mud." What's a little property damage when you're having fun?

My jest hit the floor and lay there twitching in terminal tremors.

The encounter had blown air through the banked coals of clan hatreds born generations before the tournaments began. This flare-up had involved more participants than the anointed sets of Champions and Companions. Neither family would take a ritual defeat.

Another flaw in the tournament concept had surfaced.

I said, "Bet that's got the Operators all excited." Seemed to me that nobody needed to sabotage anything. The tournament could go belly up all on its own.

Nobody wanted to stick to the once-upon-a-time formalized rules.

Hell, most people didn't want to play. If anybody was going to get hurt, they hoped that would be the shithead Operators.

Mariska finally asked, "Orchidia really is involved?"

"Orchidia truly is, oh yes!" Tara Chayne burbled maliciously. "She lost her twins. She is not happy. Some have gotten hurt already, including your dear friend K'thul Hoo, who is no longer with us. More are going to get hurt. The Black Orchid does not fool around!"

Tara Chayne sounded thrilled. Mariska was aghast. "K'thul Hoo C'thug? What . . . ?"

Moonblight added, "Orchidia might accomplish what we couldn't last time. She might rid us of the Operators and their agents forever."

Moonslight began to shake.

Only then did Tara Chayne get it.

Mariska Machtkess would be on the Black Orchid's list. Mariska was the quarry that had drawn Orchidia to my house in time to deal with the squid-headed doom.

Denvers said, "The second incident was considerably smaller and not nearly as flashy, but your guest will find it of more personal interest." He faced me. "There was an attack in which your daughter was targeted. Thank heaven, it failed."

I frowned. My daughter? What was he blathering about?

I have no daughter, nor any other known offspring. Just some informally adopted . . .

"Excuse me, sir. Your stepdaughter is what I should have said."

"Oh. Kevans? Oh! Shit! What happened? She's all right? How bad—"

"Relax, sir. She wasn't harmed and she's quite safe now, thanks be to Bonegrinder, Kyoga Stornes, and a mysterious intercessor of unnaturally large size with an exceptionally foul temper. Witnesses said that he appeared to take the assault personally."

Naturally, I got all angry impatient and demanded details only the attackers could know. Denvers, however, delivered to the extent that I wondered if he wasn't making stuff up so he could answer increasingly minute demands.

"Stop it, Garrett," Tara Chayne said. "Shut up and listen."

"Huh?"

"You're so tired you've started making yourself obnoxious. We didn't rest well last night. I suggest we do so now, in real beds, and pick it up after lunch."

Before I could commence to begin to start taking anything wrong, Denvers said, "I'll show you to the guest quarters, sir. Your associates have been bedded down in the foyer."

Guest quarters? Associates? I pushed back from the table and rose, snagging a roll as I went.

I had not yet cleared the room when the twins began to bicker, each bone weary and Mariska handicapped by the ration of terror found wriggling on her plate only moments ago.

I checked the mutts. They were all tangled up and sound asleep. Not one cracked an eyelid. All had bulging bellies. I told Denvers, "Thank you."

He nodded, gestured for me to follow.

Guest quarters were back by the kitchen and just big enough to contain a cot. The door had a lockable outside latch I pretended not to notice. Good man Denvers went away without securing it.

I was as tired as I'd been in ages. So tired that I never had a thought about how my staying out all night might cause some worry elsewhere.

86

"Is there a plan for today?" Tara Chayne asked, picking at lunch and pretending I was in charge. "Something more directed than what we did yesterday?"

"We did good work. We got stuff stirred. We got stuff done."

Denvers had produced a fine lunch. I wondered what it would take to get him to take over for Dean. It was time Dean stepped back and slowed down.

Realistically, there was no chance that Denvers would. He was exactly where he wanted to be.

The sisters had made some surface peace. Tara Chayne was treating her twin as a truculent associate in our enterprise.

I couldn't turn a blind eye to what had happened earlier, but they had no trouble because they had decades of practice.

I understood the core motives behind the shift.

There was an angry professional killer out there who might be interested in hurting Moonslight. Her place in the conspiracy needed redefinition.

I was too groggy to think about anything but aches and pains in a body unaccustomed to so much extended, unhealthy exercise.

Pain is proof that exercise is not good. Pain is nature's way of telling you to knock it off or you're going to hurt yourself.

Oh, sigh. "I was thinking about going to Constance's place, getting everybody together, see who found out what, then scope out what to do next. Especially where Magister Bezma and Orchidia Hedley-Farfoul are concerned."

I probably ought to see Morley and Belinda and check in at the house to see if anyone there had heard anything interesting. We had all kinds of people supposed to be snooping. And the Dead Man might, hopefully, be recovering.

The twins grunted in unison. Tara Chayne said, "I was hoping for something more direct. I like a plan more sophisticated than 'Let's go whale on some bushes with sticks and see what runs out.'" She eyed her sister as though willing Mariska to contribute.

Mariska had nothing.

Since her recapture Moonslight spent much of her time drifting off the way I was so much lately. Maybe we should become a couple. But of what?

Denvers still had dogs in the foyer, out of weather that had gone damp again. He felt comfortable leaving the door propped open so they could take their business outside.

They barked some, neither alarmed nor combative. Denvers went to check, came back to announce, "Some people to see Mr. Garrett. Associates of his, they say."

Tara Chayne said, "Bring them in. See if they're hungry. Unless there are a lot of them. We can't feed a whole tribe."

"There are two, ma'am. We have no suitable furniture."

That told me who the visitors must be.

Sure enough, Denvers came back with Pular Singe and Dollar Dan Justice. Singe declined the offer of hospitality. Dan looked disappointed. He was a real rat, and real rats are always ready to tuck in. You never know when you will get the chance again.

I marveled that Singe had found me even in wet weather. Maybe I was developing Lurking Fehlske syndrome.

She started out giving me an evil, accusatory look but lost that after sniffing the air and finding me not guilty. I don't know why she would suspect me, with Tara Chayne.

Females always expect the worst of us, I suppose so they can be pleasantly surprised every dozen years or so.

I asked, "What's up? Did something happen?"

"Very little. Yet. I became concerned because you failed to come home."

"Exhaustion caught up." I didn't mention our gargoyle adventure.

Trying to stagger home last night would have been tempting fate. No way would I have been alert enough to slip another ambush. Nor had Brownie and the girls been at their best.

I was confident that "they" were still out to get me.

Whoa! Hey. Kevans became Mortal Champion because Furious Tide of Light had been eliminated before the tournament's official commencement. And they had tried to get her already.

I told Tara Chayne, "We definitely need to go to Constance's place." I asked Singe, "Any change in Vicious Min?"

"Not obviously. She is restless again. With Himself asleep . . ."

"Yeah." I had to worry big-time. Min might do some serious damage if she recovered even a little, as she had before. She might do permanent damage to Dean and the Dead Man.

Singe told me, "I brought in Saucerhead and Winger and told them to protect people and property if they could but to let her go if it looked like she might hurt somebody. If Kolda's drugs are not enough. I had Kolda give her some herbals."

Once again my little girl had proven herself so thoughtful and confident that it was scary.

"I told Penny and Dean no fighting Min. They should keep our inside doors closed so she cannot get into my office or the Dead Man's room. Dean can barricade the kitchen and go out the back if necessary. Mr. Mulclar worked on the back door. Dean can manage it now. I do not think Min can get upstairs. She should only be interested in getting away, anyway. Humility will have someone there to track her if she does run."

At her suggestion, no doubt.

John Stretch is brilliant, yet I do suspect that he owes some of his success to his sister's quiet suggestions.

"That's good," I told her. She needs the occasional dose of praise. "How about Playmate and the girl?"

"Playmate has gone home. He was concerned about his business."

"He should be. Why he leaves his idiot brother-in-law in charge is beyond me. What about Hagekagome? She go with?"

The dogs showed an interest when I said the name.

"He puts the brother-in-law in charge because he hopes responsibility will bring the man to a new appreciation of reality. An indulgence in willful wishful thinking, I expect. The girl stayed. Penny has her in with her. There is something exceedingly strange about that child."

"No kidding. Both of them, actually. But some people who know about Hagekagome want to keep it secret from me."

Tara Chayne might not have heard.

Singe asked, "How old would you guess she is?"

"Fourteen? Developed but a runt. And really, really slow." Tapping the side of my head.

"I would have guessed her to be about ten, but I'm not the sort who focuses on a human female's secondary sexual characteristics. Penny says she keeps telling stories about wonderful times you had together when she was living with you. Really simpleminded stories. Going for walks, chasing squirrels, curling up in bed together."

"That never happened. I remember every woman and girl I ever shared a bed with, even when all we did was sleep. Like my cousin Hattie when we were five. I never slept with a ten-year-old. Ever. And squirrels? I haven't seen a squirrel since I was ten. Not outside the Botanical Gardens. There aren't any trees for them anymore. Firewood thieves cut the trees down and hungry people ate the squirrels."

"I know. All that. None of it sounds like you. And Penny says the way Hagekagome tells it that stuff did all happen when you were ten."

"What? No. But . . ." But.

I have seen enough to know never to use the word *impossible*. A dim and worshipful girl who had slipped a few decades in time? Unlikely, but I couldn't reject the notion. I'd get my nose rubbed in it for sure if I did.

The trouble was, there'd never been a Hagekagome in my life before the funeral. Stipulating that I did have a vague sense that I ought to know that name.

A wave of sadness welled up and nearly brought me to tears.

"You remembered something?"

"No. I just thought about Strafa. Maybe I'll go see her later."

87

Tara Chayne pulled the bell chain beside Shadowslinger's door. A weird shriek sounded on the other side. She didn't wait for a response. She opened up and invited us in.

Mashego turned up as we were reorganizing in the foyer. She told us, "We were hoping you would come today. There is good news."

I refrained from comment. Nothing good could come out of my mouth just now.

Tara Chayne asked, "That good news would be what?"

"The mistress is awake. It happened during the night."

"Excellent."

"However, she isn't herself yet. She's sitting up. She's taking food and drink—plenty of both—but she is confused and has trouble communicating."

Bashir joined us. "She doesn't seem quite sure who she is or where. She has trouble talking clearly."

I said, "Classic stroke stuff, then."

"Yes. Dr. Ted concurs, with reservations."

"Reservations?"

"He says there are anomalies. But that there always are. You'll have to ask him about that."

"I see." I glanced at Tara Chayne. She didn't appear as pleased as she might have been. Still, she was a sparkling fountain of positivism compared to her sister. For Mariska the news seemed bleak indeed.

Singe and Dollar Dan had no comment and, likely, didn't

care. They were flighty as dust motes in a sunbeam, in constant motion in relation to each other and Mariska, always making sure they were poised to counter anything she tried.

Their nostrils and whiskers, and their ears, twitched and flexed, twitched and flexed. I thought it reasonable to assume that they were catching sound and scent cues that said Moonslight was considering trying something the moment she thought she had a chance.

I faced Mariska, leaned in, looked her in the eye from bad-breath range. "Not a good idea to try right now." Which startled her totally.

She had been so busy calculating that she hadn't caught the cues she should have picked up from the rest of us.

One glance round showed her that escape wasn't going to happen.

There was a noise out front, right on time. She looked hopeful for an instant, then lapsed into despair.

Moonblight demanded, "Really? You were thinking that way? Now? Under these . . . ?" Then she understood why her sister might take an idiot's chance.

This was Shadowslinger's hole-up. Shadowslinger was back. The old sow might be confused now, but how long would that last? How long before she remembered that her granddaughter had been murdered just down the Hill? How long before she heard that Mariska Machtkess had been in with one of the Operators?

I'd be desperate, too.

For no concrete reason, though, I was sure that Moonslight had had nothing to do with Strafa's death. I was sure she knew no more about the murder than the rest of us did—despite her connections with the Operators.

I told Singe, "I just had an awful notion." I grabbed Barate as he and Kevans came in quarreling, their timing perfect. "That was you two making the racket out there?"

"What?" he snapped. He was not in a good mood. Kevans was less so. Neither showed any improvement when Bashir told them that Shadowslinger had awakened.

I told anyone who cared to listen, "I just realized that,

despite everything they've done to mess with us and hurt us, the Operators haven't been acting like they were responsible for what happened to Strafa." I laid a hard, fierce, pointed look on Mariska Machtkess and got enough force behind it to make her push back.

"He had nothing to do with what happened to Strafa." "He" presumably being her clergyman boyfriend. "He was extremely unhappy about that. It meant that she couldn't participate."

Moonslight and I faced each other with people two-deep around us now. She continued. "He was sure his people were not involved. It would be stupid to eliminate Furious Tide of Light before the contest started."

I had been thinking that for a while. "Why would Strafa even be picked when the tournament usually pulled in only young people?"

Mariska eyed me like she thought the Algarda family Mortal Companion had been stricken dim. She pointed at Barate, then Kevans, stealthily.

Oh. They had no talent to give up.

She went ahead and said it. "Furious Tide of Light was a Windwalker and more besides. She was a deep reservoir of power and talent. She never did figure out what all she could do. She wasn't that interested."

And, I suspected, she'd looked like an easy harvest.

She was always trusting and naive.

That could have been what got her killed. Not having the kind of mind that would be wary of someone rolling a big-ass siege engine up the street. I could see her watching somebody park and arm the ugly bastard without ever being more than child-curious until it was too late.

I said, "Barate, we need to get everybody together so we can share whatever we've found out. I haven't gotten much. I kept nipping around the edges of the tournament thing. The villains kept coming at me from every angle."

"Considering their success so far and the relentless interest of the Guard, they must be running short on dirty workers."

Kevans's mood did not improve. She was unhappy about everything. Plus, she'd had her nose rubbed in the fact that she had been passed over in favor of an old woman like her mother.

She was the new Algarda Champion, but one unsuccessful attack had convinced her that she wanted no part of the game. That had penetrated her shield of adolescent wishful thinking. That had gotten her attention where the murder of her mother had not.

Kevans felt compelled to say something. "I'm going to go check on Grandmother. Then I'm going to stay right here, with her, until this absurd shit is over." Her glare dared anyone to disagree or to correct her language.

All she got was an explosive sigh of relief from her father.

88

Once we started upstairs I no longer wanted to go. It had to be done, though. It could be. I had dealt with other warped defectives.

I don't know why I thought Shadowslinger's having suffered a stroke would make her more dangerous, but the conviction was there.

Her room stank of sickness and foul digestive gasses. Mashego was with her, beside the bed, patiently spooning Shadowslinger a dog-food-looking meat paste a bit at a time.

Shadowslinger looked healthier than I expected, considering how vicious strokes can be. She recognized us. She tried to talk but could not produce a sensible sentence, nor was her speech clear enough to understand. My mother was the same way after her second stroke.

Mom had trouble communicating after the first but had come up with workarounds. Worst for me had been her inability to get my name out. She called me "man" or "that man."

Shadowslinger's chow looked just awful. It probably smelled awful, too, but the stink could not break through that already in the room.

With the tact of her age Kevans said, "Isn't there a window we can open or something? This place reeks enough to gag a maggot."

No window was visible. Wall hangings kept any outside light well tamed.

Cold eyes settled on me. Where else could Kevans have acquired an expression like the one she'd used?

One pair belonged to the old sorceress herself. I thought I ambushed a glint of amusement. It went away quickly but left me reflective.

Bashir oozed through the crowd, past the foot of Grandmother's bed, to the wall on the far side. "Would you give me a hand, sir?" He wanted to take down the massive carpet that hung against that wall.

And carpet it was. You could see the wear patterns traffic had left when it graced the floor of some Venageti poobah, before Shadowslinger arranged for it to have a better home.

I asked for instructions. Bashir provided them. Straining, we lowered the hanging to the floor. That revealed a motheaten tapestry. That coming down revealed a window behind. Clearing the shades and shutters so its leaves could be swung wide demanded careful work. The wooden parts were rotten.

Bashir swung the leaves inward, right and left, so he could get the outside shutters open. Then he swung the windows outward. Constance made unhappy noises. She did not want to face the outside light.

She did not have to shrink from that. The outside world had gone completely glum and rainy. Soggy cold air tumbled inside.

I stated the obvious. "Those shutters need replacing." Paint wouldn't be enough. They had gone too long without.

Barate said, "Another of a thousand maintenance issues that have been ignored for years." He spoke toward the window. Neither his mother nor Bashir responded.

Kevans muttered something about how somebody who was too damned cheap to spend a copper now was going to have to shell out silver later. That did get a reaction from Shadowslinger, who had caught every critical inflection.

I decided to be the peacemaker. "We have bigger problems. Let's deal with them before we decide what rouge to put on the pig."

Barate said, "Much as we need fresh air in here, I think we can do without the wind and the rain."

A gust had just scattered a gallon of cold drizzle inside.

Barate pulled one wing of the window shut and the other in till there was just a four-inch gap. Mashego backed off with the meat paste and, instead, handed the old horror a pad of paper and one of Cypres Prose's stoutest Amalgamated writing sticks. Shadowslinger was able, impatiently, to communicate via head shake and clumsy block letter printing.

She used her right hand. Like most Algardas, though, she was naturally left-handed. Her left side had more coming back to do.

She let us know that she wanted to hear every detail of what had been going on while she was unconscious. She took the reports without reacting unless two or three people started talking over one another or arguing about some detail. She did show some irritation when Moonslight's role came up. She didn't seem especially surprised to learn that old campaigning pal Meyness B. Stornes had survived and was masquerading as a magister of the Church. She did get excited when she heard that Kevans had been drafted in Strafa's stead and that someone had tried to kill her.

The attacks on me and Tara Chayne were, apparently, no big deal. Only to be expected. Just a device for attritting the opposition.

Somehow the Black Orchid never came up. Shadowslinger had Dollar Dan Justice come tell what the rat men had done and seen while helping deal with Kevans's attackers. That only left her more upset.

I did my best to help Dan relax and report calmly. I also observed, "We still don't have a Dread Companion."

Shadowslinger's sleepy gaze brushed me momentarily. She was exhausted now. She was pushing herself too hard. She grunted. I couldn't tell what that meant, nor could anyone else.

Dr. Ted had remained quiet and out of the way till now. He decided that she was about to hit a wall. "Time for everyone to leave. Bashir, take them to the kitchen. They can go on with this down there."

By which he meant following up on secondary conversations concerning the evidence having to do with Strafa's death as well as the search-and-research work that had been under way.

Singe would, likely, be more use there than I would. She was in touch with the people doing the digging at least part-time.

I was next to last to go, leaving only Mash behind me. Dr. Ted had no intention of leaving.

Shadowslinger completed a laborious effort with her writing stick. She held the pad up, hands trembling. It said *Everyone out! Accept Garrett.*

You don't correct a Shadowslinger. Not when you know what she meant.

Ted and Mash both wanted to argue. Ted and Mash gave that up after one good look at Shadowslinger's darkening visage.

Visage is one of those cool words you don't get to use much. It was the perfect choice here. The terrible old woman's face had become a curtain between her interior realm and the rest of the universe. Intimations of rising storms therein left you determined to be somewhere else when the curtain rose.

Shadowslinger leaned into her writing stick and paper while Ted and Mashego made their getaway.

89

Shadowslinger's new message said CHECk HalL. for EAVEsdrop. MAKE It Go.

"Got it." I looked. Sure enough, a herd of villains lurked there, ears cocked. I borrowed Shadowslinger's pad to show them what she had to say. They moved on surlily.

I told Barate, "She'll know if you sneak back." Warning delivered while hoping that someone, preferably him, would be there to rescue me if Shadowslinger became overheated.

"I understand."

He slunk away. And I understood that he wouldn't be back. I was on my own. I would have no cover whatsoever.

I squared my handsome broad shoulders, put a smile on my handsome rugged face, turned to face the dread symphony.

With precision timing a gust flipped one leaf of the window open and flung rainy cold air inside. I scooted round the bed to deal with that.

Slowly, in words only slightly slurred, so softly it was unlikely that an eavesdropper might hear, Shadowslinger said, "Leave it. I need the noise."

Mouth arrayed to catch horseflies and other small game, I ceased all efforts to do a good deed.

Speaking slowly and straining to make each word understandable, she said, "As you have begun to suspect, my health issue is not as debilitating as I have pretended."

I closed my mouth so I could open it to ask a question. Several questions, actually. Or maybe a book full. That's the kind of guy I am. I have an inquiring mind.

Shadowslinger cut me off with a look. "This seemed a good idea at one time. It no longer is. Time has flown. There isn't much left. No more than forty hours."

I had no idea what that meant. She didn't explain. She refused to waste time on explanations. She was down to her deep reserve.

"You must end the tournament threat before time runs out."

"But Strafa—"

"Your wife will be there. She will always be there. The Operators must be handled before that can be."

I sighed. This meant a lot to her, in a strategic sense, not just personally.

I didn't get it.

As is the case most all the time in my world, something was going on and I wasn't being clued in.

She showed me a strained smile. "Break the Operators in the next forty hours. I promise you, you will be glad that you did."

Another hefty Marine Corps sigh. "I can but do my damnedest, madame." Then I had an idea. An unpleasant recollection that might be part premonition. "No one told you before. The Black Orchid has come out of retirement. She has become involved."

Nothing for five or six seconds, followed by a whole-body shudder, as though the incoming air had just added a sudden arctic chill. Several more seconds slipped away. She regained control. "Orchidia Hedley-Farfoul? Involved? How? And why?"

I told her about Orchidia's twins.

"Damn me, I should have anticipated that. The Operators should have taken her into account, too. This could be a disaster."

Wow! The Black Orchid had an impact on Constance Algarda as big as Shadowslinger had on regular people.

Orchidia Hedley-Farfoul's talent for murder must be all-time world-class.

Constance pulled herself together. "Orchidia is not incapable of reason. She is, in fact, coldly intellectual. Assuming she has sense enough to consult family, Bonegrinder will tell her the Breakers had nothing to do with her twins."

Her condition had improved dramatically again.

Funny, that.

I kept my thoughts off my face, which I can do occasionally, in a desperate moment. "Breakers?"

"It's what we called our gang when we were rebels. A weak inside joke. I use the name to include anybody interested in wrecking the Operators and tournament."

The Orchidia thing truly had her stressed. She was giving stuff away left and right.

She made another effort. "This means nothing to you. It changes nothing for you. Though you will have to move fast if you want to question Meyness Stornes without the assistance of a necromancer. I am too weak to reach him once he goes toe-to-toe with Orchidia and loses—despite the season."

Huh? "Maybe she doesn't know about . . ."

"What she doesn't know she soon will. Nothing stops the Black Orchid once she . . . Understand this. Orchidia Hedley-Farfoul might actually be the avatar of Death. Enma Ai. Death made manifest by faith."

She had lost me.

"Some believe that. Their belief may not be just fearful superstition. Divine possession is uncommon but not unknown."

No. It was not. I had seen it. It seemed improbable here, but . . . Most anything that the mind can imagine can happen in TunFaire, and certainly will in time.

Constance was wobbly from effort, and ready to collapse.

She said, "You must . . . resolve the tournament situation . . . before sunrise day after tomorrow."

"Sunrise? Day after . . . ? What? Why?" Tomorrow, come

to think, was Day of the Dead, a holy day important in some of our more successful religions. Sundown tomorrow would start All-Souls Night, significant to those who believed that it was possible to communicate with the dead.

The believers include me, though I don't put much stock in All-Souls. I have dealt with ghosts. I had a relationship with the shade of a woman who was murdered before I was born. During All-Souls Night the membrane between worlds is so thin that anyone willing to work at it can reach the dead—if the dead are inclined to be reached.

Those that aren't too lost to respond usually don't want to. Those who do are the sort most likely to become haunts anyway.

Only a few really strange folks do try to peek into the next world.

I frowned at that grim old woman. "What are you planning?"

She wasn't listening. She was slipping away. She asked the air, "Oh, what have I done?" I think. She was mumbling and facing away. "It may be too late." Seconds fled. "Nothing went the way it was supposed to." And then, fifteen seconds later, "I guessed wrong. He is too dim and too lazy to get it done in time." Then she was out completely and that looked real.

I wasn't happy. I had a powerful notion that somebody, name of Garrett, was the "he" that had her muttering about dim and lazy. Which was not even a little fair because she, like everyone else, hadn't given me any explanation of what was going on, what I was supposed to do, or why.

Stipulated, she could be right. I might be too dim. I was less flexible in my readiness to concede being too lazy.

Damn, did I wish that the Dead Man hadn't gone south for the winter! He might be able to say why a holiday that hitherto had had no mention would, according to Constance Algarda, loom large as a deadline in which the dead part might play a big role.

I wasn't going to find out anything leaning over an unconscious, stinky old sorceress while rain-laden air whipped my face through a window long overdue for closing.

I closed it.

I went down to the kitchen. The crowd eyed me expectantly.

90

"Can anybody explain how the Day of the Dead or All-Souls Night might connect with the Tournament of Swords?"

Blank looks. Of course, hardly anybody knew much about the tournaments. A week ago only a couple of us had heard of that idiocy.

I caught Moonslight shyly, indecisively, gradually, sliding a tentative hand upward while involved in a fierce internal struggle, her connection with Magister Bezma warring with a desire to see the right thing done.

She knew perfectly well that she hadn't been serving the cause of righteousness.

Not many of us ever do. Not deliberately, with benevolence aforethought.

I asked, "Has this thing just taken another unexpected right-angle turn?"

I hadn't left out much that Shadowslinger had said. I wanted them thinking. These people were not stupid. One quick mind might catch something the rest of us overlooked.

Singe eased in close, whispered, "We need to check in at home. There should be reports. And he might be awake."

"Is there a real chance that he is?"

"Probably not. But I prefer to remain optimistic."

"Good enough for me. So. See if there are enough umbrellas for everyone who wants to go."

The modern collapsing umbrella is another product of

the genius of Kip Prose. Most of those currently in the hands of the public weren't purchased by the people actually using them. There is nothing more frequently stolen than the umbrella on a rainy day. Many have a lengthy, adventurous provenance.

Amalgamated keeps prices up by marketing its more desirable products in quantities below demand. The policy encourages piracy, but the Tate old men do well at convincing the public that a deep and abiding social handicap comes with the purchase of anything that is not a genuine Amalgamated-manufactured, Prose-designed product.

None of which was germane. Just another parenthetical distraction . . .

Barate poked me in my favorite tender spot. "The coach is on its way, Garrett. Be ready."

"Coach? What coach?"

"Mother's coach. To keep you from drowning on your way. I told you about it ten minutes ago." He was worried about me.

"I'm sorry. I'm really lost, especially now that we're up against some vague deadline. It just keeps getting more confusing."

"I won't argue about that. There's more going on than we know. Keep an eye on Tara Chayne. She'll figure it out first. She knows Mother better than anyone."

I showed him my interrogative hoisted eyebrow.

"Better than me? Oh, hell yes! I never came close to figuring the old bitch out."

I stepped to the kitchen door. The rain had become a soaker. A cold, steady soaker. You couldn't tell what time of day it was, only that it was daytime. It was earlier than I thought, being only shortly after noon.

Shadowslinger wasn't big on newfangled luxuries like collapsible umbrellas. They went bad after you used them a few times, so you had to buy another. She wasn't going to play that game with crooked tradesmen.

Mash and Bash did own a knockoff that had to have its too-light stays rebent each time it opened.

They proved that couples will argue about the stupidest things by engaging in a bitter campaign to decide whether or not the imperfect umbrella ought to be left open all the time.

"It doesn't matter!" I barked in frustration. "We only have one for this many people."

Barate said, "Calm yourself, son. Being a clever old fox who's actually had to deal with weather in the past, I told the coachman to pick you up under the porte cochere."

Kevans chunked in a rare contribution. "We wouldn't want all your sugar and spice to get washed away."

That girl has issues.

Dr. Ted came back from a quick sortie into Shadow-slinger territory. "Such a spoiled, selfish bunch, fussing over a damp that you're not even out in yet. Think of the poor sodding red tops out there who have it running down the backs of their necks because their lunatic boss wants to know about every breath that one of us takes."

That was an excellent diversion. Not that I much cared about the comfort of those fools. They ought to be holed up someplace warm and dry. I was hardly ever that dedicated to my work—unless maybe I was close up on somebody that might lead me to whoever did what happened to Strafa . . .

Barate said, "Mash, I want you, thank you kindly, to go wait for the coach. The rest of us will go on making hash here."

He wanted to talk about Strafa. Unfortunately, what we knew still boiled down to little more than we had right after the event. A canvass of the neighborhood had not produced one eyewitness, nor even anyone who had noticed an itinerant siege machine—though the forensics sorcerers had determined the site from which the fatal bolt had to have been discharged.

The murderous ballista had vanished off the face of the earth.

The missing fragment of bolt had failed to turn up despite a diligent effort by Guard searchers.

Barate was more than grim when he admitted, "I hate saying this, Garrett, but for now it looks like they're going to get away with it."

"No. They won't. They may stay ahead of me for an hour, a day, a month, but not forever. We've already turned up plenty of threads to pull. We pull, sooner or later somebody will panic and do something stupid." As if they had not been doing a whole lot of that already.

Only, I might not get to yank any strings right away. Gratification might be delayed.

Shadowslinger had talked about that onrushing deadline with heightening despair. I hadn't liked it. I still didn't like it. But some feel for it had been ripening in the shadowed reaches of my imagination. For no concrete reason I had begun building a sense of importance and urgency myself.

Mashego returned. "The coach is ready."

At which point curiosity reared its head. "If Mash and Bash are Constance's only staff and you're staying here, who's driving the coach?"

That sort of question could be troubling to a guy with a twist of mind like mine.

Barate responded, "Two of our better private patrolmen, Peder and Piet Petief, handle the stable work and drive part-time. They're brothers. Twins, in fact. Reliable men."

More twins. Curious. No way that could have any real meaning, but it was interesting. Still . . . How reliable could guys be if they walked away from their regular job whenever they could pick up a bonus for handling an outside chore? Especially when that involved collaboration with horses?

I guess the index of reliability depends on the gauge you use as a measure.

91

I got water down the back of my neck, plenty, by choosing to ride up top with the driver. Piet was dressed for the weather. I only pretended to be, though I did have use of the Mash and Bash umbrella until a rogue gust snatched it away and smashed it against the face of a building.

"I need to find myself a better wet-weather hat."

"At least up here you don't have to deal with that." Piet pointed down and back with his right thumb. Someone, name of Mariska Machtkess, aka Moonslight, just would not shut up about the indignity of having to share the coach with a pack of stray dogs. Again.

"The mutts aren't her real problem." She had been friendly with Brownie when she had nothing else weighting her down.

"I know. Rat people get up some folks' noses just by managing to survive."

I grunted, shook some water off my brim. "Would you bet anything against the possibility that there was a Machtkess ancestor involved in creating the rat people?"

"My mama's stupid kids all died young."

I grunted again, this time hurting a bit. You didn't hear that expression much because it was a truth that touched most every Karentine family. Not to mention, a lot of mamas' smart kids had died young, too.

Piet remained oblivious. I sensed no malice. How could he possibly know about my brother, anyway? He said, "That would be the safest bet you ever made."

"Really? I'm not good with history."

"Oh? Story goes, a direct ancestor of the Machtkess women, and his twin brother, created the grays."

Interesting. "Twins run in their family?"

Piet was quiet for a while, then said, "I never thought about it before, but twins happen a lot on the Hill. Only not identicals. Curious."

"It run in your family?"

"Peder and I are part of triplets, actually. Him and me aren't identical. Pyotr was my identical. He didn't make it home."

All right. He wasn't an insensitive jerk. All I could think to say was "My brother, too. And my dad, right about the time that Mikey was born."

That brought up some old curiosities about inconsistent stories and some of the timing, back when, that I put out of mind as soon as I could. There was nothing there that I needed to know about now.

"Our dad, too. He was an idiot. He asked for it. Did his tour. Then he volunteered to go back. He was a hero."

So much bitterness. It was amazing. But I had no trouble understanding.

I asked, "How about we talk about something a little less gloomy?"

"On a day like today? In weather like this? This is a gift from the gods. It's them giving us a chance to get it all sluiced out."

"They've given us plenty of chances lately, then."

"You got that right. At least it's not as hot as it usually is this time of year. You know we're being followed?"

"I haven't been paying attention, but I did figure we might be."

"I reckon. You being you, as they say. This mess being what it looks like it's getting to be."

I glanced over, wondering what he meant. He sounded stressed when he said it.

He went on, "My brother and I owe you an apology, Mr. Garrett. We was on patrol . . . We should've been there when . . . We got sucked in by the diversion that day. We was pioneers in the army. We got a lust after things that go boom and make smoke. That day there was plenty of flash, lots of bang, and all kinds of colored smoke. Way around the Hill."

Had someone done any finding out about that? Maybe the bad guys made some mistake rigging things over there.

"You couldn't help yourselves."

Startled, he looked at me like I'd just given him absolution. "That's what Peder said when we found out what happened while we was off our patch. After. He bawled like a baby, he did. Everybody loved that girl. He said, 'We just couldn't help ourselves, Piet.' "

Not quite sure why, I mused, "It was almost like somebody knew exactly what it would take to get you out of the way."

Two seconds later we were looking at each other, first with big eyes, then frowning as we both wondered if I hadn't just said something important without any forethought.

Piet almost ran over a couple of people, he was so distracted.

"Hey! Godsdamn! The fuck, youse assholes? Be watching the fuck where you're goin'!"

I babbled an incoherent apology on Piet's behalf, then noted that we were on Macunado already, clattering down my block, having just accidentally missed killing one of Belinda Contague's biggest and most unpleasant lifeguards. His temper might be frayed. His dampness suggested that he had been out in the weather for a while.

I told Piet, "That's my place there where the coach is standing."

Nervous, he asked, "Does that belong to who I think it belongs to?"

"If you mean the queenpin, yes." Smug me. I'd made up a word to describe Belinda.

Her father, Chodo, had been called the kingpin.

"I heard you was friends."

"Sort of. Pretty iffy. It's a long story."

"I'll buy you a beer sometime." The offer was a sideways apology for his lapse the day Strafa died.

"Deal. And I'll buy you one back. Actually, we could go through a keg before I get it all told." And, as he brought the coach to the curb behind Belinda's rig, "You don't need to feel bad. You didn't do wrong that day."

"I know. Up here." He smacked his forehead. "If we stood where we was and then fifty, sixty people died over yonder because we wasn't there to pull them out, fuginagy, we'd have our asses in a sling big-time, anyway. For negligence or misprision or some damned thing they made up on account of somebody who don't count has got to pay. But . . ."

"Yeah. But. It keeps eating on me, too, Piet. So. Here's something you can do to help. I don't know how much, but it's something. Go see Barate Algarda. Tell him what we talked about. Tell him he should find out if anybody really looked into those explosions."

"Sure. And good luck." Mariska was getting loud. Her confidence must have gotten a boost. "You might need it."

"Thanks." I would need it less than he feared.

I had a secret weapon called ignorance.

Mariska hadn't been told where we were headed. Once she found out that she was in range of the Dead Man . . .

She screamed like a scalded baby.

Not happy, our Moonslight.

She panicked. She tried to run.

That didn't work. A lot of people helped take that option away.

92

Belinda was still inside her wagon. She wasn't alone. Morley shared the space, unhappily. They were waiting there because Penny wouldn't let anybody inside while Singe was away. Why they bothered to stay was never clear. Maybe it was a place where they could bicker without being seen.

They had not had a pleasant wait. I saw that right away. They were butting alpha wills again, presumably. Neither volunteered an explanation.

I said, "Singe will have the door open in two shakes. Dean will have something to warm you up."

Reassurances didn't help. Some folks you can't please.

"I'll ask if he can't send something out for your guys, too, Belinda." Not so much being thoughtful as reminding her that others had it less pleasant than she did.

A waste. That sociopath thing again. That inability to empathize.

Morley peeked past the edge of a curtain. "The door is open."

Sure enough. And there was Penny, hands on hips, unhappy because the cold and damp were creeping in. Because wet dogs and wetter people were crowding her, fouling the hallway.

Morley began to chuckle as we got in line.

"What?" Belinda and I both demanded.

"Garrett, you're finally living the dream."

"What does that mean?"

"What you daydreamed about when you were a kid has finally come to pass."

"I'm still lost."

He shook his head, chuckled some more. "You wanted your own harem. And now you've got one."

His expansive gesture as we stamped the water off us on the stoop included not only Singe, Penny, and Hagekagome, down the hallway greeting the all-girl dog team, but also a set of twins who pretended to be in heat most of the time.

Belinda began to snicker, too. "A harem for Garrett. It's precious. Jon Salvation could make it into a play."

Winger and Saucerhead leaned out of my old office, sleepily curious about the sudden racket. They were a dismal-looking pair. One nodded to herself and pulled back, no doubt resuming what she considered a well-deserved nap.

"He'd write a real tragedy if he put those two in it." I grinned for a moment. I can be a humble, self-effacing kind of guy, but could not long forget that this moment existed only because my wife had been murdered.

Penny scattered rags and threadbare carpets to protect the hallway floor. Even the insensitive Machtkess sisters tried to avoid dripping everywhere. Which left only the dogs. . . .

Hagekagome used the shreds of an ancient towel with one hand and loved her doggie friends with the rest of her.

She spotted me. Her face lit up. She jumped up and charged, excited as a puppy, smashed into me, pounded my chest a few times with her little fists, then just clung. She didn't tell me how much she hated me.

We got plenty of stares. I looked back at everybody, silently begging for advice. Tara Chayne gave me a nod, a reminder to be nice and gentle. Nobody else seemed particularly concerned, though Penny treated herself to a mild sulk. So I just hugged with my right arm and patted Hagekagome's back with my left hand while I tried to figure out what the hell was happening.

Whatever that might be, Brownie and the girls approved.

Mariska revealed a catalogue of expressions, beginning with bewildered and circling back round to much the same thing. She started out focused on one particularly handsome former Royal Marine and finished fixed on the supernaturally beautiful but weird kid clinging to him.

I couldn't help observing, "Something changed while I was gone."

"She got it together some," Penny said. "She still doesn't make a lot of sense, but at least she's confused in plain Karentine. So. Can you people move inside far enough for me to shut the door on the weather?"

Cold, damp air nipped the back of my neck.

Singe said, "Everyone into the office, please." Grimly reluctant. They would track in grime and moisture. Belinda and Morley looked like they wanted to change their minds about visiting but could not come up with a plausible excuse for having wasted the time they had already.

I eased Hagekagome off me, patting her head. Damn, she was beautiful, and it looked like she had matured some in the past few days. She'd be melting guys into slack-jawed puddles with a smile in another week.

She allowed herself to be peeled, went back to Brownie and the girls. Those four seemed thrilled by events. They congratulated their friend.

I checked Penny. She shrugged. I asked, "Any change in there?" with a nod toward the Dead Man's room. "Or there?" In the direction Tharpe and Winger had vanished.

"No. And no. Dean says not to expect anything there for a long time. The big woman is way out of it, but those two in there with her . . . They eat like pigs getting ready for winter." She glanced toward the kitchen. "I should go help Dean. You should close the door."

Most of the crowd had moved into Singe's office. They would presume upon my hospitality, too, also storing fat for hard times.

Dean had as much experience with Old Bones as I did. His estimate would be good. I had no time to check on

Himself. There were invaders in my establishment who had no need to know the true situation.

Before leaving to wrangle guests, Singe asked Penny, "Did anyone bring reports this morning?"

"There's always somebody banging on the door. Dean said don't let nobody in but you or Garrett. We can't be sure who our friends really are. So I ignored everybody."

Morley awarded that a surly growl.

Dean was getting all cynical and paranoid. Probably a good thing now, though it might impede the flow of information.

I asked, "Did you check the peephole?"

"You know what? I did. Every time I heard somebody out there."

Smart-ass.

"I made a list. I put it on Singe's desk."

Singe suggested, "Why don't you two come into the office, too? We will shoehorn you in. Those watching outside will inform interested parties that we are home and may be available."

93

I was thinking that most of what we had others doing had become redundant when, serendipitous, there came a discreet knock. Sourly, still not having fled to Dean's realm, Penny went to the door. I produced a head knocker, in case, while Singe conjured a kendo sword out of nothingness. Those things are supposed to be for play and practice, but you don't want to be on the downhill end without protective gear. As the Block and Relway vision takes hold, more and more people carry them for self-defense.

Even rat people get away with that. It will be interesting to see the legal weaseling after some offended rat man applies one to a particularly obnoxious human bully.

I wondered where Singe got her martial toys and when she found time to learn how to use them.

Ever the wonder child, that girl.

Penny announced, "It's an old lady."

"Old lady?" What now? Other than Shadowslinger, all the old ladies in this mess were already on hand.

Then Penny said, "And here comes somebody else. It's one of those weird guys from your other place."

"Let me see."

She was right. There was a woman out there. Old, I'm not sure she would accept. Maybe just starting to sneak down the back slope of forty. Definitely not as elderly as Penny's tone implied. But, then, the girl was just getting some traction on her teens. Everybody was old to her.

The woman turned, said something to Dex. He replied. I couldn't hear what. It was obvious, though, that Dex was agitated. He was wet and unhappy about that, too. I said, "Stand by, folks. I'm letting them in."

The would-be visitors were facing the door when I opened it, Dex behind the woman. She was maybe five feet two, down there around mom size. Anxious Dex barely kept from running her over when she awaited an invitation to step forward. I had a passing thought about malicious sprites and vampires.

Dex glanced behind him and growled. He was not fond of weather.

"Do come in," said I, pretending I was the butler. Back by the kitchen door the man who actually butled occasionally, who had stepped out to check on the fresh commotion and maybe to see what was keeping Penny, began shaking his head. He returned to the kitchen to start another gallon of tea.

The woman was in no rush. Dex, however, was. I gestured. "Penny, please take the lady into the office and make her comfortable while I try to save Dex from a galloping case of the panics."

Penny bobbed her head to the woman and gestured toward the office door. "Ma'am."

Dex protested, "I don't have a galloping case of anything."

Muted sounds of dismay came from inside the office, Mariska and Tara Chayne distressed. I was right when I guessed the newcomer to be Orchidia Hedley-Farfoul.

There was some thumping from the sickroom at the same time. Winger cursed at Saucerhead.

"Then why are you in such a big rush that you had to be pushy-rude to the Black Orchid?"

Dex started to contradict his employer but realized that he would do so in an employment-unfriendly economy— and, more importantly, the name I'd dropped hit bottom and clattered around in the tin bowl of his mind.

Elsewhere, Saucerhead cursed Winger back. They

sounded like a couple of ten-year-olds. I couldn't make out what the fuss was about.

Dex's mouth worked like that of a bass out of water. "I got it. Deep breaths. Dex Man calming down." Apropos of nothing, apparently, he added, "The wind snatched my umbrella when I was on my way over here."

"It has been a bit gusty," I conceded. "Are you calm enough to explain? Because I do have that other guest to attend to." I was still standing there with the door cracked half a foot, letting cold air in while trying to make out what a couple bearing a striking resemblance to Preston Womble and Elona Muriat were doing.

Singe's office had gone as silent as a grave—till Penny yelled, "Will you shut that godsdamn door? We're freezing in here."

Dean came out of the kitchen with his cart. Teacups, our biggest pot, cookies, and a platter of little sandwiches graced its top. He awarded Hagekagome and the mutts a fine scowl. They got out of his way with a maneuver so deft it looked rehearsed. The girl asked Dean if he wanted her to help. Dean allowed as how that was thoughtful of her and yes, he certainly could use some assistance.

That was Dean Creech being gentle, empathetic Dean, including the challenged kid, making her part of something bigger than the canine tribe.

"Dex?" Dex had witnessed and understood. Dex beamed at Dean.

Dex would have spent much of his life being excluded.

94

Saucerhead and Winger started cursing again. It sounded like somebody slugged somebody.

Penny yelled at me about the door. Again.

Dex opened his mouth, finally about to get to the reason why he had come to the house.

Vicious Min bulled out of my old office in a ferocious drunken stagger, hunched over, with Tharpe on her back and dragging Winger by the left ankle. That was a sight, Winger being as big as me. Min banged herself and Winger off the doorframe, hard. Saucerhead hung on despite getting banged against the overhead for being stubborn. Min's face had taken a serious beating. Saucerhead's, too.

He kept punching. Min tried to smash him against the ceiling. His eyes crossed, but he kept on keeping on.

And that is what made Saucerhead famous. He could take anything and keep on scrapping.

So could Vicious Min.

She headed my way, scattering Dean and his cart. The dogs went crazy when she shoved Hagekagome.

I still had the head knocker handy. And still had the door held open. I realized that and tried to do something about it at a time when I should have been concentrating on getting some serious oomph on my stick.

Things didn't work out.

Min brushed my stick aside and trampled me in a single drunken stagger. I sat down to bleed. Min flung the door wide. Rain blew in. She blew out, still dragging Winger, who never stopped screeching. She did scrape Saucerhead off on this doorframe. He fell on me, twitching some. Min realized she still had hold of Winger, let her go as she reached the bottom of my steps. Winger lay moaning in the rain.

All through the action growling, nipping dogs participated in the excitement, making the footing difficult for all two-leggers still standing. They might have continued the chase if Hagekagome hadn't gotten herself together and called them back. Then she got busy trying to lever Saucerhead off the two-thirds of me that he had buried.

I was dizzy but did glimpse a white-faced Dex pressed into the wall by Singe's office doorway, unharmed but shaken. His eyes rolled up. He sagged.

People from Singe's office broke up a clog in that doorway, came out babbling questions so vigorously that they frightened Hagekagome all over again. I got hold of her hand, which had an instant calming effect. Helping hands moved us against the wall, me, Hagekagome, and Dex, with Dean on the other side of Singe's office doorway. Saucerhead came next; then a gang of cursing souls conspired to ferry Winger back inside and into my old office, where the sorceresses among us employed such healing skills as they possessed.

Winger had suffered a concussion. She had bruises and abrasions everywhere. She had some broken bones—and yet I didn't doubt that she would be good as new before long. She was almost as resilient as Saucerhead.

I couldn't say the same for the old dread who was so critical to the Macunado household. Even an idiot should now realize that none of that would have happened had the Dead Man been on the job.

Singe and Tara Chayne both told me not to worry about Min getting away. No way could she get far or evade pursuit. She was too easy to spot and too weak to endure. Morley and Belinda agreed from behind those two, just nodding.

Then Orchidia took a knee in front of me. "I believe I've learned all I needed to know here, sir, excepting what I may be able to get from the woman who just left. I'll go find her. I have one chore to handle after that. Then I'll stop back and let you know what she had to say."

Oh, such confidence. I wish I had that knack.

She reached up, squeezed my shoulder the way Barate had one time, then gently tousled Hagekagome's lustrous hair. "You're such a good girl. You really are. Take good care of him."

Hagekagome was, at the moment, squeezed up tight against me on my left, head against my shoulder, hanging on to my arm with both hands, still shaking. She responded to Orchidia with an explosively huge smile and vigorous nodding.

Dean got his feet back under him. He drafted Penny to help pick up. Several others joined in. Some genius found sense enough to finally shut the door. And good old Dex finally began to pull himself together.

95

Dex wasn't all with us yet. He said, "Yes. Of course. Bad news brings me here. Bad, bad news." He had lost some perceived time. "Only I found more badness already cooking here."

"And I'm going to have to squeeze it out of you. Right?"

"Yes. No! I'm sorry. I'm totally frayed . . . I don't know . . . Damn! There I go!"

Gently as I could I began removing dogs and pretty girls so I could go for his throat. Morley stepped between us and helped Dex up. He suggested, "You really must get to it."

"It's Feder, Mr. Garrett, sir! Master Kyoga's son. He and his friend Konshei were killed during the night. They went to a place they had no business being at their ages, particularly in current circumstances. The witnesses the Specials caught said a monster broke in. Six people were killed besides the boys. Also something that might have been Feder's Dread Companion. It was big with scaly green skin before it was torn apart. Parts were missing, including the head. The monster also left pieces behind, so it didn't get off easy."

I heard a soft scuff, glanced toward Singe's office. Mariska and Tara Chayne stood in the doorway, both stricken, probably not for the same reasons.

Moonblight observed, "Kyoga will go crazy."

"How might he do that?" Orchidia asked. She sort of danced around Dean and Penny as they picked up.

"Orchidia . . ." Mariska breathed it. "He . . . He couldn't . . . He just wouldn't . . ."

"What, Mariska?" Orchidia asked. "Mr. Garrett?" I stared at the front door while thinking about the Black Orchid. Who told me, "My skills will be available in your hunt. I thought well of Furious Tide of Light."

It was puzzling the way she had examined Hagekagome and had spoken so gently despite the stress of the situation. That didn't fit, in a couple of ways.

Tara Chayne said, "Kyoga will go after his father now. Nothing but death will stop him. I can't believe that Meyness would sacrifice his own grandson."

"Meyness? As in Meyness Stornes? Kyoga's father?"

There was a compelling quality to Orchidia's voice. You would have to focus ferociously to keep from responding.

"Meyness Stornes. Alive, yes. One of the Operators. Possibly the chief Operator."

"Setting aside my uncertainty as to what an Operator might be, I've always thought that Meyness Stornes died in the Cantard."

"So everyone believed until yesterday." Tara Chayne refrained from mentioning that Mariska had known the truth, at least for a while. Maybe for a long time. There was some family solidarity between those old girls, however much bitterness they shared.

I doubt that Orchidia was deceived. She knew more than she admitted. She had been willing to risk the Dead Man seeing the true depth of her knowledge—though by now she had to know that he was on the snooze. Meanwhile, though, she would be fishing with the sharks.

I tried me a winsome, knowing smile, like Old Bones might be sharing with me now, but I wouldn't tell. Gentle deception. "Tara Chayne, talk to me. But wait! Dex. Was Kyoga at our house when he got word?"

"No, sir. He was at the other house with Barate, the doctor, and Richt Hauser, all heads together with Lady Constance, planning deeper protection for Miss Kevans and Cypres Prose. They had reason to believe that the Prose lad had been tabbed as Miss Kevans's Mortal Companion."

"What? Kip? I thought I was . . ." I stopped. I had assumed. There had been no "official" declaration. "How come you're bringing this news?"

"Mashego came to us in a panic. She couldn't leave Lady Constance for long. Bashir meant to join those going after Magister . . ." He stopped before the ultimate reveal, glancing toward Mariska without looking directly.

Orchidia murmured, "I see," then, at full voice, announced, "We are seeing what, in the technical parlance of the erstwhile combat zone, is classified as a level-one cluster fuck."

Sounded spot on to me. And at that moment it felt like most of the investigative work done by me and mine had no point. Old-fashioned incompetence on the Operators side made them their own worst enemies.

Kyoga and Barate wouldn't have much going in a head-to-head but strength and anger. But Richt Hauser . . . "Miss Farfoul, ma'am . . . Bonegrinder. You're family . . . How strong is he? Do you know?"

"He was quite strong once, but not so much anymore. The war used him up some, but he's still far more than a lightweight. He has trouble with memory and focus. He's old and suffers some old man's frailties."

Mariska said, "We should try to keep him from getting hurt."

Her sister and I stared, willing her to say a name. Who? Meyness Stornes? Richt Hauser?

She felt the pressure. She loathed having to open up enough to claim, "He used me." Then recast that as a query. "Didn't he?"

She knew but she didn't want to face the truth. She wanted to slough some of the emotion so part of her could always believe someone else had sabotaged her nostalgic romance.

This Tournament of Swords had been doomed from the start. Everyone involved was a clubfooted incompetent dilettante, going along for someone else's sake, or just wishful thinking, nobody ready to jump in with fanatical determination—and I shouldn't leave myself off the list. I could have been much more focused and directed.

Well, it was true that both sides were willing to hurt people.

I noted Morley observing everything with an intense new detachment, the look he got when the Black Orchid side of him wakened. I hadn't seen that in him lately.

He hadn't been that way when he arrived. Too busy bickering with Belinda. What changed? Or had he just re-membered why they had come?

I glanced around. There was too damned much going on. I needed to simplify. I needed to make me a list, prioritize it, then work my way down.

What should come first? What was critical at the mo-ment?

I wanted to dash over to the cemetery and bribe, sweet-talk, or threaten my way into the Algarda tomb so I could sit and commune with Strafa for a few hours, away from everyone and everything. I had no notion why, but the incli-nation kept building.

I could see no way that such a visit would be helpful.

The idea probably didn't really belong on my list even way down.

So. How about I start with . . . answering the door?

Somebody wanted in. John Stretch, I figured. Seemed like he was overdue. Or maybe Dollar Dan. Dan had been out of sniffing range of Singe for a rat's age. At a stretch, it could even be somebody from the Al-Khar wanting some-thing from me without having to give up anything that had been promised under the new go-along-to-get-along ar-rangement.

I used the peephole.

There was a kid on the stoop. I didn't recognize him. He was alone. There wasn't much to him, so he wasn't likely to be a threat. He looked like he was in a hurry.

"I'm going to open the door, folks. Stand by."

96

Someone crowded me from behind as I opened up.

Orchidia announced, "I'll leave now. I'll see that woman."

Still so confident. I had doubts despite what she had accomplished with Mariska's squid-headed boyfriend.

"All right. Thanks for coming." Numbly. "Be careful. And tell me if you recognize this kid."

The door was open enough. "Never seen him before." She shoved past the youngster, who seemed astonished that a little old lady like Orchidia would be so aggressive.

The boy appeared to be Miss Dreadful's age. I jumped to a conclusion, turned to holler at Penny. He asked, "You Mr. Garrett?"

"I am that lucky. Yes. I am he."

That puzzled him but only for a second. Then he ignored it. Old people do weird shit. If you didn't acknowledge it they usually stopped.

"Sir, my name is Ben Gesik. I am a junior apprentice with Trivias Smith. Master Smith sent me to tell you that the men who ordered the bronze swords came for them today. They took them even though only two blades were actually finished."

The boy talked with his eyes shut, trying to get it word for word. "The master said to tell you they removed the tracer elements. They didn't know that those would be there, but they checked and weren't surprised to find them.

Master thinks they would have become violent had they not been old and at a numbers disadvantage. They were very angry."

"I can imagine. Tell Master Smith that the tracers have become moot. We found out who the villains are and know where to find them now."

"Master will be pleased. I believe he was concerned."

The kid didn't sound like he meant just that. He sounded confused.

He added, "Master did tell me, as well, to report that the old guys meant to visit Flubber Ducky next."

"Again, tell your master thank you so much from me and if there's ever anything I can do for him, all he has to do is holler."

Singe added, "And meet our standard retainer."

The boy was done talking. He took a look around. His jaw dropped. He had spotted Penny and Hagekagome. Oh, hell yes! I sure could do something for Master Trivias's number-one junior apprentice in the department of introductions.

I was about to caution him against getting drool on my nice hardwood floor when reality slammed him, having first achieved terminal velocity. Those two were leagues out of his class. He gulped some air, made several remarks in fluent, carefully rehearsed and clearly enunciated gibberish, and began to back up. Lucky boy, he never developed the momentum necessary to flip him over the porch rail when his behind began to interact with that.

"Thank you so much, Apprentice Gesik." I closed the door gently, checked the girls. Hagekagome didn't have a clue. She hadn't noticed the boy. Penny, however, hadn't missed an ogle. She was almost smug—while narrow-eyed with suspicion that she might not have been the main cause of Ben Gesik's meltdown. She awarded Hagekagome a small, jealous scowl.

Morley was a couple of steps up the hallway, being amused. Far from him to miss that chaotic chemical weather.

Others had caught it, too, and were equally entertained, with Mariska wondering aloud why youth had to be wasted on the young and oblivious.

Hagekagome realized everyone was looking at her. She responded with a big, happy smile.

Penny decided that the old farts were entertaining themselves at her expense.

She was as smart as Hagekagome was not.

There are way too many smart females in my life.

Some might wonder, though, why, if they're so damned smart, they're in my life at all. Especially Singe and Strafa.

It's because I'm such a big old lovable fuzz ball.

I told Morley, "How about you and me slide out and take a walk?"

He glanced back. Belinda would go ballistic if he ditched her. And he was in a mood to aggravate her.

He was in a mood to tweak everybody. "Sure. You can tell me how the new kid isn't absolutely the perfect reflection of everything you ever fantasized in a girlfriend."

He just wanted to bury a needle but did bring me up short. I hadn't thought about that. Hadn't really considered Hagekagome as a girl other than to note that she was wicked beautiful. But she could not have matched my earliest teen fantasies more perfectly were I a god armed with unlimited powers and a rack of ribs.

Did that mean anything? Could it possibly mean anything? I maybe needed to find a few minutes to think about it.

97

The gods of rain were merciful. Or, more likely, were setting a trap. The heavens would open and flash flooding would commence once I got three blocks from the house. For the moment, though, precipitation consisted of a mist.

I said, "I was hoping we could do this on our own."

Morley chuckled. "That's why I love you. You never cease to be optimistic."

We had not yet gone twenty feet from my steps. We already had four canine companions, plus Preston Womble and Elona Muriat in beanbag-tossing range, not pretending that they weren't going to stay connected by a very short string.

A couple of steps onward, Morley added, "As ever, your popularity grows." Dollar Dan Justice popped into existence and fell in with us following a brief exchange with Brownie and Number Two. He had a deeper than normal slump to his shoulders.

"What's up?" I snapped, knowing it couldn't be good. "And don't ever jump out at me like that. I'm gonna have to change my skivvies."

Morley gave me a look that told me to find my patience. Dan needed to work up to his news.

I found a reserve. A very small reserve.

In the near distance Womble and Muriat fussed at each other because they had been completely surprised by Dan's advent, too. Dan said, "Thank you, sir. We lower orders have a sneaky repute to live down to."

I exchanged looks with Morley, who observed, "A smart plague is burning through the rat tribe. I'm scared, Garrett."

Maybe, but Dan wasn't clever enough to keep the snaps going. Having worked off some tension, he got down to business. "As the saying goes, I have good news and bad news."

"And the traditional question would be, which do I want first?"

"As you say." Putting on a trace of noble-class accent.

Where the hell was this guy lurking when he wasn't stalking Singe?

"Let's go with the good to start. There hasn't been a lot of that lately."

"You are going to see the smith?"

"We are. The news?"

"Right direction, then. Mud Man picked up your fugitive outside your place. He and his crew are shadowing her."

"It hasn't been that long. She can't have gotten far."

"Let me amend. Mud Man is following her and is now sure where she will settle."

Morley remarked, "And now they are divining the future. The terror grows."

Dan retorted, "And does not every rat ever born fervently wish that? No. There is no magic. John Stretch has everyone with whom he has influence poking sniffers in everywhere. Regular rats have been sent places our kind cannot access almost from the moment Furious Tide of Light went down. That sneaking and spying has begun to yield dividends. So. We now can guess where the big woman hides out."

"Didn't we find that already?"

"Different hideout, Mr. Garrett. Not much better, though. Mud Man would like to know what you want to do."

"All right. Is it on the way?" A fat raindrop ricocheted off the tip of my nose. "Are you suggesting a visit?"

"You might learn something."

"Always a dangerous proposition." I might get my ass kicked and my guts stomped out. Vicious Min, even bad sick and fighting knockout drugs, was way bigger and stronger than me. I had no desire to put her down, which might be the only way I could handle her. I was now reasonably sure that she was not responsible for what had happened to Strafa.

"Mud Man will scout the place but not closely. He knows his limitations. He believes there are other people living there."

Really? Min's kind of people? What might that mean? "As long as it's on the way. All right. I've psyched myself up. Hit me with the bad news."

"We found the ballista used against your wife."

Wham! Four feet of heavy plank, right between the eyes.

I halted so suddenly that I totally avoided being nailed by a wren's-egg-size raindrop that splooshed down hard in a puddle lapping at my toes.

The dogs closed in, faced outward with teeth bared, Number Two targeting Womble and Muriat in particular. They felt the deep shift in my emotional climate. "That is the bad news? Tell me, Dan. How can that be the bad news?"

I had a sinking, hollow feeling before he went on. He had wanted to prepare me. This was going to be bad news. It was a dead certainty: Dollar Dan Justice was about to share a secret I didn't want to know.

And I was right, but not quite the way I was anticipating.

98

"The ballista is in your cellar. It is broken down into parts and stuffed in among the rest of the lumber. Under your house on the Hill."

The dogs were so close in that I couldn't move without tripping. Morley, pale and puzzled, took hold of my left arm, in case. A good grip, I suppose to keep me from raging off somewhere without a plan, bereft of further facts.

Thinking that, but frozen otherwise, I started to lift my gaze to the sky. Toward the realm of whatever god it was who entertained himself with my misery. To see the little blonde on a rooftop up ahead, but paying her little immediate attention. "And, of course, I have an expert artilleryman on my household staff. And his alibi for the time of the killing has never been tested."

Morley observed, "The news sheds light on questions that have puzzled everyone." Never relaxing his grip.

He was right.

The first weak shakes began in my arms and shoulders.

Dollar Dan said, "Unfortunately, the critical question remains unanswered. Who? This has been checked and re-checked, Mr. Garrett, by all the best noses but Singe's, because the truth is so important. One indisputable truth is that neither Race nor Dex ever visits any part of the cellar but the wine storage. That is a separate cellar accessed by its own stair, the door to which is kept locked. None of the rats in the house—and there aren't many because Race and

Dex are aggressive about not sharing the living space—have seen either man visit the lumber cellar. But they cannot recall any other intruder, either. Stipulating that their memories become hazy quickly even when dramatic events occur. The ballista itself appears to have been stored there forever, as rats see time. So. They cannot tell us who removed it, assembled it, used it, took it apart again, and put it back where it came from. They know that happened only because whoever used it did not cover up the fact that all the working mechanisms were freshly oiled."

Morley seemed thoroughly intrigued. A smile kept tugging at the left corner of his mouth.

Dan's report was registering with me but without the crushing impact I would have predicted if asked to assess a similar situation beforehand.

Morley said, "Somebody knew the ballista was there. Mr. Justice, by some chance did your creatures see any oldtime iron crossbow bolts?" Because, of course, once upon a time, residents of the house had been connected to a scandal having to do with wartime armaments contracts.

Interesting, but now my attention had locked on to that little blonde. She was standing on an impossible slope, making no effort to hide—nor was she doing anything to attract attention. She was just there, counting on the fact that people don't look up much. I didn't see her big ugly sidekick.

Morley sighted her, too. Clever fellow, he asked, "Mr. Justice, have you been able to find out anything about that girl?"

She knew that she had been spotted when Dan turned. She began walking up the slope of the steep metal roof. A sharp eye, though, would note that there was air between her soles and the verdigris.

I learned another interesting fact about John Stretch's lieutenant. He had better eyes than the average rat man. As a tribe, ratfolk are nearsighted and much more scent-reliant than vision-dependent.

Dollar Dan announced, "We think she is a ghost."

I consulted my recollections. "She and her friend supposedly have hideouts on top of several buildings."

"That may be, yes. Such places have been found but may
not in fact be actual hideouts."

He sounded close to plaintive, which confused me. He
tried to explain. "She leaves no scents behind. Not the right
scents. Except for possibly . . . She is a ghost, Mr. Garrett."

Perhaps. Maybe. But she'd been one solid spook that
one time I got close enough to touch her.

My turn to plaint. "That could mean she's not part of the
tournament." The Operators wouldn't put ghosts on the
player roster. Spooks and zombies wouldn't work because
of the unfair advantage factor.

So I started trying to recall every detail about the girl
and her companion. Especially her companion.

Dollar Dan was not happy. He had handed me the solution to the mystery of the vanishing artillery piece, opening
a pony keg of worms, and I was just getting infatuated with
a little twist not yet ripe enough to split. . . .

I hustled back from way out there in the wanderlands,
focused on Dan, mildly aghast. Had I tapped into his secret
thoughts? Or was I daydreaming something offensive because of my own obscure prejudice?

Whatever, I felt creepy and creeped out.

"What are we doing?" Morley asked. "Besides standing
in one place long enough for trouble to find us? That wasn't
happy news, but how does it change what we're doing
now?"

"You're right. Dan did everything that could be already.
Chasing Race and Dex down would just eat time better
spent finding Vicious Min." So there I committed to checking on her before seeing Trivias Smith.

"What?" Morley demanded. He and Dollar Dan eyeballed me like I'd just turned weird. Meaning I'd hidden it
damned well before.

"Thinking about Vicious Min. Thinking about the little
blonde's sidekick. Wondering. There are differences but big
similarities, too. They could be related. The variances could

be simple sex differences. Like, who would believe that Strafa and I were the same species?"

"You have a profound point. She was an angel. You . . . You're . . . You're Garrett."

Dan probably agreed but was too civilized to say so.

I confessed, "I always suspected that the weaseling romance gods laid Strafa on me because they wanted me to become the punch line to the universe's saddest shaggy dog story."

"Shaggy dog stories don't have punch lines. They end with a whimper. Or a groan."

"Bing! And we have a grand prize winner, folks."

"That's my pal Garrett, eternal optimist, everybody. Mr. Sunshine himself."

Somehow the possibility of a connection between Vicious Min and the blonde's sidekick troubled me more than did questions raised by discovery of the ballista in the basement.

We did get moving again before divine mischief brought us to grief.

I relaxed some, actually, certain that the baddies had squandered their resources for mayhem and would now be especially short, Mariska having stepped back, depriving her boyfriend of any Machtkess connection with the grays.

I was convinced that the Machtkess history explained the gray involvement.

I hoped Moonslight had not destroyed a whole people with her bad behavior.

Grown people will amaze you with childish stupid sometimes.

99

No plan survives contact with the enemy. That is common wisdom, becoming a storyteller's cliché. It is the iron law encountered by every commander headed into action. It could be called Garrett's First Law of Investigative Dynamics, too.

Nothing goes according to plan.

We doughty adventurers, and our tails, passed the Al-Khar en route to look for Vicious Min. I had no intention of visiting. I had no intention of consulting anyone there, nor of being noticed by its denizens. Either Womble and/or Muriat rejected my script.

Maybe I should have gone a longer way.

Whatever, my crowd suddenly expanded to include Brevet Captain Deiter Scithe, Target, and a vigorously limping Helenia, who looked like there was nothing she'd love more than to take a big, steaming dump on the altar of Fortune, she was so happy to be out in the weather with me. The dogs, though, greeted her cheerfully and begged for treats she didn't have, which softened her mood from diamond to ice.

"There you are," I said. "But why?"

Scithe said, "Prince Rupert came to see the General and the Director. He wants the business involving your wife solved and wrapped."

"Why? It's none of his business."

"It's all his business, Garrett, and not just because she

was a family friend. He's the Royal responsible for 'Public Safety.' Right now that means he has to please the Hill, where people are outraged. He hopes to score political points, too."

Which made sense of a sleazy sort. Prince Rupert would be our next king, maybe not long from now. He wasn't keen on that, but he was realistic. Whatever skin he had pinched in the crimes and facts of the tournament, he had to bow to political considerations. Karentine princes who ignore politics always suffer brief, miserable reigns once they take the throne.

I didn't like it, but that was the way it was. A weasel Rupert might be, but he should be the best king we had during my lifetime. He had a knack for seeing snippets of realities outside the neverlands of his palaces.

"He also wants to see you about making you his personal investigative agent. Again."

"I have other stuff to do." The brewery. Amalgamated. Revenge for what happened to Strafa. Avoiding the bitter insanity of Karentine politics.

"He's willing to work with you on your concerns. He says you wouldn't have to give up your normal life."

"You smell that? It's piled so high a tall troll would drown in it."

"Garrett, you're being willfully difficult."

Helenia surreptitiously checked a waterlogged list, ready to prompt Scithe if he overlooked a talking point. Number Two was curious about that, probably hoping it was a treat that Helenia would give up eventually.

Scithe noted, "You spend ninety percent of your life doing nothing productive. He's only interested in buying a fraction of that."

Morley chuckled but eschewed going after the deeper dig.

"To start. That's what he'd say. But how long before he claimed he owned me body and soul, day and night, till he used me up or got me killed?" I stopped. No point working up a lather. Scithe was carrying out instructions, by the numbers, with just enough enthusiasm to get by.

He concluded, "Just come by the Al-Khar and talk."

"Some other time. Maybe after I've settled this business." Strafa's face came to me, sweetly supportive. Could I get to the cemetery today? The afternoon was getting on.

Helenia crumpled her list. The ink had run. Anything they had missed was gone. She was ready to get the hell gone herself, somewhere safe and out of this crappy weather.

Number Two was deeply disappointed.

Scithe had a point or two left but decided, screw it. "It might be a sweet gig, Garrett."

"You could be right. Volunteer for it yourself."

"I did. But he's got Garrett, Furious Tide of Light, Shadowslinger, and the Algarda clan on the brain. See him. He'll put up with you turning him down, but there's no way he'll take you disrespecting him by ignoring him."

A point worth remembering. Prince Rupert would be king. New kings close out old accounts.

Morley put that into words as we watched Scithe, Helenia, and Target head for the yellow rock pile. Target hadn't spoken the whole time.

"I know. You're right. I don't need Rupert laying for me for the rest of my life."

"My little boy is starting to grow up."

"Blame that on Strafa." I watched the red tops till they disappeared, wondering what had become of Womble and Muriat. "Let's get on with getting on." Later, I asked, "What's with you and Belinda?"

"We're two people desperately trying to make something work with somebody crazier than we are." Which ended the discussion.

I hoped their thing didn't turn darkly bad. Both were my friends. And both were dangerous and disinclined, in heated moments, to demonstrate outstanding emotional restraint.

100

"That would appear to be the place," Morley said, less fiercely than you would expect of someone who had just discovered the base of a long-sought and troublesome adversary.

Mud Man and crew were not to be seen. Dollar Dan, still tagging along, was worried. The mutts smelled something to make them nervous, too.

Adversary? Did we have that kind of relationship with Min?

I didn't think so.

I shared Morley's mood. The trouble in troublesome felt likely to shift and make for challenging footing.

This Vicious Min hole-up was sadder than the last. It was a literal hole in a wall, the sort of place an outcast, later to become known as Vicious Min, might have spent a grimly impoverished childhood.

The hole had been hollowed out of the downhill-side foundation of an enormous windmill crowning a rock upthrust that rose twenty feet above street level on that side. The mill no longer worked but did have strong wards against the usual threats of thievery, scavengers, and squatters. You could smell the sorcery like garlic in a century-old tenement. The air crackled, but the protective spells didn't reach down to the foundation on this side. Someone had figured that out and had removed blocks of stone one by one to create a man-made cave underneath the mill.

This was Beifhold's Mill, a notorious landmark from the last century. It had the protection of the Crown and city because it was unique and storied but not enough so that anyone wanted to invest in upkeep. The last maintenance I recalled was a whitewashing the year before Mom passed away. Nothing else had gotten done since the last Beifhold died in the Cantard.

The cave entrance didn't look big enough to pass someone Min's size, which might explain her need for that other place, which she hadn't shared. She did not appear to be around now, but someone was sitting outside, bent over his lap in the rain, unconscious or sleeping. He could be Min's little brother—though he still went twice as bigger than me. The dogs didn't like him. They showed a lot of teeth, for no obvious reason.

Morley opined, "It looks like a whole family lives there."

"Sad, huh? Maybe that's deeper than it looks."

"Yes. And yes, it is about as sad as I can imagine anything being."

I said, "I see why Min would get into something sketchy."

"The price of keeping body and soul and family together."

"Um. But I won't forgive her. However much I understand. Is that creature even alive?" I checked to see what Preston Womble and his henchwoman were doing. Whatever that might be, I didn't catch them doing it. They had become invisible. We hadn't caught a whiff of them since the encounter with Scithe. Speaking of which, what had become of Lurking Fehlkse? Even Dollar Dan hadn't caught wind of him lately.

At the moment he was sniffing after Mud Man. He said, "The creature is breathing, but it may be damaged or drugged."

The character beside the cave mouth was less active than a decorative gargoyle. Not only had he not moved; I couldn't detect his breathing. Had the Black Orchid gotten here already? Shouldn't there be more blood?

"See no evil," Morley breathed as a woman approached from our left, strolling toward the cave, not obviously interested and in no great hurry. She had acquired an umbrella. She stopped just out of reach of the sleeping giant—using *giant* loosely, descriptively instead of ethnically—and began speaking too softly to hear. She folded her umbrella as she did.

Giant Boy didn't twitch when she poked him.

Brownie made a snorting noise that I expected to give us away. Orchidia didn't react. The giant toppled, then slowly relaxed into a half-fetal position, on his right side, still showing no sign of life.

A chubby raindrop got me on the left cheek despite my waterlogged hat, which drooped around the brim. I glanced up. Behold, there was the blond child sitting on the hub between two sails where they were rooted in the axle that transferred wind energy to the innards of the mill. Just sitting there. Watching.

Orchidia surely sensed me, Morley, Dan, and the dogs, but she had no clue about the child in the sky. She focused on the unresponsive big boy.

That was bizarre. I had a hard time keeping my yap shut. Dollar Dan Justice had as hard a time not fussing about the absence of Mud Man.

Keeping her umbrella aimed at her victim, Orchidia moved to the cave. With her other hand she conjured one of those glow balls beloved of her kind.

She took a close look at the sleeper, her head sideways to the cave.

A fist shot out. It clipped her despite a reflex move so fast that master martial artist Morley Dotes gasped in admiration.

Orchidia staggered a dozen feet, collapsed to one knee. Morley and Dollar Dan both snagged my arms so I wouldn't go all white knight, but I had no intention of rushing in.

The big thing who ran with the blonde emerged from the cave supplely as a snake. At that range and in that light, I saw a definite resemblance to Vicious Min.

He thumped Orchidia again, deftly bound her with cords hanging ready at his belt, gagged her, stuffed her into a big jute gunnysack handed to him by another big thing who emerged from the cave after him, this one old, stooped, arthritic, and one-eyed, with a left leg that had been broken below the knee and never properly set. Old One tossed Sleeping Boy onto a shoulder, started limping. Blondie's friend tucked his sackful of Black Orchid under his left arm and followed. Neither ever looked our way.

Morley said, "Let's don't ever mix it up with those people."

"Not without me bringing my siege engine." I looked up. Sure enough, Little Bits no longer decorated the windmill hub.

Dollar Dan said, "I'm on it," and headed out after the big folks.

"Be careful," Morley told him.

"Let's see what's in the cave," I said.

"Like maybe another one of those things?"

"We should look because we came here to look instead of heading straight for the smith's."

"I'll haunt you forever if something mashes my head in."

The hole-up was empty and sad. Min's people did not live a good life.

"We know one thing for sure now," I said, eyeing the squalor. "Neither Min nor that other one qualifies as a Dread Companion."

"There's a blessing. Min was here." He indicated a bloody rag.

"I never doubted that. Mud Man followed her here. Dan will probably find her wherever those people go." I hoped he looked up once in a while. The girl was sure to notice him. "Let's go see what the smith has to say." Then maybe I would sneak off to see Strafa.

"Look here." He picked up Orchidia's umbrella, which the big folks hadn't taken along. "Not all the news is bad."

Brownie and the girls seemed to know where we were

headed right away. Brownie stuck by me, as always, while the others ranged ahead.

They didn't turn up anything. Not a Lurking Fehlkse, a Preston Womble, nor even an Elona Muriat.

We made the journey quietly. I brooded on what we had learned.

101

Trivias Smith visit provided some unwanted physical exercise but not much else. Smith handed me half a dozen tracers smashed by Operators he said were the same pair who had placed the order. One sounded like Magister Bezma in a bad mood. He had called his companion "brother." Smith wasn't sure if that meant a relationship or was a title. Did Kyoga have any uncles? I'd have to ask.

"Brother" hadn't been happy. He'd done his work, reluctantly, never speaking. He would rather have been elsewhere doing anything else.

"Probably a religious brother," I said. "The ugly one with the deformity is a magister from Chattaree, in a bad temper because his evil scheme is falling apart. His own grandson was killed."

"I fear I cannot generate much sympathy."

Morley opined, "The fool didn't just ask for the pain, he begged."

I asked Smith some general questions. He didn't mind answering. Yes, the Guard had been underfoot but hadn't interfered with business. The villains, after collecting their swords, had headed for Flubber Ducky.

We chatted briefly, me thinking he might be good to know down the road. Meanwhile, Morley showed a surprising interest in the practical side of smithery. And I thought some more about sneaking off to the family mausoleum.

The Flubber Ducky boys must have held a strategy session and decided that cooperation would be their least costly policy, going forward. They didn't hold back. Magister Bezma and his sidekick had roared in, done some damage, then carried off everything having anything to do with their order, complete or not. It all went into a generic little covered wagon drawn by a single ox. They had headed toward the Dream Quarter. And that was that, except that Pindlefix was so bold as to suggest that I should shun Flubber Ducky now and forevermore. That or suffer the burden of a thousand curses.

Morley observed, "Too bad Singe isn't with us. She could find those idiots fast. Though that's maybe too optimistic in this drizzle."

That had let up for a time but now looked like it was about to come back. On the upside, we did have Orchidia's umbrella.

"I think we know where to find them."

"Chattaree?"

"Where else?"

"Been a while."

"It has. And they'll be ready this time. Chances are, we'll be at the tail end of a line." I reminded him who would be ahead of us, in case he hadn't been paying attention.

He said, "This Bezma is one dumb shit. Your Algardas are bad enough to poke a stick in the eye, but the Black Orchid? She'll be back. Those big things weren't planning to hurt her. I've only ever heard rumors, but I know I don't want her on my case. She's like a supernatural force, not just some slick killer."

"That's what they say. That she might be an incarnation of a death spirit. A real shinigami. Look, I'm pretty sure this tournament was a jackleg operation from the get-go, a case of incompetent ambition driving the halt and blind in a scheme fancied up by a brain-dead sociopath born with no imagination."

The dogs stopped to stare.

"Be sure you let us know what you really think, old buddy."

"The only reason we haven't buried the whole mess already is that it's so stupid we can't figure it out." Or maybe because there was more than one thing going on and I kept pounding square pegs to make it a solitaire.

"Uh . . . way to make yourself clear."

"You know what I mean."

"Actually, I do. It's like trying to find a serial killer. They aren't usually smart, they just don't have any obvious connection to their victims, and the logic driving them is alien."

"That's kind of basically it."

"Here's an odd thought. Assuming you're figuring on heading on back home. How about we visit Playmate?"

"It needs doing. It would do wonders for my attitude if he turned out spanking good. But there is the matter of pending excitement at Chattaree." And of my ever-growing inclination to go see Strafa.

Something was going on way down below the surface of my mind. I couldn't get it to come out, but I had experience enough with me to know it was coming. To suspect that seeing Strafa might break it loose.

I couldn't shake Shadowslinger's dread prophecy about an onrushing deadline.

Morley grumbled, "There is Chattaree, yes." After a dozen steps, he mused, "Maybe it would have been wiser to swallow your pride and hand it off to the tin whistles."

Whoa! "Damn! I did waste a fat opportunity when we had Scithe right there. We had one of Block's top boys and Relway's own cousin besides. What more could I ask?"

"So we'll see Play on the way back from Chattaree."

I like how he remains optimistic.

"Seen the blond kid around?" I asked.

"Not since Beifhold's Mill. But don't bet a rusty Venageti fil that she isn't watching."

My own thoughts exactly.

102

The stroll to the Dream Quarter took us into a new climate zone. The sun there was trying to break through the overcast. Then the ground quivered gently, weirdly, just as a sunbeam pierced the clouds and stabbed Chattaree, painting the masonry bone white and pale golden.

"Somebody got all busy with the whitewash," Morley said.

"Yeah. I didn't notice the other day. But the light was bad then."

Clouds above went on about their celestial business. The sunbeam perished. Chattaree lost its glow.

Morley quipped, "That couldn't last."

"Looked too much like a blessing."

We came to the bench that Moonblight and I had exploited before. I decided to repeat the exercise, though the east end was occupied by a derelict. A little guy, he had not yet chosen to make the bench a bed. I scooted over enough to make end room for Morley, then leaned back and considered the cathedral, wondering, now that I was there, what I could actually do.

Brownie and the girls showed a strong interest in the bum. He was not happy about that.

Most of us have trouble seeing the unexpected. I didn't expect to be sharing a bench with Niea Syx, cathedral gatekeeper, so I failed to recognize him for half a minute. Of course, he had recognized me as we approached and now wanted to remain unnoticed, which he might manage if he didn't make a run for it.

"Niea. My man. How you doing?"

Not so good, his body language suggested.

I could not recall the circumstances of his exodus from the Macunado House. I hadn't put him out the door. Maybe Penny did. "How come you're out here?"

He gave me a hangdog look worthy of Number Two at her most artfully pathetic, rubbed his left biceps, looked like he blamed it all on me, whatever "it" might be, and said nothing.

I got some mental exercise by jumping to a wrong conclusion. "They busted your ass because we took you when we dragged Almaz and his thugs off."

Sigh. "No, sir. I got thrown down the steps when those men showed up looking for Magister Bezma. They wouldn't believe that he isn't there."

"Everyone knows the Leading General Select Secretary for Finance never leaves his quarters." Just trying to be helpful.

"True. Insiders. Which they were not. I thought I was lying. It turned out that I was telling the truth. I think."

"There it goes again," Morley said, nervously.

The earth shrugged the tiniest bit, a slight roll more perceptible than before but still barely enough to tweak the nerves. There was no sound with it, neither of breakage nor of panic. It was for sure no serious temblor.

TunFaire hadn't experienced one of those in decades.

"Wonder what that's about," Morley said. I thought he meant the shaking till I noted that he was staring at Chattaree, where tobacco-brown dust had begun to roll out of the windows and doors.

Guard whistles sounded from several directions, the extended "Woo-he-up!" indicating an emergency in progress. A Guardsman needing help puffed on his whistle in shrill blats.

Niea grumbled, "Now they've done it." With no explanation of what "they" might have done. "I don't want to be anywhere near here when the red tops start picking up the pieces."

"Damn!" I said, with feeling. Threads of lightning had begun prancing inside the roiling dust, which seemed no less dense despite its expansion outward.

The ground moved again.

"And here come some piece picker-uppers," Morley breathed. Or maybe he had made a pun and said "peace." Sometimes he can't help himself.

Tin whistles, some of them Specials, flickered into existence on all sides, rushing the dusty excitement. None of them, management or honest laborer, seemed especially motivated, however.

They had survived strange stuff in the Cantard. They were alive to see this strange stuff because they had taken time to think before dealing with that strange stuff, back in the day.

The brown dust rolled closer. I suggested, "Why don't we not stick around for a closer look at that?"

The vote of confidence in my leadership was unanimous. Even Niea joined the rout—though we didn't run. We strolled briskly, good Karentine subjects who had recalled urgent appointments elsewhere.

The lightning kept playing inside the dust as the cloud spread and became shallower. It crackled and popped behind us as we made with the heels and toes. Fingers of brown, just two inches thick now, caught up and oozed past. The brown remained dense and roiling under a slick surface that recalled liquid mercury. Two-leggers and four, we all avoided contact.

The red tops followed our lead.

Came a fourth tremor, like the involuntary shudder after a sudden, inexplicable chill. The brown began to retreat, ignoring physical law. It left a one-mote-thick walnut discoloration that behaved more like a stain than a layer of dust. It didn't puff up or transfer when disturbed.

Morley and I watched bolder folks experiment. The girls stayed back, the most unhappy of them still offering soft growls of displeasure and discomfort.

Niea Syx seized the afternoon and made like the good shepherd. On discovering his sudden invisibility, I shrugged. I doubted that he had anything useful to tell us. And we knew where to start a track if we needed to see him.

He would have been handy as a guide had we gone on with the proposed incursion. I took that off the table. There was too much excitement inside the cathedral already. Plus, red tops were gathering in numbers. Whole battalions would be getting in each other's ways soon.

I offered an alternate proposal. "Let's leave this to the incompetents already here and yet to appear." If Barate and friends were in there and stayed healthy, they could get by on Hill privilege. I shouldn't put my cream-of-the-rabble self out for notice by offering unneeded assistance.

"Then let us be off and away," Morley said. "And keep putting on a show that will thrill Jon Salvation when he turns it into a drama."

For a moment I thought he had our red top audience in mind; then the direction of his gaze indicated the little blonde on the parapet of a temple a block east of Chattaree.

Curiouser and curiouser, she.

103

Playmate was fine. He was in his little office with Kolda, playing a simple rummy game that, never mind, I couldn't figure out by watching. Naturally, once I confessed to that, I was invited to open my purse and buy myself a learning experience. Kolda was hiding out from his wife. Playmate fussed over the dogs and gave them treats they didn't need. Then we moved on, me still thinking about visiting Strafa.

I shifted course to cut through Prince Guelfo Square, to get me a hot sausage. Franklejean was hard at it selling nothing from under a giant knockoff umbrella built with brighter fabrics than anything in the Amalgamated inventory. He had made it himself. He was unapologetic. Amalgamated wouldn't produce umbrellas in the size he needed.

"I saw nothing. And nor will I ever—unless you try to sell them."

"I just don't want to get rained on while I'm working."

He had nothing interesting to report. In fact, he pressed me, hoping I had something he would find interesting. I gave up the name Orchidia Hedley-Farfoul. That left him puzzled. He knew nothing about her.

My four-legged girls loved the visit. They piled sausage in on top of Playmate's treats. Vegetarian boy Dotes, though, could work up no enthusiasm for the pork. He claimed, "You'll have these mutts too fat to waddle."

"They're like bears getting ready for the winter."

Which was true, in a way. Strays have to devour whatever they can whenever they can get it. Who knew when they might eat again?

"Winter is always around the corner. And, speaking of, what corner will you head around once we're done here?"

For the moment I lacked any urgency. I had this ever-expanding feeling that what I most wanted right then was a nap. Failing that, I wanted to see Strafa. "I don't know. I've lost my train of thinking. Where were we headed after we checked on Playmate?"

"Here, it looked like, then your place, I thought. Don't ask me, though. I'm just here to keep the pixies off your back."

While he let some problem with his sweetie cool down. Or fester.

"I think I'll go to the cemetery."

"Or to your house."

"Dollar Dan will do that once he sees where they take Orchidia. Hell, he's probably there already." I hoped Singe would find it in her heart to pretend to show some sympathy. "You can go if you want. Belinda might be waiting."

"I'll stay with you. The fact that you haven't been murdered today doesn't mean that people who hope to see you dead have given up trying to arrange it."

I started to argue. Contrary had become the Garrett ground state, it seemed. But my butt, with all its marvelous attachments, would have been well and truly deep in a sling repeatedly if people had given me the room I kept whining about wanting.

I'm overly inclined to think that I am as bad as I want to be bad. That I can handle anything that comes my way. But today had shown me that nastier things than me, by miles, were hoofing it around my town, and the tournament was all about bringing the nastiest ones out.

"Garrett shutting up on the macho teen posturing," I announced. "If you really want to hang out amongst the headstones."

"Oh yes. Definitely. I'm all about graveyards. I'm looking forward to being a resident someday myself."

Sarcasm did not become the pretty boy.

The dogs were worn down, but they agreed with Morley. They would stick to the end. Or at least until they dropped.

So we headed south and west, alternately, block by block, till we hit Old King's Way, which we followed till it T'd at First Wall Road. Once upon a time that had run along the inner foot of the original southern city wall. The cemetery had lain outside. The wall had been demolished long ago. The cemetery was well inside the city now. The sun was out down there, burning dark orange beneath the edge of the remaining overcast.

Morley indicated the sun. "How long will it be before we get another good look at that beast?"

There was that feel in the air. The break in the weather wouldn't last.

104

Ancient sextons cursed with interacting with the ever-troublesome living strained to conceal their displeasure at having to do something once black-hearted me forced them to put aside their tea and chessboard. Not a word of protest was spoken, though. One remembered me from the funeral. I was an Algarda. He was old enough to walk, meaning he knew that regular folks don't mess with Shadowslinger's kids.

The other one was more interested in the dogs than me.

Morley noticed. "Do you know these ladies?"

Obviously, the man thought that he did—though they were cleaner and fatter than he remembered.

Morley said, "There isn't much keeping our friends busy right now, Garrett." He gestured at the man from the funeral. "You and him go see your wife. This gentleman and I will enjoy a game of chess, a glass of tea, and some conversation about dog breeding." The old edge was in his voice.

"You're all back." It hadn't been so long since I'd sat a death watch beside his bed.

He had a way to go physically. I still saw the winces and slackenings that betrayed deep pain.

"Forget the wise guy stuff. Do what you have to do."

He was feeling the pain right now. No doubt pain lay behind the resurgent steel. He wanted to get done and get back. It would be a while yet before he could enjoy my adventures completely. If ever that had been the case, or could be.

"I'll keep it as short as I can." Though I had been considering taking several hours just to sit with Strafa, to talk to her, maybe to bleed off the grief and anger I'd been keeping contained.

My companion donned his rain hat and waterproof coat, impatient to move along, be done, and get cozy with his tea and his game again. A fruity odor suggested that he and his associate laced their tea with brandy.

I gestured, go. He went, cooperative because I was an Algarda. I considered letting him know he was too old and stringy for Shadowslinger's palate. Didn't seem like he would be amused, though.

The dogs spread out ahead, concerned about something. They dashed back and forth, continuously consulting. The sexton wasn't sure about them. They kept him muttering in a foreign language. His cursing increased exponentially when a dozen more dogs showed up, growling and greeting and socializing with my girls. The stay-at-homes were pleased by what they heard from Brownie and Number Two but had things to say themselves that were not so replete with positivity.

Some noise audible only to canine ears suddenly had every head and ear up, the latter twitching. The entire pack began to growl.

My companion became alarmed, too. He charged ahead, as much as an old man's body would permit. I followed, not in haste.

I had some serious aches and pains.

Cresting a slight rise, we found four unhappy men surrounded by twenty feral dogs. One dog was down, having taken a serious blow from a tool. The men all carried tools.

The dogs were not best pleased. They were reverting to pack-in-the-wild mode. Those men would be more unhappy if I couldn't get the critters calmed down.

105

"They're trying to break into your tomb," my companion gasped, astonished that anyone would commit such an atrocity.

"I know who the old guy is." Magister Bezma's sidekick and possible brother. I was surprised to see him, though the timing was right if he had collected his thugs and headed here after he and Bezma finished their business with Trivias Smith and Flubber Ducky. But why?

The henchmen were immigrant day laborers taking what work they could get to keep body and soul and family together.

Our advent, reinforcing the dogs, was all the encouragement they needed to start running. I hoped they could pawn their tools.

The dogs let them go but not the older man, whom they backed against the mausoleum door. He swung a crowbar menacingly, to little point. He survived on sufferance.

I warned, "Don't run! I can't save you if you give them a quarry."

My own old man bleated in misery when he saw the damage to the mausoleum door, forced open a crack but not enough to admit anyone. Its hang had been ruined.

Number Two and several friends squeezed inside once I pushed the burglar out of the way.

I told Brownie, "Keep this fool from running but don't hurt him," then dropped to a knee beside the injured mutt, an ugly mix of bulldog and beagle. "We're in luck. Doesn't look like any permanent damage." I fought the temptation to touch, to pet. She was wild. She was hurting. She was handling that by showing her teeth and threatening to use them.

I went to the tomb door. Squatting some, grasping its edge, hoisting, shoving, taking baby steps, I moved it enough to let me get by. My sidekick said, "There are lamps and lighters in the alcove to your right."

I eased inside. He faced off with the captive, whose body language suggested abject surrender. He had had enough. He hadn't wanted to be involved in the first place. He was just plain thrilled to be out of the game.

He wasn't so done that he was ready to lie down and die, though, just to where he was ready to let the world get on without his participation.

I lighted a lamp. The folks in charge had been on the job. There were five of those, all with fuel reservoirs full and wicks trimmed with military precision. I let the old man know that I was impressed.

"How about you reward me by hurrying it up, then, Slick? It's cold out here and I'm too friggin' old to be dancing with the bad guys, even when they're feebler than me." He indicated the captive in case I was too dim to grasp the insult.

"We'll take care of that. You. Inside with me." So I could keep an eye on him in case he wasn't as feeble as he looked. "Don't move. Don't speak unless I ask you a question."

"As you wish, sir."

I fired up two more lamps, placed them in niches prepared for them. They helped only a little. The space they had to illuminate was huge. Strafa's coffin was one of nearly a dozen. Many more resided in recesses in the walls. They had verdigris-corroded nameplates on their ends dating back centuries. Algardas had been dying to get in here for ages.

Only the most recently deceased were on display. Once the living forgot who they had been, they got shoved into a wall slot. Plenty of those remained available.

There were eleven coffins out, with room for one more. There hadn't been a free pedestal the other day. I pointed at the empty. "Sit there."

The villain sat.

The migration of a coffin into a wall was the only change since my last visit. The bad guys hadn't gotten to do whatever they'd had in mind.

"Name?" I demanded while using a sleeve to dust the glass separating me from my love. She hadn't changed. She reminded me of the girl in the story who had been so naive about accepting the free apple. I wished a kiss was enough to bring her back. Only, where to find a prince I could trust to do the necessary and then back off, leaving the girl for me?

I caught a wisp of violet coruscation from the corner of my eye, behind the captive. So. Interesting, that.

Had it been with me all along?

106

"Mikon D.—for Dungenes—Stornes."

"Brother of Meyness B.? Now going by Magister Bezma?"

"First cousin of. Meyness has been getting me into trouble since we wore dresses." Which said plenty about how old the Stornes boys had to be. Even the rich stopped putting their boy children in dresses before my father was born. "I never could tell him to shove his stupid plans back up the hole where he found them."

I recalled getting Mikey into stuff, taking total advantage of a little brother who looked up to me in awe.

"What were you up to here?" I stared hard at Strafa, willing her to open her eyes. I would forgive the cruelty of the practical joke if she would just end the game.

Others would not forgive, though. This tournament had claimed too many lives. Orchidia Hedley-Farfoul would add names to the roster of unshriven fallen. Magister Bezma, surely, had a little list of his own.

"Why were you breaking in here?"

"I was supposed to take Furious Tide of Light. I don't know why. Meyness said he needed her. He didn't explain except to say that he knew how Constance Algarda's head worked. He understood the Breaker strategy. With Furious Tide of Light we could win despite Mariska's defection."

I stared down at my wife. I heard and understood every word. The shadowed underground rivers of my mind strained to winkle out meaning, but the up-here, smelling-the-stench-of-the-mortal-realm part wasn't sufficiently engaged to generate follow-up questions.

There was an instant of impatient purple sparkle behind Mikon.

"Meyness kept the whole thing close, I think because he knew how stupid he'd sound if he explained his actual reasoning. But he did think he could make this tournament his own. He thought he knew what it was really about and that it hadn't worked before only because too many willful people were involved. This time just him and me would be Operators. We would hire done whatever we couldn't manage ourselves, using Mariska as our go-between."

I grunted. "What's the story with the swords and costumes?"

"Those are for the Ritual. At the end. When the power is taken." He volunteered no more. Since he was in full galloping confession mode I suspected that he didn't have anything else to give up.

"You snapped that stuff up before they were finished."

"There was a time problem. The Ritual has to happen just before midnight, when Day of the Dead turns into All-Souls. The Ritual is supposed to include thirteen Operator celebrants and an altar, but he worked out a way to manage with us two and some hired hands. Ten celebrants wouldn't have done anything but chant, anyway. The chant isn't critical. When we placed our orders we expected Moonslight and some hirelings to help, but nothing went right. Somebody attacked Furious Tide of Light. People kept getting in the way. The contest spun out of control right away. The first victims were the wrong ones. . . ."

"Feder and his friend," I said.

"Exactly."

"And the Hedley-Farfoul twins, Dane and Deanne."

Despite the lighting Mikon's response was striking. He practically radiated a sickly light.

"You didn't know about them?"

"No. I did not. It explains why Meyness became desperate to keep me from hearing any news. Bonegrinder . . . His enmity would be bad enough. But the Black Orchid . . . Do you have a knife? I beg you, give me a blade. I will take it outside. I won't profane your shrine. But . . . I'm a coward. I admit it. No way can I handle what the Black Orchid is going to bring."

Wow. People inside Hill culture had a total fear on when it came to the Black Orchid.

I'd been around Shadowslinger enough to wonder if Orchidia hadn't been up to some serious self-promotion, too.

I suggested, "Go to the Guard. Make a deal."

Relway loved that stuff. This guy had been in deep enough to know some sexy stuff that might be useful when the Al-Khar began butting heads with the Hill.

"Yeah. The Guard. They're everywhere. They caused more trouble than you did because Meyness discounted them before we started."

"Probably thought they could be bought the way the Watch could be."

"Yes." So. I could see that Cousin Meyness had set his feet on the road to today way back when he was a Breaker himself. The Watch in those days was an oft-drunk fire patrol whose members made more taking bribes than they did from their city salaries.

I said, "I haven't heard of you before, though several people told us that Magister Bezma had a partner. Where do you fit, really?"

"I'm his cousin. I belong to the Phila Menes Order. I have since I was fifteen. I was a chaplain's assistant during the war. I missed all the major fighting. I helped Meyness enter the Church as an immigrant named Izi Bezma, saying he was a distant member of the family. He did good work, so his situation kept improving. He never left Chattaree, so he never ran into anyone who might recognize him. For a long time I was the only one who knew, until he got together with Mariska Machtkess again."

I caught a sparkle of purple. That news irked the centipede of night.

The Phila Menes are an order that does charity work. Mikon Dungenes Stornes wasn't a bad man, he was a weak-willed guy with a true bad man in the woodpile, a cousin willing to use and discard him. He knew that despite turning a willful blind eye.

He met my gaze briefly. "You're wondering where he got the money to underwrite his scheme. He stole it from the Church. No one at Chattaree was in on it but me. Meyness's position, that he schemed and maneuvered to get, let him manage Church finances. He could take all the money he wanted. Nobody can keep track of coin donations. He was creative with numbers on paper, made some shrewd investments, and knew where enough bodies were buried to control most anyone who needed controlling."

And he probably buried some bodies himself when that was useful.

This insanity had been festering since a kid named Meyness Stornes started running with Constance Algarda, Richt Hauser, the Machtkess girls, and the Breakers. He helped wreck that tournament so he could run his own game later. But being sure of that didn't do me any good just now.

Mikon Stornes gave up on killing himself.

"I'm baffled, Mikon. Why did Meyness suddenly change up after being so careful for so long?"

"He's dying. From something slow that he picked up in the Cantard. He's spent a lot of time in the infirmary recently. He saw the Children of Light several times."

That was suggestive. The Children started out something like the Phila Menes, providing health care for the poor, but got outrageously good at it. They morphed into a gang that sold top health care to the high bidder. These days they are last-resort providers to the desperate rich—and have become desperately rich doing so.

"I see."

"I think they decided his condition was hopeless last month. That's when he stopped being patient. The point of the tournament and of being an Operator became all about collecting power for himself. If he achieved demigod status he could beat his disease."

Not so hard to understand. "And he was going to take you along."

"So he said. I never completely believed him, but he might have done. After he saved himself."

Though I understood Stornes's motivation, the rationale of the tournament still seemed loony. Fear of death is a powerful driver, especially inside Magister Bezma's intellectual community. He wasn't the first sorcerer willing to devour the world in order to beat Death.

Near as I knew, nobody had won that contest yet. At best you could buy time, a few centuries at most. The universe insisted on balance. When an Izi Bezma distorted the fabric of what Is, a countervailing force produced a Black Orchid.

Therein lay the calling of the shinigami, the death spirits. Enma Ai or Yama, in particular, could step out of the ether and deliver not only oblivion but damnation to the deserving.

Or such was the belief of some of the cults with which TunFaire is cursed and blessed. Izi Bezma, being Orthodox, might think he had found a mystical means of lawyering his way around the pitfalls that had claimed those who had failed before him.

Orchidia Hedley-Farfoul, though, might indeed be Enma Ai embodied, in the sense that she might be the device the universe chose to press Meyness B. Stornes back onto the thread the Fates had spun him at the hour of his birth.

I shook like a wet dog. So did all the mutts around me. Some chill had touched us all.

Maybe it was just my uncharacteristic, introspective ramble through realms of mystic speculation.

All so intriguing, this. I got most of it now, yet there was still plenty to mystify me. And, then, there was the whole other puzzle of Hagekagome, Brownie, and the dogs who dwelt here in the nation of the gone-before.

There was plenty I didn't yet get. Something big was missing still. Something that would make sense of what had happened to my so-beautiful gift from the good gods, now beneath that sheet of glass. Something that might be out in plain sight if I but had eyes with which to see. No doubt the Dead Man would have seen it long since.

107

I stared at Strafa for several minutes. Inspiration did not come in a flash. It was more like a slowly developing infection. "Where were you supposed to take her? And how were you supposed to get her there?"

Mikon D. took a while because he hadn't visited the place himself but eventually had me picturing the shack where Moonblight and I spent the night on the floor. Bezma meant to conduct his ritual there, with help from Mikon and his hired hands.

"There's supposedly another place if it's needed." Mikon didn't know where that was, though. Considering Bezma's jackleg style so far, it probably didn't really exist.

The how for moving Strafa turned out to be the wagon previously used to haul plunder away from Flubber Ducky and Trivias Smith's, which waited behind a big mausoleum nearby, positioned so it couldn't be seen from the sextons' shack. Mikon had been sent to get Strafa after off-loading the goods at the Hauser place.

"So, where does Bonegrinder fit?"

"Bonegrinder? He doesn't. He's one of Constance Algarda's Breakers."

"He owns that house. And he's Orchidia Hedley-Farfoul's uncle."

"Meyness probably . . . Maybe there's some intent to misdirect, or to deceive by omission."

No doubt.

"Meyness acted like he owned the place."

I had seen no sign of recent visitors during my stay there.

Mikon said, "You need to decide what you want to do. Meyness will be racing midnight. If I don't turn up in a reasonable time, he'll know something went wrong. He'll go with whatever backup he has planned. And he always has another plan."

I glimpsed something sly peeping out the corner of Mikon's downcast eyes. He was putting on a show of cooperation and contrition, but he hadn't bailed on Meyness completely. The sneaky bastard had a faint hope left in keeping the faith.

"No way will I let you take my wife anywhere. But since you've had an epiphany and mean to dedicate the rest of your life to righteous works, I'm going to let you join the rush to drive a stake through the heart of the Tournament of Swords concept."

All right. I didn't say it quite so grandiloquently, but that's what I meant. And I wanted to suggest that I wasn't as clever as I pretended, which hasn't ever been that hard to do. I wanted to get him thinking that he could manipulate me by pretending to go along to buy time.

He agreed without hearing specifics. Good thing, because I was woefully lacking on those and winging it completely.

"Let's move, then." Outside, I told Brownie, "Mikon says he'll help us. You keep an eye on him anyway. If he does something suspicious, kill him and eat the evidence."

The strays probably wouldn't attack a human, but it couldn't hurt to have the notion rattling around in Mikon's head.

The dogs looked like they understood. Several sniffed Mikon like they were checking to see if he'd be tender and tasty or tough and stringy.

I grinned at the old watchman. He kept a straight face. "I want the tomb closed up. Make any repairs that you have to. I also want to rent or borrow a coffin like the one that my wife is in." Grin controlled, I asked Mikon, "Meyness wouldn't be familiar with Strafa's coffin, would he?"

Mikon was puzzled. He lacked a ghost of a notion what I was thinking. I had only a ghost of a notion myself. It involved Morley Dotes and a recollection of a vampire we'd known. He and I were the only people living who knew what had happened.

Mikon and I collected the wagon. Me, he, and the watchman headed for the gatehouse, where I reminded Morley of the bad old days and offered my suggestion by implication. He got it, was amused, and said nothing to tip Mikon off.

After a liberal tip and my signature on a promissory note covering mausoleum repairs, Morley, Mikon, I, and my regular complement of mutts headed north, leading a covered wagon carrying a blanket-draped coffin. Though that did not have a glass top, it might pass for the one Strafa now called home.

The cemetery guys swore on God's True Name that mausoleum repairs would commence immediately in the morning. One lone mention of Shadowslinger was encouragement enough for those old men.

We were half a mile from our destination when Pular Singe and Dollar Dan Justice materialized, apparently having lain in wait.

"For three minutes, maybe," Singe said. "No longer."

"How could you possibly know that I'd be coming past here?"

"Rat rumor," Dan said. "We asked where you were. Regular rats reported a rough track. This seemed like a good place to wait."

I didn't buy it. I smelled a high bull dung content that suggested a new level of secret rat powers. That couldn't be anything but propaganda.

Singe, though, said nothing to undermine the scam.

Mikon boggled at rat folks acting like they were real people but steadfastly ignored the suggestions of rat magic.

"All right. I get it. How doesn't matter. What's happened?"

Singe is never deeply shy about delivering bad news.

What has to be done has to be done. "Barate Algarda, Kyoga Stornes, Richt Hauser, that weird man Bashir, and Shadowslinger have gone missing."

"They invaded Chattaree this afternoon. They went after Magister Bezma because of Feder and his friend. We were outside. It got exciting. There were earthquakes and clouds of poison dust. We decided not to get involved. We'll hear way more than we want after the Specials find us again." Moonblight must have ridded me of all official tracking devices. It had been a while since I'd had tin whistles underfoot.

Mikon was aghast at the idea that anyone, even from the Hill, would invade the cathedral. He would be but one of thousands so shaken. The invasion would stir a huge uproar, possibly violence, and some pointed questions from the Director to everyone involved.

The Breaker side just might have included that in their calculations.

I asked, "What's the disaster that I need to know about right away?"

"Sometime this afternoon, probably while you were at the cemetery, thugs invaded Shadowslinger's house. They tore the place up, stole everything they could carry, killed Mashego, and kidnapped Kevans and Kip. Magister Bezma led them. The sorcery holding off the private watchmen caused widespread property damage. Mashego killed four raiders and wounded so many others that the survivors weren't able to take their dead away."

"Kevans and Kip? Kidnapped?" I hadn't considered that possibility. How would Bezma know that Shadowslinger wasn't there? Or had he just assumed that she was still in a coma? "What about the bodyguards who were supposed to be protecting Kevans?"

Embarrassed, Dollar Dan admitted, "They were not there. She ordered them to go away, they were fired, she did not want their ugly asses underfoot anymore, she did not want to see any of them ever again—no more than an hour before the bad guys turned up. They are back on the job, strongly reminded that she is not their employer, and are looking for her."

How would a kidnapping fit in with the concept of a tournament? I glared at Mikon.

Mikon appeared one hundred percent chagrined. "I don't know anything about that. Meyness was supposed to be setting up for the Ritual."

"You know who we're talking about?"

"I do. Their names head Meyness's list of most-wanted gamers."

"And if he had done his research, he'd know that neither kid has any supernatural powers."

"But . . ." He didn't believe me. Or didn't want to believe me. "The girl is the daughter of Furious Tide of Light! The boy conjures all those incredible inventions. He has to be tapped into another world."

"The girl has no talent except being inventive. More so than the boy does because she does know about sorcery even though she has no aptitude for it. The boy has to be smacked in the chops with the supernatural just to recognize it. But if it's something mechanical . . . He thinks stuff up. He and the girl refine it."

Kip's best friend who was a girl but not his girlfriend, to her dismay, was his female mirror image, often more clever creatively.

I said, "I presume we know where to find our people."

Dan said, "Mud Man and Wiley Baw are on that."

"Good. I was on my way to see Magister Bezma, anyhow. Now he has me motivated. And, since his name came up, what's Mud Man's story for this afternoon?"

We resumed moving with no course adjustment. John Stretch would be waiting up ahead with word about any changes in what we needed to do.

108

Mud Man had trailed Vicious Min to one of the rooftop hideouts belonging to the little blonde and her friend. Dollar Dan had trailed the other big people and the Black Orchid to the same place. Nobody paid attention to rat people.

The blonde and her friend left Orchidia with injured Min, the slow youth, and the crippled elder.

I said, "I hope Orchidia isn't in a black mood when she wakes up."

Dan said, "She was awake before they got her to the place where they meant to keep her." Before I asked, he volunteered, "An unconscious human gives off a different odor than one who is only pretending."

"Good to know." Might even be useful, someday.

Singe made a chuckling noise. "You smell different when you are faking sleep, too." A trick I employ often when I don't feel like getting out of bed.

"I see. Good to know again." Then I yelped and jumped about a yard straight up. "What the hell was that?"

"Fireworks. Premature fireworks. It is the Day of the Dead. We should start seeing costumes once the moon comes up."

There was always a huge orange full moon, assuming the overcast let it be seen. And, as midnight approached, there would be fireworks.

Yes. Fireworks. But later.

Morley said what I was thinking. "Costumes and fireworks would make great camouflage for serious villainy."

People wouldn't pay much attention, would they? Weird and unusual were supposed to happen tonight.

Shadowslinger had anticipated that, and something else she felt compelled to go the whole mystery route about.

A second rocket went up. This one exploded huge, presenting a globe of gold and pink sparks. The dogs pulled in close, made uncomfortable by the boom and subsequent crackle of secondary explosions.

Morley laughed. "You know what that's all about, don't you?"

"I know exactly what it is. Some enterprising kid found a way to get into the fireworks magazine. He liberated some of the bigger shells." Boys try every year. It's a tradition. "The summer before the summer I went off to boot camp, Mikey and I got three star shells."

So there I was, thinking about my departed brother on an evening when you were supposed to do exactly that. Mikey and I had had a great time that summer, but the shadow of the future had begun to loom. I would be off soon, on a road that had proven cruel for so many Garrett men already.

Till the information officers brought Ma the news and Mikey's medals, I never considered the possibility that he would be the next Garrett not to come back. I'd been sure that I had a lock on a one-man lie-down six feet under in the land of the giant snakes and spiders, if I didn't turn to croc shit first.

I'm not sure what brought Mikey so strongly to mind. I mean, yes, it was that night, but I'd gotten through Days of the Dead and All-Souls untroubled for several years. Why should this one be different?

I launched a general question. "Should we consider rescuing Orchidia? She'd be handy to have around if we end up slow-dancing with a magister of the Church."

Dollar Dan opined, "It is likely that she will rescue herself when the time seems right. She may have done so already."

"Singe, for the gods' sake, lie to this guy. Tell him you'll marry him. Or tumble him blind. Or something, because he's starting to make me feel inadequate, he's working so damned hard to show off his smarticals."

"Smarticals? A new word for that special occasion when one of the Other Races amazes you by being able to tie his own shoes?"

That was kind of saying sideways that no way was she, the inimitable Pular Singe, going to be impressed by anything done by Dollar Dan Justice. He was just doing what he was supposed to, as far as she was concerned. Publicly.

But she was impressed. She was my little girl. She had grown up in my house. I knew her better than anyone but maybe the Dead Man. Dollar Dan was wearing her down.

John Stretch intercepted us soon afterward. "I stopped by your house on my way." Talking to Singe, not to me. "Those girls are not happy. Penny thinks she is going to miss the fireworks. The other one has her feelings hurt because she has not been able to spend any time with Garrett, and that is her whole reason for being with us." He turned slightly, to me. "You should give her more attention." As though I knew exactly what he meant and why.

I did not, and I tried to make that clear. "Why? She's a cute little thing . . . But she's just another stray . . ."

I'd said something wrong. I had no idea what, but all four dogs growled and showed me their teeth. I got wicked, irritated looks from some of the others.

"Godsdammit! Tell me!"

Morley was not one of the irritated. He answered with a shrug. He didn't get it, either.

"Well?" I demanded of Singe.

"I cannot help you. I should not. It cannot work that way."

"I do believe that I am about to lose my temper."

"This is one of those thing you have to work out for yourself, for good or ill. It is a moral bridge. No one can cross it for you, nor should anyone ease your way. It is all on you. And you are running out of time."

"And patience!" No shit.

I knew Singe wanted to help. She owed me. I had made it possible for her to become the prodigy that she was. But there were witnesses.

It must be true that she wasn't even supposed to offer a clue.

Irked, I imagined the Dead Man needling me with some remark to the effect that I had every clue I needed already. I should put in a little effort.

Oh, sigh. This had the feel of one of those face-offs with a moral tilting point that make life so damned uncomfortable.

I bet Belinda never suffered such quandaries. She never met a problem she couldn't solve by breaking something or killing somebody.

It sucks, this "figure it out on your own or it has no value" crap. The real truth is, people are covering their asses so they take no blame if you make the sinister choice.

Paint me cynical. Very, very cynical.

"I'll get you all, someday. You'll have the shit raining down. You'll be begging for a steel umbrella. And I'll sit there in my rocking chair humming 'God Save the Queen.'" Which is a particularly filthy drinking song about a cross-dressing fellow who has mad skills as a streetwalker but often gets into trouble because what he keeps hidden under his skirt has a mind of its own.

Singe told me, "You being deliberately disgusting changes nothing."

It made me feel better, though not much.

109

The Black Orchid wasn't where she'd been last seen, nor were any big people there, either. There was no evidence of a struggle. They had vanished right under Mud Man's whiskers. He couldn't understand how, nor even when. There were odors in the hide, thick, but no trail leading away. Even Singe could find nothing.

"Sorcery," Dollar Dan suggested, cleverly.

"Indeed." Of course, sorcery, assuredly courtesy of the Black Orchid, for whom sneaking to commit murder was a way of life.

We knew what Orchidia wanted. How would she get it? Was there any good reason to interfere?

Well, yes. Of course. I would be most unhappy if she got her revenge before I got my kids back.

Singe mused, "There is a possibility that the lady has made a pact with the big people."

That did seem plausible. The little blonde and her friend had tried to thwart the attack on Orchidia's twins. The basis for a partnership existed.

"Morley. The blond kid. Her big guy. Seen either one lately?"

"I have not. Which may mean only that they're making more of an effort to stay out of sight. I do feel like we're still being watched."

I grunted. Sometimes I got that creepy sting-between-the-shoulder-blades feeling myself. "I haven't smelled anything for at least a day."

"That might be Bell's fault. She put it out that Fehlkse's health outlook would be rosier if he stayed away."

I doubted that Lurking Fehlske would be intimidated, and recalled that Little Bit and her pal had swept the man up. I kept that to myself. "She figure out who he was working for?"

Morley shrugged. "Not yet."

Mikon seemed antsy suddenly. He might have an uncomfortable idea.

I suspected that Lurking Fehlske no longer signified. That he had no place in the game anymore. We were coming up on a crisis, if not the crisis. Despite all the other distractions, that came down to last desperate attempts by Magister Bezma to salvage something from a scheme that never really came to life in the first place.

Funny notion. The incompetent villain. In the grand stories, like Jon Salvation's dramas, the villains are all clever and brilliant and stay two steps ahead till virtue works its magic and triumphs at the end. This time, though, we seemed to be dealing with a self-deluded screwup who had spent two generations and several lives cobbling together a total cluster fuck.

Bezma/Stornes could do damage and cause pain in an effort to tie off tangled loose ends by midnight—assuming I had mined anything sensible out of the confusion. I was sure he couldn't get his dream to unfold. I was just as sure that he could still cause a heap of pain and death.

Morley said, "I may have to bail on you, Garrett. I don't have much go-power left."

I was amazed that I hadn't had to put him in the wagon already. Being selfish, though, and anxious to have the knife I most trusted covering me, I hadn't volunteered to release him from any misplaced sense of obligation.

I hoped my selfishness didn't cost him ground in his healing process.

Most of my friends were hurt these days, though, one way or another. And my wife was dead.

I tossed an inquiring glance toward the sky gods. How much of that lay at the end of a red thread of blame leading back to me?

A lone raindrop got me square on the forehead.

Some lesser deity in the rain racket had taken to sniping at me.

"John Stretch. Sir. Mud Man and Dollar Dan are bound to be wiped out, too, after this long day." No rat man was ever famous for his stamina. "Perhaps they could see my friend safely to . . ."

Morley said, "Wake up, Garrett. The vampire gambit has yet to be played."

"Oh. Yeah. So you're not going to bail?"

"Of course I am. But after that."

"Then we'd better get that done."

We didn't need to concern ourselves with where the Black Orchid might be or what she might be doing. That itch on the spine was all her. She made herself known as we closed in on the place where Magister Bezma was hiding.

She had decided that her best means of acquiring her target was to join up with folks who knew where to find him.

Morley told me, while she still awaited us just ahead, "I don't think she's here alone, either."

True. The sky gods were feeling capricious. There was no overcast at the moment. Orange moonlight was splashing in from somewhere over to the east, and that silhouetted my skywalking little friend atop a building behind Orchidia.

I said, "Good evening, Lady Farfoul. I presume that you have had your moment with Vicious Min and are now ready to rejoin me."

"As promised." Rather sarcastically.

The darkness was such that neither of us could get a good look at the other. Even so, I was at a disadvantage—though numbers and diversity of talents lay on my side of the ledger.

Orchidia seemed content to pretend that we were old pals. I know I was. And maybe we did have a deep commonality of interest.

She fell in beside me, walking carefully. "Blisters," she explained. "Not in shape for this stuff anymore. I don't get out of the house enough."

"We're all worn down to the nubs. If I understood Constance right, though, this mess still has to be wrapped up by midnight."

"The Meyness Stornes part should be. If that happens, the rest will fall into place before All-Souls ends." Before I could question her about Vicious Min and the big folks, she asked me, "You do know where to find Stornes, don't you? You are on your way to deal with him?" She surveyed my companions like she was sure that this particular crew would not have come together otherwise.

"We're on our way, yes, and working against that deadline."

"You have more time than you think."

"How so?"

"The midnight transition isn't iron, as long as Meyness Stornes is thwarted. Dawn will see the real pressure begin to build. And even then your margin should be sundown."

"His margin for what?" Morley asked, assuming that I wouldn't ask for myself.

Orchidia frowned like she thought he must be intellectually challenged, then caught my empty look and realized that neither of us had a clue.

My best pal reminded her, "This fellow here is Hill people because he shares a bed with somebody from up there. Genius isn't sexually transmitted. He wasn't born to it. He wasn't raised to it. And I only hang out with him, so I'm even further clueless."

I added, "I'm the kind of guy you have to draw pictures for."

Morley said, "He was fourteen before he could remember how to tie his shoes."

"Hey! I had it down before that. I showed it off at my

twelfth birthday party. Remember? I got it right five tries
out of seven."

The right corner of Orchidia's mouth twitched, but her
being amused didn't help. "I see what you mean. Even Furious Tide of Light may have suffered from an unjustifiably
optimistic illusion that you understood more than you did
because everyone else she knew understood."

"Finally. Somebody gets it." I put on my most charming,
big-eyed, eager-to-learn moon face—which she wiped off
the slate immediately.

"Constance should have understood that when no one
else did. Either health issues overtook her before she could
deal with it or she wanted the situation to be what it was.
What?"

"Huh?" seemed appropriate, though I thought I knew
what came next.

"Whatever, the decision to advance your education isn't
mine to make. Make your ignorance clear to Constance
first chance you get. It's possible that she miscalculated seriously." Under her breath, she added, "And that wouldn't
be the first time, would it?"

"Meaning?"

"Meaning there might have been a time when Constance Algarda secretly suffered from the same disease that
claimed both Machtkess girls, not just Mariska. Constance
was the one who brought Meyness Stornes into the original
Breakers gang."

I started to ask how she could possibly know about stuff
that happened before she was born but recalled that she
had an uncle who had been there and was now supporting
the hunt for the killer of his grandnephew and grandniece.
I didn't have to look like an idiot.

But . . . I considered the Meyness Stornes I knew by report. Old, ugly, disheveled, and dirty, with a repulsive
growth on his head. I couldn't picture an entire generation
of Hill girls straining for a chance to be exploited by him.

I tried asking Orchidia's opinion.

She rolled her eyes in Morley's direction.

All right. I got it. For ages I've watched women practically break down doors to get at Morley without understanding why. I've never heard one of them explain it in any way that makes sense. I don't expect that I ever will.

Sometimes you just have to accept what is and forget figuring out why, like accepting the Will of God. It is what it is.

Orchidia suggested, "The time for analysis is after the action."

"What?"

"There are things that need doing now. Time is running out. We should use what is left more profitably than this."

"Oh. Yeah. Good point."

Singe wanted to know our destination. I explained. Dollar Dan remarked, "The big main room there would be ideal for something on the scale of what Magister Bezma seems to be planning."

My, oh my. How could he possibly know . . . ? Kevans's bodyguard crew. Of course. They would have tracked her kidnappers. The derelict house would be swarming with ordinary rats by now.

I looked at Mikon D. Though he was intent on the cobblestones, he sensed my scrutiny. He nodded agreement with Dollar Dan's assessment. "There aren't many safe empty places with that much space," he mumbled.

110

Orchidia turned spook. After several minutes she manifested again to report, "The children, the magister, and a dozen others, mostly dead or dying, are in there. Your Mashego was a true shinobi blade master."

I held up a hand in case somebody felt like pursuing the standard Garrett strategy of charging in smashing people and things. I had a notion, though, that subtlety might be more appropriate this time.

Orchidia said, "The magister has erected an impressive array of warning spells, booby trap spells, and old-fashioned mechanical snares. He posted gray rats and gargoyles around the neighborhood, too. The grays deserted, however."

"They ran when Firé Esté and Mud Man arrived," Dan said. "Without telling their boss that they were going."

Perhaps some threats had been leveled.

The grays would be desperately dependent on John Stretch's forbearance now.

Patient henchfolk listened as Orchidia continued, asking no questions. Even I kept quiet, though I did wonder how she had gotten such a good look around in the short time that she'd been gone.

Sorcery, the rat men would say.

I told myself she had to be an avatar of Enma Ai. Death goes everywhere unnoticed until it touches someone.

I had lost control. This was no longer my operation. It

belonged to the Black Orchid. The rest of us had become supporting players. And that was good enough for me, for now. She had the tools. She had the skills. Even pursuing the ploy that was central to my plan would be more promising with her on the scene. She could do so much more than the rest of us.

Maybe fate was behind me. Maybe not every god had it in for me all the time. Maybe I'd just drawn my one random divine good hand.

Orchidia said, "The gargoyles have to be neutralized. Otherwise we'll have them behind us and they can see in the dark better than humans, dogs, or rats. Wait here."

She dematerialized before I could ask what she meant to do.

I had an idea. I didn't like it.

Morley would have no reservations. That would be his own option were the decision his to make. It was not his custom to leave live adversaries behind him. His standard of necessity was lower than mine.

He made a small gesture. There was enough moonlight to let me catch it. I nodded, got Mikon's attention. "One more time, friend. Are you going to help scuttle Bezma's plan?"

He had agreed and agreed, but I hadn't felt his conviction. He didn't want to betray his cousin, however ugly that cousin's ambition might be. He didn't truly believe that the rest of us just wanted to abort the Ritual, save the children, and wreck the tournament.

It didn't much matter what he believed, or even what he wanted, anymore. While I diverted him Morley climbed into the coffin. Mikon thought he would be delivering it empty. Part of his discomfort was his dread of Bezma's displeasure once he opened the box.

Last time we worked this grift, we delivered a coffin full of extremely hungry vampire.

Orchidia rematerialized. "We may have a problem. Two of the gargoyles had been neutralized before I got there." She described frail bodies brutally torn. "The others have fled, I hope without giving Meyness Stornes any warning. Garrett, your pretty girl has written herself into tonight's play. However cute she may be, she is no paragon of sweetness."

"Is she another shinigami?"

"What?"

I decided not to tell her that I thought she might be possessed by a death spirit. "Nothing. Let's do what we're here to do. We'll deal with that when we have to."

The blonde and her friend couldn't be a threat. They'd had tons of chances to make my life miserable and dangerous. They hadn't done so.

Whether they could be counted on to be on my side might be a whole 'nother bucket of monkey guts.

Lights had come to life inside the Hauser place while Orchidia was hunting. Several, scattered across the ground floor, feebly leaked through boarded windows. I suspected that somebody had lighted half a dozen floating-wick oil lamps. I patted Mikon on the left shoulder. "Time."

He didn't want to go. I didn't blame him. He was in a solid pinch between the devil and the deep. There was no way out but treachery, with guaranteed despair if he bet wrong. The right bet only offered a slim chance to live on in shame.

He asked, "Isn't it a little early?"

"Aren't you already late?" If his mission had gone swimmingly, he would have arrived here with Strafa a while ago.

"All right. Moving out." But before he started, Orchidia kissed him firmly, one final piece of dark psychological warfare. He didn't need her to remind him, "If there is a next kiss . . ."

A pale hope. The Black Orchid might forgive his part in the conspiracy that had claimed her children. All he had to do was . . .

I was sure Mikon had had nothing to do with those deaths. Chances were, his cousin had kept him ignorant so his conscience wouldn't lead him to do anything inconvenient.

I was equally sure that his ignorant innocence meant nothing to the Black Orchid. I couldn't find any forgiveness lying around loose myself.

"Scoot," I hissed.

Mikon started moving.

So did everyone else.

The rat people gathered in a clutch of shadow where, it became clear, they were getting in touch with normal rats, to scout and observe.

The Black Orchid became invisible. I would have stayed near Mikon myself. Maybe she was so close he'd never get a chance to betray the scale of the peril closing in on Bezma—if he was foolish enough to try.

111

A noise from the wagon . . . Morley. Very unhappy. "Garrett." He rasped it. "I can't do this. I can't handle the closed space yet. Sorry."

So he wasn't all the way back psychologically.

"I'll do it. Leave me the toys."

I lay back in the coffin a minute later. He slid the lid into place, covered it with a blanket. I began to shake.

I have problems with dark, tight places. I have bigger problems with taking up premature residence in a coffin. I launched a calming mantra from wartime days, to keep the panic at bay.

Everything lurched and shifted. The wagon had begun to roll.

Oh, did I hope that Mikon D. was more scared of the Black Orchid than he was of Meyness B.!

This really didn't seem like such a brilliant idea now that I was the guy wearing the pine tuxedo. Despite all I could do to remain calm, a big part of my head kept upchucking things that could go wrong, some stuff so unlikely that I marveled at my capacity to imagine such bizarre disasters.

The wagon stopped. I assumed we were at the door to Magister Bezma's hideout, the erstwhile Hauser stead.

The hearing inside the box was surprisingly good.

Two people responded to Mikon's arrival. I heard later that neither was a wild-haired old man with a momentous

wen. One was a gray rat man. The other, a human, demanded, "What do you want here, little man?"

A voice from the house called, "Is that you, Mikon?
What took so long?"

"I almost got caught. Twice. The first time at the cemetery. Did you know that that place is overrun with wild
dogs?"

The voice asked, "Did you get it?"

"I got it. But—"

"Excellent. Segdway. Bones. Help Mikon and Chick.
Evil Lin. Take the wagon away once they get the coffin off.
Drop it at least a mile from here and then just keep going."

Evil Lin slurred something that made it sound like he
was real excited about moving on and wanted to get to that
as fast as he could.

He was beloved of the gods—providing Orchidia overlooked him.

Any villain who didn't make tracks soon was likely to
end up celebrating All-Souls from the nether side of life's
great divide.

The coffin tilted and rocked. The foot end went high. My
head crashed into unpadded wood. That hurt like hell.
Fierce old me, I managed not to bark or whine.

I heard the wagon roll, then stop again after just seconds. Evil Lin had come down with the drizzling shit hor-
rors after catching a whiff from the clotted darkness where
John Stretch and friends were communing with their spying regular rats.

After a few seconds Evil Lin took one exaggerated step
directly away from the house where the coffin had just disappeared, making a statement. From now on he would
have no part in anything. He would go away and be seen no
more forever. And he started rolling again.

He will hear from John Stretch someday, even so, I'm
sure.

What were Brownie and the girls doing? Like about every female in my life but Hagekagome, they were probably

smarter than me and keeping their heads down. Hell, Vicious Min was probably smarter than me.

A voice said, "Set it on those chairs."

The coffin tilted, rocked, chunked down onto something that creaked. I heard what sounded like somebody agitated trying to talk around a gag. Kevans, sounding more angry than frightened.

That was good, as long as she controlled that anger.

I tried hard to picture how many people were out there and where they were located. The element of surprise would have a very short half-life. I would need to remain the center of attention long enough for the Black Orchid to strike. But our future victims were not being cooperative. Hardly any said enough to give themselves away.

The one I thought was Magister Bezma said, "There's something wrong. I feel it, Mikon. Did you see anything out there? What did you bring down upon us?"

"I saw some rat men." Which was one hundred percent true.

"They belong. They're Evil Lin's people. That's not it. There's something else. But the rats and dragons would give warning, wouldn't they?" He was talking to himself by then.

"Meyness . . ."

"All right. You're nervous. You're upset. You aren't invested in this. I understand. But be patient. Tomorrow will be a huge new day."

Another voice said something. The magister responded, "I can only repeat what I just said. Come midnight, everything will change. Come midnight, I will gain the power to heal us all. But not before."

The unintelligible voice got louder and angrier, presumably someone with a wounded friend who wouldn't make it till midnight.

Voices rose. There was a scuffle. The mutineer might have paid the usual price of failure. Or, at least, he ended up of no value to Magister Bezma—who, in turn, ended up distracted from his concern about trouble gathering on his doorstep.

He emerged from the confrontation shouting, "Mikon, where are you going?"

"Uh . . . I was going to look around outside, see if that attracted any attention."

I didn't buy it and I was inside a box, halfway panicked because I was inside a box, and couldn't see Mikon's face. How much less believable was he to someone standing in front of him who had known him all his life?

"I can't manage this without you, Mikon." Appeal and threat alike there, with the threat prevailing. "So get back in here and help."

All Mikon had going now was a stall and a hope that the trouble he'd brought with him would pull him out of the deep dung.

I suspected that poor Mikon was going to get hosed one way or another. He was one of those guys who just can't not put themselves into bad places.

Time passed faster than it felt like, trapped in there, and Magister Bezma was anxious to get on with things himself. He began ordering people around. Feet shuffled. Furniture scraped and thumped. People bickered. People complained. Kevans got very verbal after her gag slipped. She was in good shape for sure, nor was she as frightened or intimidated as she ought to be. But I heard nothing to tell me how Kip was faring. Kevans never spoke to him, which left me troubled.

I'd learn the good news or bad the hard way, once the lid came off.

Something whispered to me.

Something crossed my chest like a marching cockroach.

I came within an ounce and inch of screaming like a scared little girl.

Something was there in the coffin with me.

112

I didn't abandon reason. That was unnecessary. Violet sparks identified my roommate.

How the devil . . . ?

While we were making the changeover from Morley to me. Had to have happened then.

That didn't matter, though, did it? The critical thing was, the coffin now included a double dose of misery for whoever slipped its lid.

Could Tara Chayne be playing a practical joke? Why shoehorn that thing in here with me, otherwise? Unless inside the box was the only way to get it past Magister Bezma's wards and traps.

Kevans began barking about being manhandled, reeling off blistering threats because somebody was mistreating somebody who wasn't conscious—without once invoking her dire grandmother. The girl had guts.

Magister Bezma proved himself small by mocking her.

Mikon upbraided him for bullying a girl.

I was pleased, within limits. A man in a coffin certainly has those.

The yelling did bring home an important fact: Kip Prose was alive and probably healthy, if a little bit unconscious.

Bezma yelled some at someone about being more careful painting those damned lines. Ritualistic artistry was in progress. Kevans barked questions like a kid on a field trip

instead of the altar, or victim, meant to be offered the darkness that would facilitate Bezma's ritual.

She wasn't frightened? Was she clueless? Stupid? Sure
that help would swoop in on time? Or was she just unable
to believe that anyone could be what Bezma was?

She had Shadowslinger for a grandmother. She could
not possibly be that naive.

So . . . Algardas were weird and she was a leader in the
category.

The coffin shifted. The centipede scrambled. People outside grumbled. Bezma shrieked at somebody. Stress was
getting to him. His henchmen weren't being patient, just
out of fear. He was being cut some slack because he was
under such ferocious pressure.

Maybe he wasn't a first-water asshole one hundred percent
of the time. Maybe there were people who actually liked him.

No matter. He had my kids and his intentions weren't
good. He would've used my dead wife as a counter in his
game, too, if I hadn't gotten there first. I would cut him no
slack. I wouldn't be understanding.

Wouldn't matter if I was. The Black Orchid and the Algarda tribe were thirsty for his blood. His own son was after
him. The Machtkess sisters were stalking him. And then
there was the little blonde, her friend, and his family. They
fit in somewhere, too.

Purple sparks. Tiny, invisible claws digging in. A change
in the racket from outside . . .

Singing?

They were chanting in Old Karentine, which isn't all that
old. Most people can follow it if they concentrate and the
speakers don't rush or go all mush-mouth.

The Ritual was under way. And Kevans went right on
making her opinion clear, loudly and explicitly. Why didn't
they put that gag back in?

The coffin shuddered as somebody pulled at the lid, untroubled by the fact that it wasn't glass. Maybe they didn't
know.

Maybe Mikon really would help scuttle his cousin's game.

Maybe he'd do the right thing now that the crunch had come.

The chanting grew a little louder, a little faster. I picked out four distinct voices, two of those intermittent and unsteady. The men who had carried the coffin into the house, I presumed. None sounded enamored of their song.

The centipede crawled up on top of me. Several thousand chitinous claws scrabbled around on my face, tugging developing whiskers, getting into my nostrils and mouth, tasting like . . . I don't want to take my imagination there. I could conjure a thousand ugly ideas about where those claws had been.

The chanting circled the box.

The lid slid aside.

113

The centipede surged up and out, off my face, leaving a hundred stinging scratches. The chant ended; then stunned silence gave way to a weird, girly squeal that did not come out of the only girl in the room.

I surged up, right hand seizing the throat of an old goat with wild white hair and a repulsive growth on the front and top of his head. He wore one of the robes tailored at Flubber Ducky. The best of the bunch, I'm sure. He dropped a bronze sword. His eyes bugged. He tried to shake his head. "No!" I couldn't tear my gaze away from that monster blemish, bigger than a pomegranate and the same color, with ample decorative liver spots.

I thought about Strafa and squeezed.

The centipede had one end each around the throats of two hired hands, the youngest and healthiest of the lot. They were outfitted with robes and swords, too. They wouldn't have drawn a second glance on the street tonight. There were others, but most were barely breathing or were Mikon D. Stornes. Mikon hadn't rated his own costume or sword, even incomplete.

He moved toward Kevans and Kip, who were laid out Mandela-style atop a plank table positioned at the heart of the most elaborate and colorful mystical diagram I'd ever seen. Kip was unconscious. Kevans was not. Magister Bezma had resisted villain stereotype enough not to have stripped her down before he got to work. She was sort of

half-ass draped in one of the robes, though. Second best,
probably. And a sword lay upon her chest, grip in her bound
hands and tip between her knees. She got all loud again
before I finished crawling out of the coffin. I hoped Mikon's
intentions were good. There wasn't much I could do if he
went bad on me before I finished with his cousin.

No worries needed, though.

The front door and surrounding wall exploded inward.

The Black Orchid emerged from the debris, very much
meeting my inclination to see her as a death spirit. She was
dreadful. She gave off her own dark glow and darker sparks.
A stench preceded her. It would have been totally appropriate had she been sporting a jewelry ensemble made of
rotting baby heads and severed penises.

The wall in the back blew in. Magister Bezma's wards
and alarms hadn't been worth much. Moonblight and
Moonslight arrived. Their blazing anger did not nourish the
hope that flashed across my victim's face. Moonslight was
the more grim twin. She had a full charge of woman-
scorned going on.

The house shook so violently that even the centipede
lost its grip for an instant.

The blonde's mighty companion dropped through the
ceiling, like a stone falling from a great height . . . Actually,
he was standing on a pointed ton of stone, an inverted, stolen tombstone stele, having already penetrated the roof
and several higher floors. He drove on down through the
floor in this room, too, missing Kevans, Kip, and Mikon by
inches, stopping hip deep in hardwood. Every waking eye
looked his way. And the little blonde floated down through
the opening that he had broken.

I got my grip back. Magister Bezma passed out from
lack of air.

Morley, Singe, and Dollar Dan charged in through the
breach opened by the Black Orchid.

Everybody looked at everybody. Only Kevans had anything to say, but plenty of that, loud, filthy, and virulent, until Moonblight extended a hand the way she had in front of

my Macunado place, with similar advantage to the public peace—for maybe twenty seconds. Then something gave and Kevans started right up again.

Mikon fumbled at Kevans's bonds, finished, turned to Kip. The liberated cords and gag went right onto Magister Bezma. The moment Meyness B. was sewed up I hied my handsome but worried butt over to Kip, who did not look good. He had an ugly blue-gray hue to him. "Somebody look at this kid and see what's wrong with him." I was talking to the twins, but the death master left Magister Bezma in response. She had Kip's color coming back in seconds.

"You!" I told Kevans, finger stabbing. "Shut the hell up!" It was time. Her butt had been saved. She wasn't required to fawn or be grateful, but she could cut back on the godsdamned complaining.

Teenage girls: got to sing, got to dance, got to whine about every damned thing. And I had another one, live-in, coming up.

"You," I told Singe. "I don't want to hear a word."

She didn't say anything, either, but I knew what she was thinking. I said, "Let's get them together in one place," like that really needed saying. The bad guys were crowded together already, now absent their bronze toad stickers. "And get their costumes. We can use those." They were in no mood to resist, just standing, sitting, or lying there looking unhappy and hopeless. The one who did break for freedom smacked right into a combo mechanical and magical snare that, through absurd happenstance, hadn't inconvenienced a single invader.

"Mariska, get that moron loose. Morley, let's you and me and Mikon get the big fellow out of that hole." He had begun struggling. That just got him more stuck. I met the little blonde's gaze. She awarded me a very slight smile and a tiny nod of appreciation. In that moment she seemed more than a little familiar. But how?

The feeling that I should know her was stronger than the feeling with Hagekagome, which seemed mostly nostalgic.

Dollar Dan tied bad guys wrist to wrist and ankle to ankle with cord off a roll he found on steps leading to the second floor. That cord was the same as what had been used to bind Kevans and Kip. Kip was breathing better but sleeping. He must have been drugged to keep him pliable.

Dan made sure each healthy villain was tied between two who couldn't get around under their own power, then put a dead guy at each end attached by a tangle that only a knife would ever defeat. The bad boys were not pleased to be at the mercy of the least of the Other Races. Only one commented, though. Tara Chayne fixed him up with a throat spell that worked better than had the one she'd wasted on the sorceress's daughter.

Mud Man appeared up front. "Hey, we got it, Dan."

"Good work."

"It" was the wagon that Evil Lin had taken away, without the gray teamster. Dollar Dan had sent Mud Man to get it because he figured some of us might not be able to walk away from the scuffle.

Mud Man also announced, "There are tin whistles filtering into the neighborhood. They appear not to know what they are after, but they are looking for something."

Dan told me, "We should finish here and leave before we find ourselves trapped in an interview that never ends."

Tara Chayne grumbled, "Why the hell aren't they off riding herd on the All-Souls revelries?"

The costume folks should be out by now, in the better-lighted parts of town, since no rain had yet materialized. Pickpockets and purse snatchers would be out with them. After the fireworks the drinking and rowdiness would really begin. If the red tops were serious, they would concentrate on keeping the worst incidents nonfatal, local, and unpopular.

Hell. General Block's people would be doing that. Anyone filtering into this neighborhood would be up to something special. They would be Specials. It wouldn't be smart to count on a friendly mind-set in Deal Relway's Special fellows.

They might be under special instructions to make a special example of a certain special pain-in-the-ass-type professional snoop. They might make a special effort to catch said special guy in sufficiently special circumstances that his only way to weasel out would be to claim special immunity as Prince Rupert's personal special agent.

I said, "We maybe ought to consider getting out of here especially fast."

Special minds were already thinking along those exact lines. John Stretch had his crew, including himself and Dollar Dan, gone in a trice—not just doing a fast rat scurry but getting out in front of the Specials with intent to provide mystery shadows for them to chase.

We finished tying Magister Bezma's crew to one another. They stayed to greet the Specials. Bezma and Mikon went into the wagon along with still-sleeping Kip Prose, still-fuming Kevans Algarda, who had been tied up so long that her circulation wouldn't let her get around under her own power, along with all the weapons and costumes originally intended for the Ritual. All four dogs found ways to climb in with the people.

They had kept a low profile during the excitement. They knew when it was best to stay out of the way.

Morley brought us down to earth, dispersing a growing communal urge to do something hasty and probably foolish. "With all the talent we have here, we should be able to leave without being seen as anything but some people headed for the celebrations."

"Good thinking," Tara Chayne opined, considering Morley with that speculative look that women get around him. "We have their costumes."

Singe rolled her eyes, shook her head, and whispered, "Don't get jealous."

"Yeah? This could be fun." Too bad Belinda wasn't around to impress us with her lack of humor.

Then we were rolling with no ratfolk but Singe visible, nor any Black Orchid, nor even the little blonde's big-ass friend. Nor the blonde herself, come to that. I hadn't noticed Orchidia disappearing. I last saw her when she told me to take the gang to Shadowslinger's place. Her turning into a ghost was a disappointment but no surprise. The blonde vanishing was a bigger disappointment. I'd been all set to get to know her better.

The big guy managing to vanish was more of an amazement.

I was sure I'd see them all again.

114

Shadowslinger, Barate, and accomplices employed intimidation, negotiation, and more intimidation to evade custody. It helped that the Crown Prince was a friend and big fan of Furious Tide of Light, complicity in whose murder by an Orthodox magister had provoked the Chattaree invasion. A witness statement from one Niea Syx tilted the balance—once Shadowslinger agreed to underwrite repairs.

That promise was likely worth the paper on which it wasn't written. It would happen only if Constance found Meyness Stornes's stolen money.

Mikon said a stash existed. He didn't know how much. Meyness had thrown money away lately, arguing that there was no point having a fortune he was too dead to spend.

Shadowslinger eyed my crew and its featured captive. I observed, "You're looking remarkably hale after your debility and extended day."

She grunted, then glared at Stornes—sparing just enough attention to make sure that nobody with a grievance did anything premature.

The possibility of treasure had softened vengeful attitudes, though.

The Church's money had been filtering through Magister Bezma's sticky fingers for a long time.

Singe gave me a dirty look, knowing that I was thinking treasure, too. She figured I was well off enough already. I owned a house on the Hill.

She willfully ignores the fact that I have a house full of females, some getting fashion conscious and all too damned-liberal with my funds. How could it hurt to put together a pile too big for them to spend?

Oddly, no one objected to Singe's presence.

Bashir came in to announce, "The Lady Orchidia Hedley-Farfoul has asked to join the conversation."

Bash was holding up well for a man who had lost his wife—so thought a widower who had spent several days willfully and with malice aforethought holding up well himself. I knew what was going on inside Bash's head. The truth shone through when he eyed Meyness Stornes.

Stornes was oblivious. He had vested himself in a false conviction that the Breaker friends of his youth would make allowances.

Idiot. He could really think that way while surrounded by people whose family members would be celebrating All-Souls from the shady side because of the wicked ambition of Meyness B. Stornes?

He appeared to lose volume and mass when Shadow-slinger chirped, "Bring her in, Bashir. It would be unfriendly and impolitic to deny Orchidia a part in the process. She lost more than any of us." She laid a ferocious scowl on Kevans, who took the hint to remain silent. The girl could be intimidated by her grandmother.

Shadowslinger asked, "Richt? You want to say something about your niece?"

"Only that I suggest you be careful what you wish for."

He and Constance glanced at me. For no obvious reason most everyone moved a step this way or that, as though some silent, unconscious realignment had begun.

Bashir said, "Very well, madame." He offered Constance a shallow bow, then moved a step toward me. He murmured, "I have seen the dogs fed and bedded down, sir."

"Why, thank you." Somewhat surprised.

Out he went.

In came the Black Orchid, slightly more than a minute later.

115

Slightly more than a minute. Into that interim I interjected the announcement "My matchless resources have discovered the ballista used against Strafa."

I wouldn't say that there was a stunned silence, nor even a nervous or guilty silence.

"It's in the basement at Strafa's house, disassembled. It appears to have resided there for decades. Someone took it out, refurbished it, assembled it, and used it—then broke it down and put it back."

Singe oozed closer, till she was in actual contact on my left. She had a look on that said that this was something I should have shared with her before we ended up isolated among sorceresses, with temperatures falling.

Though it may have sounded that way, I hadn't meant to be accusing.

Then in came the Black Orchid, having overheard my announcement.

Meyness Stornes was one of the more relaxed people in the room now.

I saw no signs of guilty knowledge. People still moved, realigning. The Machtkess girls drifted closer to me.

Orchidia grabbed my right elbow almost as if we were a couple. "Are you suggesting something?"

"No. Just reporting. But part of the report has to be that Meyness Stornes had nothing to do with Strafa's murder, considering he had no access to the weapon, the timing was wrong, and Vicious Min, far from being a Dread Companion, was a hired hand. So is the one protecting the kid who keeps turning up. In fact, I'm pretty sure he's Min's brother."

Constance Algarda had become a great blank-face pile of blubber who, nonetheless, radiated the suspicion that a certain former Marine might not be as dim as he put on.

Hard to be, some might argue. Not while being deft enough to stay alive without the protection of a dedicated murder of guardian angels.

"Well?" Orchidia, but speaking to me or to the crowd?

It was a tense moment. She, for reasons unclear, was an ally for now.

"Well . . . ," I responded. "Well. It's self-evident that somebody knows more about what happened than they've admitted so far." Maybe even Dr. Ted, who could be considered a principal but wasn't with us tonight.

Bashir reappeared. "Excuse the additional interruption . . ." His eyes got big as his body arched.

The little blonde shoved him forward, demonstrating incredible strength with no leverage. She floated four inches off the floor and still moved him easily.

She was dressed the same as always. She folded her arms in front of her, sliding hands inside opposite sleeves.

Barate Algarda spoke for the first time since my arrival. Resolutely, powerfully, loudly, he proclaimed, "Ah, holy shit! This is not possible!"

Kyoga Stornes had been just as quiet—while easing closer to his father, to lay unhappy hands on if Meyness showed any sign of pulling some sorcerer's stunt. He agreed with Barate. "Oh, holy shit indeed! Nana! What have you done?"

Barate and Kyoga had called Constance "Nana" when they were little, though she was grandmother to neither. It came from some amusing toddler comment become family in-joke with sense and meaning only for those who had been there.

Barate demanded, "Exactly, Mother! What have you done?"

Constance herself showed us the fabled eyes the size of saucers.

The little girl squeezed in between Orchidia and me, as though by right. The Black Orchid yielded gracefully. The girl said, "Yes, Grandmother, you totally screwed the pooch. That spell caused a double, even a triple rebound, in time and place, both."

Suddenly, I knew why she was familiar. Suddenly, I knew who she was. Suddenly, I was a huge, ready-to-melt lump of gelatin.

I was married to her.

Well, I had been about to marry her. Then something happened that split her into a corpse and a feisty little thing that could get me a year in a work camp for thinking about us being married. . . .

She slid her left hand into mine, tugged. "They can finish up here. We have to go. We don't have much time."

Orchidia agreed. "There isn't much at all. Don't waste it being you."

Shadowslinger looked scared, compassionate, furious, self-pitying, self-loathing, and just plain crushed, all together and/or in lightning rotation. She said, "Go ahead, Garrett. I did screw up. We'll talk later. We have this part under control." A lot of eyes focused on Meyness B. Stornes. His life could get more difficult in a hundred interesting ways.

Shadowslinger made weird noises, twitched, shook oddly. I thought she might be about to stroke again—if ever she really had.

Even so, Barate was more concerned about Kevans, and about Kip because Kip meant so much to Kevans. Kyoga forgot his father. He beat me out of the room, off to get Dr. Ted. Hopefully, Ted wasn't off somewhere watching fireworks and impossible to find.

Kevans was working on a refreshed case of attitude but couldn't quite go public while her grandmother was shaking and making ever stranger noises. She didn't seem affected by the fact that her mother might now become her little sister.

Singe had no idea what was going on with Little Strafa but did get that this was no time for Garrett to mope around demanding answers to any trivial question that occurred to him. Something needed doing, and soon. I'd already mentioned All-Souls deadlines several times. She started shoving. Little Strafa pulled, demonstrating more of the power she had used to move Bashir. The Black Orchid got out front and ran interference.

Morley Dotes hadn't been invited upstairs. He hadn't gone away, either, contrary to his earlier determination. He had been amusing himself in the kitchen but now was waiting at the front door with the dogs. He and they were wide awake and seemed renewed. Little Strafa led us into Shadowslinger's garden. "Each one take a dog." She snatched up Number Two, shoved her at Singe, in whose arms the mutt wriggled just enough to get comfortable. Then she fell asleep.

Little Strafa told the rest of us, "Come on. Do it."

Brownie made it easy for me.

Morley snagged a mutt, as did Orchidia, who shuddered at the contact but forged manfully on.

"All of you crowd in facing me. Push in tight. Hold your dog with your left arm. Put your right arm around the person next to you."

Singe and Orchidia, in almost identical language, instructed me to shut up and do as I was told.

I did as I was told. I didn't say anything, either.

Brownie licked my face, then shut her eyes. I slipped my right arm around Singe as low as I could. She did the same with Morley. He got Orchidia. Orchidia put her arm around me, as high as she could get.

"Wait! Wait up!" Tara Chayne charged out of the house as if she were a hundred years younger than she was. The cluster hug fell apart.

"What?" Orchidia demanded.

"I should go with you."

Little Strafa nodded. "She's right." She shivered, cold despite that coat. She laid a hand over Morley's heart, showed him a child's forerunner of the smile that always conquered when she was a grown-up. "Please? Let Moonblight take your place? I know it's a lot to ask but I promise I'll take good care of him."

Morley checked me, Singe, and even the dog he carried, now sound asleep. Even Brownie had only one eye open. He considered the three witchy women, calculating. "Garrett?"

"I can't offer an informed opinion. I don't know what's going on. But I can say that I trust Strafa." Still, I didn't want my best friend to think I was pushing him out.

"We have a problem with time," Orchidia reminded.

"Her skills . . . ," Strafa began.

Morley presented his dog to Tara Chayne. "I understand skills." His face said a good deal more. There would be unhappy folks on the Hill if anything untoward happened because he wasn't there to prevent it, Enma Ai or no.

Orchidia said, "Your sacrifice is both appreciated and useful."

I reminded him, "You were going to bail after the raid anyway."

"Got my third wind." Morley touched two fingers to his right eyebrow in salute.

I nodded. He might do so in a state of blind exhaustion, but he would turn up at the house on Macunado.

116

Little Strafa said, "Everyone crowd in again." She rotated to face me, slightly to my right, cheek against my lower chest. She got hold of me good and Singe somewhat. I hoped she wouldn't pull some Strafa stunt and get me branded as a pedophile.

She was a kid, though, despite some grown-up memories. Her mind didn't run in those gutters.

She said, "Everybody shut their eyes."

Naturally, I didn't, so when my feet left the garden paving I watched the Algarda hovel sink away behind Moonblight. And saw Moonblight go deathly pale as she watched something behind me drop out of sight.

She was smart enough to shut her eyes; then she might have prayed. Her lips moved the whole time we were airborne.

It wasn't a long journey, but it had its moment of drizzling brown terror. Little Strafa took us over a small plaza just in time for the opening salvo of a neighborhood fireworks show. We were not high up. Rockets cracked past. They exploded overhead. I squealed. Orchidia strained to keep her response inside. Moonblight muttered in some weird Other Race language and went right on keeping her eyes shut.

Explosions above betrayed us to the people below. Most decided we must be part of the entertainment. A few beetle-browed morons yelled for somebody to jump.

Idiots! Karenta's richest resource is stupidity.

We settled onto Macunado. Two out of two witch women instantly declared, "We are being watched." They pointed, not in the same direction.

"The house is," I agreed. I waved to Preston Womble. He waved back, making no effort to be discreet. I didn't see Elona Muriat. Maybe she'd gone to the riverfront for the fireworks.

A second party was less easy to identify. They might represent Belinda Contague or General Block. They were more professional than Womble, but barely so. They would rather be off watching fireworks, too.

Singe and Strafa paid no mind. Singe hustled to the door. She used her key. Little Strafa followed her inside. I was right behind with Brownie, still napping. Moonblight and Orchidia, with mutts, brought up the rear.

Penny emerged from Singe's office. It was rare that anyone came into the house without being admitted by somebody already inside. She reddened immediately.

Singe barked, "You have been into my books again!"

"I was reading a story to Hagekagome. She likes stories. Where have you all been? We're going to miss the fireworks."

That was a diversion. Her real interest was Little Strafa.

Hagekagome, meanwhile, slipped past Penny, around Singe and Little Strafa, and glommed onto me. "Missed you! Missed you so much!" She hugged me hard with one arm while running her other hand over Brownie and sniffing. Brownie opened one eye lazily, gave Hagekagome's face a big wet lick.

Little Strafa said, "My, my." And to the sorceresses, "I see what happened. I think I get the mechanism. Grandmother overlooked natural law completely when she constructed her spell suite."

Orchidia nodded. "Yes. It seems not to have occurred to her that if she regressed you, the regressed time and emotion would have to go elsewhere, into someone equally important."

Believe it or not, I understood part of that, but the insight didn't stick.

Strafa asked, possibly with a touch of concern or jealousy, "So, who is she, then? And if she is from twenty years ago, how come she isn't as old as you?"

Ouch.

There was a new experience. I'd never seen Strafa jump into a big, steaming pile like that. That was more like something Kevans would do. Neither Tara Chayne nor Orchidia was pleased. The latter obviously considered reminding Strafa that she had kids the same age as Kevans.

Both sorceresses chose to make allowances.

There was enough grown-up Strafa in my girl to remind her that you don't yank the beards of short-tempered older women, even unintentionally.

She didn't show much more maturity with Hagekagome, though.

"Hey, you. That's my man you're climbing all over. Get off him. Stop rubbing yourself against him."

She made it sound more intimate and sensual than it was.

Whatever had happened, it wasn't simple and just physical. Hagekagome, honestly, was just trying to snuggle closer.

Tara Chayne, ever more practical than I expected, suggested, "Why don't we think of a nice, private place where we can take the girls to watch the fireworks? And talk. It's almost midnight."

Almost time for the waterfront show. "Good idea. Strafa? Are you strong enough to make two more trips fast?"

Strafa eyed me like she wondered why I'd ask such a dumb question.

Inspiration had overwhelmed me.

"Back to the street, then. Everyone." Dogs yawned, still loafing in people's arms.

People moved without asking a bunch of questions. I appreciate that when it's me wanting to get things done.

"We're outside," Moonblight said. "Now what?"

"Get into the place you were before, with your mutt. Orchidia, give yours to Hagekagome and put her in your place. Singe, same with Penny. We'll fly. You lock the door. Strafa will come right back for you."

Singe didn't like the plan. Orchidia, though, understood. Singe chose to defer to her wisdom, though she couldn't help saying, "Do not do anything stupid before I get there."

"Hearing you five by five, Mom."

Singe didn't care where we were headed. She figured I could do something dumb and inconvenient anywhere.

Orchidia chivied everyone in tight around Strafa, who rotated to face me again, adding something extra as a message to Hagekagome, who never noticed. I was embarrassed about being the object of jealousy between children—even though, in a way, both were really my own age.

Singe was locking the door as we lifted off.

Neither Dean nor the Dead Man had made themselves evident at all.

I hoped no watcher got a wild hair and tried to break in. They might actually get away with something now.

Strafa whispered, "To the ridge in the cemetery?"

"You know my mind perfectly."

"I am your wife. I will be your wife." Stated with absolute conviction and an understood "No matter what!" "The view will be a little remote, but there won't be any crowding. Not even the ghosts will get in the way of our conversation."

My wife. There might be some social difficulties till she looked old enough for the job. Say, another three or four years. Plenty of girls get married, to get out of the house, by age fifteen. They wait five more years after that, even their overly protective fathers start calling them old maids.

Maybe by the time Little Strafa was ready for a real husband, she'd want someone a little more spry than the antique fart that I would be.

117

The big fireworks show always takes place on the waterfront at the foot of the Street of the Gods. The actual launching is done from barges anchored out. That's safer. Maybe once a decade somebody screws up, does something royally stupid, and all the fireworks on a barge explode at once, resulting in a dead stupid guy who takes along any friends dumb enough to work with him, plus countless catfish whose deaths are less in vain because they get to participate mightily in numerous All-Souls feasts.

The barges were a lesson hard-learned. A century ago a thousand people died in a Great Fire following a fireworks mishap.

TunFaire has had half a dozen Great Fires over the ages.

It was chilly on the ridge. The dogs woke up and gamboled a bit, making plenty of noise. I found a good place to sit. There was moonlight enough to limn the city skyline. Chattaree's spires stood out. A tail of smoke still leaned west from the cathedral, a little orange and red at its root.

Penny and Hagekagome settled beside me, right and left, crowding in for warmth. Penny said, "I should have thought about coats."

Behind us, Tara Chayne chuckled. "Then you wouldn't have an excuse."

The first shell went up a few minutes later. The scattered fireworks we'd seen earlier were neighborhood efforts or kid stunts. I said, "I heard the Crown is kicking in this year."

Tara Chayne responded, "The army donated several tons of surplus."

Whoa! That could get showy if it included anything besides signal rockets. What they threw up at enemy Windwalkers and broom riders, flying thunder lizards, or anything else that might attack from above would be showier and louder than anything civilians ever saw.

Tara Chayne settled to her knees and hams behind me, close enough for me to feel her warmth. Hakekagome wasn't shy about snuggling up and getting a two-hand death grip on my left arm. Penny maintained a careful little gap. Nasty old Tara Chayne whispered, "Make a memory, girl," and pushed her.

Wild dogs came out of the dark. They invested no time in greeting rituals. They just made themselves comfortable. Brownie had made herself at home in my lap already.

Then the first army star shell went up. It didn't throw off fancy colors, just created a globe of ferociously deadly lesser fireballs that expanded more than a hundred yards before the fade began. No magic there, just chemistry. Chemistry able to sear holes through half an inch of steel were anyone strong enough to carry that much armor aloft.

The fire faded with "oohs," and "aahs," muted by distance.

The next shell was also surplus, less obviously dramatic. It created a cloud lighted by an inner fire that spun off lightning bolts. Those would have made passage problematic for anything sharing that airspace.

Some of the cemetery mutts raised their heads, flicked their ears, made soft, interrogative noises. Brownie answered with a sound closer to a purr than anything normally made by a dog. The others dropped their chins back onto their paws.

Little Strafa dropped out of the night with Singe and Orchidia, Singe straining to appear unflustered. Clearly, the ladies had shared a lively conversation while they were airborne.

Orchidia announced, "We ran into some gargoyles. They lit out. They didn't want to talk."

Strafa said, "They weren't dumb enough to try anything. But they did curse us in their own dialect."

They had a language?

Orchidia said, "They were looking for friends who never came home from a job in the city. They may have blamed us."

Singe asked, "What have we missed?" She eyed Hagekagome and Penny fiercely. Little Strafa also gave Penny a dark look.

"They just started."

Singe bullied a couple of mutts and made herself a place beside Penny. Orchidia did the same by Hagekagome, even laying a hand on the pretty girl's back. Hagekagome seemed pleased. Little Strafa made her place behind me, on her knees like Tara Chayne. She pushed Moonblight over behind Penny but still stayed partly behind Hagekagome. She didn't do or say anything to the pretty girl. The pretty girl paid no attention to her. She stayed where she was, snuggled up tight.

Over my left shoulder I said, "So you were actually looking out for me the last couple days?"

The fireworks began to pick up.

"After I figured out who I was. Jiffy helped me with that."

Orchidia said, "Jiffy would be the big guy."

"Um." I sort of figured.

"At first I didn't know anything. I headed for Grandmother's house. I guess that was instinct. I didn't know why, or who she was. It just seemed like the place to go." She rested her hands on my shoulders. They were shaky.

I said, "I've worked some of it out, but I can't get it to make sense without figuring in truly boggling levels of incompetence."

"Then you don't have it figured out," Orchidia said. "Though you're right about the incompetence."

A colorful barrage fixed our attention briefly; then Moonslight took it up. "Any sense anything made would likely do so only if you'd spent your life on the Hill. Only somebody who thinks like Constance Algarda could have done what she did to abort Meyness Stornes's ambitions."

"She knew about him?"

"Not specifically. She sensed a new tournament taking shape. She'd been watching for it. She called us in. Like everybody else, though, she thought that Meyness hadn't come home from the Cantard."

Strafa said, "I never made it to Grandmother's house. I ran into Jiffy and Min. They saw that I was scared and confused and crying and didn't know who I was, or where. They thought they were being kind by not letting me get to Grandmother. They had just come away from her and thought she was too wicked for any little girl to be around."

Probably true, that. "What were they doing there?"

"She hired them to investigate her granddaughter's future husband, but she paid them so much up front that they were suspicious. Min knew somebody she could pay to do the spying while she and Jiffy found out what Grandmother was really up to. For some reason Jiffy decided he had to stick with me all the time."

He fell in love at first sight and wanted to protect her, that's why. Strafa always had that appeal. It was one of her hidden powers and, possibly, the one ambitious Meyness really wanted most. Surely it would be massively more potent with Strafa looking like a lost, bewildered, vulnerable little girl.

I had no trouble understanding Jiffy being pulled in, especially if he was no brighter than he seemed.

"I tried to warn you one time, but I didn't really know what I was talking about then. You didn't pay attention, anyway. You were distracted . . ." Her hands tightened on my shoulders. "Anyway . . ."

A barrage interrupted. As it faded, Moonblight said, "Constance went almost as dark as Meyness in order to ruin his tournament."

Orchidia said, "Because she was thinking forever. She'd have no trouble justifying it to herself if she couched it as a final solution."

Tara Chayne said, "You're right, Garrett, thinking that Strafa's death was accidental, the way it worked out. I'm sure Constance intended something almost as ugly visually but slightly less permanent. She probably wanted it to look like Strafa was beyond the grasp of the Operators. That would shake their scheme to its roots. She would hunt them down while they were confused, with help from you and your friends. You would want revenge. But when she got Min together with Strafa to make the sacrifice, something went wrong. Min should have died and Strafa should have gone into a state mimicking death that would relax eventually. I'm sure you're right about that missile. Constance would have worked on it for weeks, refining the spells and layering them on for timed release. But it bounced off a bone inside Min and took out Strafa for real."

"Yeah." Not quite incompetence, that. More like malicious Fortune. We saw absurd stuff like it all the time during the war. "So, after that she let the scam run anyway, but she ducked out on us by faking a stroke."

Tara Chayne said, "The stroke was real, it just wasn't as bad as she made out."

"So . . . let me get this. Vicious Min is alive but she should be dead. Shadowslinger meant to murder her when she hired her. My Strafa is dead, but Min's murder was supposed to make it so she could be revived."

Tara Chayne, Orchidia, and Little Strafa agreed: That was the exact situation.

"So, what's the deal with this Strafa? And where does Hagekagome fit? Or does she?"

The pretty girl answered the mention of her name by trying to snuggle closer.

"She fits," Orchidia said.

118

Tara Chayne said, "Here is where the theory gets esoteric. The practical aspects of what happened may take years of study to work out."

"Since it looks like you all are finally willing to talk about this stuff, why not fill me in even where you don't think I'll understand? I can fool you sometimes."

Orchidia said, "Strafa, Singe, and I talked this over on the way here. Singe believes that the smoothest road forward is the direct one."

"Thank you." Three large goat carts would have been needed to haul that load of sarcasm.

Singe said, "Don't make me reconsider."

Her sense of humor is atrophied. Better not risk her going totally serious.

Little Strafa said, "When Grandmother's spell activated, it not only did what she wanted it to, but did what the laws of nature required. She hadn't taken those enough into account, probably because she never looked past what she wanted right now."

Orchidia said, "Constance is a master. Her spell suite would have performed exactly as designed if that bolt had struck the sacrifice's heart. But once it ricocheted into the protection Strafa was trying to weave—"

Moonblight interrupted. "That's what made the missile stray. Strafa being Strafa, she probably tried to protect Min first."

Little Strafa said, "I can reclaim no memory of anything that happened between the time I left Garrett that morning and when I ran into Jiffy and Min. I'm not sure how many hours or days I lost, then gained by going back."

Definitely weird, that great leap backward.

They were picking at something I thought we had covered before. Then I saw that there was more to it. Why did we have Hagekagome and Little Strafa? "Was Strafa supposed to be regressed?"

Tara Chayne said, "No. A temporal tremor created her and the other girl, both."

"Out of legend," Orchidia said, harkening back.

"Huh?"

She indicated Hagekagome. "That has happened before. In folklore."

Tara Chayne said, "I'm sure the point of the exercise, for Constance, was a false death for Strafa that would make the Operators scramble to replace her in time to do the Ritual tonight."

I didn't get that. The midnight changeover from Day of the Dead to All-Souls might be particularly potent, but I suspected that the Ritual did not have to happen at any specific hour.

Maybe midnight tonight was just the best time to do it using a skeleton crew.

Orchidia said, "Meyness apparently wasn't that distraught about missing the chance to harvest the power of TunFaire's only Windwalker."

"Could that be because Furious Tide of Light had no healing powers to mention?"

"Ah. Yes." Cold, cold. The Black Orchid had emerged. I tried recalling Dane and Deanne from the heyday of the Faction. Had they shown any talent for healing?

They hadn't impacted my consciousness much. The talent I recalled was one for shaping life-forms. They had helped the Faction create monster bugs. "I see what he must have been thinking."

"He was wrong."

"In so many ways. But that's behind us. That's all settled. Talk to me about Hagekagome. Who is she? What is she? How can she possibly be so devoted to me, and have those stories about our wonderful times together, while I have no clue? I've never suffered egregious and persistent memory loss. And how can she be only this old if she's been pushed forward in time? If Strafa got younger?" Fact, though. The girl had been gaining on Penny, fast, from the moment she attacked me.

And my own Strafa didn't get younger, did she? My own Strafa got dead. Little Strafa was a whole different creature. So why shouldn't Hagekagome be a whole different creature, too?

But . . . ? Different from?

Orchidia made a joke. "Dog years."

"Huh?"

Penny hadn't contributed much but awed responses to the flash and bang over yonder, so far. Now she found a reserve of daring, leaned her cheek against my arm, and said, "Hey, Hage!"

Must have been a game they'd made up. Hagekagome responded, "Hey, Dread!" Sleepily.

"Hey, Kage! Who is that boy that you're in love with?"

"Mikey Garrett. Hey, Dread! Who is that man . . . ?"

The game went a couple of rounds more. I lost it, becoming frozen in a moment.

Hagekagome tightened her grip even more when she said my brother's name.

All the evidence was there.

I plummeted into the deep, dark well of my mind, headed down and away further than I'd ever fallen before.

119

The roar over the river kept me from getting lost.

Game over! became an anchoring thought, though it made no sense in the circumstances.

I could not interrogate Hagekagome, or anyone else, because of the racket from the waterfront. The fireworks guys were moving toward their big finale. That looked likely to roll on longer and louder than ever, thanks to the generosity of Karenta's Royal Army.

Mikey. Hagekagome had confused me with my little brother. No one had yet convinced her that she was wrong.

How hard had anyone tried? Had anyone, other than Penny, even worked that part out?

Hagekagome being misinformed helped explain why I didn't know her. Mikey had had time for a girlfriend or three after I went off to war. But that didn't explain why I thought I should know her name. I was sure that I'd heard it before. Neither Mikey nor Mom had been the sort to write letters. Neither had been the sort to afford a scrivener and the post, nor had any mad need to communicate ever befallen them. I wouldn't have heard about a girlfriend from a letter.

Too, Playmate knew the name. He must have heard it before he went to the war zone. Mikey was gone before Play got back.

Maybe Mom mentioned Hagekagome after I came home, during the short while that I had her—mainly as an emotional sparring partner. She hadn't been able to get her mind around the fact that I was a grown-ass man who had survived the ugliest that the world could fling at me and no longer ought to be treated like a slow eight-year-old.

Even with all the information at hand, I kept missing the last point. I knew I had it all. I just couldn't look at it from the right angle, despite a lifetime spent in this bizarre city. Despite a civilian career spent eyeball-to-eyeball with the mystical, supernatural, implausible, and sometimes downright logically impossible. After having dealt with several varieties of ghosts and undead. After having coped with gods and demons, devils and giant insects, and intelligent fungi. After having battled shape-shifters, racialists, coin collectors, vintners, and similarly fantastic creatures, I still failed to see the obvious. The simplest explanation. The step right out of folklore obvious once my lady companions piled on the hints. But I could call an excuse: Hagekagome was neither a fox nor a crane.

Moonblight sighed. "My forehead is getting sore, being banged against a wall . . . But time flies. Midnight has gone. The slide has begun. It could go very fast now. I have no choice, however much you all want to nudge and hint so he can work it out for himself."

Hagekagome held on to me even harder than she had been. I glanced down. Moonblight made a jewel of a tear in the corner of her eye. Several dogs had crowded in close to her, including all four who had gone adventuring with me. Brownie had turned in my lap and now extended overboard enough to rest her chin on Hagekagome's right thigh.

More than anything, I was having trouble getting past the fact that Hagekagome thought that I was Mikey. Poor child, to be so wondrously beautiful, yet so dim.

Little Strafa's fingers on my shoulders now shivered constantly.

Moonblight asked, "Are you being willfully slow? I've heard that you often pretend to possess the reasoning capacity of a twenty-year-old stump."

"I'll stipulate the incapacity but not that I'm doing it on

purpose. I'm the most frustrated one here. I know that I should get it. I know that I keep looking at it wrong."

"For goodness' sake," Orchidia said. "Your brother brought home strays . . ."

And *Bang!* The last great barrage began, lighting the city brighter than day. And *Bang!* The truth exploded inside my head. The implausible, impossible truth.

I remembered where I'd heard the name Hagekagome.

Mikey had brought home a sweet, beautiful little black-and-white stray not even old enough to wean. She had been in bad shape. Thunder lizards had had her cornered when he intervened. She had lived at our house for a while because even hardhearted Mom hadn't been able to make such a loving, pretty, and badly injured little thing "run away" before she was well enough to make it on her own.

She hadn't been my pup, my friend. She had been as devoted to Mikey as any dog could be. But even I had shed some tears when Hakekagome wasn't with us anymore.

Mikey had named her that, making the name up from words he had learned from a foreign trader kid he met on the waterfront. It had something to do with a game like hide-and-seek that he learned about from the foreigner—who might have been a girl, his first infatuation. He spent a lot of time on the wharfs for a while.

Of course, that was me thinking. I am the one who sees all history in terms of the females involved.

That Hagekagome spent a summer and part of an autumn with us. She and Mikey had done all those things she told Penny about. But then my cousin Gesic came home missing an eye, an ear, an arm, and a leg, and there had been no one else to care for him during his remaining days. We couldn't support Gesic and a dog, too. Even Mom cried—and had enough emotion invested that she insisted Mikey had to deal with this one himself. How grim he became! My little brother, always so cheerful before, was never the same afterward. Always glum, never smiling.

I now knew how he had resolved the cold equation. He had taken Hagekagome to a place where wild dogs lived and left her with them. And she had not found her way home. Or she had understood well enough to know that, no matter what, home could no longer be there. So, because she loved Mikey so much, she made his life easier by choosing not to follow him.

I got misty just thinking about it.

I hugged Hagekagome back so hard that Strafa began to growl.

I would never tell Hagekagome that she had confused me with my brother. Never.

I knew what all this meant now. That of all the nights of my life, this would be the saddest. A massively stupid error by a sorceress with good but mad intentions had collided with an old kernel of pain and had breathed in life that belonged to my wife-to-be, without intent, accidentally, and agonizingly cruel.

I couldn't get tangled up in the mechanisms of how and why. I just accepted the fact that a cute dog who had loved my brother had come back as an incredibly beautiful, if not very bright, young girl who also loved Mikey with canine depth and commitment.

I could accept that because I had been chin-to-chin with strange stuff throughout my career. I expected the strange to keep right on, heading down the road, unless Strafa's death did what Tinnie Tate's incessant nagging had failed to accomplish, which was to break me down.

Truth. I didn't have to get into these things if I wanted to avoid them. I had the gigs with the brewery and Amalgamated. I had inherited wealth, little as I wanted that. I no longer had any need to work. I could sell the business to Singe. She was sure to make a raving success of it, with never a drop of blood being shed. If I felt compelled to hit the mean streets looking for an ass-kicking or head-thumping, I could always sign on with Prince Rupert.

I was going to have to learn to swim in rare social waters, like it or not. That was one cost of having become involved with Furious Tide of Light. Her being gone would not excuse me from being Mr. Furious Tide.

My grandmother-in-law, if no one else, would make sure I was out in front from now on, the curtain behind which the more bizarre crew lurked. Me. Garrett. The mask of normalcy disguising the Algarda tribe.

I glanced back at Little Strafa. Her hands had become shakier. Maybe it was just the intense moonlight, but she also seemed to have developed a deathly pallor.

Hagekagome had become a little more shaky, too. Her grip on my arm seemed almost desperate. She panted like an overheated or frightened pup. Brownie and her friends were restless, too. Number Two emitted the occasional doleful whine.

An old childhood story, based on legend or rural folklore, told of a fox girl who fell in love so deeply that the local gods gave her permission to take human form to be with the man she loved. The catch—and there is always a nasty one where gods are involved—was that it could be only for a short time, and then she would die. But so deep was her love that she made that choice, trading a long magical life—foxes being magical as well as natural creatures—for the brief time she got to share with the one she loved.

I found a part of me thinking I should mention that story to Jon Salvation next time we got together. It would make a sweet tragedy. Only it would be like him to throw in some ugly commentary on his own bleak species by having the human lover just shove the fox girl aside after she sacrificed everything, maybe going after some bimbo with enormous hooters instead.

Penny said, "We should do something besides just sit here talking. Time is not our friend. It's almost up for Hage."

And of course, Garrett, the ultrasensitive wonder child that he is, absolutely conformed to the negative expectations of his female companions despite having had his nose rubbed in the fact that Hagekagome and Little Strafa were part of a twisted real-world iteration of the tale of the fox girl, thanks to the efforts of various less than competent sorcerers.

Singe launched a sigh of exasperation. "Is your brain made of cheese? Or chert? They are going to go, Garrett. And it won't be long. The process has begun."

Hagekagome was shivering badly now. "I'm so cold," she whispered. "I'm so sad. I don't want to leave you."

Boy genius that I am, my first impulse was to ask, "Little Strafa, too?" instead of answering Hagekagome's need. A whole murder of crow women read me beforehand. Snarls, hisses, and growls came at me from every angle, slowing me down. Making me pause long enough to digest what Hagekagome had said, so I was able to respond with a satisfactory "I'll always be with you, Little One. I'll always have you in my heart, till we're together again."

It didn't seem possible, but she squeezed my arm even tighter. She was shaking even more. I told her, "Don't be afraid. You were always a good girl."

"I'm not afraid. I just don't want to leave you."

Penny got up and came around to Hagekagome's other side, moving Orchidia to do it. She glommed on to the pretty girl, tight. "Hey, Hage."

"Hey, Dread."

Brownie made a whining noise. So did Number Two. Orchidia and Little Strafa repositioned themselves so they could both contribute warmth from behind.

Hagekagome hit me once, weakly, over the heart, with her left fist as she forced her way over to rest her left cheek against my chest. Her big brown eyes sparkled in the moonlight, diamond tears. "I love you. I love you more than anything."

And then she closed those beautiful eyes.

120

There was a disconnect in reality for a moment, like there was a one-half-second fade to black that might, in truth, have lasted a thousand years or an entire cycle of the universe. When it was over I had another dog in my lap, an ancient black-and-white female who had to have set a record for life span in dog years. All the strays pushed in around me, sniffing, whimpering, and giving her face goodbye licks.

At that moment I decided I would honor Mikey's love by laying Hagekagome down beside my own love. She would have a fine funeral, too.

We were entering a season of funerals. We had to see off Kyoga's son, Orchidia's twins, and the marvelous Mashego. And maybe Vicious Min as well. We hadn't heard anything more there.

John Stretch would report.

I had a more immediate concern.

Strafa clung to my back as fiercely as Hagekagome had clung to my arm, shaking. "Tara Chayne, Orchidia, I don't think I can survive losing her again."

Moonblight responded, "You can handle this. You're a grown man. A war veteran. You're just tired and feeling sorry for yourself. Hike up your big boy britches and get on with it."

There she went, kicking me into the land of what the hell is going on? again.

Orchidia suggested, "Time is less friendly than we thought only an hour ago. The dog girl reverted sooner and faster than I expected."

So Little Strafa's time might come sooner, too.

Singe asked, "What can we expect?"

"More of that." Orchidia indicated Hagekagome. The old dog looked sad in the moonlight. Strays looked at me like they thought I should do something.

Looking at Brownie, Number Two, and the others I saw something I'd missed till now. These were Hagekagome's children. Well, more remote descendants than that, probably. But she was their beloved and honored matriarch and they had shown her to her heart's desire before she'd had to leave them.

I levered my stiff old bones upright. I needed help. It had been a long day, yet there remained more day to be lived.

I lifted Hagekagome. She was heavier than I expected. I headed downhill. The Algarda Mausoleum lay just over a hundred yards distant. Moonlight painted the graveyard crisply spooky. Everybody, dogs and all, came along.

Little Strafa crowded me as tightly as Hagekagome had earlier, grimly aware that she was running out of time.

She was not comfortable with it, the way Hagekagome had been. For a time there had seemed to be a chance of living to grow up and become the wife . . . But that hope had gone. She wanted to kick and scream and fight, but there was no throat to wrap her little fingers round.

We were halfway to the mausoleum when Tara Chayne delivered a heartfelt rendition of "Oh, shit!" while looking back upslope.

The big guy stood where we had sat watching fireworks. Where Hagekagome had left us. He spotted Little Strafa, boomed a question loudly enough to waken babies a mile away.

That would bring the sextons out.

I told Strafa, "You're the only one who can handle this." She stopped to wait while the parade moved on. A min-

ute later I found myself developing a grudge. The mausoleum remained as we had left it earlier, open to anyone
daring enough to disturb the dead during All-Souls.

I passed Hagekagome to Orchidia, eased inside, found
the lamps, fired them up, then went back for Hagekagome.

Jiffy stood calmly and respectfully out of the way, Little
Strafa holding his hand. She was calmer now.

I swapped a lamp for Hagekagome, carried her inside.
Orchidia lighted my way. Tara Chayne followed. Brownie
came, too, the only mutt with courage enough to enter.
Singe and Penny chose to stay outside.

I placed Hagekagome on the available plinth. I was
teary again. Orchidia drifted to the doorway, bellowed at
Little Strafa to get her butt in here; her presence was required.

Strafa did not comply.

I couldn't help myself. I swept dust off the glass between
me and my wife, raised my lamp for a final sorrow-filled
look . . .

Trick of the lamplight, Strafa seemed to have gained
some color.

An outcry rose outside, Penny and Singe both shouting
for me, "Now!"

Little Strafa was having a seizure. Jiffy had her in his
massive arms, controlling her, but was at a loss over what
else to do. He passed her to me the instant I was close
enough; then he just stood there looming with wet cheeks.

The violence of Strafa's seizure waned to a bad case of
the shakes. She opened her eyes for a moment, slammed
her arms around my neck, and squeezed till it felt like she
might break something.

I settled to the grass and held her. There was nothing
else I could do. Nothing I could think to do. Penny and
Singe tried to comfort me.

Little Strafa's shakes weakened. She opened her eyes
one last time, forced a sad smile, touched my cheek with the
tips of the fingers of her left hand, whispered, "Love you.
Forever."

She stopped shaking. She stopped breathing. Then, a few minutes later, she stopped being.

There was another of those fade-to-black moments, after which we all gawked at my empty lap.

Jiffy went somewhere to be alone with his pain.

I sat there amid family and dogs and wandered off into the lost realm that had been so attractive lately.

Murmuring and shuffling brought me back.

Orchidia and Tara Chayne were easing out of the tomb, a sagging but breathing grown-up Strafa suspended between them, too weak to lift her chin.

I took a quick look eastward before I rushed in.

No. We didn't get to add dawn light to the drama. Not yet.

ABOUT THE AUTHOR

Glen Cook was born in 1944 in New York City. He has served in the United States Navy and lived in Columbus, Indiana; Rocklin, California; and Columbia, Missouri, where he went to the state university. He attended the Clarion Writers Workshop in 1970, where he met his wife, Carol. "Unlike most writers, I have not had strange jobs like chicken plucking and swamping out health bars. Only full-time employer I've ever had is General Motors." He is now retired from GM. He's "still a stamp collector and book collector, but mostly, these days, I hang around the house and write." He has three sons—an army officer, an architect, and a music major.

In addition to the Garrett, P.I., series, he is also the author of the ever-popular Black Company series.

Also in the gritty Garrett P.I. series from
Glen Cook

<u>Introducing Garrett, P.I.</u>
Includes *Sweet Silver Blues*,
Bitter Gold Hearts, and *Cold Copper Tears*

<u>Garrett Takes the Case</u>
Includes *Old Tin Sorrows*, *Dread Brass
Shadows*, and *Red Iron Nights*

<u>Garrett For Hire</u>
Includes *Deadly Quicksilver Lies*,
Petty Pewter Gods, and *Faded Steel Heat*

<u>Also Available</u>
Angry Lead Skies
Whispering Nickel Idols
Cruel Zinc Melodies
Gilded Latten Bones

Available wherever books are sold

or at penguin.com

R0160

THE DRESDEN FILES

The #1 *New York Times* bestselling series

by Jim Butcher

"Think *Buffy the Vampire Slayer* starring Philip Marlowe." —*Entertainment Weekly*

STORM FRONT
FOOL MOON
GRAVE PERIL
SUMMER KNIGHT
DEATH MASKS
BLOOD RITES
DEAD BEAT
PROVEN GUILTY
WHITE NIGHT
SMALL FAVOR
TURN COAT
CHANGES
SIDE JOBS
GHOST STORY
COLD DAYS

Available wherever books are sold or at
penguin.com

S602

Want to connect with fellow science fiction and fantasy fans?

For news on all your favorite Ace and Roc authors, sneak peeks into the newest releases, book giveaways, and much more—

"Like" Ace and Roc Books on Facebook!

facebook.com/AceRocBooks

Penguin Group (USA) Online

What will you be reading tomorrow?

Tom Clancy, Patricia Cornwell, W.E.B. Griffin,
Nora Roberts, William Gibson, Catherine Coulter,
Stephen King, Dean Koontz, Ken Follett, Nick Hornby,
Khaled Hosseini, Kathryn Stockett, Clive Cussler,
John Sandford, Terry McMillan, Sue Monk Kidd,
Amy Tan, J. R. Ward, Laurell K. Hamilton,
Charlaine Harris, Christine Feehan...

You'll find them all at
penguin.com
facebook.com/PenguinGroupUSA
twitter.com/PenguinUSA

Read excerpts and newsletters, find tour schedules
and reading group guides, and enter contests.

Subscribe to Penguin Group (USA) newsletters
and get an exclusive inside look
at exciting new titles and the authors you love
long before everyone else does.

PENGUIN GROUP (USA)
us.penguingroup.com

S0151

P.O. 0005221020 202